Los Vryosos
(The Radiant Ones)

Los Vryosos

A Tale from the Varrio

ADAN HERNANDEZ

This book is a work of fiction. Names, characters, places, and incidents are either products of the author's imagination or are used fictitiously. In most cases, English translations are included in italics after words and phrases in Spanish and Caló. See the glossary on page 337 for more information. All illustrations by the author.

FIRST EDITION

Hernandez, Adan.
Los Vryosos: A Tale from the Varrio
    341 pp.
    ISBN 10: 0-978642-00-7
    ISBN 13: 978-0-978642-00-6
    Library of Congress Control Number: 2006928431

I. Title

10 9 8 7 6 5 4 3 2 1

For my gente, my parents Juan and Olivia, and my late wife Debi.

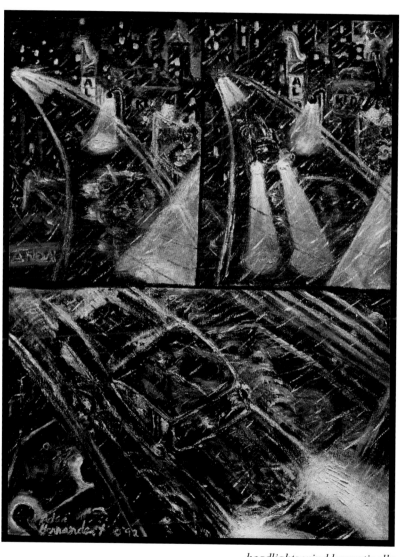

headlights wind hypnotically

a flash of lightning splits the darkness

maddog gafas glow an eerie red

the cars race on the high overpass as city lights strobe by

gunshots echo, sending him crashing through the guardrail

the windshield shatters violently

aparición

One

Aparición
Apparition

The night is cold. Hazy. A silent cityscape in the rain. A pair of head-lights winds hypnotically around an overpass. The flashing red blades of a squad car.

From the steering wheel of the speeding car, the night is dream-like. Heavy drops pepper the windshield, melt the road ahead into a liquid urban wash.

Above, a blinding flash of lightning splits the silence. Glistening darkness. Deep roaring thunder rolls across the sky, leaving in its wake the wailing of the siren, which fades then emerges. An audible premonition.

Cold heavy raindrops splat and stream away on the windshield. The car speeds faster.

Maddog gafas on a face shrouded in darkness peer back through the rain-streaked car window. They glow an eerie red, reflecting the

nazul awakens

menacing flasher blades now bathing the back window with an electric tint. The car stereo weeps with a melody that transcends time and place.

♫ "Estás sellado…por el destino." *You are sealed…by destiny.*

Chelo Silva's tragic voice fills the soul with a painful longing for eternal existence.

♫ "Que tú serás…mi compañero." *That you will be…my companion.*

The cars race on the high narrow overpass as city lights strobe by.

♫ "Y que iremos por un camino…" *And we will go down a road…*

The squad car speeds alongside the '57 Chevy. Gunshots echo in the night.

♫ "Hasta que alguno de los dos…" *Until one of us…*

Inches from his ear, the rearview mirror explodes.

♫ "Se muera…" *Passes away…*

Gripping the steering wheel tighter, his desperate hands swerve sharply away, sending him crashing through the guardrail.

♫ "Hasta que alguno de los dos…"

A sense of falling grips his stomach.

♫ "Se muera."

The windshield shatters violently, shifting time into a slower crawl. The melody echoes away.

♫ "Se muera."

Through the blinding smoke and flying glass illuminated by the dusty headlights, a faint image of la Virgen flows mysteriously upward in silence. He travels down into a dark void.

His restless sleeping eyes struggle to see. Beads of sweat glisten in the pale light.

♫ "Iremos juntos…juntos por la vida." *We will travel together… together through life.*

Slowly, his eyes open and search weakly for their place in time.

♫ "Hasta que el cielo…" *Until the heavens…*

They follow the melody to a clock radio nearby.

♫ "Otra cosa nos decida." *Decide something else for us.*

He sighs in relief to be home.

♫ "Estás sellado por el destino."

nazul hurries to get ready

Next to him, on a half-open window, cheap curtains rise and twirl with the cold breeze. Outside, twilight.

He takes a deep breath and stares out the window. The movement of the curtains caresses the revelation. That was no ordinary dream.

On the wall behind his bed, hubcaps reflect a glint of sunlight. The day is breaking.

"Nazul! Despégate los ojos!" *Nazul! Unglue your eyes!* A man's voice outside his window startles him.

He sits up in bed. "Ey!" He slaps his radio into silence. "Elías, ¿Qué pasó?"

"Carnal, you gotta take the carburetor back to Prieto's. Aquellos *burros*, por andar con sus pinches chistes, te dieron el carbulador de un Mercury." *Those* burros, *for always screwing around with their damn jokes, ended up giving you the carburetor to a Mercury.*

"¡Ayi voy!" Nazul jumps out of bed and hurries to get ready. He flicks on a lamp as he struggles to pull up a pair of wrinkled, oil-stained khakis.

The tiny, cramped room could pass for a varrio auto parts store after taxes. Oilcans, engine belts, car jacks, and tools of all kinds litter the area. A transmission in the process of being rebuilt sits on a rubber tarp on top of a coffee table. Considering the tenants, the place looks neat.

Nazul reaches for a worn-out work shirt hanging on his bedpost. Beside it, on a shelf turned into a mini altar, a twelve-inch porcelain figure of la Virgen prays silently above a lit vela jar. He stares at her momentarily, her sharp rays glistening in the flickering candlelight.

The intense dream is still like a shroud clouding his being. She was there. Apareció. Pero qué quiere decir eso? *It was an apparition. But what could it mean?* La Virgen's pure porcelain face reflects the warm glow of the candle flame. It seems she could almost look up at him and answer.

As Nazul throws on his shirt, he makes his way through the next room cluttered with santos. Some still lie in boxes with cards and flowers.

Buttoning his shirt, he stops at the doorway to a tiny kitchen. An old man with his back to him slowly sips on a cup of coffee, unruffled by Nazul's hectic pace. Empanadas lie invitingly in a basket on the table. Nazul stops for a moment to absorb the scene as though it were something sacred. Somehow even more so today.

don pablito studies nazul

"'Apá, ¿Cómo amaneció?" *Dad, how are you this morning?*
The old man slowly turns his smiling, weathered eyes to him.
"M'ijo, buenos días. Qué lindo día del Señor." *Son, good morning. What a beautiful day of the Lord.*
Nazul walks to the kitchen sink and starts washing up. The cold water could wake the dead.
Through the steam rising from his coffee cup, the old man carefully studies him. "Nazul, ¿Dormites bien?" *Did you sleep well?*
Toweling dry, Nazul gazes out the kitchen window for the answer.
"Sí. Pero tuve un sueño muy espantoso." *Yes. But I had a very mysterious dream.* He cracks a grin like it's no big deal.
The old man seems to know that certain dreams aren't to be taken lightly. He looks into his coffee. "Tal vez tu vida va a cambiar." *Maybe your life is going to change.*
Nazul reaches into his back pocket and pulls out a greasy black comb with a few blades of dry grass still stuck to it. He slides it through his jet black hair. "Sí...pero ojalá que cambie despacio." *Yeah...but I hope it changes slowly.*
Grabbing an empanada, he kisses the old man on top of the head and heads for the door. "Lo miro al rato, 'Apá. Voy de prisa." *See you later, Dad. I'm in a rush.*

With classic grace, the old man gets up from his chair and peers out the half-open kitchen window as Nazul strides quickly away. He mutters softly to himself, "Sueño mensajero." *Messenger dream.*

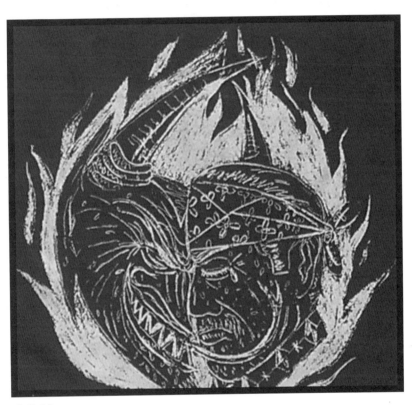

el diablo

Two

El Diablo y la Luna
The Devil and the Moon

Nazul walks down a narrow, two-lane varrio street. It's late December, and the tall pecan trees are shedding their sienna and gold leaves by the hundreds. A light drizzle makes him shiver. He pulls out a navy blue wool cap from his back pocket and puts it on.

The faint sounds of polkas, rancheras, and an oldie here and there add a little warmth to this dying varrio. Abandoned houses, tiny family-owned grocery stores, and boticas line the crater-covered streets like ruins.

Not long ago this was a beautiful place full of cultura and bright expectations. After 'Nam everything changed. Too many veteranos brought back with them a cursed addiction to drugs and started preying on trusting gente to support their vice.

Nazul walks by a boarded-up panadería. He glances at the dense graffiti that now covers the walls, thinking about how most of the varrio chavalos have given up trying to do right en un mundo chueco, un mundo donde nomás gente rica culera rifa en la mera. *In a wicked world where only greedy rich people stake claims in the real craps games of life.* He shakes his head at the crossed-out tags on the wall of the deserted bakery and breathes out a cloud of steam. Messages of death. Byproducts of poverty and familias crippled by drugs and ruthless gangs. Now they were settling every dumb dispute with plomazos.

He crosses over to la Calle Montezuma. Muchos sueños han muerto aquí también. *Many dreams have perished here too.* Neighborhoods like this one en el Weso have earned notorious names like las Colonias, el Indio, Ghost Town, el Alto, and here, where Nazul lives, la Tripa: *the Intestine.* Some say if you're an outsider and cruise in, you'll come out with your tripas in your hands.

Nazul figures he's been damn lucky so far. No vato loco has given him grief yet. That could all change in a heartbeat. They're everywhere now.

He smiles when he thinks of Elias' confrontations. His camarada did have a few run-ins with little wacko punks and drugged-out vatos who were trying to rob or steal from the helpless people in the varrio. Most cowered in Elias' maloso presence.

Nazul takes a deep breath and exhales the hopelessness so deeply felt in these streets. 'Virgencita, what did we ever do to offend you so much that you would ignore our desperate pleas in our prayers to you for so long?' he thinks to himself as he kicks a syringe into a storm drain.

An unusual sound snaps Nazul from his trance. Someone, a grown man…crying? He reluctantly turns down the alley to investigate.

Behind the carcass of a washing machine he finds un señor llorando. He looks around, wonders what to do. Nazul leans down tentatively to the man, who sits siesta-style, sobbing into his lap. He doesn't look like a tecato or a wino, but a hardworking señor que le cayó algún desmadre. *Who was hit with some disaster.* "¿Necesita ayuda?" *Do you need help?* El señor ni le da la vista. *The man doesn't even look at him.* Nazul is waved away by the man and hurries back to the street, ashamed to have intruded.

Again he stops. What if the man is hungry or needs a few bucks? Maybe he had la luz turned off and his family is freezing. He pulls out his wallet to see if he's got any feria. A five and two ones. Taking them out, he returns to the alley. It is now silent.

Puzzled, Nazul looks around at the layers of old box springs and leftover corrugated roof metal pieced together to form walls and fences in the alley. Light rain falls on the trashed-out spot where the man had been sitting. The indentation of his body on the moist weeds is still there.

Damn. Nazul checks every escape route. El señor se desapareció. *The man has disappeared.*

Nazul returns to the street and continues on to Prieto's, the image of el señor nagging at his heart.

"¿Qué fue eso?" *What was that?* he wonders out loud. Nazul walks on in the icy drizzle and a memory from his childhood days comes spilling out into his mind.

Biting wind.

A freezing, dark grey afternoon in Memphis. The ice-covered ground cracking and breaking under the weight of his scuffed-up, dark leather shoes. His five-year-old feet numb from the cold. Gente picking cotton in the field. The plants dark, brittle, heavy with the dirt-covered cotton, sustenance of migrant workers. The unmerciful wind beating on the bent bodies picking the frozen commodity.

He inhales the scene. "Mi gente. Trabajadores de pura gloria. Los trabajadores. Ellos también era gente *vryosa.* Nunca maldecían a Dios por su miseria. Y siempre estaban listos para ayudar a otros aunque fuera el mismo gabacho que los engañaba y los tenía en la ruina. No tenían nada. Lo poco que tenían te lo ofrecían. *Mi* gente." *The workers. They were also people of radiance. Because they never cursed God for their misery and were always ready to help others, even if it was the same racist white man who was the cause of their suffering. They hardly had anything, but what little they had, they would offer it to you.* My *people.*

His 'buelita enduring a blinding toothache as she worked. Wrapping a red weathered scarf around her face to try and keep her cheek warm, her eyes teary from the unbearable pain and cold. In those days finding a dentist who would work on Mexican Americans was unheard of.

Nazul arriving with his tío Ben, who had come from the barracks where they lived next to the cotton gin. He had taken some pregnant women home who had collapsed while picking. His tío hadn't wanted to bring him, but Nazul cried his way into his truck. Back then his driving ambition was to be the best cotton picker among his gente. His father's oldest brother, tío Carlos, now held the record at fifteen hundred pounds a day; Nazul's father, Juan, was a very close second.

The gente bent over like windblown cattle, beasts of burden in a field of dark ice. A life alien to the promising, pampered lives of their ruthless white patrones. The year: 1958.

If the cotton wasn't all picked before we headed back to Corpus and Robestán to spend Christmas in our beloved hometowns, we wouldn't get paid, and most wouldn't even have enough to feed their families.

"¡Nazul! ¡Vete para el bos! ¡Hace mucho frío para tí!" *Nazul! Go to the bus! It's too cold for you!* His beloved 'buelita Maria calling to him over wind gusts that chill the bone, her cheek swollen.

Close by, 'Apá stands up stiffly, echoing 'Buelita. "Nazul, ¡Tú no tienes negocio aquí! Ya te dijo tu abuela, ¡Vete pa'l bos!" *Nazul, you have no business here! Your grandma already told you, go to the bus!*

On the way to the bus, walking by Martinita, Mama's lovable friend. She always had time to grab him and pinch his chubby cheeks. But on this day she endures her own freezing hell and only gives him a tearful smile. Her ankles exposed, scraped. A pair of torn leather shoes with no socks were her only protection from the icy ground.

Opening the double doors of the bus, startled. Former grocery store owners who had lost their tiny business back in Robe are now newcomers to the labores: un señor, his wife, and teenage son. They sob from the cold in a huddle by the bus's heater, which isn't even on. Ashamed, el señor hides his face from Nazul.

On the way home from the field, a clump of shivering bodies with their muffled weeping crowding as close as space will allow to the bus's heater.

These images were the seeds of Nazul's political consciousness.

Up to that day, he had never seen a grown man cry. 'Cuando un hombre llora, a los niños les da miedo.' *When a grown man cries, the kids feel a deep terror.* Nazul recalls the chilling certainty that things were really wrong. He thinks, 'La cosa es que they were like gods in my sight. Then I had to see them weep at my feet from the wet, numbing black ice they had endured all day. Back then no tenía la mente para entenderlo. Ahora pienso que los que les causaban tanta miseria, ni merecían la *presencia* de los trabajores. ¿Cómo *podían* tener el poder para quebrar a gente tan linda?' *Back then I didn't have the mind to understand, but now I think that those people who caused them so much suffering didn't even deserve their* presence. *How* can *they have the power to break people of such character and dignity?*

He swallows their pain. "Donde quiera que estén," *Wherever you may be,* he glances at the misty trees in the horizon, "quiero que sepan que para mí you will always be lo más lindo, trabajadores de pura gloria." *I want you to know that for me you will always be the most beautiful, workers of pure glory.*

As he walks, he recites a polka in his mind that he once wrote:

> Esta canción se la mando
> a mi gente de Robestán
> Y aquellos años pasados
> a mis abuelos que ya no están.
> Labores llenas de vida
> retumban en mi memoria,
> De una gente tan linda,
> trabajadores de pura gloria.
>
> Mi Robestán:
> ¿En dónde están
> Aquellos años pasados en las labores de Robestán?
>
> Se acabaron esos tiempos,
> laguna que se secó;
> Ahora las nubes lloran
> porque esa vida se marchitó.
>
> *I send this song*
> *to my people of Robstown*
> *And those years long past*
> *to my grandfathers who are no more.*
> *Fields full of life*
> *resound in my memory,*
> *Of the most beautiful people,*
> *workers of pure glory.*

My Robstown:
Where has it gone?
Those years gone by in the fields of Robstown?

Those times have ended,
a lagoon that dried away;
Now the clouds cry
'cause those times have passed away.

Carruchas with their loud radios pouring out polkas and Christmas songs come and go as Nazul arrives on Guadalupe Street. Nazul is reminded of Elias and Elsa's kids, Oralia and Joey. He smiles at the thought of their excitement when they see the presents he has stored away for them. Christmas is just around the corner, and the varrio's constant pitfalls seem to ease up just long enough to allow kids a moment of unforgettably joy.

When Elias got laid off from Kelly Air Force Base, his ingenuity as a first-class mechanic came in handy in el Weso. Just about every other car that rolled into Nazul's house to see el curandero had some kind of mechanical problem. Elias and Nazul would often spend their days jumpstarting or fixing the old beat-up carruchas in their yards. Back then they were dos vatos sin jale. *Two vatos out of work.* That's what Elias' wife, Elsa, would call them, shaking her head in resignation.

Grateful gente praised their mechanical ingenuity in the varrios like preachers. Soon, five other viejitos or señoras would be knocking on their doors with their belching, rattling, or smoking carruchas. In no time Elias and Nazul had a thriving business as backyard mechanics.

The winter day is dark, with low, brooding clouds. Young mothers with their children, señoras, y señores brave the cold morning at bus stops on this busy artery in el Weso. Nazul takes in the scene. He's wondering if the fierce winds, flash floods, and electrical storms that have been so frequent this fall could be part of the new world order the Mayas predicted.

As he nears Prieto's Auto Parts at the corner of Guadalupe and Trinity, Nazul glances at the bus stop and freezes on the spot.

It's her.

He can hardly breathe.

Suddenly it's Christmas time a year ago and he's at the bakery—la Poblanita. Warm, comforting smells fill the shop—pan dulce, fresh tamales. Floorboards creak and a bell on the door jingles. Nazul is looking up absently from the glass display case full of huesos azucarados, cuernitos, marranitos...The bell jingles again, making him glance back absentmindedly. He starts to look back at the pan dulce, but instead freezes as this vision of a woman walks in. Y como un menso, he stares at her almost openmouthed—numb to his surroundings. The panadero asks him something about cuernitos and snaps him back to the pan dulce.

"Ah, si, ah deme...cuernitos." He glances back at her and finds her staring right at him. She looks away. Is she nervous? He can barely feel his face. Amor sagrado. *Sacred love.* She is the one. The only one. He's embarrassed when he figures out she is with her little sister and jefita, porque they must have seen him gawking at her.

Nazul grabs the pan dulce bag and has to resist wringing it to dust as he walks to the register.

"Hola, Consuelo. Cómo están las muchachas? Y que bonitas. ¿Qué se le ofrece?" *Hello, Consuelo. How are the girls? Such beautiful girls. What can I get you?* the panadero's wife asks her mother.

As he grabs for his change at the register, Nazul glances back and finds her staring seriously at him—again. Her beautiful, dark eyes seem to invade his being. Una mirada que penetra su alma...desenterrando los secretos de sus sueños más eternos. *A look that penetrates his soul...unearthing the most eternal secrets of his dreams.*

For the next few days, Elias would ask him something and find Nazul staring into space. "Blue-Boy. Ey. You're braindead, ¿que no?" he would chuckle. "Chinga, we been working too hard, vato."

"No." Nazul had looked away, then to the tool-ridden ground. "Es que miré a la mujer de mis sueños." *It's that I saw the woman of my dreams.*

Elias stood there openmouthed, then smiled wide. "Pos, ese Blue-Boy," Elias slapped him on the back with a grease-covered hand. "Ya era pinche tiempo. Yo pensaba que ya te ibas a hacer sacerdote." *It's about fucking time. I was already thinking you were gonna become a priest.*

Y ahora aquí están. Esos ojos. Esa mujer. *And now here they are.*

Those eyes. That woman. Directly in his path at the bus stop. He stands riveted to the spot. She glances at him for a moment, then looks away. Nazul's rapture is interrupted by a troubling uncertainty associated with the woman before him, as if este amor está envuelto en una gran oscuridad misteriosa. *As if this love is wrapped in some great and dark mystery.* He is shaken back to the present and tries to position himself casually to stand at one end of the bus bench. From there he can take her all in.

¡Hijo! She looks so damn good in that vintage '40s black skirt that reaches to her chamorros. Y qué chamorros tán lindos. *And what beautiful calves.* Her skirt is thick y tiene diseños Aztecas bordados con hilo dorado por la hem. *And has Aztec designs embroidered with gold thread on the hem.* She wears a black jacket, fits her real good, also '40s-style. From behind, a colorful embroidered image of Emma Tenayuca, the valiant heroine of the poor workers, leader of the San Antonio pecan shellers' labor struggle, gives solidarity to the image of the woman she is. The image somehow fits perfectly with her energy, Nazul muses.

He is reminded of the sound of a train wailing in the night. A heaviness he can't wrap his mind around. Tragedy foretold or a restless imagination, he can't be sure. He shakes the thought off and finds himself staring again.

The striking Chicana—Nazul figures her to be in her late twenties, más o menos—leans gracefully against a street lamp, lost in the newspaper now, acting like their rapt gaze never happened. A black leather briefcase sits beside her on the sidewalk. Two señoras sit chatting about novelas on the bench. Un señor ya grande in a janitor's uniform leans on the telephone pole nearby.

Nazul is overcome with yearning for this woman, to be close to her. The power of his emotion seems completely out of place at this morning varrio bus stop. Es ella. Nadie más. *It's her. No one else.* She's a gem in a junkyard, here in his path.

He looks down at his wrinkled, oil-stained work pants thinking, 'Estoy bien loco. What chance do I stand? What would she want with a backyard mechanic? A Chicana like her is probably impressed by slick vatos with wheels, maybe even by some educated vato with a promising future.' He breathes in deeply and devours her with his eyes as if he may never see her again. It strikes him that she looks important: businesslike and varrio-trucha at the same time.

nazul encounters luna at the bus stop

me llamo bond, james bond

She doesn't give him another look. A car rolls by blaring out the Texas Tornados' polka version of "Frosty the Snowman," leaving in its wake the raw smell of gas. Nazul knows that it's time to bust a move.

Like a stray varrio dog, Nazul walks up beside her to cross the street to Prieto's. He looks up at the traffic light. A todamadre! It just turned red. He glances at her. His heart thumps in his throat like a Li'l Rob Chicano rap hit. Before he loses his nerve, he finds himself blurting out a stupid line heard from tourists who get lost in the varrio: "Excuse me, señorita, but can you tell me how to get to the Alamo?" He tries to be funny with his bolillo line.

For a few long, painful seconds Nazul bears her indifference. "What?" she finally blurts out, annoyed. Meanwhile, the two señoras clock the real-time varrio novela with amusement.

Nazul regroups, tries another angle: "If your car isn't working, I can fix it for you."

She slowly turns her eyes to his. They lock in a dreamy stare. Her eyes then slowly travel down his pathetic getup, ending at his scruffy, grease-stained shoes.

Nazul feels numb, unable to swallow the huge lump in his throat that now blocks his airway.

Just when he is about to fall off the curb from the suspense, she speaks again. "I don't even know you." She shrugs her shoulders so sensuously that it makes his balls ache. The backs of his knees feel weak.

He swallows the lump and catches his breath. With a sophisticated air, he grabs his smudged collar. "Me llamo Bond, James Bond." He tries to crack her sheet of ice. The two señoras bite their lips to keep from smiling.

The Chicana gives him an unamused glance: "Me llamo lost. Get lost," and looks back down at her paper. Nazul walks stupidly across the street with his tail between his legs to the muffled giggles of the señoras. The Chicana smiles at the señoras, then stares long and seriously at Nazul's back.

Nazul bursts into Prieto's Auto Parts. It's just as he left it: Two vatos wait around for a part they can't get cheaper anywhere else. Chuy, el Picudo, a short, burly Chicano in his late forties, leans across the long, beat-to-shit, oil-stained counter on the business side, exchanging chisme with Plutarco, a tall, thin señor in his sixties. Plutarco is sitting on a high stool next to the counter, half reading *La Prensa* and half listening to Chuy's lies. Both are dressed in work clothes that have taken years of abuse. Nazul shakes his head at the sight.

Chuy and Plutarco give Nazul a serious look as if they don't know him but already don't like him. They're setting the stage for a little varrio theater to entertain the two bored vatos in the shop.

Nazul struts toward them. "¿Qué pasó, chavalones? ¿Qué están haciendo?" *What's up, little punks? What are you doing?*

Chuy glances at Nazul, then back at the two vatos. "Nos mira aquí platicando y pregunta que '¿Qué estamos haciendo?'" *He sees us having a conversation and he asks, 'What are we doing?'*

The two vatos hide their grins, embarrassed for Nazul. Nazul isn't flustered as he approaches the counter, checking out Chuy and Plutarco with a grin. "Chinga, ¿Porqué mejor no se casan? Así pueden dormir juntos también?" *Fuck. Why don't you two just get married? That way you can sleep together too.*

Nazul glances over at the two vatos, who burst out with half-muzzled carcajadas. He turns back to Chuy and Plutarco, who are still hanging on his remark with their dead serious Gregory Peck looks. He locks on Chuy and raises an index finger to him.

"Por andar con tus chistes horribles, me dites el carbulador de un Mercury, menso." *For always boring us with your ugly jokes, you ended up giving me the carburetor to a Mercury, dummy.* He drops the oily rag with the carburetor on the counter with a thud.

Chuy's eyebrows and nose bridge meet in a disbelieving frown. "¿Que? ¡No puede ser! ¡Yo *nunca* me equivoco!" *What? It can't be! I never make a mistake!*

Nazul gives the vatos his Garfield the Cat look. Chuy grabs the carburetor and looks under it mysteriously. He smells it. Nazul is impatient. "¡De volada! Doña Tomasa needs the car by tonight!"

Chuy clicks out of character and walks off to get the right part.

"Imbecile," Nazul mutters.

Chuy runs the shop now that Prieto is too old to distinguish a radiator hose from a muffler pipe. His two daughters didn't want to be around sweaty, oil-stained men all day. Prieto's two sons have both died, one in a drive-by three years ago. Prieto's other son was killed in 'Nam in '68 at age twenty. That was a very dark Christmas in el Weso many years ago, Nazul recalls.

Plutarco is checking out Nazul with a mischievous grin. "Oyes,

Blue-Boy, ¿Cuándo te vas a casar *tú,* maricón?" *Ey, Blue-Boy, when are* you *getting married, pussy?*

Nazul frowns. "No me quieres volver a ver, ¿o qué?" *You don't want to see me again, or what?*

Plutarco looks at the vatos. "Sí. Cuando te dejen que salgas pa'fuera a regar las matas." *Yeah. When she lets you go outside to water the plants.*

They all have a good laugh.

Plutarco is a lifer of el Weso. He's always hanging around the shop when he isn't roofing homes or mowing the sprawling lawns of rich gabachos in Alamo Heights. He passes his days joking around with the regular vatos that come and go, vatos that seem to spend a third of their lives working on their junkpiles on wheels. It always amazes Nazul how these vatos, when they get together to discuss a car problem, seem to know chingos about even the late-model, computerized cars.

Sometimes Chuy pays Plutarco a few bucks to go fetch a part across town. Plutarco is a dependable and honest compadre to all who have the good fortune of knowing him. Not a day goes by that he doesn't end up in some amateur mecánico's driveway tinkering with the odd electrical problem in somebody's carrucha. Electrical problems can drive any backyard mechanic to a drunken parranda. A retiree of Kelly, Plutarco has the ingenuity and patience to track down the culprit wire. Nazul doesn't see this patience in many of the younger vatos in the varrio.

Nazul taps his fingers on the counter, impatiently.

Chuy finally returns with two carburetors and carefully compares them, taking todo su pinche tiempo. *All his sweet time.*

Nazul slams his hand on the counter. "Ey, órale! Sácate la daga!" *Pull the dagger out!* He glances at the two vatos, who are grinning. "No nomás estás *menso* y *horrible,* pero eres *pachorrudo.*" *You're not only* ugly *and* stupid, *but you're* slow. The two vatos can't contain their laughter.

Chuy makes a decision and hands the right carburetor to Nazul. "Ten, miserable." He mouths every syllable with damning emotion.

Nazul grabs the carburetor and heads out the door. "Ay los wacho."

Chuy clocks Nazul. "Te bañas!" *Make sure to bathe!* The vatos burst out laughing.

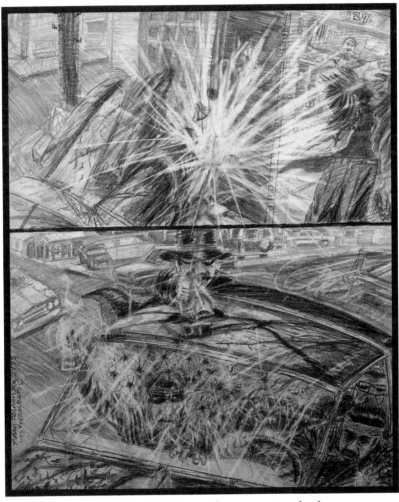

a camaro crashes into a hydrant, heavy firepower rains death

"Te purgas!" *Make sure to take your laxative!* answers Nazul without looking back. The vatos laugh even louder.

Nazul opens the door and the world explodes! The morning calm is shattered. Automatic gunfire. Frightened screams. A cherry red '69 Camaro filled with young gangsters comes crashing into a fire hydrant at Nazul's feet, sending water gushing in an upward arc. Nazul leaps back inside the shop for cover.

Five punks knock heads inside a black, '67 Ford Mustang as it screeches and skids, finally ramming into the back of the Camaro. The Mustang flips to a smoking stop with its trunk open, its back to the Camaro, which ends up facing the traffic light at an angle.

From a dark, '74 Olds Cutlass in the middle of the intersection across the street, heavy firepower rains death on the chavalos in the Camaro and Mustang. The Cutlass is no more than forty feet from the two cars.

Inside Prieto's, everybody dives for cover. The rounds cut into the Camaro's windshield, making popping sounds and sending glass shards shooting up into the cold wet air. Stray bullets penetrate Prieto's in quick succession, puncturing stacked oilcans and sending streams of oil to splatter the counter and walls like dark brown blood. Pieces of splintered wood fly off the counter, leaving trails of dust.

Outside, shotgun blasts and automatic fire fill the intersection con la madre de desmadres. *With the mother of all fuckups.*

Breaking out their own firepower of Uzis, Lugers, shotguns, and TEC-9s, the chavalos in the Camaro and Mustang return fire.

The thumping bass of "Family Affair," a rap hit by Kid Frost, resonates from the Camaro and bounces off the walls of the tiny businesses like the erratic beat of an inhuman heart.

Sticking their weapons out the passenger windows of the Mustang, the young gangsters answer with deafening reports that bounce off the four corners of the intersection. Greyish smoke hangs heavy over all three cars.

A vato in the Cutlass's front passenger seat sticks two .44s out the window and sprays the Mustang with hot lead. Blood splatters and frantic hands thrash about in death throes, releasing their hot, smoking steel to fly up in the air and clatter to the street.

For a few seconds the shooting stops. Nazul looks up from his cover. From the Cutlass, Sunny and the Sunliners pour out "Put Me In

black maddog sunglasses fly through the air, a stream of blood falls away

Jail" in a mournful refrain.

The clicks of fresh clips slapping into metal can be heard in the background.

The shooting heats up again and Nazul ducks down. It's definitely a conflict between an older ganga and a younger one. The rhythms pounding from the Camaro fill the air with a surprisingly captivating melody.

A young gangster kisses the floorboard in the front seat of the Camaro and winces. Armor-piercing rounds tear holes through the engine and right through his legs. "Aawww! Chingadamadre!!!" The stereo plays.

The vato yells and curses, both from the fear of death and the pain of the deep burning wounds. "Chingadamadre!"

The wounded gangster spits saliva and blood as he writhes on the floor of the car. His homie lies screaming in fear and agony across the front seat and console next to him. Flying glass and hot metal shards cut into him also. "Take that culo out!" he yells at his homies behind him. "Take him out!"

Three vatos in the Camaro's back seat open up with their Glocks and Uzis. They lean out the windows and over the roof, trying in their panic to find the vato with the weapon tearing through their only shield. Their eyes are a stark mirror of their terror as they struggle for their lives.

Screams from crouching bystanders lure Nazul's head up. He spots a shattered pair of black maddog sunglasses flying through the air above the Cutlass. A stream of blood falls away. Time drags down into slow motion in the midst of this living nightmare.

Nazul glances to the bus bench where the Chicana and the señoras were. Of course, they're gone.

He can barely make out the tops of some heads behind parked cars outside the 7-Eleven directly across the street. The Chicana huddles with the señoras and señor, who are terrified. "No tengan cuidado." *Don't be afraid.* She shields them with her arms. "La Virgencita nos proteje." *The Virgencita will protect us.*

More screams. Chuy, Plutarco, and one of the vatos in the shop peer up. They see two vatos step out on the driver's side of the Cutlass firing automatics. A rash of bloodcurdling slaps of lead on meat and bone suddenly silences the last firepower coming from the Mustang.

The two vatos from the Cutlass look like hardened criminals

in their '50s attire and black bandanas, compared with the younger chavalos in their Nike sports caps and Polo sweatshirts.

Through the smoke and water spray, the older vatos shift their focus. They coolly approach the dripping Camaro, which straddles the toppled hydrant, unable to move. Incredibly, the engine is still running. It revs high as the vato on the floorboard pushes the accelerator with his hand. The tires spin wildly, causing the Camaro to lurch sideways but still stay stuck on the hydrant.

The chavalones inside duck as lead whizzes by their heads.

The older vatos strut right up to the hood of the Camaro.

The two wounded chavalones in the front seat of the Camaro peer up and start shooting wildly through the shattered windshield. They are finished off instantly by the varrio assassins in a stunning flurry of firepower.

Not to be outdone, two chavalos crawl out of the Camaro's back seat onto the sidewalk and street, one with a smoking sawed-off shotgun and the other with a red hot Uzi.

They miraculously survive a barrage of hot lead as they flinch, duck, and yell, looking for an opening to answer back.

While one homie falls to the street with his shotgun and blasts the two veteranos in the ankles from underneath the Camaro, the other chavalo is able to mow down the soldados in an Uzi heartbeat.

One vato falls back onto the hood of the Cutlass with a bloody thud.

Gunsmoke hangs thick over the street like a fireworks display.

Only one vato remains in the Cutlass. El mero chingón, the one they really want. He sticks his hand out to fire over the hood. A dozen bullet holes surround him on the windshield.

The chavito in the street with the Uzi empties his clip at him. Pieces of chrome trim from the door's frame fly off as the last rounds are spent.

The other chavito is gripped by fear. He operates on pure adrenaline, struggles to keep his legs from buckling like crackers as he stands on the sidewalk with the sawed-off. As he nervously reloads, the shells scatter on the pavement under the gushing arc of the water from the hydrant.

On the street side of the Camaro, the chavito scrambles with a fresh clip. In his clumsy rush, he snags the clip on his inside jacket pocket and can't pull it out.

The vato in the Cutlass steps out.

Leaning in and picking up a .45 from the front seat, the chavalo with the shotgun stands and empties ten rounds at the vato. As the vato stands clear of the open Cutlass door, a bullet shears off an earring from his left ear. More rounds whiz by, making his jacket fly up from the lead.

In the back seat of the Camaro, the last chavalo claws on the floorboard for a fresh clip that's almost out of reach under the front seat.

The vato approaches the Camaro.

Jet black maddogs under a black paño. A black cap with its visor flipped around to the back. A gunmetal grey Salvation Army jacket, dark brown, baggy Dickies worn low, a half-smoked frajo dangling from the side of his mouth, and a Glock in each hand give him the look of the last vato you'll ever have a problem with.

Death crowds in with the chavalos in the Camaro and they make their last stand against the vato. Their consciousness drags to a nauseating crawl.

The vato fires back effortlessly, tearing a hole over the engine and blasting the Camaro's thumping stereo into silence. Now Sunny rules the airwaves.

For the chavalos, time jerks forward with a head-splitting jolt. Their blood runs like ice through their veins as they numbly gather their wits. The vato has turned his attention to the sawed-off on the sidewalk.

Before the chavalo on the sidewalk can stop shaking long enough to slap shells and level off, the vato blasts him in the chest, sending him slapping his head against the weathered wall of Prieto's, dead before he hits the ground.

On the street side, behind the open door of the Camaro, the chavito with the Uzi inserts the new clip. The vato struts toward him with all the coolness of well-greased iron balls. The lone chavalo in the back seat of the Camaro fires wildly through the jagged hole in the windshield, but only punctures the trapped cars of bystanders.

The Uzi erratically lays down a row of holes in front of the vato, taking out chunks of asphalt from the street.

The vato continues his approach. Clouds of steam pulsating from his nostrils are the only sign that he is human. A seasoned varrio war veteran, he picks his shots carefully, making each one count.

He fires, the impact ripping the Uzi from the chavalo's hands with a violent flip.

Grimacing in agony, the chavalo tries to shake the pain off his hands.

He slips on the wet, oily blacktop, avoiding another blast of lead that nearly blows off his head. He dives behind the Camaro, stumbling toward his last chance of escape down the sidewalk.

From the back seat of the Camaro, his homie also bails out on the sidewalk side. As he stands and his head clears the Camaro's roof, he empties the last three shots from his automatic at the vato.

Nothing.

The vato closes in chingón, his eyes dark. The chavalos run off, terrified for their lives. He checks for a clean shot. One chavito clears some street signs, a telephone pole. The vato fires. The .45 finds its mark, piercing the kid's back. He goes crashing into a makeshift fence in front of a tiny varrio barbershop. He's dead within seconds. From behind some garbage cans, a trembling viejito rolls onto the sidewalk, his stomach bleeding a red pool onto the white concrete.

Half a block away, the other chavalo runs for his life. Panicked, he foolishly sprints across the street, becoming a clear target. The vato takes him down, winging him in the heel. The chavalo's nerves recoil. He flips into the air and crashes back down to the pavement. Dazed and bloody, he struggles to get up again and limps toward some cars across the street.

A young Chicana mother with two toddlers hides behind the parked cars. She sees the chavalo come limping in her direction, breathless with fear. The vato, clearly now just toying with the chavalo's life, fires at him with both .45s. He misses, but the rounds ricochet and ping on the cars, dangerously close to the young mother and her niños. She pleads for her children's safety as she cowers amid their painful cries.

The chavalo feels the warm wet pain at the end of his leg. Weak and dizzy, he is drawn to the pleading mother, to her protection.

"Perdóname, 'Amá." Shots slam into the car near her and she falls to the street, trying to cover her kids with her body. The chavalo's heart and mind are instantly imbued with clarity. He limps out of the family's range, feeling his life draining away.

A muffled explosion bellows in the distance. Whizzing. A jolt. He feels outside himself, unable to control his movement. Suddenly the varrio becomes blurred, surreal. He feels the warm blood flow from his chest, sees it steam, struggles to breathe in its pool on the pavement. The tips of the vato's shoes are closing in. The young mother's pleading cry turns to a muted lament for this boy she doesn't know, for his mother, who cannot protect him.

Back at Prieto's, the young Chicana from the bus stop has come out of hiding. She is frozen, watching, trembling to the bone. She hears the mother's screams. She desperately looks around for help.

The Chicana starts walking down the calle towards the vato. "Los niños!" *The kids!* she screams. "Los *niños*!"

Standing outside of Prieto's, Chuy, Nazul, and Plutarco gauge her movement. They are unaware of the viejito lying on the sidewalk down the street.

The Chicana sees the vato walk calmly up to the chavalo. The mother screams for his life. She yells again, "Somos Raza! Aquí viven nuestros niños!" *We are one race! Our kids live here!*

The vato stops dead in his tracks. He looks around, puzzled. He stares at the Chicana over his shoulder. He sees her stretch her arms out to him.

"Aquí viven nuestros abuelos! Respetalos! Te lo pido!" *Our grandparents live here! Respect them! I beg you!*

The vato looks down at his bloody hand on the cohete, then around to the crying mother nearby.

Worried, the señoras start walking after the Chicana.

Nazul moves quickly to her and waves the señoras back. Gently, he urges the Chicana not to get too close and tries to escort her back to safety.

The vato turns back to the chavalo, who is nearly unconscious. He stands over him. Points his Glock. "Este es por mi carnalita." *This one's for my little sister.* He breathes out deeply.

In a last act of defiance, the chavalo spits blood up at him. "Pinche, Diablo!"

The thunderous blast of the Glock slaps its echoes against the walls of the surrounding buildings, leaving only the faint weeping of huddled bystanders.

All is silent as the vato walks calmly back to the Cutlass. His head cocked back, he chuco-struts to another song by Sunny now starting to pour out of the car.

♫ "Smile now, cry later."

The vato looks menacingly around at anyone who might be foolish enough to challenge his macho authority.

♫ "Smile now, cry later for you."

Only a few viejitos brave his stare. He ignores them with a sadistic grin. As is usually the case in the varrio, not a single siren can be heard.

Back at the intersection across from Prieto's, Nazul holds the dazed Chicana against his chest. She trembles and mutters to herself, "Co-cobarde." *Coward.*

♫ "My friends tell me…you could never belong to me."

Her breath is choppy. She raises her eyes to look into Nazul's… then to the bloody scene, numb.

♫ "So I'll smile for my friends and cry later, yeah, for you."

"No puede ser," she whispers hoarsely. "La vida no puede ser tan horrible." *Life can't be this horrible.* She swallows gulps of grief.

Nazul sees the vato approaching and discreetly shields her from his view. Except for the blaring song echoing against the silent walls, the intersection is eerily quiet.

The vato arrives at the still-lit and smoking Cutlass.

♫ "I wouldn't be crying…if I didn't love you so-o-o."

He drags his homie's bloody body off the hood and drops him onto the street like a bag of cement.

♫ "I'll smile for my friends—"

Streams of blood run down to the curb and melt into pale tints of brownish-red with the hydrant's spray raining on the scene.

Almost casually, the vato walks to the driver's side and tosses one of the guns into the passenger seat. He sticks the other Glock into his belt. He looks around one last time.

Nazul has his back to him. The place suddenly feels like time has come to a standstill.

Then the vato looks toward Prieto's. Through the water spray, Chuy and Plutarco are staring back at him with hate in their eyes. The vato locks on to their stares with his dark maddogs.

They hold theirs on him.

He reaches into the Cutlass and cuts the stereo.

Deafening silence.

Nazul senses the tension and looks around to find the vato staring at Chuy and Plutarco. The vato walks toward them.

When he gets ten feet away, the vato stops and slowly lifts the Glock's barrel and levels it at Plutarco, the tip of it red from the chavalo down the street. His deep voice penetrates the silence: "Yo soy Diablo! El que me relaje…lo entierro!" *I am Diablo! Whoever rats on me…I will bury!*

The vato's maddogs could be the last thing they ever see, but Chuy and Plutarco don't even flinch.

"Cobarde!" *Coward!* The Chicana's voice startles Nazul and the cringing gente, who are dreading the explosion from the .45. "Mátanos a todos!" *Kill us all!* Diablo grins and stares Chuy and Plutarco down.

Suddenly, another voice across the shell-ridden lanes strikes a nerve.

"¡Nomás *culeros* usan cohetes!" *Only* chickenshits *use guns!*

Diablo turns so fast his neck pops. He looks inhuman in his dark, impenetrable maddogs. The air is again taut with tension as Nazul stares him down. Diablo's mouth forms into a scowl as he points the Glock at Nazul, his hand trembling with rage.

"Cobarde! Pelea como hombre!" *Coward! Fight like a man!* the Chicana yells as the señoras struggle to hold her back.

Nazul glances at her for a second.

"¡Aquí vive mi hermanita! ¡¡Mi hermanita!!" *My little sister lives here! My little sister!!* The Chicana's stare is cold. Determined.

Diablo stands frozen for a moment. He looks around to the gente, who seem to awaken from their trance. He turns back to the Chicana. She stares him down. He nods chignon. "Orale, ruca. ¿Así lo quieres? Atodamadre." *All right, ruca. Is that the way you want it? Fucking great.* He lowers the barrel.

Diablo grins at Nazul sarcastically. "Te rayates, culo." *You lucked out, asshole.* He steps quickly back to the car, his eyes never leaving Nazul. He throws the gun in the Cutlass, and in the same motion he reaches into his back pocket and pulls out a push-button fila. *Switchblade.* He pops the nine-incher.

What looked like a ghost town is now starting to come alive with terrified but curious onlookers expecting to be mute witnesses to the last few moments of *another* vato's life.

His head cocked back, Diablo struts chuco-style toward Nazul. His aura radiates death as he handles the fila with killer confidence.

Some señora yells, "¡Córrele Nazul!" *Run!*

"El no tiene defensa!" *He has no way to defend himself!* Her voice hoarse, the Chicana yells over the señoras trying to detain her.

Nazul looks around to the ground. He sees a skinny green tree switch about three feet long lying on the sidewalk. He picks it up and

diablo pulls out his push-button fila

slices the air with it a couple of times, making whipping sounds as Diablo arrives. Running the length of the blade across his red tongue, Diablo grins with a malicious scowl at the sight of Nazul holding the varita. Nazul awaits the inevitable.

Suddenly Diablo lunges at him like a rabid varrio dog.

Nazul is a blur as he jumps away. With perfect timing, he whips Diablo's face twice with the switch.

For a moment Diablo is stunned, a red cross on his leather face. In a blind rage, he lunges at Nazul again, only to get a bonus across the mouth. Diablo checks his lip. Blood.

Faint emergency sirens can now be heard wailing in the distance. Diablo turns to Nazul, who hasn't budged an inch. In one last attempt, Diablo flings his fila, missing Nazul's head by a hair.

Nazul stands unflinching.

With sirens closing in fast, Diablo half walks, half runs back to the bullet-riddled Cutlass, tension still hanging thick in the cold, misty air. Reaching the driver door, he turns to Nazul.

"El que apuesta conmigo…siempre pierde todo." *Those who bet with me…always lose it all.*

He trains his 'dogs on Luna and nods chingón. Then he looks back to Nazul. "Ya estás bien entrado." *You're in deep.*

Nazul calmly shrugs his shoulders. "Pos, ¿pa'qué me la cantas? Aquí estoy." *Well, why sing me a tune? I'm right here.*

In a rage, Diablo jumps into the Cutlass and tears away, running over a dead body and leaving a cloud of burnt rubber.

Onlookers seem strangely inspired. They crane their necks to get a better look at Luna and Nazul as they tentatively gather around the bloody carnage. Three teenage girls clock Luna as she kneels down to a chavalo gasping his last breaths. A señora hands her a rosary and the Chicana clasps it around the bloodied hand of the chavalo and lifts her eyes up in prayer. Las señoras weep for the waste of such young lives, shaking their heads in disbelief as the varrio slowly slides itself back into real-time. As Nazul drops the switch, a teenage chavalo quickly runs and grabs it. He stares at Nazul as he slices the air with it.

Chuy and Plutarco, followed by Nazul, run over to the viejito who got shot and is now starting to moan. He's bleeding badly.

Sirens blaring, two squad cars recklessly screech to a halt, almost clipping the bystanders, who jump away. Four cops jump out with their Glocks and pump-action shotguns ready.

Cautiously, the two vatos inside Prieto's step outside to assess the damage.

Immediately, the cops point their weapons at them. "Hold it right there! Get on the ground!"

The Chicana yells at them, "They didn't do anything! They're gone! He's gone."

Chuy yells from thirty feet away to the cops, "Eh! This señor is bleeding to death! Where's the ambulance?"

The cops are still preoccupied with the two innocent vatos sprawled on the sidewalk. They get busy searching them for weapons, frisking every pocket. Two cops, combat-ready, sneak into Prieto's searching for other suspects.

The Chicana yells at them, "Call an ambulance!"

One cop yells back, "Shut up! We know what we're doing! We're in charge here!"

"¡Estupidos!" The Chicana runs to help Chuy, Nazul, and Plutarco, who are picking up the viejito and carrying him to Chuy's '68 GTO parked behind the smoking Camaro in front of Prieto's.

The old man is near death. They load him into the back seat with the Chicana. Nazul jumps in the front passenger seat. Chuy throws the car keys to Plutarco, who runs around and jumps in the driver's seat. They peel away, honking the horn at the small crowd.

The GTO races through the varrio streets, its horn blaring. It only slows down at the intersections.

"Dios es muy grande. Dios lo bendiga. Lindo es Dios." *God is very huge. May God bless you. Beautiful is God.* The Chicana cradles the señor in her arms as Nazul hands her his shirt. She wads it up and applies pressure to his wound. "Que la Virgencita me lo cuide." *May the Virgencita protect you.* She tries to soothe him.

Arriving at the hospital, Nazul and Plutarco burst through the emergency room double doors carrying the bloodied viejito, hoping he can still be saved. The medics see the blood and quickly help them through.

Her clothes stained with blood, the young Chicana walks slowly behind them, knowing it's too late.

Un señor and his wife approach her in the waiting room.

"M'ijita, ¿Qué pasó? ¿Estás herida?" *My child. What happened? Are you injured?* The señora holds her hands out to her. The Chicana grabs their palms and squeezes tight. Her eyes watery, she swallows a lump in her throat, trying to maintain.

"Vamos a rezar por ese señor." *Pray with me for that man.*

"Are you his next of kin, or a friend?"

The Chicana looks up to see Plutarco and Nazul, their clothes brown-red with blood, resignation in their faces, as the young intern talks to them.

"Yeah, I knew him." Plutarco nods, glancing down at his bloodied hands.

She sees only darkness.

The ride back to the varrio is a journey of reflective solitude. Silent. Her eyes weary, the Chicana looks darkly out the back window to see the gente as they walk back from the scene of the shootout. 'This is my gente. Humble. Dirt-poor,' she thinks. "How can viejitos or kids or *anybody* live in this hell?" she blurts out.

Plutarco checks her in the mirror. "Los jovenes de hoy en dia, andan perdidos. No tienen vergüenza ni respeto a nada." *These kids nowadays are lost. They don't know shame or have respect for anything.*

Nazul just stares blankly ahead. He's thinking about his Don Pablito and how he'd like to shield him from this ruthless world. He glances at the old, '40s-style, weathered walls of the varrio buildings, electrical lines, windows, and doors as they drift past. 'If these streets could tell a story, it would be a high drama about survival, about real people, a forgotten people of the shadows.'

Wailing sirens fill the cold air as they arrive back at Prieto's.

The last of the bodies are being loaded into the ambulance. Chuy is outside with a water hose, washing the blood into a storm drain. The red-stained water streams over the brown and dirty pink chalk outlines of the bodies.

A Live-Eye news team is packing up its gear as a homicide photographer takes the last few shots.

"*Nobody* saw *nothin'*?" A white rookie cop with his pad and pencil stares at twenty-odd people with his mouth open. He glances at Chuy, who washes the blood past his boots. The cop's gaze follows the stream of water down to his boots and back up to Chuy.

"What about you? Got any identification?"

Chuy rolls his eyes. "*Identification?* That old man was *dying.*"

"I'm guessin' you didn't see anything either."

"Move your family over here and let's see how well *you* see." Chuy cannot contain his sarcasm.

The rookie throws his hands up in resignation. "We can't make an arrest without witnesses."

"Well, if you put down your taco long enough to patrol these streets, maybe *you* could be a witness."

The rookie loses his patience with Chuy. "Either way you slice it, nobody lives forever."

Chuy bugs his eyes at him. "Mind if I try, officer?"

"Yeah, keep talking." He gives Chuy a threatening stare.

Plutarco and Nazul walk toward Chuy. He can tell by their faces that the viejito didn't make it. The Chicana walks behind them. The rookie sees the blood on their clothes.

"I already called his familia. They're on the way to the hospita." Chuy shakes his head.

The two señoras walk out of the crowd and approach the Chicana, one of them holding her purse and briefcase. Folding his pad with a flop, the rookie cop walks off with a smirk.

Elias arrives breathlessly. He checks out Nazul. "Carnal, estas bien?" Nazul nods yes. Elias sees Plutarco also looks all right, despite the bloodstains from the viejito. "Y el Chore?" *And Shorty?* Nazul nods yes about Chuy. Elias shakes his head, looking around to the remains of the shootout. "I had to drive Elsa to work. I just got back. Cabrón, there were screaming ambulances everywhere." He crosses himself toward the chalk outlines. "You got the carburetor? I'll take it with me. I got the chavalos in the car." Nazul walks into Prieto's and comes back with the car part. He hands it to Elias and gives him a Razas handshake. Elias takes off down the street. "Ay te wacho en el canton. Ay te wacho, viejo," he nods to Plutarco. *See you at the house. See you later, old man.*

The last ambulance pulls away and goes crying through the varrio streets. Nazul and Plutarco walk into Prieto's and come out with paper towels and a spray bottle full of soapy liquid to clean up the blood-stained GTO.

Scrubbing the back seat, Nazul stops and looks around outside to the few gente still left. "Oyes, Plutarco, la muchacha. ¿Pá dónde se fue?" *Ey, Plutarco, the girl? Where did she go?*

Plutarco wipes the steering wheel. "Se fue." *She left.*

Nazul: "Ni le preguntamos su nombre." *We didn't even get her name.*

Plutarco collects the bloody towels from Nazul and throws them in a garbage bag that Chuy brings them. "Luna."

Nazul stops cleaning. "¿Qué?"

Plutarco: "Her name is Luna."

"¿La conoces?" Nazul scrubs the floorboards.

"I knew her jefito. Her familia es puro Weso. Ella es una mujer maravillosa." *She is a marvelous woman.* Plutarco leans in to help scrub the caked blood in the seams of the custom diamond-pleat upholstery. "Her jefe was a cop here en el varrio until about five years ago. Pero he wasn't like some of these pendejos we saw today."

They decide to take out the bottom half of the back seat to get to the blood underneath. They set it on the sidewalk and crawl back in to continue cleaning. Nazul is still hanging on Plutarco's story. "And? What happened five years ago? ¿Y por qué es maravillosa?" *And why is she marvelous?*

Plutarco doesn't look up. "Lo mataron." *They killed him.* He steps out and walks into Prieto's for more paper towels.

A minute later he returns. Nazul has stopped cleaning and is now clocking him. "Chinga, parece que te estoy sacando una pinche muela. *Fuck, I feel like I'm pulling out one of your damn molars.* How did he die?"

Plutarco slowly clears his throat, accepting the fact that Nazul isn't going to go away. "Well, there was this clicka. Unos vatos, muy malillas, aquí en el varrio." *Some really bad vatos here in the varrio.* He stops for a minute, distracted by the sound of two drunks fighting a few feet away on the sidewalk. He turns around and checks them forcibly clawing at each other over a cuarto de bironga. *A quart of beer.* He yells at them, "¡Ey! ¡Vámonos de aquí! ¡Váyanse a pelear en su hogar!" *Ey! Get out of here! Go fight in your own damn yard!* He rolls his eyes wearily at Nazul. "Pinches winos. ¿Cómo ellos nunca tienen cancer?" *Damn winos. How come they never get cancer?* He gives Nazul a varrio-trucha glance. "Porque no tienen feria, chinga." *Because they don't have any money.*

Nazul is still staring at him.

Plutarco clears his throat. "Bueno, ah, los culeros andaban diliando chiva y les causaron chingos de problemas a la pobre gente de aquí." *Anyway, those chickenshits were dealing heroin and caused a lot of problems for the poor people here.* He nods his head. "'Taba gacho." *It was bad.*

Nazul sees Plutarco calmly stepping out again and playfully grabs him by the collar. "¿Maravillosa?"

Plutarco grins and nods at his curiosity. "You like her that much, eh? Pinche joto." *Damn wimp.* He changes gears. "Oyes, I just want to tell you que…ese jale con la varita," he shakes his head in disgust and checks Nazul up and down with a grin. *That shit with the switch.* "Nah, tú ya no vales verga." *Nah, you ain't worth a fuck anymore.*

Nazul leans in to Plutarco's scruffy face. "¿Y? ¿La *clicka*?" *And? The* gang?

Plutarco: "'Ta bueno, hombre. Cabrón, ¡cómo eres necio!" *All right, man. Damn, you sure can nag!* He pushes his face away. Nazul releases his collar cautiously.

"Well, the cops knew what was up with these cabrones, but they either didn't give a shit or were supplying them with the chiva to make feria out of the gente's misery." He looks away at a three-legged, war-torn varrio dog limping by on the asphalt, sniffing hopefully at the stains of blood.

"¿Y luego?"

Plutarco takes a deep breath. "So Luna's father and his close friend and partner, a gabacho named, ah, Fischer, went to their ganghouse to serve a warrant. There was a big shootout. The varrio talked about it for weeks."

"Chinga, and I can't even get you to talk about it for two minutes." Nazul throws down his damp towel. "¿Solo que así se murió?" *So that's the way he died?*

Plutarco nods as he looks away. "Only el gabacho survived that balaceada. But he got badly wounded and almost died. I heard he took seven plomazos. El Mexicano, Guadalupe Ríos, como una docena. Later Fischer told the news that if it hadn't been for his partner, he wouldn't be talking."

"¿Y la ganga? ¿Qué tántos vatos?" *And the gang? How many vatos?*

"Inside la ganghouse they bagged eleven tecatos. *Junkies.* Chinga, parecía una pinche guerra." *Fuck, it was like a damn war.*

Plutarco looks at Nazul, who has drifted off, picturing the events in his mind. "¿Vites? *See?* Don't be cynical. Some gabachos are good." He heaves a halftoad and spits on the curb. "Pero, very few."

Nazul gazes out the windshield. "Luna. Qué lindo nombre. Maravillosa." *What a beautiful name. Marvelous.*

Rolling his eyes at the low clouds, Plutarco shakes his head, grinning. "Pinche empelotado. *Damn hopeless romantic.* She wouldn't give you la *pinche* hora del tiempo. *The* damn *time of the hour.* Nadie chinga con ella." *Nobody fucks with her.* He looks around. "Ey, Blue-Boy, what you should be thinking about is that vato Diablo. Pónte trucha. Es de los más *fríos.*" *Watch out. He's as* cold *as they come.* Plutarco looks away, thinking. He locks back on Nazul and whispers loudly, "Ni le des la espalda." *Don't even turn your back on him.*

Una carrucha rumbles by on the street, leaving a white cloud of toxic smoke. With watery, burning eyes the vatos go coughing around the corner of the building. "Chingau! The city should hire ese vato to exterminate zancudos." *Mosquitos.* Plutarco spits again and continues. "Anyways, ese Diablo ha matado a chingos de vatos. Dicen que es hijo del Carrasco. Otros dicen que del Copetón. Pero estamos seguros que es una pinche máquina de desmadre. Los vatos más malillas lo conocen como el Rey de las siete muertes." *Anyways, Diablo has killed a lot of vatos. Some say he's the son of el Carrasco. Others say he came from el Copetón. But we are sure of one thing, that he's a damn killing machine. The baddest vatos in the varrio know him as The King of the seven deaths.*

Nazul looks away, concerned for the gente now. "Si ese vato anda chingando con la Raza, *alguién* le va a tumbar la corona." *If that vato is fucking with our people,* someone *is gonna knock his crown off.*

"Simón. Pero ese *alguién,* vale mas que tenga la gracia del Señor a su lado." *Right. But that* someone *better have the grace of God on his side.* Plutarco rubs his watery eyes and breathes deeply, trying to exhale the near-death experience of la balaceada. "No se había visto hace chingos. Yo creo que estaba encarruchado." *He hasn't been seen around for a while. He must have been in the slammer.*

Checking his back, Blue-Boy looks around to make sure they're clear. He whispers, "Elías no le va a agarrar cagada. El sí, lo manda para un pozo *más* hondo." *Elias ain't gonna take his shit. He'll send him to a deeper hole.*

Plutarco just nods his head, worried.

aparición #2

Three

Horas luminosas
Illuminating hours

Praying fervently, the curandero works his healing over a frail viejita at his altar. She sits on a chair in the center of the tiny, ten-by-ten-foot room. Nearby, her grandson waits. The five-year-old youngster looks up at dozens of santos elbowing for space on the walls of the tiny room. Quietly he watches, in awe of their divine magic.

Don Pablito rubs holy water on the viejita's neck and arms as he prays. He tells her to relax, then starts popping her neck, arms, knees, and back. She winces slightly, but it's a welcome relief. Don Pablito wipes his hands on a clean white kitchen towel. His hands seem swollen, curiously oversized from the many people he sees each day.

Sitting on a short stool, he faces the viejita and speaks. "Cuando le empiezan a doler sus huesitos y está en su casa, abra un bote de tomates enteros. Póngase el tomate en todos sus dolores por una hora o menos. ¡Y ya no coma carne! La carne está muerta y nomás le da muerte a su cuerpo. Por eso le duelen sus huesos. Después la puede dejar ciega, también. De vez en cuando está bien. Y tome pura agua distilada. Y váyase a andar en el parque por una hora, siquiera tres veces por semana. No ande en el mall. Ahí no hay naturalesa. ¿Eh? ¿No ve que la naturalesa—los arboles, la tierra—le absorbe su energía negativa y le da la buena energía? En el mall nomás hay puro cemento y el aire acondicionada no es saludable. Es todo por hoy." *When your bones begin to hurt and you are at home, open a can of whole tomatoes. Put the tomatoes on all of your pains for an hour or less. And don't eat meat. Meat is dead, and it will only give death to your body. That is why your bones ache. It could leave you blind as well. Once in a while it is okay. And drink pure, distilled water. And take a walk in the park for an hour at least three times a week. Don't walk in the mall. You won't find nature there. Don't you see that nature—the trees, the earth—absorbs your negative energy and gives you good energy? In the mall there is only cement and air-conditioned air, which are not good for your health. That's all for today.*

Don Pablito smiles as he watches her stand up briskly and turn to get her worn-out purse. "¿Sus piernitas le están sirviendo bien ahora, eh? Usted no tiene negocio vivir su vida en una silla de ruedas cuando es tan buena señora. Y vive su vida con respeto a la ley de la tierra," he says. *Your legs are serving you well, no? You have no business living your life in a wheelchair when you are such a good lady. And live your life with respect to the law of the land.*

The viejita feels as light as a feather from the treatment.

"¿Si, verdad? Mis hijas que son *enfermeras,* no lo pueden creer. Gracias, Don Pablito. ¡Muchísimas gracias! Me siento veinte años más joven." *Isn't that right? My daughters who are nurses cannot believe it. Thank you, Don Pablito. Many thanks! I feel twenty years younger.*

Don Pablito looks through his thick tablet to see who is next. But in response to the viejita, he points his index finger at a dominant picture of Jesus. "Las gracias, déselas al Señor." *Give your thanks to the Lord.*

Humbly, the viejita turns and prays with gratitude, crossing herself with genuine emotion. Her grandson mimics her.

She takes his tiny, smooth hand into her wrinkled, weathered palm and opens the door to step out. The living room/waiting room area is as jam-packed with gente as the altar room is with santos. Gente of all ages turn to look, and señoras stop their gossip in mid-sentence as the viejita and her grandson step out and walk past. They hold their gaze on Don Pablito as he reads out the next name.

"¿Diana Parker. Eh?" Don Pablito squints to make sure he has read the name right. A few puzzled looks from the gente are exchanged.

A beautiful white lady in her mid-forties, her face covered in a black veil, gets up from the edge of the room, followed by a Chicana. Eyeing the unexpected patient quizzically, el curandero shows them into his office.

As the viejita reaches the front door, she takes out two dollars and fifty cents and puts the money in a glass jar that sits almost hidden away against the wall. On both sides of her, the living room walls are covered with the photos of gente who have been healed by el curandero. Even a few crutches hang from nails and hooks on the wall.

"Yo me llamo Graciela y—" *My name is Graciela and—*

Don Pablito interrupts her and speaks directly to Diana Parker. "What can I do fer joo, Mees Parker? Are joo here to see eef eets all true?"

Pulling her veil away from her face, Diana fidgets a little on the tiny stool, her eyes fighting back tears. "No. Well, yes. I mean, I have breast cancer. The doctors gave me radiation, then chemo, and now they tell me it's spreading rapidly. And I just don't know what to do." She chokes back tears. "I-I don't trust them anymore."

"So, m'ija, had joo heard about me before? Why are joo come to me now?" Don Pablito wipes his hands on the white kitchen towel as he eyes Graciela suspiciously. "Joo make dee doctores jur gods, and now look. Joo wants me to beeld a house with burnt wood. Jur body is sacred. El doctor is good eef joo get in a car accident. But he cannot cure dee cancer. Only joo ana jur Creador can do thees."

El curandero takes her soft arm in his huge hand and turns it slowly, scanning her light skin. "I see seek peoples since before joo were born. An I can see dat joo don' haf no canser." He nods his head with assurance. "Joo do haf toxeen from dee chemo, but esersize, fruits, ana vegetables can get jur body backs to healthy agane."

He lets go of her hand and stares deeply into her eyes. "But who am I fer joo to beleef? I haf no beeg buildins. An where ees my degrees? Do joo see dem on dees walls? I has only my repootachin. An I don' charge joo tousands of dólares." He gets up and looks through his tablet for the next name in line. Then he looks up at Diana with mercy. "Joo and dee Maker. Eef joo beleef."

Desperate, the woman pleads with moist eyes and a glimmer of hope. "How *do* I believe? They told me you can cure anything."

"I don' cure *no*seen." Don Pablito throws down the tablet. "Only joo ana God!" He gives Graciela a stern glance. "An eef joo queet been angry, slowy down, an eet right, joo don' get seek."

"So you're saying the doctors don't care about me?"

"Eef dey deed, joo would not be here." He takes a deep breath like he's seen it a thousand times. "I has neber seen so many seek peoples than now that doctores are so powerfuls."

"So, you're saying doctors are no good? There must be some that are good."

With his massive palm, Don Pablito points to the tiny, photo-covered door. "Der are some that are gud. Ders dee door. Joo go find it. I cannot help joo. I can only tell joo dat de doctor who gets reech from the peoples' meesry will not haf the power to heal."

Diana turns his words over in her mind. It seems every time she sees a doctor she feels closer to the grave. "So, you can't do anything for me?"

"No." Don Pablito lights a vela on a low shelf next to his weathered leather stool. As far as he's concerned, their time is up.

Hopelessly, Diana looks to Graciela for help. Her friend's eyes are trained on the dozens of photos that compete for space on the small, wooden door. Graciela looks back at Diana with eyebrows raised, then back to Don Pablito, who seems indifferent. "Don Pablito, I know you care about this woman. Help us. Do you know of a healer who can help Diana?"

There's a long silence as el curandero puts down a rosario, which he was draping over his fingers. He slowly looks up at her. "Well, I know a man fer a few jeers who has dee power of da land to help peoples. Se llama Don Huerta. He's a good man. Hees son Joseph was a doctor who got very seek. And when dee doctors told heem hees gonna die, Don Huerta safe hees life."

Diana glances at Graciela. She's coming to grips with a vital truth. "So doctors can't even heal themselves?"

"Drugs ana surgery don' heals bery good. Haf jur doctor efer espeek 'bout what joo eat, 'bout de water joo drink? Haf he efer espeek 'bout how joo can keep healthy from gettin' sunshine and exserciseen and *acteen right to oders*?"

Diana's mouth drops open. She is clearly vexed by this last question. She wants to ask about it but stops short.

Don Pablito looks her in the eyes seriously. "Canser ees a bery beeg beesiness. Joo are da loser. El doctor y los beeg drugs companies—dey are weeners."

Diana's eyes light up.

Don Pablito goes on, dipping his hand in a shallow clay jar of water. With a dripping forefinger, he makes the sign of the cross on her forehead. "M'ijita, remember, when joo get angry or joo worry too much, joo make too many toxeens in jur body. De body cannot process it, an dis make joo seek. But all joo need ees to eat right, be happy, exsercise, ana joo get wells."

Diana nods, lost in thought. "If Don Huerta is so gifted at healing, why don't more people know about him?"

Don Pablito chuckles. "Dees humble peoples treating oder humble peoples. Joo go. See for yourself. Don Huerta lif aquí on Calle Trinity. He does hees work der at hees home. Hee werks only fer donacions. Eef joo reech or pors, heel treat joo dee same. What doctores do dat? Eh? Don' be 'fraid. Hees treatment is *material,* ana joo donna haf to haf faith to get well. He don' says he can treat canser 'cuza he would goes to jail fer saying eet, even eef it is true. But he weel get jur body helty enof dat it cana cure itself of anyting." He holds out his hand to Diana. "Ana donna worry nomore! Do esaklee as hee tells joo ana joo ara goins to be wells."

Diana stands to take his hand with a new glow of hope in her eyes. "Thank you, señor." She leans to kiss it.

Don Pablito pulls it back and flicks his wrists to the heavens. "Geef jur tanks to jur Creador."

"Ah, how much do I owe you?" Diana digs in her purse.

Don Pablito looks at Graciela and nods. He points his finger at the door to Diana with a grin. "Go!"

The voices of two vatos working under a beat-up '80s Monte Carlo filter up into the muggy, cold December day. They are exchanging ideas underneath the jacked-up car in the front yard next door to the curandero's house.

"A ésta transmisión, el último mecánico put Perma-Tex en el oil-pan gasket. *In this transmission, the last mechanic put Perma-Tex on the oil-pan gasket.* When it got hot, the Perma-Tex melted and seeped into the exhaust lines. We're gonna have to take it out and clean all that shit off, then replace the front and rear seals."

The two good-looking vatos slide out from underneath, their hands and arms covered with grease that could scare the hell out of soap.

Elias is about ten years older than Nazul but looks as strong and fit as any middleweight boxing champ. They wipe off what they can of the grease with rags that look even greasier.

Nazul reaches for his soda in a cup on the hood of the car.

Elias looks around for his and finds it on the ground next to the jack. A huge Texas fly is glued to the tip of his straw. Angrily, he bats it away. "Pinche mosca culera!" *Damn sonofabitch fly!* He picks up his soda and looks at it with a frown.

Nazul gives him a sly varrio glance. "Dat moscota drank it all?"

Elias takes a sip. "No. I slapped him on the back and he spit it back out."

Nazul turns to the Monte Carlo with questions. "So, how are we gonna do this job? Tú que sabes." *Since you know about this.*

Elias thinks about it for a moment as he pops the lid from his soda and chews on some ice. Though it's cold and drizzly outside, the vatos are shining with sweat.

"This is a 305 engine with a 350 transmission. We're gonna take off the transmission mount and remove the differential bar. We gotta take out the starter también. With a rolling jack we're gonna pull the trans down, then remove all the trans-lines and passing gear."

Nazul is listening attentively. "That's it?"

"We pull out the booster and front seal and clean all that shit off with gasoline. We replace the modulator, the oil-pan gasket, and trans-filter. Then we put it back in and fill it up with fluid. That's it."

The vatos gather their tools and get ready to work. Elias' kids, Joey and Oralia, burst out of the front door of the house, slapping the screen door against the wall. They shriek and giggle in their wild game of cat and mouse, traversing the tool-ridden yard. Nazul and Elias, used to their antics, sort out their tools.

Nazul grins affectionately at them like they're his own kids. In a way they are. While Elias would go pick up Elsa at work, Nazul would double as a babysitter. His love for them has opened up a whole new world. He looked forward to their Christmas like a doting padrino. *Godfather.* He smiles at their carefree abandon, secretly wishing the children could always remain young and innocent and part of his life.

"Oralia! Don't play near the street." Elias jacks up the Monte

Carlo. "Play over here in the grass, Prieta." He points to an area under a fifty-year-old pecan tree, a safe distance from the street.

Out of nowhere a white, jacked-up '68 Malibu comes tearing around the corner, its tires screaming. The slick street causes it to swerve sideways wildly. The car veers dangerously close to the grassy area where Oralia is playing, unaware of the danger.

"Oralia!" Elias drops the jack handle and sprints to her. From the other direction, Nazul trips over a toolbox as he follows in a rush. Joey, who had been whipping the air with a tree switch, runs behind Nazul.

Elias picks up Oralia in one scoop.

The two-door Malibu straightens out into the street. Inside, five Chicano punk gangsters in full gang regalia stare Elias down, taunting him. Two of them grin defiantly.

"¡Estúpidos!" Elias hands Oralia to Nazul, who takes her and Joey away toward the house. A couple of viejitos from inside Don Pablito's house come out to see what the commotion is.

"Fuck you, buey!" On Elias' side, the punk riding shotgun yells at him as the Malibu's wheels start spinning again. Unable to catch traction, it swerves as it tears away.

Elias looks to the ground for a rock, picks one the size of a fist, and hurls it forcefully at the car. It bounces off the trunk and cracks the back window. The Malibu screeches to a halt. Reverse lights glare as it smokes back to Elias, who is waiting.

Nazul is huddled with the two children behind Elias' primer-grey '67 Nova. Joey looks up at him with scared eyes. Shielding the kids from view, Nazul monitors the confrontation through the car window. It quickly gets out of hand.

Elias glances briefly toward Nazul as the Malibu arrives. "Carnal, wacha los chavalos." *Watch the kids.*

"Do you know who you're fucking with, puñata?!" With a black paño tied around his head, low over his eyes, the punk gangster leans out the front passenger window not ten feet from Elias. Three gold earrings decorate his right ear. Before Elias can answer, he pulls out a .25 automatic and points it at him.

"Choot 'im!" The driver looks about eighteen. He wears a black cap and sports tattoos on his neck and arms.

Elias walks right up to the .25 until it's pointing at his stomach. "You better kill me, pinche huerquillo, joto," he whispers loudly.

"Choot!!" the other punks yell out. The punk's hand starts shaking. He fires.

The bullet goes straight through Elias' left side and ricochets off the Monte Carlo.

Behind the Nova, Joey jumps when he hears the loud pop. Nazul watches through the car window. Joey whimpers, "I want Daddy." Nazul hugs the kids closer to him and keeps his eyes on Elias. "Daddy's coming in a minute. Don't worry," Nazul exhales in a whisper.

He doesn't see Elias even wince as he grabs the punk's hand and gun, forcing it slowly upward as the punk yelps in pain. He hears a loud snap as Elias breaks his wrist.

"Ahhh! Ahhhhh!!!" The punk hangs his broken hand like a puppet. He's sweating from the pain. The driver pulls out an automatic from his waistband, but can't get a clear shot at Elias with his homie rocking back and forth in agony.

Gauging his move, Elias leans down to their level and punches the punk on the side of his head, sending it bouncing off the driver's face. Now they both rock back and forth in serious pain. Another huerquillo in the back seat pulls up a sawed-off. Elias grabs a golfball-size rock, and before the chavalo can aim, flings the rock. It crashes into his right eye. The chavalo drops the shotgun and squirms around. Elias pelts the vatos in the back seat until they're huddled on the floorboards.

Four señores stand by the front door of Don Pablito's house, watching with amusement.

Elias looks down at his own wound and his anger starts to build. "'Ora les voy a poner una chinga bien dada!" *Now I'm gonna give you the mother of all beatings!* Elias whispers loudly again as he flings open the passenger door like a madman bent on murderous destruction. He's pissed but partly acting. He really just wants to teach them a lesson.

The driver frantically tries to jet off, but the car is still in reverse.

Elias almost grins from their predicament as he leans down and grabs another rock. The Malibu jerks back and forth, trying to find a gear.

The smoking carrucha swerves wildly, tearing away with crying tires.

A few people slowly come out of the curandero's house. They see the blood now trickling down Elias' side and left leg.

Nazul finally looks down at Joey and Oralia. Their small bodies shudder. They sob softly. Nazul squeezes them close to him. He would give anything to shield them from these volatile streets. "Carnalitos, look at me. Your daddy's safe. Nothing's going to happen to you, okay?"

"But the gangas…" whimpers Joey.

"It's okay now. I need you to stay down here while I go help Daddy." The kids look up at him with wet cheeks. They nod obediently and Nazul gets up.

"Elías, andas herido." *Elias, you're injured.* Un señor watches him as Elias looks around to see if the kids are okay. Nazul gets closer to Elias and sees the blood. He whispers loudly, knowing that little angels are listening. "Carnal, they shot you…"

Finally acknowledging his wound, Elias looks down at the bloodstain, which is seeping through his clothes and becoming painfully obvious. "Simón. But it went through. Take me to Don Pablito."

Nazul looks around to the Nova. "Oralia, Joey, go inside the house and wait there for us." He doesn't want them to see the blood. "Daddy's okay." The two kids scamper into the house like scared kittens.

A team of señores is ready to assist Elias. With a grin he waves them off, indicating he can walk into the curandero's house on his own. "No se asusten. Es nomás una rozada." *Don't worry. It only grazed me.*

Inside Don Pablito's, the gente are all on their feet, checking out Elias' wound. Paranoid, some still peek out the window to make sure the danger has passed.

Don Pablito is waiting for him with the altar-room door already open. "Pásale, m'ijo," *Come in, my son,* he says quietly.

Elias walks in with Nazul and eases himself down on a cot that Don Pablito has prepared. The curandero helps Elias remove his shirt. Don Pablito has a pile of clean white cotton towels sitting on a shrine table. He folds a couple of them for thickness and applies pressure to both wounds. The white towels slowly turn red. He replaces them and looks carefully at the wounds on Elias' side and back.

Don Pablito goes into his kitchen and soon returns with a concoction of herbs: green pecan shells and roots, finely ground into a dark mud.

The curandero folds the white towels thickly over the mud and ties them in place around Elias' waist, front and back, with long strips of white bedsheet that Nazul tears for him to keep the bandage in check.

Don Pablito glances at Nazul and nods. The wound is a safe distance from any vital organs. He's going to be sore as hell in the morning, but all right.

los muertos

Four

Los vivos mueren; los muertos viven
The living die; the dead live

"Ay, honey, no quiero que levantes nada pesado. Cuídate." *I don't want you picking up anything heavy. Take care of yourself.* Elsa fusses over Elias' wound as she saunters in with a huge, steaming plate of every Chicano's favorite dish. Elias is laid out on the couch and sits up with slight discomfort so she can lay the plate on a TV tray resting on his lap. He looks down hungrily at the carnitas-en-sopa, along with chícharro, calabaza, and fideo adorned with a huge helping of whole beans straight from the pot. Gracing the edges of the plate are a couple of green serrano peppers.

Their home is small but cozy, with secondhand furniture and only two bedrooms. Elsa and Elias have meager possessions, but their warmth is more precious than any hefty bank account.

The kids sit by the TV at a kiddie table with little chairs and munch down their food as they watch a Christmas cartoon about Rudolph the red-nosed reindeer. In front of the living room picture window, a Christmas tree twinkles.

Outside, the night is falling.

Elsa brings her plate in one hand and sets it down on a coffee table beside Elias. Her other hand sets down a dozen tortillas wrapped warmly in a kitchen towel. She looks at Elias to make sure he is comfortable.

Elsa is a devoted mother who works part-time in a downtown hotel as a cleaning lady to supplement the family income. Elias and Nazul are weakhearted workers, always helping out la gente with car parts and cheap labor. But if Elias didn't work at home and wasn't there when the children got home from school, Elsa would never consider working outside of the house.

"Don Pablito did a good job on your wound." She takes a big bite of tortilla, folded to scoop up a mouthful of fideo and beans. Elias devours his food, comforted by his family's glow.

Elsa jumps up with a couple of warm tortillas for the kids. Elias glances at her as she kneels down by them. He smiles inside. The last one she always thinks about is herself.

His thoughts drift to the time when they first met. She was only seventeen. That late spring he had just finished his tour of duty as a Marine. Two years in 'Nam had left him with a whole new appreciation for everything innocent and simple. He lost two buddies from the varrio to sniper fire. Then he was back in San Anto catching up with los bailes. Those classic nights of live music and dancing at grand west side clubs like el Patio Andaluz. Sunny and the Sunliners, The Royal Jesters, The Mystics, Rudy and the Reno-Bops, and Joe Jamma were all the rage of the times. The west side sounds.

Those nights were a capirotada of unfolding yearnings; long-awaited curadas replenishing the core of his being.

At the crack of dawn one cool morning, his family was awakened by his tío Lalo and his tía Cuca with their young family passing through from Robstown, Texas. They were starting their migratory trek up north to work the fields and hopefully make some good money at the expense of brutally long hard work.

His tío Lalo was a strong, healthy man with hundreds of hours of work logged on his powerful back. He had an infectious smile and a quick wit. Whenever they would wind up living in scary, desolate, out-of-the-way shacks, it was hombres like Lalo who would fearlessly walk out into the creepy night to check out a scream or whatever his frightened, superstitous wife, Cuca, would imagine she heard hidden in the strange surroundings.

Elias' father, Chito, and his mother, Güera, caught the migratory bug. Since Elias was home from the war and their three young daughters, Gloria, RosaMaria, and Teresa, were out of school for the summer, a sense of adventure was in the air. It had been a long time for Elias. You never really distance yourself from the restless spirit of the migrant worker. A spiritual bond with the earth compels you to roam and explore its beautiful form.

Bay City, Michigan was the first stop to pick cucumbers and hoe beets. Then on to Traverse City with its hilltop orchards of huge, red cherries that seemed surrounded by a massive mirror from the waters of Lake Huron gleaming in the sun.

By early August they were weary travelers burnt a deep, dark brown. Transformed by the hard work, you felt you'd acquired a noble character.

Your first long day of working the fields and a night sleeping on a sagging, cheap cot had you wondering how you were gonna drag your defeated ass to the nearest highway and hitch a ride back home. With your back frozen stiff in the shape of the cot, you were so sore even your hair would hurt. The next day blisters would plague your feet and you'd be trudging through the field with your feet in burning buckets. By the end of the week, working from sunup to sunset with no time to recuperate, you were on the verge of catching fever or pneumonia.

By the second week, if you weren't in the intensive care of your jefita, you felt like a totally new person in body and mind. You were a true trabajador de la gente. *Worker of the people.* No glory was earned more dearly.

Teenage girls worked right along with the men. The mothers not only suffered the fields, they went home afterwards to cook giant dinners for the hungry workers. In the morning they would wake up at three o'clock to prepare breakfast and lunch, rolling out by hand sixty tortillas, minimum requirement.

Elias considered women to be superhuman. Their work wasn't to be able to afford a new car or fancy clothes, but just to get by. Their love and devotion to their families drove them to accomplish impossible feats.

He met Elsa in Florida as dozens of pickers from all over converged on the orange groves in the still twilight of early morning. She was one of them. He remembers how he couldn't breathe or feel his feet when their eyes first met and she spoke to him.

"I've never seen *you* here before," she remarked with confidence. "You must be one of those *educated* Heespanics we keep hearing about." Her eyes pierced right through his rugged character. If he had a granite will, with a character to match, Elsa was still on a higher level. He felt her chip away at his indestructible wall.

"No," he stammered. "I mean, I *am* educated. If you consider a high school diploma an education. Pero no soy un Hispanic," he mumbled foolishly. Chicanas like her had a way of making you feel like a fool and traitor if you embraced the celebrated white man's world. They had a good point. School always seemed to cost you your identity in the eyes of the ones who really gave a damn about you. It started with the strict rule of not uttering a single word in Spanish and continued with a forced feeding of every gory detail of European culture.

Elias recalls how he couldn't take his nervous gaze off her luscious mouth. He had managed to stammer something that made sense. "You never went to school? You seem very smart." He fumbled with his belt, which slung the bucket from his shoulders. There the oranges were thrown while you were up in the trees. He felt uninitiated into her world of orchestrated finesse.

"What for, so I can learn how great white people are?" She cocks her head sideways and glances up at him with a charm that he finds irresistible. Her long dark hair had a luster any cover girl would kill for. Her timelessly beautiful Aztec features could bump any screen goddess into oblivion. "I have all the education I need right here with my gente, who care about me and what *I* think. They've *shown me* what is *great.*"

Elias had fallen for her right in the middle of that conversation.

"I dropped out in the eighth grade. Who's got time for an education when you need to figure out how you're gonna eat first?" She turned and walked off, disappearing into the orchards without another word.

At lunchtime, fifty or so people gathered between two trucks, a huge canvas stretched between them for shade. Elias noticed his sisters talking and giggling with Elsa across the small fires and smoke from the gente's cooking. They kept looking at him.

As they got up to go back to work, his sister Gloria walked by with a sly grin and kicked him on his boots as he tried to sneak in a ten-minute nap. "She *likes* you. You better get a real job."

With summer waning, Elias courted Elsa under the careful eyes of her father, Jesus. Jesus and his wife, Elida, had two younger daughters and a ten-year-old son. To Jesus, Elsa was his consentida. He knew, regretfully, that the day his prieta would marry and leave them was upon him. In those days, if you lay down with la hija de un señor, it wasn't to see if you were compatible or not. It was for life. Or death.

The harvest was almost over. Elias' dad was already talking about leaving early the next week. Elias couldn't bear to leave Elsa behind. He proposed. She accepted.

Everyone was happy and sad at the same time: happy for their new love, sad to be leaving their familiares. Elsa's father, Jesus, took it very hard. He didn't attend the quick wedding. He wasn't ready. Instead he went on a killer parranda. On the third day after the wedding, he showed up at the couple's motel room door. He hadn't eaten or slept. He was past drunk but, amazingly, in total control.

"Súbanse a la troca," he blurted, and he simply walked around and climbed into his old pickup.

Elias and Elsa looked at each other, puzzled, but quickly followed and got in beside him, not knowing what to expect.

He lit the truck and drove without a word to a nearby grocery store. Reaching into his shirt pocket, he pulled out a hundred dollars and stuck it in Elsa's purse. He told them to pick out all the groceries they needed for their trip to San Antonio and to keep whatever was left. In those days a hundred dollars was serious money.

Jesus looked at his daughter, her face glowing with tears of gratitude. He struggled to hold his composure as he tried to talk. "Tú me has ayudado *mucho* a mí, prieta." *You have helped me very much, dark one.* He swallows his loss hard. "No es nada pero, por favor, acéptalo como un regalo para tu boda y como un símbolo de mi agradecimiento." *It's nothing, but please accept this as a gift for your wedding and a symbol of my appreciation.*

Elsa hugged her father amid sobs. "Te me fuiste muy pronto." *You left me too soon.* Tears streamed down his sunburnt face. He pulled her back to look at her. "Pero, más que nada," *But more than anything,* his Adam's apple traveled up and down his muscular throat, "quiero que seas feliz." *I want you to be happy.* He braved a smile.

Elsa hugged him again. She cried openly for the world of childhood she was leaving, for the señorita she would never be again. Most of all she cried for her father's heart.

After the embrace, Jesus took out his paño and wiped Elsa's eyes. He looked over at Elias. Elias remembers how good it felt to make his announcement.

"Don Jesus, no me la voy a llevar pa' Tejas. Aquí nos vamos a quedar. Siquiera por unos cuantos años." *I'm not going to take her to Texas. We're gonna stay here. At least for a few years.*

Elias saw a huge weight lift from Jesus' shoulders as he took a deep sigh of relief. He looked at Elias proudly. "Sé que eres un buen muchacho, de hembra firme. Ahora, te voy a abrazar a ti!" *I know you are a good young man, of firm lineage. And now, I'm gonna hug you!* He playfully leaned over Elsa, smothering her as he tried to hug Elias. Elias remembers all this history, the way Elsa had laughed and cried at once as they started their life together.

Now she is beside him, finishing her cold dinner. Elias glances up at the old oval portraits of her parents and his where they hang on the living room wall. They seem greyed with time. How the years melt away into nothing but memories. 'Maybe it's all just a dream,' he thinks.

He looks out the window to the last fading warmth of sunlight. The cold wind blows the dry leaves from the tall pecan trees. They go sailing away, catching the last rays of light, twirling like hazy afterthoughts laced with gold.

el fantasma de robestán

Five

El Fantasma de Robestán
The Phantom of Robstown

Nazul, fresh from a shower, combs his jet black hair in front of a small round shaving mirror hanging from a nail on the wall. A little lamp on his dresser is the only light. He's shirtless in a pair of grey Dickies work pants. The house seems dark and eerily quiet.

Nazul leans down and clicks on the cheap clock radio by his bed. Ramon Ayala's "Mi Golondrina" trickles out.

He turns around and walks to his closet. A colorful tattoo of the Aztec icon and saint la Virgen de Guadalupe graces the center of his muscular back. From high up on the shelf he pulls down a neat stack of small, dusty boxes and lays them on his bed. He opens one box and pulls out a black pachuco hat in protective plastic.

As he uncovers it, an image of his 'buelito, Julian, enters his mind—"Nazul, ésto era de tu 'apá. Esto es sagrado. El Fantasma de Robestán. El castigador de hombres malos." *Nazul, this belonged to your father. This is sacred. The Phantom of Robstown. The punisher of evil men.* His grandfather's eyes would bug out mysteriously, rousing a curiosity that could not be restrained.

The memory fades away with those mysterious words.

From the other boxes he pulls out a '40s topcoat and a matching pair of pleated pants, along with shiny calcos, also in protective plastic. All solid black. He frees the chuco hat from its cover and lays it on the bed. Staring at the collection, he runs his hands over each one.

He leaves it all lying on his bed and goes back to the mirror to lather up his face and shave a three-day-old stubble. A small washpan filled with water sits on a little table underneath the mirror. He grabs the razor and gets ready to shave. He stops and takes a long look into his reflection. He locks on the black chuco hat reflected in the mirror. Its power over him had always been like a religion he could not deny. His 'buelito Julian's trembling voice echoes in his mind, again from a distant past which now seems like another life.

"El Fantasma de Robestán." In his mind Nazul sees Julian packing some of his belongings. Soon Nazul would go to live with Don Pablito. Except for a few tías in Robstown, Nazul's immediate family had all met with one disaster or another. A significant lineage of los Kuculkánes could end or flourish with him. Nazul Kuculkán. Years back, young Maria and Julian had gone to see a renowned curandera on the outskirts of Vera Cruz, near a small town called La Media Luna. She told them they would have only one grandson, that she would watch his soul closely, and to her he would be known as Manco Capac. "A Cha Chaquella. Warrior of the Clouds."

Juan and Olivia, Nazul's parents, were killed in an auto accident up in North Texas, where the family was picking cotton. Nazul was nine when his grandma finally told him the story. Nazul's heart had ached at the sight of his 'buelita in such a tortured state as she recounted the event.

A steaming summer had faded into fall and an unusually early cold wind brought sleet down on the vast fields of unpicked cotton. Down from the arctic came a pouring rain which was like a frozen sheet. Nazul's family was driving home from the fields. The drunken gabacho's Buick veered wildly, nearly hitting the truck Julian and Maria were in. Instead, it plowed into their son's Chevy following closely behind.

The loud boom, followed by the sound of grinding metal, caused his 'buelitos to look behind them in time to see both cars tangled like two crazed machines, flipping and spinning around the street in a violent cogida of death. They pulled over and ran back to the disastrous wreck to find a five-year-old Nazul totally naked and crying in the middle of the street. Somehow there was not a scratch on him. The drunk rancher miraculously pulled himself out of his mangled Buick, staggered across the street, and collapsed. He survived that incident, and in spite of Julian's protests, wasn't even arrested by the Hillsboro cops. Instead, they had threatened to throw Julian in jail if he didn't leave town immediately.

Two days later, when Nazul's grandparents were driving back to Robestán heartbroken and on their way to bury their dead, the drunk gabacho zoomed by them again, guzzling on a whiskey bottle and swerving in and out of his lane, an insult to their grief.

That wouldn't be the end of it. Nazul's mind winds its way to the fate of his tío Carlos, his father's only brother. Carlos had been there in Hillsboro too.

"'Apá, todavía ando batallando con el carro. Ustedes váyanse pa' Robestán. No nos quieren aquí. Allá los miro." *Pa, I'm still having problems with the car. You all go ahead to Robstown. They don't want us here. I'll see you there.* Those were the last words Julian heard from Carlos as they left Hillsboro.

Carlos knew what he had to do. He stayed back in Hillsboro, crouching at the side of the road where his brother had been killed, waiting for the drunken gabacho. He didn't wait long. When the drunk's pickup came careening along the road, this time with his son next to him in the front seat, Carlos stepped out and hurled a fist-sized rock through the windshield. They lost control and rammed a tree. The son was unhurt, but the drunk fell out the open door, his mouth busted and a gash on his forehead. He staggered to his feet and reached into the pickup for his gun. Frozen in fear, the son watched Carlos beat his father to death on the spot.

Nazul had learned about his people's ways of enforcing justice in a racist land from such stories. He had also learned that this law of the land carried a price.

Tío Carlos never made it out of that county. Los Tijerinas, compadres de Juan y Olivia, had been late in leaving Hillsboro. As they drove out of town en route to Robe, Carlos sped by them, followed by two wailing police cars. They saw the cops shoot out the tires of Carlos' Ford, then try to run Carlos over when he came to a stop and got out. The Tijerinas stopped to help Carlos when they saw the police beating on him with clubs. When the cops started firing on the Tijerinas' truck, the whole family inside it, Carlos wrestled a gun away and engaged them in a shootout. Carlos took three rounds in the back but managed, with the help of Don Tijerina and his sons, to stagger into the back of the Tijerinas' lona-covered truck. As they sped home to Robestán, Carlos bled to death. Before dying, he asked Irra, one of the sons, to ask his parents to forgive his venganza.

Nazul's grandparents tried to remain strong for him, but they never got over their terrible loss. Sometimes Nazul would come home unannounced to find his 'buelita crying alone, emotionally crippled by the cruel memory of the loss of her sons.

♫ "Y tú que te creias, el rey de todo el mundo." *And you who thought, you were the king of the whole world.*

In the background, the Sunglows belt out a soulful rendition of Cuco Sanchez's "Fallaste Corazón." In his dim bedroom, Nazul decides to rinse the soap from his face.

clavado

Six

Don Julian

There's a gentle knock on the bedroom door. "¿Nazul?"

"'Apá, pásele." *Pa, come in.*

Don Pablito opens the door to find Nazul sitting on his bed beside the black pachuco outfit. He exhales a sigh of worry. "Nazul, ¿Qué piensas hacer?" *What do you intend to do?* Nazul looks at the floor with guilt. "No siembres semillas de odio." *Don't sow seeds of hate.* He knows the power the pachuco outfit has over Nazul.

Nazul tries to soothe his concern. "No, 'Apá. Chico, el pintor, quiere que sea su modelo para una pintura de pachuco." *Chico, the painter, wants me to model for a painting of a pachuco.*

Don Pablito's eyes seem to pierce to his soul. Nazul had learned to live with the fact that not much can be concealed from el curandero, who could tell what was ailing his patients just by looking at them. He seems relieved by Nazul's excuse, but is still cautious. He raises his index finger to make a point the way Julian used to. "Cuando tu abuelo Julian estaba en su cama de muerte y me pidió que te cuidara, le prometí que *siempre* te guardaria tus pasos." *When your grandfather was on his deathbed and asked me to take care of you, I promised him I would* always *guard your steps.* He glances at the pachuco threads, then back to Nazul. "Anda un desquieto en las calles." *There is unrest in the streets.* He takes a deep breath. "Antes que salgas esta noche, ven por tu bendición." *Before you go out tonight, come for your blessing.*

Nazul finishes dressing as Don Pablito dissolves back into the darkness of the hallway.

'Buelito Julian. Nazul's mind wanders over memories of him. After 'Buelita Maria passed away, Julian refused to go on with life as usual. Nazul would wake up in the middle of the night to find him gone. After frantically searching the varrio streets, he would finally find him weeping and trying to climb the tall, locked gates of the San Fernando Cemetery, where Maria lay.

Nazul remembers the stories of his 'Buelito Julian, the ones he could tell only after Maria had passed away.

"A ver, Don Julian, platíquenos la leyenda del Fantasma de Robestán." *Let's see, Don Julian, tell us the legend of the Phantom of Robstown.* Don Pablito was there, as he was now almost every evening, to help Nazul care for Julian, who was quickly deteriorating after the loss of his Maria. Julian brought out the pachuco outfit, and after setting it on the kitchen table where Nazul and Don Pablito were drinking cocoa, he announced to Nazul that it had belonged to Juan. He then simply turned around and walked away, back to the bedroom from which he had come.

With 'Buelita, his companion of sixty years, now gone forever, it was hard for him to focus too long on the details of this world. His consciousness was already treading on the next, sometimes daring to go back to his past. He hardly ate anymore and refused to take care of himself. Nazul and Don Pablito were the only threads holding him to this existence.

Nazul opens the boxes to reveal the black outfit. He calls out, "'Buelo, usted nunca me ha enseñado este traje de 'Apá. ¿Qué significa? ¿'Buelo? 'Buelo." *Grandpa, you've never shown me this outfit of Dad's before. What is this about? Grandpa? Grandpa.*

Suddenly, Don Julian appears at the bedroom doorway.

"A ver, Don Julian, platíquenos la historia. ¿Para qué nos deja en suspenso?" *Let's see, Don Julian, tell us the story. Why do you leave us in suspense?* Don Pablito sips on his cocoa and bites on a bean tamale. By the time he looks up, Don Julian is there. He holds an index finger up in a humble gesture to begin his story.

There was something beyond cinematic when 'Buelito told a story. Gente of his time immersed themselves in the rich art of storytelling. You could almost experience, firsthand, the atmosphere and rich drama when they would recount a tale.

"En esos tiempos," Don Julian begins, mouthing the words slowly with poetic expression, "¡los cuarentas en Robe, andaba un gabacho ranchero que, en vez de pagarle a los Mexicanos por el algodón que le piscaban, los asesinaba!" *In those times, the '40s in Robstown, there was this white rancher who, instead of paying Mexican workers for the cotton they picked for him, he would assassinate them!*

El curandero and Nazul nestle themselves into more comfortable positions on their hard wooden chairs.

"Yo trabajé por ese gabacho. Pero, ya para el tercer día, sospechaba que algo no estaba parejo." *I worked for that white man. But after the third day, I suspected something wasn't on the level.* He levels his palm out.

"En todo Robe, no encontré a nadie que quería ni hablar de ese ranchero, Meester Heller. Porque él, como todos los bolillos de esos tiempos, cargaba la ley en su billetera." *In all of Robstown, I couldn't find anyone who would even talk about that rancher, Mister Heller. Because he, like most white people of those times, carried the law in his wallet.*

Nazul and Don Pablito are glued, imagining the time.

"Llegó el momento de cobrar mi pago. Llevé mi fusil. Cargado. Y le dije a Maria, 'Prepara todo en caso que tengamos que viajar de repente.'" *The time came for me to collect my pay. I took my shotgun. Loaded. And I told Maria, 'Prepare everything in case we have to leave suddenly.'*

Don Julian sits down and rotates his cocoa in round, gentle movements. "Como estaba la noche fría y andaba una tormenta alrededor, no batallé para esconder el fusil en un sobretodo, largo y oscuro." *Since the night was cold and there was a tempest growling nearby, I didn't have any trouble hiding the shotgun in my long and dark overcoat.*

'Buelito looks away into his past, dreamily. "Solo que fui para su rancho afuera del pueblo. Ya le había trabajado una semana. El quería que le trabajara dos semanas, pero yo le dije que no. Yo no le trabajo a nadie por dos semanas sin pago. Esa es *mi* ley." *So I went to his ranch on the outskirts of town. I had already worked for him one week. He wanted me to work two weeks, but I said no. I don't work for anyone for two weeks without pay. That is my law.*

Julian leans in to Nazul. "En esos tiempos, muchos bolillos eran muy cabrones con nosotros. Y hasta la fecha." *In those times, many white people were very shitty with us. And to this day.* He sips his cocoa.

"En esos días, tu tío Carlos," he looks at an engrossed Nazul, "tenía, creo, veintidos años. El fue conmigo. Y tu 'apá, Juan, todavía no se casaba pero andaba interesado en tu 'ama, Olivia. El andaba en Alis, allí cerca de Robe, trabajando con Pedro Monguía. Un buen amigo desde que eran niños. *In those days, your Uncle Carlos was, I think, twenty-two years old. He went with me. And your father, Juan, wasn't married yet, but was interested in your mom, Olivia. He was in Alice, Texas, close to Robstown, working with Pedro Monguía. A very close childhood friend.*

"Le dije a Carlos que me esperara en la troca. Que si algo me pasaba a mí, que se huyera y se llevara a toda la familia lejos de allí. Le dijé que dejara la troca calentada. *I told your Uncle Carlos to wait for me in the truck. That if anything happened to me, to take off and take the whole family far from there. I told him to leave the truck lit.*

"La troca estaba parqueada cerca de la cochera lejecitos de su casa." *The truck was parked near the shed a ways from his house.* He motions with his hand and eyes the distance of the truck from Heller's house.

"Solo que fuí a la puerta de Mr. Heller y toqué. Su esposa contestó y me dijo que pronto salía. Era muy amable ella. Me dió una taza de cafe mientras esperaba. Ya empezó a lloviznar y el airenonazo," *So I went to Heller's door and knocked. His wife answered and told me he would be out soon. She was very sweet. She gave me a cup of coffee while I waited. Then it starts to rain, and the wind,* Julian stiffly stands and mimics with his hands the problem with trying to hide the shotgun under his coat, in the wind, "me volaba el saco y tenía cuidado que se me enseñara el fusil. *The wind blew my coat around, and I was afraid that my shotgun would show.*

"Ya de rato sale el Heller, con una risota y portándose como un amigo de atole. Ya andaba hasta pedo. *After a while Heller comes out with a big grin and acting like a friend of grit. He was already drunk.* "El cabrón sabía un poco de español. Yo creo para chingarnos mejor. Pero le dije que no venía a platicar, sino que venía por mi pago porque mi familia necesitaba provecho. *The bastard knew a little Spanish. I guess to fuck us over better. But I told him I hadn't come to chat, but to collect my pay because my family needed provisions.*

"Me dice el cabrón, '¿Por qué tienen ustedes familias tan grandes? ¿Cómo se aguantan con tantos pinches huercos?' *He tells me, 'Why do you people have such big families? How can you stand so many damn brats?'*

"Le dije que para mí los niños eran una bendición de Dios y que mi familia era una cosa sagrada. Solo que no me gustaba oír a nadie, menos a él, que hablara de mi familia con babosadas. Se ríe y me dice el cabrón, 'Yo no tengo *ningún* huerco que me pida esto o este otro. Todo lo que tengo es para *mí!*'" *I told him that for me, children were a blessing from God and that my family was something sacred. So I didn't want to hear anybody, especially him, talk about my family with stupidity. The bastard laughed and said, 'I don't have* any *brats to ask me for this or that. All I have is for* me!'

Julian takes a dry bite of an empanada he's been contemplating. El curandero and Nazul pour themselves a warm-up of cocoa and wait for the story to continue. They hated for it to be even halfway over.

Don Julian continues. "Le contesté, 'Bueno,'" he clears his throat, "'¿Qué quieres que haga? Arretácate todo lo que quieras. Yo no soy tu juez. Yo nomás quiero mi pago.'" *I said, 'Fine, what do you want me to do? Stuff yourself all you want. I'm not your judge. I just want my pay.'* Julian leans in to his audience seriously. "Se puso muy colorado. Como que no aguantaba la rabia. *He got all red. Like he could barely contain his rage.*

"Me dice, 'Ahorita *mismo* te voy a pagar.' Como ya estaba lloviendo, me dijo que me esperara en la troca y luego me traía mi pago. No quise que se pusiera sospechoso, solo que me fuí para la troca. Y el se metió a la cochera, que allí estaba," he motions with his hand, "a cruzar la calle de mi troca. *He tells me, 'I'll pay you* right *now.' And since it was raining, he told me to wait in the truck and he would bring my pay. I didn't want him to get suspicious, so I went to the truck. And he went into a shed that was across the road from the truck.*

"Nomás entró a la cochera, y Carlos se salió de la troca y se escondió en el oscuro en un lado de la cochera. Yo me hice para el driver's side de la troca y así lo esperamos. *As soon as he went to the shed, Carlos slipped out of the truck and hid beside the shed. I moved to the driver's side and waited.*

"Ya de pronto sale el Heller, tirándole tragotes a una botella de wiskle. Pero la otra mano, como estaba oscuro y lloviznando, la traía escondida así por detrás." *Soon out comes Heller, taking huge gulps from a whiskey bottle. But his other hand, since it was dark and raining, he had it hidden behind his back.* Julian holds his right hand behind him, emulating Heller hiding something.

"Se me acerca a la puerta de la troca donde estaba yo sentado, y yo bien sabía que en la mano derecha cargaba la traición. *He got close to the door of the truck where I was sitting, and I knew well that in his right hand he carried his betrayal.*

"Puse mi brazo izquierdo en la manejera, así." *I put my left arm on the steering wheel, like this.* Julian puts up his left arm and rests his hand on the imaginary steering wheel of the truck. "Y con la otra mano, acomodé el fusil por debajo de mi brazo izquierdo." *And with my other hand, I positioned the shotgun under my left arm.* He positions an imaginary shotgun under his left arm, pointing out the driver's window facing Heller.

"Estaba bien oscuro y el cabrón se asoma para adentro de la ventana y me pregunta, 'Dónde están tus hijos?' *It was pitch black and the bastard leans to look in the window and asks me, 'Where are your sons?'*

"Le contesté, 'Mira, aquí están mis hijos.' Y le dirigí su vista por debajo de mi brazo izquierdo. De repente, un rayo partió la noche. *I answered, 'Look, my sons are right here.' And I directed his vision under my left arm. Suddenly, lightning split the night.*

"En eso se fijó, y miró el par de cañones que los tenía apuntados a su mera cara!" *With that, he looked and saw the two barrels pointed right at his face!* Julian leans in to them with raised eyebrows. "Creo que se le quitó hasta lo pedo y se fue tropezándose pa'trás en el zoquete." *I think that sobered him up, and he went stumbling backwards in the mud.*

Julian gently sips his coffee with all the patience known to man while Nazul and Don Pablito hang anxiously like a couple of nail-biting comadres enduring a cliffhanger in a killer novela.

Julian finally continues. He holds his finger up to the imaginary darkness. "De repente, Carlos lo sorprende por detrás! Y hasta lo hace que grite de susto como una vieja. Le quitó Carlos la pistola. *Suddenly, Carlos surprised him from behind! And he even made him scream like a hag from fear. Carlos took his gun away.* "Yo me bajé de la troca con el fusil, listo. En veces cargan *dos*." *I stepped down from the truck with my shotgun ready. Sometimes they carry two.* He holds up two fingers matter-of-factly. "Pero Carlos lo esculcó y nomás le halló una daga. Para que su esposa no viera nada, nos lo llevamos pa' detrás de la troca y Carlos lo hizo que se hincara en el zoquete. *But Carlos frisked him and only found a dagger. So his wife wouldn't see anything, we took him behind the truck and Carlos made him kneel in the mud.*

"Y yo le puse el fusil en la mera garganta y le prometí que el cobarde que no me paga por el trabajo, que tanto hace sufrir a mi familia, entonces me paga como el marrano que es, con todo. Esa es *mi* ley. No la ley de culeros." *And I put the shotgun right on his throat and promised him that whoever didn't pay me for the work, which makes my family suffer so much, pays me like the pig that he is, with everything. That's* my *law. Not the law of chickenshits.*

Julian looks into Nazul's soul with his weathered eyes. "Hoy la ley está un poco mejor. Pero en esos tiempos, el cobarde me hubiera matado como un *perro,* y a la ley le hubiera importado *pura madre.*" *Today the law is a little better. But in those times, the coward would have killed me like a* dog, *and the law wouldn't have given a* damn.

He leans back and takes another dry bite of his empanada and chews it slowly.

"Solo que el Heller se puso a temblar como un chihuahua nervioso y empezó a llorar y rogar por su vida como imbécil. Lo echamos a la troca y nos lo llevamos varias millas de allí, para que su esposa no lo oyera chillar." *So Heller started to tremble like a nervous chihuahua and cried for his life like an imbecile. We put him in the truck and took him several miles from there so his wife wouldn't hear his cries.*

'Buelito Julian continued, raising his palm to show the winding road they were on. "Solo que nos lo llevamos, yo y Carlos, por la carretera zoquetosa. Los relámpagos y truenos estaban fuertes y el Heller se estremecía de susto. La tempestad ya chiflaba por las líneas elétricas y mecía la troca cuando lo bajamos al zoquete. Le sacamos la billetera. Estaba *llena* de biles. *Miles* de biles. Pensé yo, 'Este cabrón no ha trabajado tanto para estar tan *rico*. Sus manos están muy

blanditas. Como las manos de una mujer cremona.' Era dinero de trabajadores que él había asesinado!" *So we took him, me and Carlos,
down the muddy road. The lightning and thunder were powerful, and
Heller shook with fear. The tempest whistled and moaned through the
power lines and rocked the truck when we took Heller out and threw
him in the mud. We took out his wallet. It was* packed *with dollar bills.*
Thousands *of dollar bills. I thought, 'This bastard hasn't worked hard
enough to make all this money. His hands are too soft. Like the hands
of a pampered woman.' It was money from workers that he had assassinated!*

Julian makes two fists, trembling with the rage he felt. "Quién sabe
a cuantos los traicionó. *Todos* eran *mi gente.* Gente como *yo.* Porque
todos semos del mismo rancho! Me entró una rabia que nunca había
conocido. Lo hice que se hincara y le puse el fusil en la mera cara. Le
dije, 'Eres el demonío. Prepárate a *morir, cobarde!*'" *Who knows how
many he betrayed. They were* all *my people. People like* me. *Because
we are all from the same ranch! A rage I had never known overtook
me. I made him kneel down and put my shotgun right in his face. I told
him, 'You are the demon. Prepare to* die, coward*!'*

Julian throws his hands down around his feet. "Pos, no se me tiró
a los pies, abrazándome las piernas pidiendo misericordia como un
cobarde descarado! *Well, damned if he didn't throw himself at my feet,
hugging my legs and pleading for mercy like a shameless coward!*

"Le dije, 'Cállate el hocico! No te mato todavía. Pero, si acaso tú
me tratas de arruinar a mi o a mi familia, o quizás a un buen amigo...
entonces...una noche despertarás en tu cama, mientras que te destripo!
Entiendes ese español?' *I told him, 'Shut up! I'm not gonna kill you,
yet. But if you try to ruin me or my family or maybe a good friend...
then...one night you will wake up in your bed as I disembowel you! Do
you understand that Spanish?'*

"Naturalmente que me prometió todo. Estaba al punto del cañón.
Carlos le dijo, 'Si algo le llega a pasar a mi 'apá, aunque sea un castigo
que le caiga, te prometo que en todos los días y noches de su velorio, te
castigaré! Y cuando lo sepulten, te *quemaré vivo!' Naturally he promised me everything. He was on the business end of a cannon. Carlos
told him, 'If something happens to my father, even if it's a tragedy that
befalls him, I assure you that in all his days and nights of vigil, I will
torture you. And when they bury him, I will* burn you alive*!'*

"Le dije al Heller, 'Por hacerme batallar por mi pago, ahora me

das *todo este dinero!' I told Heller, 'For inconveniencing me for my
pay, now you will give me* all this money*!'*

"Solo que lo amarramos con mecate para comprar un poco de
tiempo y allí lo dejamos en un diche arrastrándose por el suelo como
la vibora que era. *So we tied him up with rope to buy a little time, and
we left him there in the ditch, squirming on the ground like the snake
that he was.*

"Llegó fuerte el chubasco. La llovizna nos picaba la cara con la
fuerza del aire. Nos fuimos directamente para la casa y recojimos a
toda la familia, hasta a compadres y comadres, y nos alejamos de
Robe. Como estabamos impuestos a viajar, como Apaches, no batalla-
mos para huirnos pronto de allí. *The storm arrived with a vengeance.
The rain stung our faces with the force of the wind. We went directly
home and gathered the whole family, even relatives, and we took flight
from Robstown. Since we were used to traveling, like Apaches, we
didn't have a problem rushing out of there.*

"Pero, tu 'apá," he looks at Nazul, "acuérdate que andaba trabajando con Pedro Monguía en Alis escarbando una noria treinta millas de
allí. Carlos me dijo que nos fueramos nosotros y que el iba por Juan.
Eso es lo que hicimos. Pero antes de que Carlos llegara a Alis, la ley lo
paró. Lo golpearon mucho y lo llevaron con Heller. El mismo quería
matar a Carlos. Pero primero quería castigarlo para ver si Carlos le
confesaba donde estabamos nosotros. Eso fue lo que nos dijo nuestro
amigo, el cherife, McKinney. McKinney era bolillo pero era buen
hombre. Ayudaba a la gente. El mandó a un amigo de nosotros para
avisarnos aquí en San Antonio donde estabamos escondidos." *But your
father, remember that he was working with Pedro Monguía in Alice,
digging a well thirty miles from there. Carlos told us to leave and that
he would go for Juan. So that's what we did. But, before Carlos arrived in Alice, the law stopped him. They beat him severely and took
him to Heller. He himself wanted to kill Carlos. But first he wanted to
torture Carlos to see if he would confess to our whereabouts. That's
what our friend, the sheriff, McKinney, told us. McKinney was white,
but he was a good friend. He would help our people. He sent a friend
of ours to tell us here in San Antonio where we were hiding.*

Julian glances at Nazul and el curandero, whose unblinking eyes
are bloodshot for fear of missing a slight gesture or fleeting facial expression from Julian.

"Y el McKinney fue y le dio razón a tu 'apá en Alis que los chotas tenían a Carlos prisionero y que lo estaban castigando. También le informó que a nuestra casa en Robestán, le habían prendido fuego, quemándola todita! Le explicó a Juan todo lo que había pasado esa noche. *So McKinney went and gave an account to your father in Alice that the cops were holding Carlos prisoner and that they were torturing him. He also informed him that our house in Robstown had been set on fire and burned to the ground. He explained to your father everything that had happened that night.*

"Ese chota, el McKinney, no podía hacer nada por Carlos porque el era uno solo y los méndigos policías y Heller le hubieran arruinado a toda su familia. El tenía una familia muy grande. Pero, a pesar de todo, era un *buen* amigo. *That cop, McKinney, couldn't do anything for Carlos because he was alone in this, and those damned policemen and Heller would have ruined his whole family. He had a very big family. But, despite all this, he was a good friend.*

"McKinney le dijo a tu 'apá que los cobardes planeaban castigar a Carlos toda la noche. En la mañana cuando se les acabara todo el trago, lo iban a matar." *McKinney told your father that the cowards planned to torture Carlos all night. And in the morning, when they ran out of liquor, they would kill him.*

Nazul and Don Pablito are on the edges of their seats with suspense as Julian slowly gets up to walk away. His life was a daze without Maria. Nazul and Don Pablito look at each other, puzzled.

"'Buelo," Nazul stops him, "y luego ¿qué pasó?" *And then what happened?*

Julian stops and thinks for a minute. "Oh, si. Bueno. McKinney halló a tu 'apá en Alis en un baile, como era viernes. Juan andaba vestido en este traje de pachuco. Así se fue a buscar a Carlos sin decirle a Pedro Monguía nada. No quería que Pedro también sufriera la venganza de esa ley maldita. Pedro tenía dos niños y su esposa estaba esperando cama. McKinney también quería echarse el compromiso, pero Juan insistió que no, que él solito se engargaba de Carlos." *Oh, yes. Well. McKinney found your father in Alice in a dancehall, since it was a Friday. Juan was dressed in this pachuco outfit. That's how he went to look for Carlos without telling Pedro Monguía anything. He didn't want Pedro to also suffer the vengeance of that murderous law. Pedro had two kids and his wife was expecting another. McKinney also wanted to take on that responsibility, but Juan insisted that no, he himself would be in charge of rescuing Carlos.*

After a few moments of silence, Julian looks off again to that night. "La tormenta se calmó por un rato y un silencio lindo arrullaba la tierra negra. Llegó Juan a la cochera de Heller donde habían cinco chotas con Heller, golpeando a Carlos y amenazándolo con la muerte. *The storm had calmed down for a while, and a beautiful silence came over the dark earth. Juan arrived at Heller's shed, where five cops and Heller were beating Carlos and threatening to kill him.* 'Let's cut off his huevos and stick his verga in his mouth. He isn't gonna talk anyways.' La risa de los cobardes retumbaba en la cochera. Carlos estaba casi inconciente de tanto golpe. *The laughter of the cowards resounded in the shed. Carlos was almost unconscious from so many blows.*

"Afuera dos carros de policia estaban estacionados. De repente uno explota. Salieron los mensos corriendo pa' fuera cuando el otro carro también, boom!" *Outside, two cop cars were stationed. Suddenly one explodes. The iditos ran outside when the other car also, boom!* Julian makes Nazul and Don Pablito jump in their chairs with his special effects. "Explota en sus caras, azonzándolos y volándole los zapatos de los pies a dos policias. Los rumbó contra la pared de la cochera con su fuerza! Y nadie estaba seguro de lo que ocurió después." *It explodes in their faces, knocking them senseless and blowing the shoes off the feet of two cops, the force thrashing them against the wall of the shed! And nobody was sure what happened afterward.*

Julian leans in to Nazul for effect. "Tu 'apá les había cortado las líneas de gas y les echó vuelo. Se levanta un chota, todo bombo, pero con la pistola en la mano. Y Heller resulta, como siempre, en el suelo, buscando su pistola en el zoquete. En eso se les aparece el Pachuco por detrás." *Your father had cut the fuel lines and set them on fire. One cop gets up all rattled, but with gun in hand. And Heller ends up, as usual, on the ground, searching for his gun in the mud. Just then the Pachuco appears to them from behind.* Julian holds up his index finger again. "Nadie sabía que la esposa de Heller, oyendo las explosiónes, salió pa' fuera a fijarse y fue testiga de lo que sucedió después." *Nobody knew that Heller's wife, hearing the explosions, went outside to look and was a witness to what happened afterward.*

Julian looks at them with total seriousness. "Un humano," he whispers discreetly, "es capaz de hacer cosas increíbles cuando le amenazan la vida de su gente." *A human is capable of incredible things when his people are mortally threatened.*

With his index finger ready, he turns away. "Mrs. Heller vió cuando un chota, con la pistola lista, cayó como muerto al suelo. Y en su lugar apareció una forma negra. En eso, Heller halló su pistola. Gritando de miedo y coraje, le descargó todas las balas a esa sombra que como quiera se le acercaba! Le gritó Heller, '*Qué chingaus eres?*' Pero, la sombra pesca a Heller del pescuezo. Y levantándolo contra la pared de la cochera, le contestó...con la muerte. Porque a pesar de todo el desmadre que ya había hecho, Heller iba a seguir matando a la gente decente. *Mrs. Heller saw when one of the cops fell like dead weight to the ground. And in his place there appeared a black form. Just then Heller found his gun. Yelling from fear and rage, he unloaded his gun at that shadow that still kept approaching! Heller yelled,* 'What the hell are you?' *but the shadow grabbed Heller by the throat. Picking him up against the wall of the shed, he answered him...with death. Because in spite of all the misery he had already caused, Heller was going to continue killing decent people.*

"Cuando Mrs. Heller vió esto, se metió gritando y loca de susto pa' dentro de su casa. Y allí se quedó por tres días con el susto muy *fuerte.* Ni los chotas ni nadie podía conbenserla que saliera para que les dara más clara razón de lo que había pasado. Especialmente cuando le preguntaron que si estaba segura que Heller le descargó la pistola al fantasma. Porque sí habían casquillos, pero no podían hallar nada de sangre en ninguna parte." *When Mrs. Heller saw this, she ran screaming and crazy with fear back into her house. And she stayed there for three days with a* paralyzing terror. *Not even the cops nor anybody could talk her into coming out and giving an account of what had happened. Especially when they asked her if she was sure Heller had unloaded his gun at the phantom. Because they found the spent shells, but could not find a sign of blood anywhere.*

Julian gets eerily serious. "*Más,* se asustó. Y su susto espantó a muncha gente de esos pueblitos que ni querían salir pa' fuera en la noche. Decían que el oscuro tenía ojos. Pero no es que eran ignorantes. Sino que nuestra gente cree y *sabe*...de cosas increíbles y *maravillosas.* Para el pecador, son *muy* espantosas. Es otro poder. Son castigos negros que manda *la ley de la tierra.*" *She got even more scared. And her fear struck terror in the hearts of many people in those little towns so that they didn't even want to venture out at night. They said that the darkness had eyes. But it's not that they were ignorant, it's that our people believe and* know...*of incredible and* marvelous *things.*

To a sinner, they are very *terrifying. It's another power. They are dark curses sent by* the law of the land.

Nazul unfolds the topcoat and finds six bullet holes where the chest would be. "'Buelo, ¿Cómo aguantó 'Apá esas balas? Y ¿Porqué no sangró?" *Grandpa, how did Dad endure those bullets? And why didn't he bleed?*

Julian looks at him with a sly grin as he leans in for effect. "McKinney le preparó un disco de acero que usan los tractores para calaberiar y se lo enganchó del pescuezo con cuero por debajo de la camisa. El aseguró a Juan, quien andaba loco de prisa, que sin esa protección, tal vez lo hubieran herido o matado y no le salvara la vida a Carlos." *McKinney prepared an iron disc that is used by tractors to till the land, and he hung it with leather strings from Juan's neck, under his shirt. He assured Juan, who was crazy with haste, that without that protection he could easily get wounded or even killed, and he wouldn't be able to save Carlos' life.* Julian looks at Nazul with a twinkle in his eye. "Nazul, tu 'apá era un hombre que se entendía a lo que necesitaba hacer." *Nazul, your father was a man who commited himself to what needed to be done.* He chuckles.

"Oh," Julian thinks for a second, "el chota que cayó como pesomuerto al suelo, también sabía español y después dijo que él se dió en sí cuando Heller le gritó al fantasma, '¿Qué eres?' y que el fantasma le contestó, 'La ley de esta tierra.' Cuando dijo eso, el chota dice que sintió un temblor en la tierra. Y con esos testigos empezó la leyenda del Fantasma de Robestán, La Ley de la Tierra. *Oh, the cop who fell like dead weight to the ground also knew Spanish and later said that he came to when he heard Heller scream and yell at the phantom, 'What are you?' and that the phantom answered, 'The law of this land.' When he said that, the cop said he felt the ground shudder. And with those testimonials began the legend of the Phantom of Robstown, The Law of the Land.*

"El muerto, que *vive! The dead one who* lives!

"Por mucho tiempo después, los chotas tenían cuidado de amenazar a la Raza. Después oímos historias falsas que se les había aparecido ese fantasma a gente mala, y que a otros los mató de susto. Porque decían que se aparecía en noches cuando andaban tormentas o chubascos que aullaban con un aire maldito y traicionero, que les volaban los techos de laminas a los jacalitos de la gente pobre de esos tiempos. Y otros lo nombraban 'el Gato Negro.' Contaban que era un gato que se transformaba en persona cuando castigaba y por eso nadie lo podía pescar. *For a long time afterward, the cops were afraid to threaten our people. Later we heard false stories that the phantom had appeared to evil people, and that he had caused others to die of fright. Because they would say he would appear on nights when there were tempests or twisters that would howl with a deadly and treacherous wind, a wind that would blow off the tin roofs of those shanty homes of the poor people of those times. And others called him 'the Black Cat.' They would recount that he was a cat that transformed into a human when he would strike, and that's why nobody could catch him.*

"Nosotros estabamos muy a gusto aquí en San Antonio y la pasamos muy bien con el dinero de Heller. *We were very comfortable here in San Antonio and got along very well with Heller's money.*

"Después oímos que Mrs. Heller nunca quiso volver a su casa y que los chotas de esa noche también se habían huido de Robe porque alguién, Pedro Monguía," *Later we heard that Mrs. Heller never went back to that house, and that the cops of that night had also taken flight from Robstown because someone, Pedro Monguia,* he whispers, "les quemó las casas como a nosotros. Con gasoline. Que el Gato Negro no los dejaba que vivieran en paz. Y nunca podían pescar a los culpables porque todos decían que habían visto al fantasma ahí. Solo que después de varios años, nos movimos pa' tras pa' Robe y vivimos ahí muy a gusto." *Monguía had burned their homes like they had burned ours. With gasoline. That the Black Cat wouldn't let them live in peace. And they could never catch the culprits because everyone would say that the phantom had been seen there. So after a few years we moved back to Robstown and lived there very comfortably.* Julian looks at his audience. They are silent with intrigue. "Y esa es la leyenda del Fantasma de Robestán. El muerto que vive." *And that is the legend of the Phantom of Robstown. The dead one who lives.*

'Buelito Julian.

pachuco con jumper cables

Seven

Pachuco con jumper cables

Outside, drops of light rain patter in the stillness. Nazul rolls the pachuco threads over the calcos into a neat bundle and places them in a plain-looking shopping bag with the felt brim carefully on top, folding a Mexican-style poncho on top of it to keep the rain out.

Nazul walks to the altar room, where el curandero waits with a black rosary hanging over his clasped hands. The tiny, saint-packed room exudes a strangely ominous power, with two burning candles emitting a surreal golden glow.

Nazul sets his bag at the entrance, but Don Pablito gestures to him to bring it in. He sets his bag beside him as he kneels on the floor on a small weathered rug. It is woven with Aztec designs, thick and old. Reaching into his shirt, he pulls out an old black rosary that he wears as a necklace. He kisses the crucifijo, holding it up in his praying hands while he bows his head.

Don Pablito dips his left hand into a small clay jar and sprinkles Nazul with holy water from San Juan de los Lagos, a gift from the gente in return for his healing. He lays his wet hand on Nazul's head as he prays silently for a minute, letting the water trickle down Nazul's torso inside his shirt.

Nazul is completely silent, eyes closed, humble and serious. Don Pablito's bendiciones always make him feel lighter somehow. As if all is right with the world. He felt protected from harm by a delicate, yet formidable energy of some sort.

True curanderos never work for a price, since, as Don Pablito would say, the power would be denied. Educated people who can't be convinced of such *nonsense* are to Nazul too smart for their own good.

A Nazul le encanta leer. *Nazul loved to read.* He has read a lot of books pertaining to his Raza. Don Pablito has also provided him with tales del Niño Fidencio and other great mysterious curanderos. He warns that in recent years many false curanderos are sprouting up and taking advantage of the gente. Their deceit doesn't last long since they are cursed from the start for their audacity.

Nazul has also been given writings about visions from a couple of the local viejitos who toil in the hot sun for a buck. These writings are extensive, filled with divine messages. Nazul treasures them. The writers might be wearing old T-shirts with moth holes and shoes tattered by the years, but Nazul is always humbled by their wisdom.

Nazul knows viejitas who are like saints to even the fiercest tecatos in the varrio. They would spend their days looking in on poor familias living on the edge of survival. Always dressed in their trademark long black dresses, black socks, shoes, and veils, their knowledge of life is astounding.

Nazul is saddened by the fact that the knowledge of his varrio elders is not recognized by society, where it could help so many people. And there are so many sick people today. Yet, for the 'well-educated,' these masters of energy are considered just quacks. What is common knowledge to the curanderos and to the firme in the varrio, the most learned in America could only hope to grasp. There are many viejitos in the varrio who shun medicine and are very healthy into their nineties. Yet, their 'educated' children are dying in the prime of their lives because they don't believe in the wisdom of their own gente. Como quiera, the varrio educates those who are open to our elders' wisdom. A curandero's wisdom doesn't span hundreds, but thousands of years. It does not originate from a self-serving, money-obsessed mentality. This sabiduría is revealed to gifted human beings from a higher intelligence. The curandero's mysterious power is a gift to be shared openly. What better formula for the longevity of our species? Formal education, though a necessity, is nevertheless notorious for sidestepping common sense, for not giving a deep-rooted, significant culture its place. In the end, for way too many, such arrogance is its own costly and terminal reward, Nazul figures.

After a few minutes Nazul stands, kisses Don Pablito on top of his head, grabs his bag, and heads out the door. "'Apá, voy también a dejarle el carro a Doña Tomasa. Después vuelvo." *Dad, I'm also going to take the car to Doña Tomasa. I'll be back.*

Nazul cruises down Trinity in a '67 Ford Fairlane. The streets, now dark, seem like a ghost town. The night belongs to las clickas. Even stray dogs seem to seek shelter after dark.

The Fairlane pulls into the cramped driveway of a modest two-bedroom house in the heart of the varrio. Nazul steps out with his bag of pachuco threads and knocks on the wrought iron door. The gente are like prisoners in their own homes, with window guards that double as fire traps.

Una señora in her fifties answers cautiously. "¿Sí?"

"Soy yo, Nazul. Le truje su carro, Doña Tomasa."

"Ay, sí, Nazul. Espérame un momento. Te debo cuarenta dólares." *Wait for me a moment. I owe you forty dollars.*

Nazul looks down the wrought iron screen door as three little kids come running up to it. They giggle and laugh. He can see the scraggly Christmas tree with a few meager presents lying around it. Doña Tomasa watches the kids while her daughter works. Thirty seconds later, Doña Tomasa comes to the door to find Nazul gone. She rushes out onto the sidewalk. "¡Nazul!" She sees him half a block away. "¡Nazul, te debo cuarenta dólares!"

Nazul turns momentarily without breaking his hurried stride. "¡Quédese con ellos! Es un regalo de Elías por su negocio! Feliz navidad!" *Keep them! It's a gift from Elias for your business! Merry Christmas!*

With the cool wet breeze blowing her hair around her face, she watches him fade away with gratitude in her eyes. Her nietos at her side, she gathers them to her and nods her head to Nazul. "Mira, m'ijos, ese es un buen muchacho. Así van a ser ustedes." *Look, kids, that is a good young man. That's how you're going to be.* She smiles at the distant shadow. "Qué la Virgencita me lo cuide. ¡Gracias!" she yells out, but Nazul doesn't hear her as a '76 Firebird rumbles past him on the street with a deafening rap song bouncing bass beats off the quaint little homes. The leaves in the street scatter and roll in its wake as the nightly racket of gunshots and emergency sirens emerges, as if on cue, in the distance.

Nazul strolls down the darkening varrio street. At El Paso y Chupaderas he does a double take when he sees a tiny home shot to hell with bullet holes. A child's yellow and red tricycle lies abandoned in the front yard.

Nazul walks down the varrio streets with his chuco outfit in the bag. He stops for a minute to gaze at a classic, fenced-up tire shop, closed for the night at Chihuahua and Brazos. Sirens wail.

Nazul studies the tiny building with a thoughtful grin. Just about every rincón and cranny se mira como que it's either known, slept, or wrestled with a pinche tire. On the smudged walls, tapas hang by the dozen. They brighten up the otherwise dull, twenty-foot grease spot.

Next door to the tire shop, an overgrown garage is covered with a powerful mural of la Virgen surrounded by the sad solemn faces of gente, young and old, trained on the viewer. Dissecting the image are cruel barbed-wire lines, precariously close to their eyes and faces, a memorial to the fencing off of the gente's culture and existence.

Nazul gives a coded knock on a side door. "Tan-ta-ta-tan-tan."

A minute later an older Chicano with a greying goatee peers out with his tired eyes. He holds a paintbrush dripping with purple-cobalt oil paint and squints to focus. "Eyy vato, you made it."

"Pos, ¿no te dije?" *Well, isn't that what I said?* Nazul walks into the dim interior. A polka plays on a beat-to-shit, paint-smudged radio nearby. At the far end of the thirty-foot studio, the silhouettes of two vatos in their late fifties are deep in conversation in the darkness, warmed only by a couple of velas and a dingy lightbulb hanging high overhead. They haven't noticed him enter.

Nazul turns to Chico, who is looking at his bag. "Did you bring the pachuco threads, ese, o ¿me trajiste algo para Chreesmas?" *Or did you bring me something for Christmas?*

"Simón y chale."

Chico smiles. "You got me again. I admire un vato de palabra." *A vato of his word.* Chico looks around the crammed studio. "You can change over there." He points to a two-foot-square area where a push broom might fit.

Chico goes back to his painting in the only bright spot in the place, under another light bulb hanging from the ceiling.

A couple of brushstrokes and he's in another dimension.

Nazul looks around and is amazed that arte can be so obsessive to its creador. The place is crammed to the ears with what look to him to be paintings and dozens of drawings everywhere. All set in the dead of night. The artworks are crammed sin respeto on the walls. The rest end up as expresiones mudas, stacked against anything that'll stand still long enough. He doesn't know it, but in this slice of the art world, Chicano noir tira parada. *Is without equal.*

Like captured illusions of the Chicano consciousness, the paintings pull you into their world, and before you know it, you're dreaming.

Nazul looks up. The tire shop next door seems to have contaminated the studio already. Hubcaps have infiltrated the place, coming in through the ceiling, nailed flat in willy-nilly fashion like a flying saucer invasion.

The polka ends when Chico trips over the electrical cord and abruptly cuts off the radio. Nazul now hears the two vatos at the end of the studio as they turn to check the radio, then quickly return to the argument they're more interested in.

"But how can they *shit* on the only ones who give a damn about them?" one vato can be heard saying.

The other vato is determined too. "Because when one of us hurts," he holds up his little finger, "we all hurt." He spreads out his hand.

The other vato nods in agreement. "Gangas can be good. Back in the '60s we organized all the clickas que nomás andaban con sus travesuras. *That were just causing mischief.* They helped us to campaign. For the first time in history we got our gente into the seats of power. They were Clickas, Ph.D. Pero wacha los huevos de este vato today. You think those culeros give a fuck about that? No! Because the pinche TV has 'em so colonized que they don't even know us anymore. We aren't their heroes."

The chubby silhouette gets more comfortable on his stool and continues. "Wacha, un pinche perro tiene más derechos que un Mexicano."

Check it out. A dog has more rights than a Mexican.

"¿Qué?" The other vato is perplexed. "A ver, a ver, I got you on this one, vato. A ver, ¿Cómo tiene un perro mas derechos?" *Let's see, let's see. How does a dog have more rights?* With a grin, he squints into the darkness of the studio toward Nazul and Chico. "Oyites, Chico, listen to this, man."

El chubby: "Mira, un vato, some time ago—you probably read it in the paper and it was all over the pinche TV—bueno, ese vato mató un perro. *Killed a dog.* He got cuatro años in the big house. ¿Verdad? Bueno. Ahora look at that gabacho rancher en el Valle que mató a un mojadito in cold blood simply porque le pidió agua, porque él y su compañero se murían de sed. *Now look at that gabacho rancher in the Valley who killed a poor illegal in cold blood because he asked him for water, because he and his companion were dying of thirst.* That pinche Nazi got sent home to his family. ¿Qué no?"

"Oh, you're right. Simón."

Nazul lifts his leg to pull up the pachuco pants and knocks over a vase full of worn-out paintbrushes, scattering them on the floor. The two vatos in the back try to make out who he is.

Chico turns around and focuses. "Blue-Boy, you don't need to wear the trama'os. They're not gonna show."

"Eyy! El Blue-Boy!" Nazul turns to catch José Rivera-Barrera, local mesquite-wood sculptor, approaching him with a big, humble smile. José gives him a Raza handshake. "I didn't know you were here, ese."

"Simón, carnal. I'm here to pose for a pintura."

Nazul walks over to the other vato sitting on a barstool. "Ey, carnal, you're Benny Solis, from La Raza Unida Party. Del Vidrio."

"Qué pasó, Blue-Boy. Ey, I'm too old to go running to shake hands como José. Pero quiero que sepas que en mi libro, eres chingón. Pero mucho cuidau." *I want you to know that in my book, you're killer. But be very careful.* He holds up a cautious index finger.

"El respeto es mío." *The respect is mine.* Nazul humbles himself to these two veteranos de la Causa. Vatos like Benny, from Crystal City, Texas, changed the course of history for all Raza, fighting for basic civil rights so that Mexican Americans would be treated like human beings instead of cattle. Vatos and rucas of his generation had their lives threatened in their struggle with relentless racism. To Nazul, gente like Benny were true Raza.

"Y, vato!" Benny playfully points an accusing finger at José. "Este vato, te estaba rayando *todo* el disco!" *This vato was scratching your record all up!*

They all have a good laugh.

José is originally from Kingsville, Texas. Somehow, Raza from all over seem to gravitate to cultura-rich San Anto. José is a constant fixture at Chico's studio, but when he starts a sculpture, he disappears for a month at a time. A humble, caring man with a quiet yet formidable power, his grace is a rare reflection of a Chicano's true identity.

José, already used to the parade of models in Chico's studio, checks out Nazul's black pachuco topcoat. "So, you gonna pose, eh?"

Nazul nods.

Benny chimes in. "Simón, Chico already described it to me." He holds his hands up, panoramic-style. "It's gonna be a masterpiece de la Raza!" He stops to think. "Shit, we need our *own* museums. What kind of art history are our children going to claim? These babosos don't even want us to speak Spanish." Their laughter resounds through the smoky studio.

Chico is disrupted from his trance in front of his painting and starts planning his next artistic obsession.

Benny continues passionately. "Simón, we need Raza representing our accomplishments, people who know what we're about."

José grins at Nazul about Benny. "Chinga, you sound like a salsa commercial."

Chico approaches with a camera ready. "Orale, Blue-Boy, did you bring the gafas?"

Nazul digs in his topcoat pocket and pulls out a pair of maddogs, slips them on. "Pos, ¿no te dije?"

Chico grins. "Chinga, vato. Why don't you just shoot me?"

Nazul turns around to a small, grease-smeared mirror barely finding a six-inch space on the cluttered wall. He checks his look like a vato maloso. But the mirror is a foot to the left. The vatos chuckle.

Benny snickers into his fingers mischievously. "Chinga, Chico, préndele la pinche luz." *Chico, turn the damn light on for him.*

José: "No puede ver a Ray Charles ni pintado." *He can't stand to see Ray Charles, even painted.*

Chico uncovers the front end of a hollow '57 Chevy at the far end of the studio, which he had covered with a tarp to keep the dust and paint drops off the shine.

He grabs a pair of jumper cables hooked to a car battery on the floor beside the front end and hands Nazul the cables, opens the car's hood and stations it with the hood bar.

"Now, carnal, all you have to do is lean in to the battery inside the hood and touch the cables together to make it spark in front of your face. Pero con cuidado."

Positive and negative meet. The sparks fly. Chico quickly starts snapping photos.

drive-by asesino

Eight

Morir soñando
To die dreaming

Nazul walks by a cantina. The night is cold, electric. A ranchera filters out.

Nazul is deep in thought about that morning. Los cohetazos. *The gunshots.* The lágrimas in her dreamy eyes as she leaned against his chest. Anticipation mixed with tension hangs heavy in the wet air.

The air brakes of a city bus catch Nazul's attention. As the bus pulls away, a striking Chicana is left standing in the night.

Nazul blinks in disbelief. "No puede ser." *It can't be.* All day long, Nazul has not been able to get her out of his mind, the way she felt up close. The cool breeze blows her hair in swirls around her beautiful face. Nazul catches his breath. "Luna." Her name escapes his lips as if stored away deep in his soul. She's wearing a long, dark dress with dark flat shoes and a matching jacket that glistens dark blue, reflecting the light.

He swallows hard. He's got to talk to her. She starts walking across the street in a hurry towards him, then turns away down the sidewalk past a closed molino. Soon she is obscured from his view.

Nazul starts walking faster. The traffic is light but steady.

"Luna!" His voice is nervously deep and doesn't carry. Instead, the cool wind and the loud exhaust from the passing mufflers carry her name away into the air.

He reaches the corner, lit up from a single yellow bulb under the canopy of the molino. He sees her walking past El Gallo Giro Lounge. The deep blue and electric red tints from a neon beer sign bathe her hair and clothes as she walks by.

Nazul takes a deep breath. "Luna!" he hears himself say.

She turns around to see, but still keeps her stride. She seems confused.

As the neon glow lights his approaching silhouette, she sees his face and takes a deep breath. Undecided. She waits. "Nazul." She looks down and away as she bites her lip. The memory of the morning's events bears down on her like a dark shroud.

Nazul's smile warms her and grounds her in the present. After changing back from the pachuco threads at Chico's studio, he's wearing his usual varrio attire—a navy blue work shirt with a white patch that reads 'Azteca Tire Shop,' navy blue Dickies, and a Goodwill store brown jacket.

As their eyes meet again, neither knows what to say. They stand in a novela moment, each gazing into the other's soul.

Her mouth opens. Short of breath, her voice is somewhere deep in her chest. "Nazul, right?"

Nazul is speechless. Since that morning, an undeniable connection has developed between them. He nods. "Luna, right?" They both smile at their awkwardness.

"Did I give you my name?" She tries to recall.

"No, ah—" It's a struggle just to dip into his memory. "Ah, Plutarco told me. Plutarco." He tries to smile his dumbness away.

His charm relaxes her and they start walking slowly. She fixes her gaze on him. "Nazul, about this morning. I'm confused. I'm sorry if I got you in trouble—"

"Naw, it was gonna happen." He shrugs. "We're surrounded by it." Nazul sounds convincing. "Forget about that. It was loco this morning." He presses on. "But, if it's okay, I want to talk about you. ¿Quién eres? *Who are you?* What do you do?" He can't take his eyes off her.

"I teach." She looks at him with mysterious grace, her eyes watery as she tries to control her emotions.

"A teacher? ¡Qué lindo!" *How solid!* He looks down.

She chuckles uneasily. "What about you? Someone told me you were a varrio machanic?" She tilts her head slightly. She's irresistible.

"Simón, there ain't a broken-down varrio I can't fix." They laugh together.

Nazul opens his mouth to ask more, but she beats him to it. "Were you born here in San Anto?" They walk slowly down the dimly lit street. The carruchas rattle and roll by.

"No, I've lived here most of my life, pero soy de Robestán, close to Corpus. I've heard it said it's the birthplace of the pachuco."

Luna checks out his attire. "So, are you a pachuco?" She looks into his eyes. An electric magnetism hypnotizes him.

"Todos somos del mismo rancho." *We're all from the same ranch.*

"'Del mismo rancho?'"

"It's an old saying from the labores of Robestán."

"Which means?" She likes his sense of history.

"That means all Raza is connected by our identity and struggle. A pachuco is just another symbol of our stance against oppression. Those are Benny Solis' words. It's also a tribute to the Chicano civil rights movement and Crystal City, el Vidrio, where it all began."

Luna is left openmouthed by this mechanic's varrio-trucha education.

"So, are you a pachuco?" she presses.

He looks seriously into her eyes again for a magical moment and nods. "Pachuco, Ph.D."

She bursts out laughing. "Ohhh, maybe *you* should be the teacher." The night is transformed into a timeless dream.

Far off in the distance the night train groans.

"Luna—"

Before he can continue, she interrupts him by reaching into his half-open shirt and pulling out his rosario into her beautiful hands. "A crucifijo." She looks at him.

Nazul looks down at her hand. Her fingers stroke the sculpted body of Christ hanging at the end of the rosario. "Era de mi abuelita."

It was my gramdmother's.

"Qué lindo." Luna looks up into his eyes.

Tires squeal. A jet black '59 Impala hangs a U-turn in the middle of the street and rolls up to them. In the front passenger a hardcore gangster leans out to them in a flipped black cap and black maddogs. Diablo.

"Eyy, Blue-Boy, you got a varita for this?" He levels a TEC-9. His gold tooth catches a ray of light as he grins at his catch. Three dark silhouettes accompany him. A dreamy rola by Sunny pours out of the stereo.

Nazul and Luna are frozen.

"Whasamata? Did I catch you at a bad time?" For a second Diablo gets dead serious, expecting Nazul to bust a move. His death mask turns into a sadistic grin. "*Nadie* se burla de mi! Bamos a tirar el welton, ese Blue-Boy." Nobody *laughs at me! Let's go for a cruise, ese Blue-Boy.*

Nazul looks at Luna, not knowing what to do. "Vete de aquí." *Get away from here.* He whispers, "Por favor."

She looks deep into his eyes. "No." Her voice trembles. She may never see him again. Across the street a squad car rolls by slowly, oblivious to the high-stakes drama.

Nazul holds his eyes on her, wondering if this is la última mirada. *The last look.*

"I got chit for patience, homes." Diablo cocks his nine, menacingly.

Nazul steps toward the car. Diablo opens his door and leans forward so Nazul can squeeze into the back seat between two vatos.

Diablo clocks Luna with his dark, soulless eyes as Nazul holds his breath. "And you, masota," he stares at her long and hard, "te admiro." *I admire you.* He nods chingón. "Pero, si me cruzas, te juro que tu familia…morirá soñando." *But, if you cross me, I swear your family…will die dreaming.* He spits on the sidewalk.

Disturbing images cut through her being, but she stares Diablo down, knowing that he's going to do whatever he wants no matter what. "Como te dije, eres un cobarde." *Like I told you, you're a coward.*

She nods her head.

Diablo grins and puckers a kiss at her.

Luna looks up to see the squad car, which has made a quick U-turn and is rolling back up to the red light, fifty feet away. Diablo swivels around and sees it, then looks at Luna. He leans out the window to her. "Dale shine, masota. Tú sabes que a mí me importa verga." *Shine it up, babe. You know damn well I don't give a fuck.* Luna is frozen, the bloodbath of that morning still fresh in her mind. If the Impala drives off, Nazul is as good as dead. She starts to wave at the cops just as their flashing lights flick on. They screech away to the call of some other emergency. She clutches her stomach as the Impala fades away, Diablo grinning out the window at her.

The strike of a matchstick in the darkness casts a warm glow of life over the santos in the curandero's altar room. They glisten with strange metallic light, like wondrous souls trapped in suspended animation.

Don Pablito is lighting holy candles around the room. The twenty or so candles give the tiny room a sense of mission. With divine patience and grace in every move, Don Pablito kneels down on the oval rug with his rosary in his hands. He prays directly to la Virgen de Guadalupe, the gateway to the Creador.

Her sharp golden rays pierce the thick, smoky atmosphere in the room. Her gaze is serene. Don Pablito's eyes, a masterwork of wrinkles, seem transformed into the innocent eyes of a child. His whispered prayers seem to possess a tangible energy. Rising up and out of the room, they float off into the cold wet night.

The train moans as it approaches the Guadalupe Bridge. Storm clouds are forming overhead. Nazul is startled by a flash of lightning inside the Impala as it heads toward the bridge. Thunder rolls across the sky like the lumbering footsteps of an angry giant.

♫ "Slowly, slowly, but surely…our hearts fell in love. Slowly, slowly, but surely…we drifted apart."

A rola by Henry Peña and the Kasuals pours out of the stereo.

Tight on Nazul's every escape option, the vatos are silent, like the static calm of a lightning bolt before the blinding flash.

Raindrops quicken their taps on the windshield, melting the cityscapes ahead into glistening globs of light and shadow, electric colors of a varrio night. Windshield wipers sharpen them into perfect 3-D, only to let them melt again…

One of the vatos flanking Nazul in the back seat checks him. He's in his late twenties, with a black paño tied low over his eyes. "Blue-

Boy, eh?" He grins defiantly. "Well, tonight you're gonna have something to be blue about." They all chuckle except for Diablo, who is eerily quiet, grooving coolly to the car stereo and staring ahead at the Guadalupe Bridge. This narrow concrete and steel overpass separates the glitzy downtown affluence machine from el Weso, a stranger lurking in the shadows of the American Dream.

Nazul knows that this could very well be it. Discreetly, he grabs for his rosary in the darkness. Holding the crucifijo, he snaps it from his neck. The beads fall silently onto his lap and roll to the floor. Again a lightning bolt splits the night. The thunder fades into the nerve-wracking yelp of the night train, which is about to cross their path underneath the bridge.

Sunny's gruff voice bathes the scene with varrio glory as "The One Who's Hurting Is You" plays on the radio.

As the Impala reaches the top of the bridge, the other vato turns to Nazul. "This is where you get off, vato maloso."

Diablo turns around to face Nazul. "El que empiece algo conmigo, vale más que lo acabe. Porque yo sí, lo voy a acabar!" *The man who starts something with me better finish it. Because I will!*

A sharp yelp from the train below assaults Nazul's nerves again. Diablo opens his door and steps out so the vatos in the back seat can squeeze pafuera. The rain falls heavier now. Nazul steps out with one of the vatos at his side. The rat-tat-tat of the cold raindrops peppers their dry clothes. The other vato gets stuck in the doorframe. Diablo grabs him by the back of the collar and pulls him out. "De volada. Me estoy mojando, baboso." *Hurry up. I'm getting wet, idiot.* Diablo climbs back in and slams the door shut.

One with a fila, the other with an automatic, the two vatos force Nazul to the edge of the bridge. The train lets out a deafening roar as it rumbles under them, the ground trembling.

One vato yells at Nazul above the thundering monster. "You got three choices, Blue-Boy. You can either jump, get shot, or both!" They laugh at their sick humor.

Except for a timid car rolling by in the opposite direction, the place is lifeless.

They force Nazul right to the edge, to a four-foot-high railing of rusted-out, round metal beams.

The other vato yells at Nazul, "Blue-Boy, aquí se acaba tu corrido. We click to la rola: los Muertos, por donde pasamos, se tropiezan con los cuerpos." *Blue-Boy, your ballad ends here. We click to the hit: the Dead, where we cruise by, they trip over corpses.*

Nazul looks down to the railway cars thundering by underneath.

Just then, Diablo rolls down the car window and yells out at them, "*Eyy,* órale, tengo que tirar l'agua! Se me anda *reventando.* Escríbele una pinche carta!" *I have to take a leak! It's about to* burst. *Write him a fucking letter!*

Nazul looks down at him with varrio disgust. He yells, "No tuviste los huevos pa' matarme como un hombre. Eres un rey de culeros." *You didn't have the balls to kill me like a man. You're a king of chickenshits.*

Diablo just stares back.

Confused, not used to Diablo not answering a line like that with a shotgun blast to the mouth, the two vatos grab Nazul by the hair to shove him over.

Diablo finally replies. "Simón, soy un *culero.* Y un culero te quitó *todo.*" *Yeah, I'm a* chickenshit. *And a chickenshit took* everything *you've got.* He starts rolling up his window.

From Nazul's left, the vato with the gun shoves him with his gun hand. Nazul grabs it and stands teetering on the edge as two rounds blast off over his head. The other vato lunges in with his fila, but Nazul uses his homie's arm to shield himself. His homie yells out as the fila stabs him. A second lunge. Yelping again, the vato starts losing control of the situation. He wraps his legs around the metal rails of the bridge, buying a few seconds as he supports all of Nazul's weight with one arm. Nazul, still holding the crucifijo in his left hand, uses the sharp metal cross to cut into the vato's fingers. His grip on the gun loosens.

The vato with the fila looks for a clear jab at his target, but Nazul manages to twist the automatic around. He fires at the vato. The hot lead finds his shoulder and spins him around. He stumbles to the pavement.

Diablo glances indifferently out his fogged-up passenger window, nodding his head in disgust as he calmly lights a cigarette with an old-fashioned metal lighter. "Puñatas," he breathes to himself. The mulatto vato beside him at the wheel just nods simón.

As the vato's legs lose their hold on the guardrail and they both fall away, Nazul empties the automatic at Diablo. The rounds send the chrome trim flying off Diablo's window frame in an arc. The last round cuts through the window and blasts Diablo's lighter out of his hands. The lighter ricochets off his maddogs, which shoot away violently in several pieces, cutting a huge gash on his cheekbone, adding to his already scarred-to-shit face.

The driver recoils his hand from the steering wheel as the bullet, continuing on its trajectory, ends up blasting the tip of his little finger off. "*Ay! Cabrón!*" A spray of red tints the windshield.

Outside, Nazul and the vato fall to the stream of boxcars below.

Nazul crashes through the slat-wood roof of a boxcar while the vato lands on the edge with a loud crack and tumbles over the side.

Up on the bridge the injured vato outside the Impala gets up painfully and peers over the edge into the inky blackness. No sign of life. Just rumbling, creaking boxcars.

Diablo holds his cheekbone and pulls up on the door lever, then angrily kicks open the car door. The cracked car window crumbles off. "Tenían que hacer sus cagadas." *You had to fuck it up.* He glances angrily at the broken window, then trains his death look on the vato outside who is walking to him, holding his bleeding shoulder. "Nunca puedo tener nada machín con ustedes puñatas!" *I can never have anything smooth with you jackoffs!*

The tall vato stands there, not knowing whether to get in the car.

"Te vas a subir, ¿o no?" *You getting in, or not?* As Diablo stands up to let the vato in, he notices the blood streaming from his shoulder. "You better not bleed all over the back seat like last time, culero. This is diamond-pleat." His dark menace checks him up and down for drips.

Inside, the bleeding vato takes off his cheap dark jacket and removes his T-shirt. He folds it and applies pressure to soak up the blood. He checks the cherry red seat for any drips.

Diablo gets in and slams the door shut. With a scowl he glances over at the driver, the mousy-looking mulatto, who is diligently wiping the splatter of blood from his little finger off the dash and stereo with his sleeve. His busted finger is wrapped tightly in his paño.

Diablo follows the blood drips down to his cassette player. "Chinga! Chingada madre! You fucking bled on my Sunny tape." He grabs the tape and flings it angrily at the driver, bouncing it off his forehead. "¡Dále! ¡Vámonos a la verga de aquí!" *Stomp it! Let's get the fuck outta here!*

Without warning, the car dies. The driver hits the ignition. Not even a click. The Impala starts rolling backwards on its own as the driver frantically slams the brakes. They don't respond.

"Hit the brakes, menso!" Diablo looks at the driver, who stomps on the brake pedal to no avail.

"Chingau! No jalan!"

The Impala gains momentum.

"Hit the gears, Raton!" the vato in the back seat yells.

Diablo looks nervously behind him to see where they're going to land.

"The gears no jalan!" Raton, the driver, is frantic. Not even the steering wheel responds. "What da fuck!?"

With a mind of its own, the Impala goes careening down the steep slope. As it reaches the bottom it swerves wildly to the right, flipping over in a grassy area, and ends right-side-up in the Aztlán-Apache creek.

The three shook-up vatos sit in silent disbelief. The smell of gasoline and dirty water fills their nostrils in the smoky, dusty darkness.

Suddenly the headlights turn back on and the car starts revving up. Raton yells in panic. Los malosos look at each other with superstitious fear. Diablo tries to get the hell out, but his door is jammed from the rollover. The driver's side door is jammed too. The headlights flash on and off eerily.

Diablo lunges out of his broken window and is followed by the other two whimpering vatos, who fight each other to be next.

aguila que cae

Nine

No plomeen a la Virgen
Don't shoot the Virgin

Milling around the front yard in the cold wet night, two Muertos, black paños tied low over their eyes, stand by the sidewalk in front of an old, condemned, graffitti-infested shack that once was a home. Neighbors up and down the street have long abandoned the entire block, leaving behind shells and ruins. Except for the glow coming from the broken window of the shack and a dim street lamp down the block, the area is dark.

The two Muertos stand by themselves smoking a toque. They act like they don't know the two young headbangers who are pulling out a boombox from a beat-up white Pinto parked on the curb. The two punks sport spiked mohawks and long raggedy T-shirts ripped in strategic places that hang like black rags from their wimpy frames.

Metallica, Marylin Manson, and some other satanic images scream from the shirts. Their dirty, greasy black jeans adorned with chains end in a jumbled clump, half hiding their steel-toed boots. They look like something KISS might puke up, shamefully out of place in the varrio, especially in la Tripa. Worst of all, they're Hispanic.

They crank up the boombox full-throttle and a Megadeth hit shatters the calm of the still night. They try to be cool, grooving to the indistinguishable ranting of some pissed-off white dude. The two Muertos look at each other with disgust.

Brujo flings his frajo. "Damn, Meco, why'd you have to invite your primito over here? Parece que 'stán retarda'os." *They act like they're retarded.* He scowls.

Meco is a tacuache-looking vato who seems to have been kicked around the varrio 'til he found a home with los Muertos. He is ill at ease. "Shit, Brujo, you don't know this huerquillo. He's been nagging me to death that he wants to see Diablo about joining la clicka. He'll probably just piss Diablo off and get maimed. Maybe then he won't follow me around anymore."

Brujo is a bald, shady-looking character who could pass for an overweight cuervo. *Vulture.*

They see three shadows approaching from down the dark street behind the Pinto. They both pull their cohetes from their waistbands and check them for ammo. Squinting, they try to recognize somebody.

As the shadows get closer, Meco puts his gun back. "That chuco walk is Diablo's. ¿Qué chingaus pasaría?" *What the fuck happened?*

Quickly, they both walk to meet them.

Diablo is walking ahead of the other two, his face frozen into his usual scowl. But tonight he's late for his chiva and his telenovela. He's in no mood for nonsense.

As Meco reaches Diablo, he notices the gash on his cheekbone. "Carnal, where's your gafas? What—"

Before Meco can finish, Diablo shoves him aside. "Hazte a la verga!" He keeps walking.

Meco decides to ask the tall vato with the shoulder wound instead. "Ey, Tripa, where's Spooky? What the hell happened?"

Tripa just keeps walking. "Se lo llevó el tren, some weird shit. Pregúntale a Ratón." *Ask Ratón.* He motions with his head behind him. "I'm too tired to talk, chinga."

Last in line, with a bloody finger wrapped in a paño, the driver, Ratón, answers Meco. "That pinche Blue-Boy, he was peor than a pinche cucaracho to kill. Pero, something weird happened. Andábamos de malas. We were on a bad roll, ese." He looks up at one of the acid punks stupidly ambling up behind Diablo, who has just passed them up without a glance. "Who's that pendejo?" The boombox squeals like diez marranos atorados. *Ten stuck pigs.*
A look of mortal fear washes over Meco's face. "Homer! *Wait!*"
Too late. Homer, all doped up and grinning, taps Diablo's shoulder from behind.

Diablo swings his arm around with a plomero in his hand and smacks Homer in the mouth, knocking him on his ass. Without losing the rhythm of his swing, he blasts the screaming boombox off the roof of the Pinto. Homer's friend, inches away, dives to the pavement.

Dead silence as Meco runs up to Diablo. Homer is stunned, looking for his teeth and marbles on the ground.

"Chinga, parece que me están rayando toda la pinche madre!" *Fuck, I feel like I'm getting cussed all to shit!* Diablo trains his death look on Meco, then on a groggy, bloody-mouthed Homer. "¿Quiénes son estos *jotos*?" *Who are these* faggots?

Meco helps Homer to his feet. The other dude by the Pinto is thinking about running away down the dark street. Meco tries to calm Diablo. "Mero, cálmala. Es-este es mi primito, Homer, and his camarada over there is Jamie." Meco motions for Jamie to come.

Jamie's legs quiver when he realizes he's go to get closer to the *real* Megadeth. He slips on the muddy lawn but composes himself, only to trip over a hairline crack in the sidewalk.

The other Muertos watch with sadistic amusement as the two pendejos deal with the hole they've dug for themselves. Diablo had an effortless way of taking any vato with huevos and turning him into a mumbling pendejo. Much less these wimps.

Jamie walks up next to Homer.

"Y ¿qué chingaus quieren?" *And what the fuck do they want?* Diablo stares them down to the ground and into their graves. The metalheads sweat bullets in the freezing night.

"Me-Mero," Meco swallows hard. "They wanna know if they can be Muertos."

Bloody-mouthed, Homer foolishly puts out a limp, sweaty hand. "He-he-hey, du-du-dude, I-I—"

Diablo ignores Homer's smooth white hand. He tries to make out their T-shirts in the dark with a pissed-off fashion opinion. He calmly puts his cohete back in his waistband. The punks breathe a sigh of relief. Maybe they're not going to die in the next breath.

With both hands Diablo grabs their T-shirts at their chests, gripping a couple of inches of their soft skin in the process. He rips their T-shirts down the front in a jerk, leaving them hanging askew from the neck, suspended only by the thread rings. "Babosos! You think those jotos give a fuck about you?" Diablo yells at their grimacing faces. "Estúpidos. Get the fuck outta my sight!"

The two punks seem to get a jolt of high voltage up their asses at Diablo's command. They spring forward from their frozen positions, only to trip and stumble on their hanging rags. They make their way to the Pinto, pathetically holding their torn shirts up to their chests like two girls trying to hide their titties. Diablo clocks them with a stone face.

Los Muertos bite their lips and taste blood to keep from bursting out with laughter. Meco has lost his standing gacho.

When the punks reach the Pinto, they pick up a few of the large pieces of the boombox so as not to be litterbugs on Diablo's turf.

Jumping into the safe haven of their Pinto, they anxiously rev 'er up. Rrr-rrr-rr…RR-r-r, click. The battery is dead.

Diablo y los vatos watch from the yard in cemetery silence.

The two punks sit motionless for a moment in the painfully still darkness. Again he tries it. Click, click. Nalgas.

The window rolls down slowly. "Can-can anybody give us a-a-a jump?"

"*Chingada madre.*" Diablo pulls out and pops his nine-inch push-button fila. He struts to them with a rage like he is going to disembowel them where they sit.

With panicked whimpers the punks jump out of the Pinto and stumble down the street for their lives. They disappear into the darkness.

Tripa blurts out a tee-hee. Diablo turns to him slowly. "Yo juego contigo?" *Do I play around with you?* Tripa turns to marble.

The four vibrating statues watch silently as Diablo walks to the ganghouse door, opens it, then slams it behind him.

Tripa, despite his shoulder wound, falls to the wet grass, squirming with uncontrollable snorts. "Meco, that's your badass primo? Haa-haa! Ahhaa! My tía Martinita's got more huevos in her titties! Haa-haah-aaahhhaaa!"

The other vatos join in, unable to contain it any longer. They cackle and snort like possessed hyenas.

Suddenly a dark car with the headlights off rolls out of the darkness toward them. The vatos quickly go for their automatics—shic-chic, shic-chic. Two run and hide on the lawn side of the Pinto. The other two get down on the ground in the dark, muddy wetness.

The car slowly rolls up behind the Pinto. The vatos recognize it. It's the Cutlass from the shootout that morning, now sporting a new windshield and Bondo-filled bullet holes. The vatos on the ground get up with muddy elbows and knees. "Chingada madres" can be heard.

Tripa and Ratón with the bloody finger go in the ganghouse to tend to their wounds.

The front passenger steps out carrying an AK and a shotgun. Like Cuco Sanchez, he's bug-eyed with a flat, round face. His body is short, frog-like, and he wears his black paño Aunt-Jemima-style.

Meco walks up to him. "Ese, Sapo! You get the hollow points?"

"Hollow like your chompa." *Head.* Sapo directs him to a box on the floorboard of the Cutlass. The driver opens the trunk. Inside lies enough firepower to let a paranoid Colombian drug lord sleep like a baby. Grenades, Uzis, TEC-9s, AKs, and some boxes of ammo.

"Killer, you been riding around with no lights and carrying this shit?" Meco questions the driver.

"Ey, Diablo wanted the shit." Sapo slaps a clip into an AK and plants a sloppy kiss on it. "What are we supposed to say, los juras won't let me drive around without lights?"

Brujo pulls out a grenade and fingers the clip. "Baboo-o-ososs, you vatos scare me."

Killer pulls out his paño and grabs some shells.

Ratón peers out the rickety front door of the ganghouse. "Ey, Killer, Diablo wants you and Meco to go pick up the Impala by the Guadalupe Bridge in the Atzlán-Apache creek!"

"What about all this shit?" He throws his hands down at the artillery.

"Jump-start the Pinto. Fuck, I don't know." Ratón shuts the door.

Killer walks over to the Pinto, jumps in, and hits the ignition. It purrs right up. "Whose is it, anyway?"

Meco and Brujo look at each other, surprised that it started.

"Ahhh, you don't know him," Meco mumbles.

Meco jumps in, the Pinto's headlights glow, and they purr away.

Two fresh vatos emerge from the ganghouse. The taller one flips the bill of his dark cap to the back, over his jet black hair. The other vato wears his traditional black paño low over his eyes, hiding them halfway. They are both wearing long-sleeved, black and grey checkered wool shirts with khaki pants. Aztec warriors ready for the night.

"Ey, Bad-Boy, Huevo, look at all this new shit." Sapo introduces the vatos to their collection. "We gonna start stockpiling the shed again, ese. Diablo's órdenes."

Bad-Boy, the tallest of the four, sports a thin mustache and a teardrop tattoo under the corner of his right eye. He looks like a ladies' man and a man killer. "These look brand new, homes. We'll break 'em in tonight." He nods chingón.

Huevo is a little heavier and goofy-looking, with buck teeth. "Shit. This is one ride I don't wanna be on. Fuck!" He nods his head. As a weak polka trails out of the Cutlass, they use handkerchiefs to handle the ammo and load the assorted firepower.

The vatos are restless tonight. They sigh and pass around a joint, releasing the tension that hangs heavy in the air, though the menacing storm seems to have dissipated into a hushed, dripping stillness.

With a frown Sapo squints into the darkness down the sidewalk. Flashes of silvery yellow light float toward them. He can't imagine what it is. "Wacha, vatos, ¿Que chingaus es eso?"

"No sapo, Rana." Huevo doesn't even bother.

"You gonna start that shit? You're the only grown man I know who's still afraid of the cucuy." Bad-Boy glances up only briefly, then goes back to loading his AK clip.

Sapo tilts his head like a curious puppy trying to identify the intruder. A grin of recognition forms on his frog-face. "A la verga, es el Dirtys."

The vatos exchange disgusted looks.

"Ese, Dirty Rick." Sapo is the only one to acknowledge him as 'el Dirtys' comes into view.

El Dirtys sucked on one too many baggies of glue. He's wearing a silver and yellow Elvis-style shirt with a Dracula collar. Its metallic-looking material screams, reflecting any light near it. When he walks, it sends off flashes of microwave light one might find emanating from a quasar or supernova.

His thick red polyester pants are short enough to reveal yellow socks. The pants are gathered potato-sack-style around his waist. His shoes are shiny white plastic. He tries out his clumsy chuco-style walk.

"MR. SHOWTIME!" Sapo smiles wide.

Dirtys grimaces as he gets ready to talk. It's like he's about to sneeze or is taking a long-held whiz. He's a stutterer. "Eeeey-ey-ey eesse-see ho-ho-homie!" Eyes half-lit, his speech is slurred and his lips drool. He's like an overdressed borracho on a killer parranda. The rest of the vatos keep their distance as he nears. Sour looks cross their faces when they catch a whiff of his B.O. His hair gleams with el Perico hair grease, combed Flaco Jimenez style with a drippy curl hanging on his forehead for good measure.

"Sa-sa-sapo-o-o, ¿n-n-o ab-ab abla-ates con Di-di-aaaa-blo de mi-mi-mi?" *Sapo, did you ask Diablo about me?* Dirty Rick sways with his marijuano look softly trained on the only vato who will stand close enough to communicate with him.

Sapo keeps loading shells into a shotgun, trying not to breathe too deeply. "Ya te dije, Dirtys. Diablo said chale." *I told you, Dirtys. Diablo said no.*

Six feet away, Bad-Boy glances sourly at Dirtys' getup. "Besides, yur momma dresses you funny." He nods. "Por anka la chingada." *Way the fuck out there.*

Diablo bursts out of the ganghouse, causing the old torn-to-shit screen door to slap loudly against the wall. All the vatos turn to look. A trail of smoke from his frajo follows his silhouette like a smoking gun. The outlines of two rucas in babydoll dresses stand at the doorway, watching him leave. Diablo is sporting a new set of maddogs.

Diablo crosses the yard toward the vatos, the frajo glowing red as he takes a huge drag.

Dirtys sees his ticket. He intercepts Diablo's chuco stride. "Dia-dia-diaaaa-a—"

Before Dirtys can blurt it out, Diablo sticks his menacing face into his, "Nooooo!!!!" Dirtys grimaces as if enduring the blast from a shotgun. The smoke from Diablo's frajo makes him look even more pissed as it billows out of his mouth and around Dirtys' face.

Coughing babas, Dirtys stumbles back. "Ye-ye-ye-yeesss-sir!" He salutes him like an idiot.

Ignoring him, Diablo walks to the vatos, who are looking away to hide their grins.

"Hava-hava-haaave a n-n-n-niiice ev-eve-eve-ning!" Dirtys is all Miss Manners.

"¿Dónde están aquellos burros?" Diablo asks impatiently.

Just then the Impala's headlights turn the corner. It rolls up to the vatos as they quickly gather an assortment of weapons to load in.

Diablo opens the passenger door and waits impatiently for Meco to step out. He jumps in the front passenger, still enjoying his frajo. Killer, Sapo, and Huevo go around to the driver's side and squeeze into the back seat. Bad-Boy jumps in the driver's seat while Meco stays behind to keep Dirtys company.

Diablo turns to Dirty Rick, standing in the front yard waving goodbye a dozen times in his overstated fashion statement. Diablo almost cracks a grin. "Ya vete pa'la casa! Antes que encandiles a un pinche carro y te machuque!" *Go home already! Before you blind some damn car and get run over!*

The vatos burst out laughing. Con gritos they tear away, leaving Dirtys waving goodbye in a cloud of burnt rubber and exhaust smoke.

The Impala cruises down the varrio streets. Inside, the vatos are heavy with thought.

They glide down a few blocks, hang a right on Montezuma Street, then a left on Chupaderas. It's pitch black and quiet as the Impala rolls up to the curb between two small houses deep in slumber.

Bad-Boy lights a frajo as he glances out the broken passenger window past Diablo. The thick grey smoke hangs around his head. "Este es el cantón. This is the puto who turned our homies into altar boys."

Diablo trains his maddogs on the dark, quiet home. They all watch the silent twinkling of Christmas lights on the eaves and window frames.

In the back seat Huevo leans in to Diablo. "Este vato, Elías, a la mera gravota, que es *Azteca*. *This vato, Elias, without a doubt, is pure Aztec.* Purple Heart, Silver Star. Todo el pinche pedo. *The whole fucking package.* El vato saved half his platoon en 'Nam, including his gabacho captain, who fainted. He survived siete plomazos and got stabbed in the head with a bayonet." He chuckles. "Huevos de fierro. *Nadie* le tira parada." *Balls of steel.* Nobody *stands up to him.*

Sapo looks out the back window. At the house next to Elias', a Virgen shrine glows pale lavender in the front yard. "What about la casa del Blue-Boy? There's only a curandero who lives there. Es *buena* gente." *He's* good *people.*

Huevo is feeling goofy. "Two houses? Man, I shoulda packed a lunch."

Except for Diablo, who is totally serious, the vatos giggle and snort. Killer catches the groove. "Do we get a frajo break?"

Snorts and tee-hees come to an abrupt end. Diablo turns to them. "¿Quedaron bien?" *You think you made out?* He reaches between his legs in the inky darkness and cocks his Uzi. He opens his door and steps out facing the houses. He checks the clip.

Five seconds go by. Puzzled, Diablo turns around to find the vatos still sitting in their seats.

He leans in to them. "Estos pendejos," he nods at the defenseless hogares, "apostaron con la muerte y perdieron." *These idiots gambled with death and lost.* Diablo tries to justify the coldness of his act with his macho poetry.

Bad-Boy and Killer step out, but Sapo and Huevo look deeply troubled.

Sapo: "Vato, it's Chreesmas. Can't we wait 'til Ferubary?"

Diablo levels his Uzi at them. "Entonces, me pintan venado," *Well then, you can paint me a deer,* he whispers coldly.

With heavy hearts the vatos slowly step out. The biting breeze numbs their faces. Taking deep breaths, they cock their AKs and shotguns.

"No plomeen a la Virgen," *Don't shoot the Virgin,* Diablo says. The vatos look at each other, shaking their heads. Sapo is teary-eyed.

The stillness of night is turned into a raging firestorm as they open up on the two homes.

An ambulance screams by a modest two-story house on the busy corner of Guadalupe and Zarzamora. Its flashing lights dazzle the night with their urgency.

Luna is in her bedroom. Her weak lamp casts a warm light in the small room. She still wears her dark outfit, which now makes her feel like she's in mourning. She lies silently on her bed and stares at the dimly lit wall. The oval-framed portrait of her father in his Marines uniform stares back silently with a proud face.

A decorated war hero, he escaped death several times only to get killed in the streets where he grew up, the streets he loved so much.

"Luna, the news is on." A little girl's voice outside her closed door.

She opens the door to her ten-year-old sister. "Thanks, Estrella. Come on, let's go." Luna's bedroom is upstairs, and they both trot

los muertos open fire

down to the modest living room/kitchen area, still decorated in early-'60s style.

Consuelo is sitting on a flowered couch, watching the broadcast. The girls flop down beside their mom. A bright Christmas tree in the corner is surrounded by wrapped presents.

"The gang problem in San Antonio's west side is again spilling into the streets, as was witnessed today. A wild-west shootout, involving up to fourteen gang members, took place in front of horrified onlookers in the middle of the intersection of Guadalupe and Trinity at approximately eight a.m. today. Police say *all* except one of the dead were confirmed gang members. A bystander died later at Robert B. Green Hospital. Law-enforcement officials have likened the city's west side to a war zone." Video clips of the massacre follow featuring pools of blood, bodies covered with yellow tarps being loaded into the ambulances, the bullet-riddled, cherry red Camaro, and the chalk outlines of the dead bodies.

The three sit totally quiet, not wanting to miss any details. Consuelo finally grimaces. "Ay, m'ijita. I can't believe you were there. I hope you crawled under a car."

Luna nods. She holds Estrella tightly under her arm.

"In other news, the body of a young Latino male was found on the railroad tracks under the Guadalupe Bridge tonight."

Luna sits stone-faced, her blood rushing to her feet. "Virgencita, no," she whispers to herself, squeezing Estrella's arm. Her sister looks up at her, puzzled.

"Sources say he fell or was pushed from the bridge. Police say it appears to be gang-related. The victim remains unidentified."

Consuelo shakes her head. "Ay, when will it end?"

Luna numbly glances at her, then down to the floor.

Luna walks into her room and closes the door, leaning her whole weight on it. Mechanically she walks to her window and opens it. A cold breeze blows across the busy intersection, making her curtains dance. She stands there letting the breeze blow on her. She leans out and gazes blankly at the cruel night. Police and ambulance sirens wail. In the streets below, dogs bark and howl. A cantina around the corner, with its obnoxious jukebox, pours a rola out onto the breeze. It carries the sound in muffled then louder waves that drift away to Luna's window.

♫ "Smile now, cry later, oo-oo-ooo. Smile now, cry later for you-oo-oo, for you-oo-oo…"

A train moans in the distance. Luna stares at the dark. She buries her head in her hands and nods. "¿Porque me siento culpable? No fue mi culpa. Virgencita, no fue mi culpa." *Why do I feel guilty? It wasn't my fault. Virgencita, it wasn't my fault.* She weeps.

A long wet tongue licks a pair of closed eyes. The eyes squint hard, painfully. "Baa-aa-aa, baa." The sound of sheep enters Nazul's consciousness. He moves. Sharp pains sear his body. "Baa-aa-baa." He opens his eyes to a blur, feeling like he got run over by a garbage truck. As he tries to sit up, his left hand cramps with agony. He looks down at it. In waves, sharp blades of pain shoot through his head. Opening his bloodied hand, he sees the crucifijo that he clutches. Blood drips down around it from the cuts in his palm.

"Baa-baaa." Dazed, he slowly looks around to find himself the center of attention among a crowded group of fluffy white sheep. The wooden slats that surround him are spaced a few inches apart, sending slices of pale blue light across the sheep, packed in like cotton balls. "Baa-aa-baa." A boxcar.

Their hot breath hits the cold air and puffs of white steam trail upwards. He squints again and shakes his head, trying to get a sense of perspective. The smell of plasma makes him reach down to the darkness of the floor. His right hand comes up dripping crimson.

Struggling to stand, he leans back against the wooden slats for support. He looks under him. Two sheep lie crushed to death in a pool of blood. He looks up. A gaping hole in the ceiling tells him how he got there. Then it dawns on him: El Diablo anda suelto en la noche. *The Devil is loose in the night.* "'Apá!" he whispers breathlessly.

He sticks the crucifijo in his pocket and peers out through the slats. He's at the stockyards. No one around. A lonely bright spotlight illuminates the area. Looking up again, he sees his only way out.

With moans and groans he climbs up the wall of the boxcar, using the gaps in the slats as a ladder. He makes his way through the jagged hole and takes one last look down. To his amazement the sheep, now silent, are all looking up at him like a crowd of perplexed 17th-century British stargazers. Nazul squints to make sure he's not dreaming.

He climbs down the outside of the boxcar and makes his way home. Hours must have passed, but how many? He moves as fast as his aching back will allow.

Fifteen minutes later he nears his home.

He can make out a car outside. It's Chuy's cherry red '68 GTO. He freezes with fear. "'Apá!" As he wobbles closer, he makes out the "Police Restricted Area" ribbons lying torn on the ground, blowing in the late night breeze.

He panics, then runs with searing pain to the kitchen door and bursts in. "'Apá!" His eyes search but are afraid to see.

To his relief, Chuy and Don Pablito are sitting at the kitchen table drinking coffee and are startled to their feet. Chuy splashes his lap with coffee and winces from the burn, brushing it off his pants. Both are instantly relieved to see Nazul in one piece.

Nazul breathes out the agony of not knowing in one long exhale.

"M'ijo, gracias a la Virgen que estás bién!" *Son, thank the Virgin you're all right!* Don Pablito grabs him and holds him tightly. Nazul buries his head in Don Pablito's comforting shoulder for a long moment, his eyes welling up for their precious time on this earth together.

"¿Yo? ¿Cómo está usted?" *Me? What about you?* Nazul pulls him back as if checking for bullet holes.

"Yo estoy bién…" Don Pablito looks down at the floor. Nazul is again gripped by the throat with a sickening dread.

"Pero," Don Pablito looks out the window towards Elias' house. A razor-sharp blade of jagged ice slices through Nazul's being. "Esta noche," *This night,* he swallows hard, his words trembling, "Elías y su familia fallecieron." *Elias and his family passed away.*

Don Pablito can't stand to look at Nazul.

Nazul is stunned speechless, feeling outside himself, like his soul has left his body. He looks to Chuy to somehow discredit what Don Pablito has said.

Chuy looks down. His jaw twitches. Tears stream down his expressionless face and drop on the cold floor. Nazul's legs give way. He falls to his knees and buries his face in his hands as he crumbles to the floor. His grief cripples him, folds him into himself. He convulses in sobs. "Noooo! No puede ser! Noo…no."

Don Pablito and Chuy look down at him helplessly.

Outside, Elias and Elsa's house is dark. Yellow police ribbons hang from the pecan trees in their front yard like a curse.

Above, the brooding storm clouds start once again to weep down on the grieving earth.

nazul collapses to the floor

Ten

Días en azul, noches en infierno
Days on blue, nights in hell

Temporarily escaping the terrible reality of his waking hours, Nazul lies asleep on the floor in the same crumpled, defeated pile where he collapsed.

Outside, the day is breaking.

"Nazul." Don Pablito leans down and touches his shoulder to wake him. Neither he nor Chuy have slept a wink. They are both bleary-eyed. "Nazul…"

Nazul groans as he comes around.

He wipes at his bloody mouth and swollen eyes and looks around. The agony of the present creeps across his face. Taking a deep, painful breath, he shudders in disbelief. Slowly he staggers to his feet. His back and legs feel like they've been cast in iron.

"Blue-Boy, es mejor que no te quedes aquí." *Blue-Boy, it's better not to stay here.* Chuy pours himself another cup of coffee. "Don Pablito sabe de un lugar donde te puedo llevar." *Don Pablito knows a place where I can take you.* He glances at Nazul, groggily. Chuy is the rock to lean on that Nazul and Don Pablito need right now.

Nazul looks at el curandero through red, worried eyes. "Pero, 'Apá," his voice is deep and strange, "no lo puedo dejar aquí a usted." *I can't leave you here.*

Don Pablito touches his shoulder reassuringly. "Almas perdidas me han amenazado, hasta en otras existencias muy antiguas en el pasado. No. No me harán daño a mí." *Lost souls have threatened me in the past, even in other ancient existences. No. They won't harm me.* He nods his head timidly, yet there is power to his words.

Nazul squints, looking around to the bullet holes in the walls. He follows the trail down the hallway, his aching back straining to hold him up.

Opening the door to the altar room where Don Pablito sleeps, he peers in.

As he focuses, he is amazed to find the room totally untouched by the assault of gunfire. He focuses again to make sure he is awake.

Puzzled, he looks back at Don Pablito.

This small room, where miracles have changed the lives of so many, seems immune to evil. If only Elias and his family had slept here.

At the other end of the hallway, el curandero gently looks back from the kitchen. "No tengas cuidado de mí, m'ijo, es un lugar sagrado." *Don't worry about me, son, this is a sacred place.* He looks down at the floor with regret. Tears well up in his eyes, nearly swollen shut from a night of grieving, and stream down his leather cheeks. "Si mi Dios me hubiera dado el derecho," his gaze motions to Elias' home, "yo cambiaría mi lugar en esta vida con la de ellos." *If my God had given me the right, I would change my place in this life with theirs.* He nods his head firmly, "El Señor tiene un plan supremo con esto que pasó. Tal vez ellos sacrificaron sus vidas por el bien de todos. Todos sabemos antes de nacer, dónde y cómo va a acabar nuestra vida. Y estamos de acuerdo con eso." *God has a supreme plan with what happened here. Maybe they sacrificed their lives for the good of everyone. Everybody knows before they are born where and how their life will end. And we are in agreement with the outcome.* He glances at Nazul and Chuy. "¿Yo quién soy para cambiar o condenar eso? Nadie." *Who am I to change or condemn that? Nobody.*

Wiping his eyes with the sleeve of his shirt, el curandero ponders the bullet holes in the walls. "El hombre que hizo esto...carga un dolor muy grande en su vida. El...ha sufrido mucho." *The man who did this...carries severe grief in his life. He...has suffered much.*

Nazul believes him that he's safe here, but isn't as forgiving about Diablo. Diablo definitely hasn't suffered enough. Nazul's mind wanders. It starts running away from him. 'Elias. His beautiful family. No!' The weight crushes him.

"Alístate." *Get ready.* Don Pablito snaps him out of his downward spiral with his más-chingón-than-life power.

Nazul trudges into his room.

A duffle bag sits on the bed, already prepared for him. He pulls his rag of a shirt off his back with a long groan. Two football-sized, bluish-red bruises mar his lower back. There are foot-long scratch marks higher up on his back and shoulders.

He finishes undressing and steps into the shower.

Now that he's alone, the weight is like a boulder on his neck and shoulders. 'The water, the water will wash it away.' Leaning his head against the wall, he cries quietly, muffling his convulsive weeping with his hands. 'No puede ser. Por favor Virgencita, que no sea verdad...' *It can't be. Please, Virgencita, don't let it be true...*

Una estrella cayó
Del cielo negro
Ya nunca amaneció
El sueño se acabó
Cometa de castigo
Cometa de castigo,
Que el cielo mandó.

Dame una vida alma quebrada
Un mundo oscuro bueno pa'nada
Ya no hay nadie aquí
Quien castigar

Dame a mí
Total control

De todos los que pecan bajo el sol
Ya late en mis venas
El castigo

Yo perdí tu bendición
Caí de cara en el panteón
Recojo mi derecho y
Mi desgracia

Cuando oí, ten fe, ten fe…yo nunca comprendí
Cuando oí, ten fe, ten fe…yo nunca comprendí

Nunca supiste nada de mí,
Ni de mi raíz que penetra muy hondo aquí
Yo soy el México
D'este destino

Mil naciones yo vi crecer
Y cuando cayeron por no creer
Siento en mis venas el castigo

Cuando oí, ten fe, ten fe…yo nunca comprendí,
Cuando oí, ten fe, ten fe…yo nunca comprendí…

Nazul is numb. He has no memory of his loss. Strangely he feels protected from himself. At least for the moment. After taking care of his back, Don Pablito finishes patching up his hand.

Nazul kisses Don Pablito on top of his head as he gets ready to leave with Chuy. This time it's a sad goodbye.

Before Nazul can reach the kitchen door, Don Pablito calls him. "Nazul." He stops in his tracks. Slowly turns around. "No siembres semillas de odio." *Don't plant seeds of hate.* El curandero holds up his index finger like his 'buelito used to when making an important point.

"Nadie tiene el derecho a la venganza. Porque todos somos pecadores, o no estuviéramos aquí en éste mundo." *Nobody has the right to avenge themselves. Because we are all sinners, otherwise we wouldn't be here on this earth.* El maestro's eyes tear through Nazul's flimsy shield. "Solo uno…guarda ese derecho. Y El hace un trabajo permanente." *Only one…has the right. And He does a permanent job.* He levels his palm down firmly. His eyes look heavenward, then travel back down to meet Nazul's. "Acuérdate el dicho, en la tumba de Cuauhtémoc…" *Remember the saying, on the tomb of Cuauhtémoc…* Nazul looks at him and nods silently, regretting the law el curandero has laid down to him. "Nos vemos en sus resos…" *We'll see each other in your prayers…*

Chuy hands him his pair of maddogs to help shield his grieving eyes from the world, which is starting to come alive outside.

A light drizzle taps on their heads as they step out in the crisp morning. They climb into the GTO with Nazul's duffle bag.

The storm is highly charged. It seems to have no end. Gusts of wind blast through without warning, spreading debris into the streets and yards, sometimes whipping it up, sending it sailing into the saturated sky. A dust has blown in from some far-off county. The lightning blasts the darkness with explosive brilliance, lighting up the dust in creepy reddish flashes.

As they pull away, they pass by Elias' house.

The bullet holes are visible. Nazul closes his eyes. His hands writhe; he struggles to maintain reason.

Anger starts to take root inside. 'Semillas de odio…'

"Chuy, take me by Chico's cantón." Nazul looks at him seriously.

Chuy checks Nazul, wondering what he has in mind. Nobody can interfere with this kind of venganza. The GTO purrs away down the wet varrio street.

Nazul looks up to the pecan trees raining leaves. He reflects on the words of Don Pablito.

When Nazul was still a teenager, Don Pablito and Julian took him to Dr. Urrutia's house near Brackenridge Park to view the sculpture of the Aztec warrior prince, Cuauhtémoc. Majestically stationed on the front yard of the cozy three-bedroom home, Cuauhtémoc bent his bow far back, the arrow pointed at the sun, while he rested one knee on the ground. Nazul remembers how getting close to such a work of art transformed his life. The words engraved on Cuauhtémoc's tomb awakened in him a wisdom he must have known in another time. 'Solamente las horas luminosas…cuentan en la vida…' *Only the illuminating hours…count in life…*

Nazul ponders Elias and the Aztec warrior who ruled his life.

cuatemoc

The thought melts into an image of Quetzalcoatl engraved in stone. The image is the low relief façade around the entrance to a strangely beautiful building in downtown San Anto. This splendid and masterful structure sits right on the river. Its architecture is adorned with low relief Mayan designs true to the originals.

Chuy pulls over and looks up at the fire escapes on the seven-story building. "Blue-Boy, este es el edificio que recomendó tu 'apá." *This is the building your father recommended.*

Nazul looks up at it with curiosity.

"Dijo Don Pablito que subieras las escaleras de lumbre hasta el piso de mero arriba. Ahí hallarás un cuarto vacío con ventanas redondas al lado del rio." *Don Pablito said to climb the fire escape to the top floor. There you will find an empty room with round windows facing the river.* Chuy holds up his right hand for a las Razas handshake.

Nazul lowers his gaze with gratitude. "Chinga, Chuy, gracias."

"Carnales pa' qué son?" *What are brothers for?* He looks down at the bag beside Nazul's duffle with curiosity, causing his eyebrows and nose bridge to meet in his varrio frown. "Oye, Blue-Boy, ¿pa' qué quieres ese traje de pachuco?" *What do you want with that pachuco outfit?*

Nazul thinks for a long minute. "Era de mi jefito, Juan. Es nomás para que me de fuerza…" *It was my father, Juan's. It's only to give me strength.*

Chuy believes him, sort of.

He watches as Nazul climbs like a cat, unnoticed, up the fire escape with his two bags. Nazul reaches the top floor and peers in. Except for a few boxes around a couple of pillars, the room is empty. He checks the huge wooden window. It's open. He waves to Chuy down below. Chuy slowly takes off.

Nazul climbs in and surveys the area. The round windows facing the river are like portholes and swivel open. He checks the only door to the long room. It's locked from the inside. Opening it, he finds a long stairwell that ends right at the door. Beside the door, inside the building's huge dome, which graces its top floor on the front, eight-foot-high gears turn with squeaks and grinding noises as they lower and lift the elevator below. The attic evidently has not been used in a while. Once a gambling casino with secret rooms for the town's elite, the building is now a luxury apartment complex for privileged residents.

Nazul clears an area and takes out a thick Indian blanket from his duffle bag. He spreads it out on the cold concrete floor, exposing its rich Navajo designs of red, green, and black. He reaches into the duffle bag again and pulls out yerbas, santos, and miracle velitas which el curandero packed for him. He places them neatly on the blanket with care.

A delicious aroma hits him and Nazul pulls out a basket filled with a dozen warm bean tamales wrapped in foil. There are empanadas, pan dulce, a huge block of white cheese, two dozen corn tortillas, and a spill-proof container filled with freshly chopped pico de gallo. Nazul sighs. A man could be happy here.

At the bottom of the duffle bag, wrapped in black velvet cloth, there is a framed eight-by-ten photo of Elías y su familia. It used to sit on his end table by his bed. Nazul loses his appetite. Memories take over.

It's a sunny summer day. Nazul and Don Pablito are there with them as usual. Chuy had bought a camera and was trying it out. Elias and Nazul are covered with grease after squirming out from under a car. Impishly, Joey is spraying them with a garden hose as Elsa and Oralia jump away from the spray, shrieking with laughter.

"It can't be real. Joey y Oralia en el cielo. Pos sí, son angelitos. *Joey and Oralia in heaven. Of course, they are angels.* This world isn't good enough for you." He nods his head in sorrow.

"No los pude salvar. No pude hacer nada." *I couldn't save you. I couldn't do anything.*

He turns his eyes to the porthole window. A beam of morning light shines in. Pure.

From his shirt pocket he pulls out a two-by-three-inch plastic image of la Virgen framed with black cotton thread. The material is frayed from the years. He runs his fingers over her Mexican face, pure and forgiving. It was a source of consolation when he was a boy. His grandparents gave it to him when he took his first communion at the age of eight. "Virgencita, por favor, pídele al Señor que me perdone." *Virgencita, please, ask the Lord to forgive me.*

en mi casa no me quieren #3

Eleven

Semillas de odio
Seeds of hate

Chuy is deep in thought as he purrs back to Guadalupe Street, groggy from the sleepless night. He sighs deep and hard. '¿Qué irá a hacer este muchacho?' *What is this vato going to do?* He glances over to the train tracks that intersect below as he glides over the Guadalupe Bridge.

'Don Pablito made a promesa to Nazul's grandfather that he wouldn't let his seed perish from the earth, that his lineage would continue. And now, esta tragedia. Elias, Elsa, the kids. It's gotta be some cruel nightmare that escaped its dimension.' He comes to a red light.

He knows that el curandero, though old and fragile-looking, has the power of los Vryosos. Chuy watches two varrio dogs chase a vato across the street. They tear viciously at his lower pant leg. He shakes them off and races around the corner. Just another day in el Weso.

He picks up his train of thought about Don Pablito. Chuy is fascinated with the power of his prayers.

When Chuy first met el curandero, the experience wasn't without its life-altering edge. He pulls away from the intersection of Guadalupe and Brazos and comes to a stop on the curb in front of Prieto's. It's too early to open. He sits there thinking as the sleepy street slowly comes alive with gente.

He remembers working with a road crew in Marble Falls for several months. Las bandas aventaban el suelto into the hot blacktop as Chuy and his crew, all Mexicanos, would spread the hot, sticky tar mixed with pebble filler over the road. The mixer, powered by a compressor, would flap and churn in the red hot sun with loud, nerve-wracking claps, keeping the tarred asphalt loose and spreadable. They were building a highway. There he met Chente, un señor maravilloso, un mojado.

"You stupido wetback! Don'tcha understand any fuckin' English, you worthless moron? I toldja never to let that black tar seep over to the other side! I'm gonna lose this fuckin' contract onaccoun'a yur pendayho ass!" Big John was a six-foot-four, heavyset redneck, a mama's boy who came from a privileged home of ranchers and cowboys near Boerne, Texas.

Like most mojados, Chente spoke just enough English to get by on the job. He spoke his mind the best he could with a thick accent. "Ey, Big John, I deedn. I doos my jobs! De macheen ees leaking. Ees old. We needs a newer ones." Chente would stand up to the devil if he thought he was right. Everything with him had to be on the level and in the open. He never settled for cheap assumptions. This mojado worked harder than anybody else for one-third the pay. Big John hated him because Chente had a way of making him eat his words in front of the whole crew. Sometimes with just two words, since he could barely put them together sensibly. Other times with just a gesture. The only reason John tolerated Chente was because this mojado was damn smart. He had gotten Big John out of many a blunder with his ingenious solutions. Still, more often than not, Chente had to swallow John's cussing and verbal abuse. The threat of a call to la migra was implicit in all his dealings with Big John. Any day Chente could be shipped off to el otro lado without pay. All day long you would hear John cussing Chente and ordering him around like a wicked stepmother. All Mexicans were idiots, leeches, or slaves to Big John.

Despite having to work with this ball and chain, Chente refused to take Big John's shit or cower at his threats.

Chuy recalls one night. It was just a week before Big John's record-setting payday. A quarter of a million dollars in three months' time. But John had to finish this contract on time to qualify for a hefty bonus and to land another. Big John was banking on dry weather to finish up quick. There had been no hint of rain for weeks.

That night the crew was hanging out with Big John at the house he had rented for the job. He made out like a bandit charging his workers rent for their rooms while placating the local residents who had made complaints about too many Mezkins staying at the local hotel.

The gang was sitting between the dining and living rooms at a poker table, playing dominoes, cards, and guzzling beer. Big John was drunk, as usual. A faint electric glow emanated from the living room area. The sounds of macho talk and constant gunfire came from the TV.

John was guzzling tequila like it was spring water. Chente walked in, fresh from a shower and sipping on a Big Red. Big John started in on him.

"C'mon you dumbass, you think yur too damn good to drink with us!? I thought all you Mezkins were macho shit or something!" His red, thirtysomething face was arranged in a permanent arrogant scowl. "That sugar water is for pussies."

It drove John crazy that Chente never drank. Chente had a self-control that was beyond his comprehension. He had heard that Chente could drink anyone into the grave. "I only drinks alone," was all Chente said. He paused and looked around at the cold birongas. "Or wis someones." He broke out into an easy, infectious laugh. Despite the hell he endured daily, Chente was always de buena onda. Los señores who worked alongside him admired him for that and for the fearless way he handled Big John, but never let on for fear of Big John's petty scorekeeping and the retaliation which was sure to follow.

Nobody had the last word over this Texan.

"Toldja. This Mezkin is a pussy. He has to wash and iron his own apron while his wife's out with her Sancho."

At those words, a dark cloud cast its shadow over Chente. He grew strangely serious as he held his eyes on Big John, intently nodding his head. He took a deep breath. "Ahrighty, Meester Big John, so ju want me to dreenk wit ju? Ahrights." He lifted the lid on the cooler and pulled out a cold Bud, popped it, and took a gulp. He pulled a cigarette from a pack of Marlboros on the table and lit up with a kitchen match. "Pero, I promees my wife I wouldn't dreenks anymores. Because den I tells animals like ju...de troose." He nods.

"'De troose,'" Big John mocks Chente's pronunciation. "What the hell is 'de troose,' stupido? Learn how to talk, why don't you? Then maybe someone'll listen to yur 'troose.'" Big John pushed the half-empty bottle of tequila at Chente. "Put that piss-water down and have a real drink, joto."

Chente ignored his challenge and pulled up a chair. The TV went inexplicably silent. "But I am animal too, Big John. 'Cause I breaks mi promesa to peoples dat trust me. Innocent people, Big John. Eh?" He holds up his beer to him. "De troose ees dat de hate ju haf for me...weel keel ju. Jes. And...I am a man, Big John. A man! And I know some tings. Ju also do know some tings, but the most important tings...el Mero only let mojados like me, de nobodies, know it. Dat ees de troose." Chente stared at Big John and guzzled half his beer. The crew was eerily quiet. Big John stared back for a minute, then got up to bang on the side of the TV. The sound of gunfire resumed.

Chente still held his eyes on Big John as he came back to the table. "What the fuck, 'de troose?' Yur just an illegal chickenchaser." Big John smirked at the guys, who returned dry smiles, their timeless faces toasted a rich brown from their toil.

"Sí señor," smiled Chente, nodding. "Dee fuckeen troose." The guys tried to squelch their laughter. Chente went on, "I know, John, ju tink I'm estupid because I don't espeak a good Engleesh. Ees okay. I learn." Chente calmly sipped his beer.

Big John seemed to get more agitated by Chente's calm. He stood up. "You know, Mezkin man, maybe in yur country yur a man 'cuz the standard's a lot lower down there." Big John towered over Chente, who smiled slightly at one of the guys listening. "Here yur nothing, just an illegal, over here breakin' our laws, and there ain't nothin' you could ever teach me. I got me an education from the best and I put it to good use gettin' rich, like I'll be next week."

Chente turned his head up at Big John curiously. He had an idea. "Ju know, Big John, let's sees eef a pendejo like me knows anyting. Let's say I tells ju dat I haf some bad news fer ju about tomorrow and de next day an' maybe efen de nex' week."

"Whatayoutalkinabout? What news? That I might call in la migra just before the money rolls in?" Big John cackled.

"Ees about de money, jur right, John. Ju see," Chente looked down at his boot, propped on the rung of the chair, and pulled back on the leather flap, which had nearly torn off from the sole, "I really need some new boots. Tomorrow ees Sunday, dee only day Mejicanos can go to town. So…I weel go anda buy some new boots."

"Yeah? Shit don't scare me like that. What do yur damn beat-to-shit boots have to do with my money?" Big John grinned at the crew.

Chente stared at John and the TV again went dead. "De ting ees dat efry times I buy new boots, eet rain. Eet rain a lot. Sometimes for weeks. If dat happen, John, ju lose big money." Chente gulped down the rest of his beer and looked around the table.

John shook his head for a long moment. "Yur a sick pendejo mojado. What the fuck. It rains. That's not what the weatherman said. Dry and sunny. All week." He looked around to the vatos with a smirk. "A wetback like you knows more than state-of-the-art radars? It ain't gonna rain and I'll betcha a hunnerd on it." Big John slapped a hundred dollar bill on the table.

Chente's grin spread into a huge smile and his eyes sparkled. "Orale, Meester Big John." He pulled a wad of twenties from his pocket and put them next to the hundred.

Big John was never the same after that Sunday, Chuy recalls. Chente went to town and came back to the house wearing brand new Red Wings. The very next day, torrents of water washed away the beautiful blacktop, which was still setting. The uninsured Caterpillar slipped down the muddy banks of the swollen arroyo and flipped over. From the heavens thunderous explosions crashed down, blinding lightning, sheets of rain. The town of Marble Falls was declared a disaster area. Big John became quiet and dark. He seemed to grow shorter. Not long afterward, while working the Caterpillar, Big John had a heart attack and died.

Chuy catches himself awestruck at the magic of his gente and wonders if Don Pablito's prayers can save Nazul. Then his mind wanders back to the job in Marble Falls. When the job ended, Chuy's wife Dulce came to pick him up.

His right shoulder hurt to the point of passing out. He had worked the heavy, compressor-driven, handheld street hammer. The brutal long hours and constant vibrations and jolts to his arms and shoulders had taken a terrible toll. He had already been to several doctors in San Antonio, but his shoulder seemed to be going from bad to worse. It was excruciatingly painful to hold his arm up to the steering wheel. Dulce had seen a cop on the side of the road on her way there, and not having a driver's license, was afraid to drive back. And since it was a good day for it, Chuy had a blowout. When the tire blew, he strained his shoulder further trying to control the car and bring it to a stop.

As he was trying to fix the flat with one arm and a bad attitude, they both saw a man, perhaps in his seventies, walking by on the other side of the road. Moving briskly in the direction they were headed, he didn't even bother to look their way, even though they were the only ones around for miles. Chuy was cussing at the lug nuts, which he couldn't put enough leverage on. They looked at each other, then at the distinguished-looking señor who walked with the air of a king. He wore a ragged old shirt and dirty muslin pants. An old leather sack hung from his shoulder. His silvery hair was shoulder-length and stringy under a sweat-stained straw hat.

"Mira, ¿De dónde salió ese Indio?" *Look, where did that Indian come from?* Chuy wiped the sweat from his brow, catching his breath.

Dulce stared at him for a long, silent minute. She looked around. "Apareció del aire." *He appeared out of the air.*

Chuy scanned the desolate area for an answer. "Sí, ¿verdad? Yo no vi que pasamos a nadie. Solo que haya salido del bosque." *I didn't see us pass anyone. Unless he came out of the brush.* He nods. "Sí. Salió del bosque." *Yeah. He came out of the brush.*

After an hour or so, Chuy and Dulce were back on the road. The light was starting to dim as night approached. They had driven for two hours toward twinkling city lights when they saw the Indio walking by the side of the road. Chuy pulled over and offered him a ride. Gratefully he accepted and climbed into the back seat of Chuy's twin-cab.

"¿Cómo está? Yo me llamo Chuy, el Picudo. Ah!" Chuy hissed and groaned with pain as he offered his right hand over his shoulder to him for a handshake. When el señor grabbed Chuy's palm in his, Chuy felt an electrical current run through his body and jerked his hand away. Stunned, he stared ahead in silence. "Oiga, parece que tiene una corriente corriendo por sus manos." *Listen, it seems like you have a current running through your hands.* He strained to find him in the darkness of the reflection in his rearview mirror. There was a long silence behind him. Then, just as he was about to say something else, el señor spoke up. "Si, pero nomás los *animales* lo sienten." *Yeah, but only* animals *feel it.* Chuy knew he was referring to him but didn't say a word. He recalled how he lost his temper and was cussing at the tire when el señor was walking by. He probably heard him and that's why he referred to him as an 'animal'...He decided to change the subject. "Oiga, ha avanzado mucho en tres horas...¿Alguién más le dio ride?" *Listen, you've gotten a long way in three hours...Did somebody else give you a ride?*

Another long stretch of silence, then, "No." Chuy and Dulce exchanged puzzled glances. Chuy: "Señor, ¿Usted va a México seguido?" *Do you go to Mexico often?* "Si...Como tres veces al mes." *Yes...About three times a month.* "Oiga, y ¿Cómo le hace ahora que tienen en el border todo ese state-of-the-art surveillance y infrared radar y todo?" *And how do you do that now that they have all that state-of-the-art surveillance and infrared radar and all?*

El señor took another full minute to answer. "No. A mí no me molesta." *It doesn't bother me.*

Chuy's curiosity about the old man was quickly replaced by his piercing shoulder pain. "Ahhh." He looked over to Dulce. "A ver mamá, dáme otra painkeeler." *Give me another painkiller.*

"Pero ya te tomaste cinco." *But you've already taken five.* Dulce started to reach for her purse on the floorboard.

"Pero, no me hacen nada." *But they don't do anything.* Chuy rubbed his shoulder, groaning.

"M'ijo, si me permites, te puedo untar un aceitito del Niño Fidencio." *Son, if you permit me, I can rub some oil of el Niño Fidencio on it.* This man's voice seemed to take all his pain away.

"Sí. Por favor." Chuy strained again to find him as the man seemed to dissolve into the darkness of the cab. "Oiga, ¿Cómo se llama usted?" *What's your name?*

"Don Pablito." El señor leaned up to him. "A ver, hágase la camisa para un lado." *Let's see, move your shirt aside.*

Chuy felt a warm, earthy-smelling oil being rubbed on his shoulder from behind. "No sé si me va a ayudar, porque ya he ido con varios especialistas…y parece que hasta me duele más. Me dijieron que me van a tener que operar." *I don't know if it will help, because I've already been to several specialists…and it seems to hurt worse. They told me that they were gonna have to operate.* "Ellos saben mucho del cuerpo, como el diablo. Y son muy buenos mecánicos. Nomás que el dinero es el dios de muchos doctores. Y en eso está la ruina. Saben mucho. Pero las cosas *más* significantes…las sabe nomás la gente que aquí no quieren." *They know a lot about the body, like the devil. And they're very good mechanics. Except that money is their god. And therein lies ruin. They know a lot. But the most significant things…are known only by people they don't want here.* El señor rubbed him all the way up to his neck. Chuy heard him whispering something but couldn't make it out.

In his mind Chuy remembered Chente's words about las cosas más significantes and the reference to men as animals with Don Pablito's. As Don Pablito rubbed the oil on Chuy's shoulder, he felt his whole body vibrating with a hot, tingling sensation.

"Oiga, Don Pablito, me siento muy curioso." *Listen, Don Pablito, I feel very funny.*

"Sí. Es que tu alma puede hallar el perdón muy facil." *Yes, it's that your soul can find forgiveness easily.* Don Pablito finished rubbing and pulled his hand away. "A ver m'ijo, mueve el brazo." *Let's see, son, move your arm.*

To Chuy's astonishment, his pain had disappeared. "¡Ya no me duele casi nada!" *It hardly hurts at all!*

"¿Qué?" Dulce is openmouthed with joy and intrigue.

"Está traumado por el asalto del dolor pero ya se siente bien. Pero, ¿que clase de aceite me untó? Muchas gracias." *It's traumatized by the assault of the pain, but it feels okay. But what kind of oil did you use? Many thanks.*

"Las gracias dáselas al Señor," *Give your thanks to the Lord,* Don Pablito corrected him sternly. "Aquí me puedes dejar." *You can leave me here.*

"¿Qué?" Chuy looked around at the pitch black of the surroundings. To the east, where they were headed, the purple-red sunrise was warming some rainclouds above it. "¿Aquí?" He pulled over to the side of the road.

"Me oyistes bien." *You heard right.* Don Pablito opened his door and stepped out without another word.

"Pero, ¡espere!" Chuy jumped out of his seat and followed the man around the back of the truck. Dulce turned openmouthed at what just happened as she strained to see el señor. A crack of thunder bellowed in the distance. Chuy yelled again. "Oiga, muchas, digo, ¿Qué tanto le debo?" *Listen, thanks, I mean, how much do I owe you?* Don Pablito gave him a hard, sobering stare. "Yo no me enriquezco con la miseria de la gente." *I don't enrich myself from the misery of others.* He turned abruptly and started walking away in the direction they had come from.

"Perdóneme. No quería insultarlo, nomás que estoy muy agradecido por su curada." *Forgive me. I didn't mean to insult you, it's just that I'm very grateful for your cure.* Chuy followed him, looking at his raggedy shirt, which barely covered his body, and decided to offer him his. "¡Espere!" El señor stopped and turned with a sigh. As Chuy started to pull off his shirt, something inside of him made him stop, and he decided not to.

"No tengas lástima de mí." *Don't feel sorry for me.* Don Pablito looked at him sternly. "Así prefiero vivir." *This is how I choose to live.*

"Pos, ¿Pá dónde va? ¿Necesita un lugar donde vivir?" *Well, where are you going? Do you need a place to stay?*

El señor was starting to walk away, but stopped and turned. "Tal vez me vaya a vivir en San Antonio en unos cuantos años. Pero primero tengo que cumplir con algo." *Maybe I'll go live in San Antonio in a few years. But first I have to finalize something.*

Chuy crinkled his nose at the coincidence. He yelled, "Pos, de allí soy yo. Allí vivo por la Montezuma. Todos me conocen. Me dicen Chuy, el Picudo. Nomás pregunte por mí y yo le hallo donde vivir. Okay?" *Well, that's where I'm from. I live on Montezuma Street. Everybody knows me. They call me Chuy, el Picudo. Just ask for me and I'll find you a place to live. Okay?*

El señor just nodded with a smile as he walked away slowly. "Sí, m'ijo,"—his voice seemed to come from nowhere and faded back into the imposing night—"Yo y tú, nos vamos a volver a ver. Ya verás." *You and I are going to see each other again. You'll see.* And with that, Don Pablito seemed to dissolve into the night.

A year later, Chuy was working with a camarada from the varrio remodeling a house. Chuy fell off the ladder and landed wrong on his right foot. The doctors put a cast on it, but the foot kept getting swollen. Instead of healing, it became infected and ugly. He made failed attempts with the doctors to get his foot mended. The bills piled up and Dulce was getting frantic. Chuy remembered Don Pablito and the ointment from el Niño Fidencio. He decided to go to Mexico and find the site where el Niño lay. Back then it was common knowledge in old-fashioned Raza communities that el Niño could heal people from his grave.

El Niño only lived to his early twenties. He died of exhaustion from the constant bombardment of sick people who sought him out. He never turned anyone away and often couldn't even find time to eat or sleep. It was a well-known fact among la Raza that el Niño could cure anything.

"Estás loco? Como vas a manejar con ese pie?" *Are you crazy? How are you going to drive with that foot?* Dulce's nerves were already frazzled from economic hardship. "¿Y de dónde vas a sacar para el gas?" *And where are you getting money for gas?*

"Pos yo nomás te estoy diciendo que voy a ir." *Well, I'm just telling you I'm gonna go.* Chuy got ahold of a serrucho and started to saw through the cast.

Dulce knew that when he got something into his stubborn head, it was no use.

As they drove off, Chuy, using his left foot crossed over his right to step on the gas and brakes, rolled his shoulder, thinking about the night he met Don Pablito.

Dulce's family was there to greet them when they arrived in Allende, Coahuila. They lived in a little ranch house with a few chickens and goats scurrying around.

When Dulce went in to get some sleep, Chuy and his compadre, Eudencio, decided to go and find la capilla del Niño Fidencio, two hours or so away in Espinazo.

A couple dozen people stood in a line leading up to a middle-aged man in a black missionary robe. The sun was starting to swelter around the half-block encampment built in some unknown order. With the help of crutches, Chuy wobbled up the little dirt path with Eudencio and they made their way to the center, where the line formed. Chuy looked around at the few cars that lined the main dirt road. Two assistants came to them with a couple of corn tortilla tacos of beans and rice wrapped warmly in a paper towel.

Chuy and Eudencio thanked them and started to eat hungrily.

They thought those little tacos would only stir up their appetites. But minutes later their hunger was totally satisfied.

Squinting up at the cobalt-blue sky, Chuy seemed to hear the sound of an electrical current humming first low and then higher in the atmosphere above them. He looked back around to his compadre. Eudencio had gone to sit on a nearby concrete slab.

El señor in the black robe was saying something, but Chuy couldn't make it out. A few poeple who looked like helpers sat around his feet while two others walked slowly down the line.

Chuy heard some yelling and cursing. He turned his head to see a Hispanic man wearing a big Mexican straw hat. He was being pulled out of the line by the two helpers. They forced him down the line past Chuy, despite his angry protests.

"No! Váyase de aquí!" The two helpers, dressed in ropa indígena and brown leather sandals, escorted him to his car and off the premises.

As the helpers marched back, Chuy asked them what was wrong. One of them stopped and pierced his soul with a cold stare, then just walked off.

Chuy tried to find someone to ask about this, but nobody would look at him directly. Finally un señor up ahead gave up his place in line to stand with Chuy. He looked at the pissed-off man tearing away in his Cadillac. He glanced at Chuy. "No. Es que no quieren gente aquí que nomás viene a burlarse." *It's that they don't want people to come here just to find something to ridicule.* El señor spoke with a calmness that was soothing. "Cuando llegué yo, todavía estaba oscuro y me puse a platicar con ese señor. El me dijo que era doctor y científico y que él no creía en éstas tonterías. Nomás quería venir a ver de que se trataba. Y yo he oído de otra gente que han corrido porque les proponían hacer de este lugar un negocio comercial. Quien sabe como, pero si saben esos fidencitos quienes son los que nomás vienen a burlarse. Y los corren de aquí." *When I got here it was still dark, and I got to chatting with that man. He told me he was a doctor and scientist and that he didn't believe in all this nonsense. He just wanted to see what all the fuss was about. And I've heard of other people they had to run off who came here because they wanted to make a commercial business out of this place. I don't know how they know, but they do, and they run them off.*

"Que curioso." *How funny.* Chuy's nose crinkled in a varrio frown.

Time passed, and as Chuy got closer to el señor in the black robe, he started to make out a woman sitting beside his feet. She was dressed in black and wore a veil over part of her face. She turned and looked toward Chuy.

To his astonishment he recognized her. His body went numb. He could feel his heart throbbing in his throat. He couldn't believe it. A few years earlier Chuy had been at her funeral in Múzquiz.

Now he was close enough to make sure. 'Sí ¡es ella!' *Yes! It's her!* He looked around for Eudencio and called him over with a gesture. Eudencio was looking his way, seemed to be looking right at him, but didn't react. 'What's with him?'

Chuy remembered that this woman, Chavela, had lived a few houses down from his mother's in that little ranching town. They said someone had put 'un mal' on her and disfigured her face, which looked like a frog's. And it still does. She had died from the curse.

By the time Chuy got to el señor in the black robe, he had forgotten all about his foot and just nodded dumbly. He was instructed to say a few exclusive prayers at the little chapel close by.

Chuy wobbled off with the assistant and was directed to a small chapel fifteen feet away with a glass window. As he knelt uncomfortably on the stone step, he peered into the chapel and saw what looked like human bones bunched together amid old rags that might have been somebody's clothes, now rotted almost to dust. Chuy shook his head feeling que estaba perdiendo la razón. *Like he was losing his reasoning.* He decided prayer was the only way to save his common sense. He prayed like never before.

After he finished his worship, Chuy wobbled over and stood between two four-foot-high concrete walls that ran up and down the encampment. There was a space of about two feet between them where stone steps crossed through. He put down his crutches and looked around for Eudencio. He was nowhere around. Chuy still couldn't get the image of that woman out of his mind and wanted to know if Eudencio had seen her.

He looked down at his foot, wondering how he'd get someone to look at it.

The electric current sounded lower now and seemed to hang right over his head. He looked up to see thin, flimsy clouds race by at a supernatural speed. He lowered his head. The strangeness of it all was unnerving.

Far off in the distance Chuy saw a bright figure approaching in a dusty, watery mirage which seemed to melt in the heat waves…

As he neared, Chuy saw what looked like a herd of goats laboring in front of the figure, which now looked like a man. Goats? No, dogs? Time seemed irrelevant…He couldn't measure minutes. Sometime later he realized that the animals were pigs, strutting in perfect formation in front of…Don Pablito? He squinted to shake the sweat from his brow. It was him, and he was headed right for Chuy. Something fluttered by his ear and Chuy was jolted from his concentration. He scanned the windy surroundings. When he looked back, el curandero was amazingly close.

The seven pigs, in three-by-three formation with one in front, came right up to his feet. Looking up at him, they stopped in perfect timing with the halt of el curandero.

Chuy was amazed by their apparent intelligence. Their eyes were like a human's. He could imagine them speaking quite easily and telling him, "Hastealachingada." *Get-the-hell-outta-the-way.* Chuy barely gathered his composure to speak to el curandero. "Hola, ¿Cómo está?" He extended his hand to him, hoping he could get close enough to shake.

"Yo te conozco a ti?" *Do I know you?* Don Pablito's face was covered in dust. He squinted up at Chuy, disregarding the hand.

Chuy had a hard time not noticing the pigs, still at perfect attention, looking up at him. He knew that a pig is the hardest animal to train to do *anything.* It seemed impossible that they were acting that way. "Sí. ¿No se acuerda que me curó el hombro cuando le dí un ride allá en el norte?" *Don't you remember healing my shoulder when I gave you a ride over there in the north?*

Silence. Then, "No. No me acuerdo." *No. I don't remember.* El curandero just nodded his head indifferently, as if he wanted to be on his way.

Chuy held up his foot to him slightly. "Pues vine porque me lastimé este pie y los doctores no me lo pudieron aliviar." *Well, I came because I hurt my foot and the doctors couldn't heal it.*

"Y ¿Qué quieres con nosotros? Ya escogiste tu dios." *And? What do you want with us? You've chosen your god.* He gave Chuy a crippling stare. "A la gente los aruínan los doctores. Luego la gente viene aquí. Los curamos. Y luego vuelven con los doctores a chequearse. Los vuelven a desgraciar o asustar y nunca acabamos!" *Doctors ruin our people's health. Then the people come here. We cure them. Then they go back to the doctor to get checked. The doctors scare or screw them over again and we never see the end of it!* Chuy felt embarrassed by Don Pablito's statement. "Solo que ¿No me puede ayudar?" *So you can't help me?*

"No." El curandero waited an uncomfortable minute, then, "Pero, sí te vas por esta vereda," he pointed with his chin, holding on to the leather satchel on his shoulder and what looked like agave threads in his left hand, "allí está un jacalito con el techo de hoja de palma. Allí está un hombre que te puede ayudar." *There is a hut with a palm roof. There you will find a man who can help you.*

"Gracias." Chuy starts to move out of the way, then stops. "Oiga, Don Pablito, allá en la fila está una mujer a los pies del maestro. Es que ella se murió hace varios años." *Listen, Don Pablito, over there on the line is a woman at the feet of the master. It's just that she died several years ago.*

Don Pablito nodded his head indifferently. He looked Chuy in the eyes. "Y tú sabes algo de eso? De la muerte?" *And what do you know about that? About death?*

"No. Nada. Bueno, me hago a un ladito para que pasen los animales." *No. Nothing. Well then, I'll move out of the way so that the animals can pass through.* Chuy grabbed his crutches and wobbled off the path.

"Sí, porque por donde pasa un animal, pasan los demás." *Yes, because where one animal passes, the others follow.* Don Pablito's stare made him feel numb.

Chuy felt like a worm, embarrassed that he had insinuated that Don Pablito was also an animal. He was still confused by Don Pablito's words, by his cold indifference at meeting him again. Chuy didn't know why, but he had always considered himself animal. He had even told friends this in pláticas and parrandas. *Conversations and drinking binges.*

Suddenly Eudencio was standing right in front of him. Chuy was startled once again by all the strange occurrences in that mysterious place. "¡Eudencio! ¡Oyes, me asustates!" *Eudencio! Man, you scared me!* He looked around, confused. "¿Pa' dónde te fuiste?" *Where did you go?* Chuy's whole body shook.

Eudencio was mild-mannered and wonderfully humble. "¿Por qué? Aquí he estado todo este tiempo." *Why? I've been here the whole time.* He seemed confused by Chuy's question. "Pero, te iba a preguntar a tí la misma cosa. Te desapareciste!" *But I was gonna ask you the same thing. You disappeared!*

"¿Yo?" *Me?* Chuy felt overwhelmed by confusion. It was just too complicated to try to describe with words. "Ahh! Olvídate. Vamos. ¡El curandero que conocí en San Anto, lo vi aquí! Y me dijo que fuera para este jacalito por esta vereda." *Forget it. Let's go. I just saw the curandero I met in San Anto. And he told me to follow this path to a straw hut.* He wobbled onto the path with a confused Eudencio.

"Mira. Ese es Don Pablito." *Look, that is Don Pablito.* He turned Eudencio's attention around to el curandero fading over a dusty hill nearby.

Eudencio squinted. "O sí. Ese es un hombre muy misterioso. La gente mala le tiene un grave miedo. Dicen que puede matar con solo una mirada." *Oh, yeah. He's a very mysterious man. Evil people are gravely scared of him. They say he can kill with just a look.*

They arrived at the jacalito Don Pablito had described. Chuy tried to knock, but the walls were made of mud. He called out, "¿Hay gente?" *Are there people?* An eagle's shadow flowed over the dusty trail. Chuy squinted up at it. "¡Hola!" Nothing. "¡Hola! ¿¡Se encuentra gente!?" *Hello! Anyone home!?*

An old grey-bearded man peered out through the dry palm leaves that formed the door. He looked at Chuy, then at Eudencio.

Chuy wobbled around to a more comfortable position to speak to him. "Me dijo un señor que usted me podía ayudar con mi pie." *A man told me that you could help me with my foot.*

El señor looked down at Chuy's swollen, decaying foot. "Ah, sí. Pues, pásele." *Ah, yes. Well, come in.* He stopped Eudencio. "Usted espérelo aquí." *You wait here.*

Chuy walked in and found two cots across the room from each other. These were the only furnishings, except for a small table in the corner with two old wooden chairs. The sun streaked in through a round opening in the ceiling. Dust trails danced up to the light from the dirt floor.

El señor was dressed in a plain beige cotton shirt and ankle-length pants with dusty leather sandals. He pulled one of the cots across the room towards the other one. He had Chuy sit on one and rest his bad foot on the other. He peeled the moist, dirty gauze bandages from Chuy's foot.

"¡Caray! ¿Por qué te esperaste tanto para buscar curada?" *My, my! Why did you wait so long to get it looked at?* El señor winced at the condition of Chuy's foot.

"No, sí. Es que fui con los doctores en San Antonio donde vivo, y ellos me la atendieron." *It's that I went with the doctors where I live, and they treated it.*

Shaking his head, el señor seemed disappointed in Chuy.

Chuy groaned as el señor turned his foot slightly, trying to straighten it out or something. He placed his huge hands on the ankle and sole of the foot, holding them there and slowly applying more pressure until Chuy's foot felt like it was in a vise. Chuy winced quietly, but it started to feel better immediately. El señor held his hands gently on it now, and Chuy could feel the heat from his hands coursing through his foot and ankle. He started to sweat.

Finally, el señor got up and walked slowly to a leather bag by the table and pulled out a jar. He twisted the cap off the recycled jelly jar and scooped up three fingers full of gooey wet stuff. It looked like it had some kind of blades of grass or herbs in it. It felt like mud.

After applying the mud to Chuy's ankle and foot, el señor rewrapped them. "Ahora sí. Te puedes parar." *You can get up now.*

Chuy took a painful step to his feet and reached for his crutches. "Muchas gracias. Me duele, pero muy poquito." *It hurts, but very little.* He applied a little weight to it.

"Bueno. No soy el Niño. Yo creo en dos horas podrás caminar." *Well. I'm not el Niño. I believe in a couple of hours you can walk.* After clearing his throat, el señor looked Chuy in the eyes. "M'ijo, no hagas muchos corajes. El cuerpo es muy inteligente y te cuida de cosas más graves. El cuerpo sabe que si sigues con coraje y falta de pacencia, te puede dar un ataque de corazón o puedes hacer alguna tontería. Lo de tu pie fue una llamada de atención, para que te sentaras y te calmaras. Dale gracias a tu cuerpo que tanto te ha cuidado. ¿Eh? No es facil ser Mejicano. Acuerdate de tus abuelos, como ellos guardaban la gracia de vivir bien." *My child, sometimes we get too angry or we worry too much, and that is when these things happen. The body is very intelligent and protects you from greater harm. The body knows that if you continue in the bad road of anger and lack of patience, you can have a heart attack or maybe do something stupid. So your body causes you to break a leg so you will sit down and relax. Give thanks to your body for taking such good care of you. Eh? It's not easy being*

Mexican. But remember your grandparents and how they guarded the grace of living right.

El señor smiled and Chuy felt a peace he had never known. He thought how hard it is being a Chicano. The rage we endure because of a system that dedicates itself to making our lives unbearable. "Gracias." He nodded his head appreciatively. "Le puedo ofrecer dinero?" *Can I offer you any money?*

El señor shook his head. "Nosotros no cobramos por lo que hacemos." *We don't charge for what we do.* He pointed his finger skyward. "Nomás le pedimos a él. Ese pago es verdadero." *We only ask Him. That pay is truthful.* Tilting his head, "Pero, si me quieres dar un poquito, sí te lo acepto. Nomás para que me sostenga. La mayoria de la gente aquí somos pobres." *But if you want to give me a little, I'll accept it. Only to sustain myself. Most of the people here are very poor.*

Chuy pulled out some wadded-up bills mingled with a couple of quarters, nickels, and pennies.

As Chuy started to count the ones, el señor stopped him by putting his hand gently on Chuy's. He started picking out only the small change. El señor nodded thank you to Chuy, holding his gently closed fist to his chest. "Con esto tengo. Gracias." *This is all I need.*

His grace left Chuy hypnotized. In Mexico it wasn't uncommon for the poor gente there to offer what little they had to you, even if they went hungry themselves. '¿Quiénes son esta gente? Y ¿de *dónde* son?' *Who are these people? And* where *do they come from?*

"Y mucho cuidado con el agua y la tierra en los varrios pobres allá en San Antonio," *And be very careful with the water and the soil in the poor varrios over in San Antonio,* el señor said matter-of-factly.

"¿Qué?"

"El agua." *The water.* El señor leaned in to him. "El agua es peligrosa en esa ciudad, pero nomás en los varrios, eh." *The water is dangerous in that city, but only in the varrios.* He was serious. "Nomás tome agua destilada. ¿Okay? Y los capitalistas, también, han echado mucha ponzoña en la tierra allí en la area de Kelly. Hemos recibido a mucha gente con enfermedades de alli." *Only drink distilled water. Okay? And the capitalists have also poisoned the soil there in the area of Kelly. We have treated many of our people who have gotten diseases from there.*

Chuy was still digesting the information as he shook his hand

and turned around to step out into the yellow light from the shadowy, musky interior of the jacal.

He looked around for Eudencio, who, once again, was nowhere in sight. There were some rocky hills around. Chuy looked down at his foot and turned it slightly. He felt it getting better by the minute.

He started to limp on it now as he trudged around looking for Eudencio. Feeling the mysteriousness of the place creeping up behind his knees and into his spine, he looked down at himself. "Estoy aquí...Soy de a de veras." *I am here...I'm for real.* He slapped his beer gut. "¿Me desaparecí otra vez?" *Did I disappear again?*

As he looked up to walk on, he came face to face with a breathless Eudencio in a cloud of dust. The jolt made him lose his balance, but his compadre caught him with a smile.

"Chinga! Eudencio, te desapareciste de vuelta!" *Damn! Eudencio, you disappeared again!*

"Oh no. Me fui pa' detrás de esa lomita a hacer mi negocio." *I went behind that little hill to do my business.* He smiled with relief, pointing at a small hill nearby.

Chuy dropped his shoulders with a sigh. "Vámonos." *Let's go.*

Two hours or so later his foot was almost as good as new.

One stormy night, years later, Don Pablito showed up at Chuy's house on Montezuma Street. Chuy put him up for the night. The next day Don Pablito was taken to see un señor in his sixties who lived in the varrio and was dying of cancer. El señor was bedridden and had already prepared himself and his family for his death. Instead, that night he had dinner with his family, Chuy, Dulce, and Don Pablito.

The day after that one of the sons, moved by el curandero's healing powers and his refusal to accept money, decided to give Don Pablito a house he owned, a few blocks away from Chuy's.

Don Pablito has been there ever since. Sometimes his appointments are scheduled a week ahead of time because of the many people he sees. When people ask him if he heals on Sundays or wants to rest, he tells them, "No. Cuando me muera descanso." *No. When I die, I'll rest.* Like el Niño Fidencio, he didn't like to turn anybody away, but the people here respected his space.

el blue-boy

Twelve

El Blue-Boy

As the varrio comes alive in the wet morning, rare sunlight peeks through the thick clouds. A pair of varrio dogs fight over a piece of soiled Pampers on the street. They chase each other and almost run into a pair of beautiful legs hurriedly clicking down the sidewalk in flat black shoes.

She jumps out of their way. "¡Ay! ¡Pinches perros! *Damn dogs!* Get a life, cabrones." Luna seems more optimistic in the fresh light of a new day. Cars roll by with their rolas playing as she makes her way to the bus stop. She is wearing a smart, dark green skirt suit with a shiny black purse and her black briefcase.

Down the street, inside Prieto's Auto Parts, Chuy and Plutarco are quietly discussing something when the door chime catches their attention. It's Pete, a local gangster wannabe who decided the life was too damn risky. Pete, with his usual permanent varrio snarl, is sporting a red muscle shirt in the freezing weather. His build is thin, with arms that hang like wet noodles. He could easily pass for a weasel. His arms are decorated with amateurish, half-finished tattoos that some borracho must have started in a back alley until they passed out. Some tattoos have grown a mind of their own and have crawled up his neck and one side of his face. With a front tooth missing, he smiles at Chuy and Plutarco, throwing his head back like a vato-chingón. "¿Qué pasó, chavalones?"

"Ese, Pete!" Chuy grins at the sight of him.

With a varrio frown, Pete focuses his bloodshot, hungover eyes on Plutarco. "Oyes, Plutarco, no voy a poderte esquinear con 'el roofing' hoy. Tengo que ir al Brady Clinic pa' que me saquen estas balas. Wacha." *Ey, Plutarco, I'm not gonna be able to help you with the roofing today. I have to go to the Brady Clinic so they can pull out these bullets. Check it out.* Pete pulls his shirt up and turns around to show two slugs embedded in his lower back. There is no sign of blood.

Plutarco and Chuy are perplexed.

Chuy's frown forms again as he tries to figure Pete out. "Oyes, Pete, a lo mejor ya estás muerto. No se mira nada de sangre." *Ey, Pete, maybe you're already dead. There's no sign of blood.*

Plutarco throws in his two cents. "No, hombre, este vato le vendió toda la sangre al blood bank. Ahora corre con agua tibia." *Naw, man, this vato sold all his blood to the blood bank. Now he runs on warm water.* Laughter.

Pete tilts his head, bugs his eyes like an insulted chuco wannabe, and clocks them as he heads for the door. "Yyyy…Ahí los wacho."

Grinning mischievously, Chuy watches him leave. "Ey, Pete, ya que estás ahí, diles que también te saquen la bota del culo." *Ey, Pete, while you're there, tell them also to pull the boot out of your ass.*

Roaring laughter.

Comically, Pete bugs his eyes again and snarls his lips even more. "Yyyyy, vato, no oyites lo que le pasó al último vato que me dijo ese jale?" *Didn't you hear what happened to the last vato who said that to me?*

As Luna walks in all the ruckus stops, and Pete stumbles out like a pendejo.

Chuy and Plutarco lose their smiles and look at each other discreetly. Luna senses that they're hiding something.

Plutarco greets her. "Buenos días, m'ijita."

She looks like she's on a mission. "Buenas." Her breath is short and choppy, with her heart beating fast against her chest and up to her throat. "Ando buscando razón de Nazul. ¿No lo han visto?" *I'm looking for word about Nazul. Have you seen him?* Chuy and Plutarco look at each other and down at the floor, not knowing what to say. Plutarco looks away.

Chuy glances at Plutarco and sighs. "M'ijita, anoche pasó una gran tragedia." *My child, last night a great tragedy occurred.* Luna holds her breath.

"El vecino de Nazul y toda su familia fallecieron en un drive-by." *Nazul's neighbor and his family perished in a drive-by.* Chuy swallows hard.

Luna breathes out at last. "¡Dios mío! Qué lástima." *My God! What a pity.* She covers her face with her hands. "I think I saw that in the news." She slides her fingers down her face, her beautiful eyes sparkling with tears. She's afraid to look at them. "Y, Nazul? Was he the one killed last night at the Guadalupe Bridge?" She shuts her eyes, bracing for the blow. "It was also in the news." She grits her teeth.

Chuy's and Plutarco's eyes are glazed over in resignation.

"No sabemos de él." *We don't know about him.* Plutarco shakes his head as an afterthought, avoiding her gaze. His eyes seem to sparkle with moisture as he stares out the window at the gloomy day. He clears his throat and swallows his grief.

Luna is aware of the danger of a loose tongue in this varrio and doesn't press. She pulls out a handkerchief from her black purse and wipes her tears. "Tengo un grave miedo que algo le ha pasado." *I have a grave fear that something happened to him.*

Chuy and Plutarco fight for composure.

Luna studies their faces for a hint of the truth. She locks on Chuy's swollen, red eyes. She ponders his nervousness and thinks, 'It *had* to be him. It must've been Nazul. He's been in mourning, probably up all night.'

Plutarco looks out the large, patched-up glass window. "En este varrio es mejor no tenerle cariño a *nadie.*" *In this varrio it's better not to care for* anybody.

Luna swallows her fears again and takes out a card. She hands it to Plutarco, her hand shaking. "Si saben de Nazul, por favor, llámenme a este número." *If you hear about him, please, call me at this number.*

Reluctantly Plutarco takes the card. He looks deeply into her pained face. "M'ijita, pídele a la Virgen que te de fuerza en estos días negros.

Y hazle una promesa. Nosotros también rezamos por tí y Nazul." *My child, ask the Virgin to give you strength in these dark days. And make a promise to her. We will also pray for you and Nazul.*

Her eyes plead to Plutarco for an answer about Nazul, but he just looks down at the floor. She walks out. Across the street the bus driver waits patiently for her.

Luna looks out the bus window, fighting back tears. An old, beat-up carrucha, full to capacity with a Chicano family, pulls up beside the bus at the light. In the back seat a little girl cries out the passenger window to an indifferent world. Her tears stream down her chubby cheeks.

A group of teens sits in a classroom. A TV screen blares out the local news. "Gang violence held its grip of death on a west side neighborhood last night. Authorities say at least twenty people have fallen victim to the murderous gangs in this area." The video shows Elias' house shot full of holes and two small tarp-covered bodies on stretchers being hauled off to the ambulance.

"All were gang-related deaths. Police now say a rise in gang violence is predicted as revenge for the killings is sure to follow, with no end in sight. Roberta Roberts is on the north side. Roberta?"

The camera cuts to Ms. Roberts, about to interview a woman in her thirties who lives in snooty Alamo Heights, notorious for its celebrated racism.

Roberts gives the camera her screen-goddess look. "We've been interviewing concerned citizens all over the city and have gotten the same response: People are fed up with gangs. Here we have Mrs. Strickland. Mrs. Strickland, can you share your thoughts?"

Mrs. Strickland sips on a bottle of mineral water before she goes on.

"Boyyy-howdy! We want the mayor to know that we demand every hoodlum who even looks like a gangbanger be thrown in prison. And throw away the key. I have kids. What if these murderers decide to have a shootout in our neighborhood? We need to hire a lot more police officers to catch these losers and put an end to this violence. Now. Even my five dogs seem jittery."

"I guess Mrs. Strickland has said it all, Mary. Back to you."

"Is your cat too fat? Well, we have received a flood of calls on this subject. Sooo—we've devoted a whole half hour to pet diets! Also, if your dog is hopelessly overweight, this segment is for you. And we'll hear from a rock diva who says she is *outraged* at rumors printed about her in magazines stating that she is a drug fiend. Finally, a businessman will announce his plans to donate fifteen million dollars to his alma mater. The donor says he wants to give back to his prestigious university to show his appreciation for his success. That's all coming up—" Click. The screen goes black.

The teens all turn around to find Luna holding the TV remote control. "Buenos días. I think we've all had enough enlightening news for one day, don't you?" She scans their faces. Her group includes ten teenage girls and fifteen boys, all from the varrio.

With her education Luna has managed to scrape together a meager fund to run this center, 'Los Vryosos.' Teens who are trying to stay away from gangs and trouble with the law, or those who have simply dropped out due to the relentless degradation of their culture, are always welcome here. Luna stresses the importance of education, but even more important, she teaches how to best use what you've got: your ingenuity, wits, and hard work. Learning to read is high on her agenda. She wants the kids to gain the motivation to learn. She is their teacher. To most of these youths, she is a beacon of light in their dark worlds; to others, she is like the mother or father they never had.

The center consists of a long, twenty-by-fifty-foot room, which the kids themselves remodeled. It has an area where twenty-five desks sit facing a blackboard. Luna's desk sits at the front of the class by a large TV. The front door is by her desk, and the back door is at the end of the room. On the other side are a few picnic tables always stocked with fruits and salads where the kids eat lunch. Beside the tables, a noisy window unit keeps the room warm in the winter and cool in the summer. There are two fruit juice machines near the tables.

One of the teenage girls speaks up. "You know, Luna, we can't even stand to watch TV anymore. All those pendejos act like we don't even exist, except to tell the world what murderers we all are. What about all the honest, hardworking gente?"

Luna's head drops slightly. "You're right. The media has a nasty habit of treating our gente like we don't count. Most of you are very, very talented, yet you are never noticed or bankrolled by talent entrepreneurs. And our parents' brave struggles just to put food on the table are ignored as well. But that's okay. We know who we are. We don't need their approval." She looks around to the other faces. "Anybody else want to comment?"

A vato speaks up. "And all those stupid, lily-white Hollywood movies. Nobody gives a damn about us. What we think. Our stories. Yet our gente trip over each other to pay to see their pendejo movies."

"Simón," a fifteen-year-old vato speaks up. "And those babosos care more about their pinches gatos than the lives of our kids!"

"Yeah," another vato joins in, "their pets eat better than my little sister." Laughter.

Luna: "Yes. Maybe their pets can take care of them when they're sick, or need someone to pick them up off the floor. I have heard of dogs able to dial 911." More laughter. But Luna doesn't join in, and the kids notice that her easy humor is absent today. Their laughter is short.

Luna continues, "Okay, gente. This is Friday. Who has work lined up for today? Let me see the hands." Seven kids raise hands. "Now remember, be on time and follow instructions. And try to wear a happy face," she stresses with an upward glance.

"Like this." A vato makes a retarded-looking smile. The class breaks down.

"I was hoping we could continue to talk about the importance of visualizing our dreams in life." She pans the class. "I know you all have dreams." She sees a droopy-looking vato who stayed up too late and is trying to stay awake, but still raises his hand. "Octavio?"

"Sirol, I dream of being an art dealer and selling Chicano art in New York and Europe." He drops his hand like a heavy weight.

"The world needs someone to do that. You will be brilliant at it. Maybe you can think about what you need to do to prepare for that important work." She moves to a girl in the front row. "Graciela."

Graciela could easily be a fashion model. "I dream of being a teacher, like you. I want to help make our schools a place where Chicanos want to learn."

"Thank you." Luna takes a deep breath, trying hard to keep her sorrow in check. She notices the kids' concern and smiles to reassure them. "Coming from you, that compliment is very dear to me. Because all of you are *my* heroes. Graciela, your plan is attainable and very necessary for our gente.

"Remember, class, when you visualize your goals, you set the wheels in motion." Luna pans their intent faces. "Visualizing and believing in yourself and in your abilities can actually attract, even create, the circumstances which will help you to realize your dreams. What we think about ourselves is very, very important. And—" she notices Octavio has crashed out on his desk and is starting to snore. The kids giggle.

"Octavio?" Luna's voice cracks his snooze.

"Uh?" He opens his droopy eyes.

"Octavio, if you want your dreams to come true, you have to stay awake."

Some of the baddest vatos, like Silent and Azteca-Boy, were originally attracted to Luna's program because they heard she keeps you rolling in the aisles.

"We have to set realistic goals and put them into action. How do we do that? Lorena?" She motions to a seventeen-year-old girl with Selena lips and her hair in a bun like 'Chiquita Banana.' Her clothes are varrio-trendy, a dark pullover shirt and navy blue workout pants with double silver stripes on the side.

"I want to sing, Luna. I found a group I can practice with every day now, and I'm starting to really think I can do it."

"Excellent. Lorena, you *are* doing it. Taking these first steps toward your goal is very brave. Each step will mold you, and you'll begin to see clearly what you need to do next. You are in charge. Nobody can take that away from you." She slaps her hand varrio-style. "Dale shine, carnala." *Shine it up, homie.* She turns to the class. "Your thoughts are so powerful that they actually shape your life. That is why we have to be very selective about what we allow ourselves to dwell on. This is the science of the mind and the secret to success. Your belief in your goal is more important than the facts. That means that what you perceive to be true can actually alter reality in order for you to attain your dreams. Think about that for a minute." Her eyes find nothing but focused faces…depending on her. Some of them for their very lives.

"We will have times when things are rough, of course, but we have to maintain a natural outlook on life, which is always slanted to the positive." The class hangs on Luna's every word.

"And we have to be persistent with our goals. Anybody can get going when the going is great. It takes a person with resilience to seal the deal. Everyone in this room has already proven they possess this. We have to throw our belief in the face of a society that wants us only to see our failures. Remember your parents and grandparents and the way they handled the most overwhelming odds. To them struggle was a way of life. Learn from them, not from MTV. We need to listen to the people who care about us first. Be honest and generous. Lose anger, greed, and envy. They block the creative forces and waste energy. Who can think of something we can do that will create positive energy in our lives?"

Two girls: "Do your part to help others when you can."

"Good!" Luna checks her class. "Yes! The secret to enduring prosperity is to help each other. Because this science is one you can set your watch by. Any more comments?" She reaches for a book on her desk. "Let's look at our reading books. Octavio, wake up."

"Huh? Oh, yeah." Octavio sucks up his drool and grabs the book tucked under his desk.

Two vatos start arguing over a pencil. The argument heats up and they start cussing.

Luna slams her book down. "Stop it! Please."

The two teens abruptly comply. They are startled and concerned by her reaction.

Luna, with paper-thin emotion, "Payaso, Osito, por favor, no more fighting." Her hands resting on her desk, she drops and nods her head in resignation.

"Luna, what's the matter?" Osito.

She looks down for a moment. "I just…"

"Ey, Luna, you got it." Payaso hands Osito the pencil.

Luna looks up at her class. Intent, caring faces clock her every move.

Lorena carefully speaks up. "Luna? Is something wrong?"

"I…just worry…about you." Luna cups her hands on her face and tries to rub away her anxiety for Nazul. She worries for the vatos in her class who might get caught up in the vicious cycle of violence from the recent shootout. Taking a deep breath, she stands in front of the class. "I know that some of you probably knew of someone who was a victim of the recent gang violence. If so, it's good to talk about it."

After a brief silence, a fifteen-year-old vato speaks up. "My homeboy, Chato. We grew up together. He liked to play with guns. Now he's dead."

A girl wipes a tear. "He was so talented. A good singer, and he could really dance. I'm gonna miss him." She starts sobbing as two girls come to comfort her.

Luna hangs her head. She swallows hard and looks back up at her class through cloudy eyes. "Life can be very cruel sometimes. I am aware of this. But there are gente who are working tirelessly to change your odds. Yes. There is also a lot of *good*." She struggles against her own encroaching hopelessness.

"Ey, Luna."

"Azteca-Boy?"

"Who do you think you're talking to? We're calle. *Street*. We know what's up. Clickas are everywhere. They rule."

A girl cuts in. "The house behind ours has been shot up five times. Yesterday a cop finally shows up. But he's there to arrest my mom. Okay? My mom holds two jobs. She gets busted for not being able to afford car insurance. That's a lot of good."

"Our gente has it hard, I know." Clasping her hands, Luna feels their frustation. "But I have high hopes for all of you. And I know you won't let me down. You won't let yourselves down either. You struggle many times more than the average American just to claim what is rightfully yours: a chance to build a real life. The opportunity to work at what you want to and have a decent chance at success. To have America care about *you,* for a change. To claim your share of the American Dream."

Luna walks down the aisles of her class. "All of you here, Chicanas, Chicanos, are the descendents of the indigenous peoples of America. Azteca, Maya, Inca, Tolteca, Apache. Your ancestors, whose blood runs in your veins today, realized some of the most incredible achievements in art, science, mathematics, and government. Their legends and monuments leave even the world's most celebrated scientists and engineers in awe, gasping in the sun for comprehension of their incredible feats." She looks into their souls. "You *are* this Raza. You are capable of incredible achievements. Your abuelos y abuelitas, on whose shoulders you now stand, worked themselves into the grave to give you this chance. They have suffered many hardships just to get you where you are today. Think about that and cultivate that seed of greatness. You can be as good as *anybody* at *anything!* You will shine. Who are we?"

The class chants enthusiastically: "Los Vryosos, dale shine!"

Luna: "So, everybody do your workouts. You can dance if you want, just don't get carried away and break the furniture like last time. Then you can take a break for chalupas. Remember, I don't want to see anyone drinking sodas or anything with sugar while you are eating.

That is why there are so many problems with our health: diabetes, high blood pressure. Remember, you can eat sweets an hour or so after eating. I still don't recommend soda. Don Huerta is coming to talk to all of you next week about proper nutrition. Don Huerta says that if you live on a diet of only fruits and vegetables and exercise regularly, you will not only look a hell of a lot better, but you'll feel great, and you will be ten times smarter than the average bear. So, is that worth it? I think you will hate me now and thank me later." She smiles and perks up. "Hey, I just made a song: 'Hate me now, thank me later, woo—ooo ooo.'" The whole class bursts out with giggles at her silliness. She seems to be over what was bothering her. "Mira, people, we can eat meat once a week, or if the urge is too great. It's okay. But every day, no. It's too taxing on the body."

There's a knock at the door. "Okay people, take your break." Luna dismisses the class and goes to answer. She opens the door to a wonderfully dressed Chicana in her early forties. "¡María! Ay, Qué bién te miras." *Maria! Ay, you look so good.* Maria is a little on the heavy side. She exudes confidence and grace as she waves and smiles to the kids, who recognize her at once.

"It's Maria Rosales," one of the rucas blurts out. Chavalos always know when somebody gives a damn about them, even if they have never met.

Maria is the main newscaster for independently owned Azteca TV in San Antonio.

Luna invites her in, but Maria instead beckons Luna outside the partially open door for a more private talk. She glances cautiously at the curious group. They know that something is up.

"Luna, listen," Maria whispers loudly. "I have very little time, but I wanted to tell you in person. I haven't found out anything about that vato from last night." Maria whispers loudly, making sure the coast is clear. "The cops are keeping a tight lid on his identity. Ongoing investigation bit. They probably want to make sure it wasn't one of their own who did it, chinga. A white cop was killed here not too long ago and they are rabid to find the killer. That little Chicana who was kidnapped for three days then found dead, they didn't give a damn, and every time I pressured them to do something it was always, que les dolía el culo or some pathetic excuse. Her family had to get their own volunteers to go comb the varrios for her. They're the ones who found her."

Luna shakes her head. "When are things going to change for the better here?"

"No, but when they killed that cop, there were TV announcements and a twenty-five-thousand-dollar reward y todo el pedo. The cops do a great job of finding the culprit when the crime is against *them*. Oh, they excel in protecting *themselves*. And they are grown men with guns!" She grits her teeth and squints her eyes in disbelief. "There are a few good ones. But, like the doctors, try finding one." She takes a deep breath. "And remember that fourteen-year-old girl who disappeared on the south side six months ago? Well, her mom called the police I don't know how many times, but they kept telling her that there was nothing they could do and that she probably ran away. She was missing for almost a month and had been kidnapped by this old pervert who had her tied up in his house. She escaped *on her own* and made it home, lucky to be alive. So now when this rich lady disappears a few weeks ago from Alamo Heights, they ran a huge article on her in the paper saying she was a 'real' person or something like that, and that crime is unheard of in their neighborhood. Well, now the Texas Rangers are scouring the area for her and we're getting a blow-by-blow account about her case in the news. It's like they're implying that poor people are not 'real.' Babosos."

Luna shakes her head in accord. "What's wrong with these pendejos?" She gives Maria a look of gratitude now. "Ay, Maria, thank you anyway for helping me." Luna casts her eyes downward.

Maria studies Luna's face. "Luna, who is this guy? And what's he to you? Es algo más serio, ¿verdad?" *It's something more serious, right?* She searches for Luna's eyes behind her lustrous black hair.

Luna's eyes start to water as she gazes up at her. "No se, María." *I don't know, Maria.* She nods slowly. "Pero this is just between us, okay? 'Cause we're carnalas." She breathes deeply. "Apenas lo conocí…y no se que me ha pasado. Ya me hace falta." *I just met him… and I don't know what's happened to me. I need him.* She looks away. "Maybe when two people meet in life-threatening circumstances, they develop a powerful bond. Like they're afraid that their chances of being together…are very limited." She looks back to check on her class, then back at Maria. "Still, what's with me?"

"What's with you? Mujer, this vato has gotten under your skin and you don't know what to do with that."

"No, Maria. Me estoy volviendo loca porque no se si está vivo o

muerto." *I'm going crazy because I don't know if he's dead or alive.*
"Ay, m'ijita." Nodding her head, Maria hugs her. "No sé que más
decirte. *I don't know what else to tell you.* But I'm glad you told me
and got some of it off your chest so you can breathe, chinga." She
rolls her eyes heavenward. Her gaze comes back to Luna's determined
eyes. "M'ijita, guard your heart. Ya no te preocupes por él. Tú bién
sabes que estas calles son muy crueles para el amor. *Don't worry about
him anymore. You know very well that these streets are very cruel for
love.* I don't know what else to tell you. Does Consuelo know?"
Luna shakes her head.
The two women brave smiles for each other.
"I gotta go. Pero, mira, I'm taking your mom to lunch today so
she can meet and talk to the anchorman, Antonio Tello, from la es-
tación Mexicana. So he can tell her what he's uncovered about the
drug industry and hopefully get her to stop taking those pinches pills.
Okay?" Luna smiles with appreciation and gratitude. Maria gives
Luna a strong smile. "No te preocupes, m'ijita. ¿Okay? Acuérdate
que lo bueno siempre sobrevive." *Don't worry. Okay? Remember that
good always triumphs.*
"Maria, tú, si, eres mi homie." *Maria, you are truly my homie.*
Luna strokes Maria's locks. "Again, gracias for being there, carnala."
She looks away, then remembers something. "Oh, sí, can you still pick
up Crystal at the courthouse? She's there with her jefita because she
missed too much school and the pinche principal ordered her mom
to appear before a judge." She touches Maria's shoulder. "She's the
smartest in her class, but since she is a lesbiana, the kids make fun of
her. And her pinche teacher, instead of looking out for her, exacerbates
the problem by telling her in front of the class, 'I have no patience for
this wierdness.'" She rolls her eyes.
"Pendeja." Maria looks away with exasperation. "They just don't
give a damn. It's not about teaching, it's about control. Making them
all wear uniforms so everybody looks like stupid yuppies. Might as
well have Hitler as the superintendent, chinga." She checks her beep-
ing cellular and answers it. "Yeah, Lila, I'm running a little late. Can I
just meet you there? Orale, bye."
"I know, Maria. These kids, more than anybody, need to express
themselves to mature. Dressing up is a way for them to deal with problems at home, or other serious issues." Luna checks on her class, peeking through the wooden door. "The way they dress is not a pendejada.

For many it's a way to keep their sanity."

"It's like they don't want our kids to show even a hint of being Chicano." Maria sighs. "But it's okay for the cops and everybody to dress up like pinche cowboys."

Luna playfully peeks around the door to her students and smiles, then turns back to Maria. "I had to go look for a student's early immunization records at this elementary school in the varrio yesterday, and there's these three Hispanic teachers belittling another bilingual instructor. A beautiful woman inside and out. They were saying, 'She's teaching them how to grow corn, pick it, make the masa just like the Aztecs, and roll out tortillas! When are these kids ever going to fit into society if we don't get the Mexican out of them?'" She glances at a single mother with three toddlers waiting in the cold for the pinche bus across the street and shakes her head. "It's sad to see that the ones educating our kids, whether they're Chicano or not, have no sense of validity in our history, our cultura." She looks at Maria. "They call themselves *teachers?* They can't even have compassion for these kids' chaotic existence. Can you imagine how much self-esteem that bilingual teacher is giving them? She's giving them a life! Estos bueyes get an education, and yes, they do come back to the varrio, but they come back feeling like they're above the poor gente here. They call themselves masters of this and that because of their degrees, but let's face it: If they don't care about a real education for their poor students, they're not masters of shit."

With a palm Maria sweeps her remark away. "No, ¡cállate! Good bilingual teachers are leaving the profession in the varrio in droves. They'd rather work at Foley's, chinga. Why? Nobody knows why. Why? Because the pinche schoolboard has 'em so muzzled, you can't even get a pedo out of them. How 'bout the teacher who came out with the story about the principal who threatened activist parents with la migra. She got canned real quick. She *feared for her personal safety.*" Maria grits her teeth.

"How can things improve if teachers can't even express what's going on?" Luna checks the chavalos. "In this school system, if any teacher shows any solidarity or embraces the cultura of la gente here, they are made to look like troublemakers or idiots."

"Tell me something I don't know." Maria glances at her watch. "Oyes, mi fiel, I gotta pintar venado. Chinga, don't get us going. But let's catch up at my jefita's for dinner tomorrow night, ¿trucha?"

As Maria walks off, she yells at the young mother with her children at the bus stop. "M'ijita! ¿Quieres ride? Vente." *My child! Do you want a ride? Come on.*

The Chicana nods yes appreciatively, surprised. Maria crosses the street to help her get her kids into the primer-grey, hubcapless '69 Nova.

At lunchtime the girls are deep in gossip at one end of the long room, amid folding chairs and a small, secondhand coffee table. At the other end a group of vatos has gathered to exchange the latest varrio news amid the drone of the AC unit.

A vato with the words 'El Silent' tattooed on his neck has cornered the attention. "Simón, I heard it from Brujo's sister."

Luna walks over to the tables near the vatos to clean up a few leftover pieces of paper from lunch. Just then the loud heater unit cuts off. She can make out what the vatos are saying. The group has gathered in a huddle, obscuring her from their view.

"Who?" one vato asks.

Silent: "Some vato named El Blue-Boy?"

Luna freezes, but she slowly continues her cleaning. She's got to know.

Another vato: "Los Muertos threw him off the Guadalupe Bridge?"

"Sí, sordo." Azteca-Boy, close to the source, gets impatient.

Luna feels her heart pounding in her chest. Her stomach starts turning into a knot.

"Who's he?" Another confused vato.

Azteca-Boy: "Chinga, what are we, Central Intelligence? El vato las dio! *The vato cashed in!* Who the fuck knows who he is?"

"Shit, ese vato tiraba parada." *Shit, that vato was straight up.* Another vato nods his head, frío.

"Vale más que lo creas." *Better believe it.* He thinks for a minute with the vatos' gaze locked on him. "Pero stranger shit has happened en éstas pinches calles." *In these damn streets.*

They finally notice Luna listening and break out with another subject. "Ey, ah, did you finish the mural?"

Luna walks off. She throws the papers in the garbage and steals away through the back door.

Outside alone, she leans against the weathered wall of the stucco building and grits her teeth as the breeze caresses her jet black hair.

Four girls step out to look for her.

"Luna, what's the matter? What's bothering you?"

Luna shakes her head. "I can't tell you. I'm sorry."

The vatos step out. Now the whole class is outside, a huddle of concern. When one member of a family hurts, the whole family suffers.

la tierra del sol

Thirteen

El tren
The train

The night is falling hard en la Tripa...Dark, menacing storm clouds are slowly devouring a reddish-purple sunset.

A pair of black calcos walks with purpose down the darkening streets. Polkas, rancheras, a Christmas jingle, and an oldie here and there from the tiny businesses and homes mingle with the sounds of gunshots and crying ambulances in the distance.

Down a rainsoaked varrio street, half a block away, an angry woman is calling out to Attorney Ruiz.

La sombra, in black calcos, moves toward the voice for a better look, hiding behind some bushes between a closed panadería and an abandoned house. He sees a disheveled Chicana in her thirties carrying a three-year-old girl on her hip. She walks quickly toward a chubby man in an impeccable suit who is trying to slither away.

"Attorney Ruiz! Don't act like you don't hear me! Your hearing was sharp as a dog's when you wanted my money!"

Attorney Ruiz looks around to the sleepy homes and decides to stop and try to discredit her, in case people are listening. He is five feet away from where la sombra is hiding.

The angry Chicana catches up to him.

"I don't know you. I don't know what you're talking about!" He raises his voice so that anybody listening can hear. "I just came here to help this poor old señora," he motions to a house a few doors down, "in case she needs any legal advice, and now you're accusing me of what?"

"Like the 'legal advice' you gave us? My husband is married to a wheelchair. I have three kids to feed, and you ripped us off with our insurance claim. You promised us you would double our claim if we let you borrow it for one week. All you have given us back is your bullshit!" She consoles the little girl, who is starting to cry. "It's okay, m'ija." She turns her wrath on him again as he starts to leave. "I have been calling you for a month, and your secretary keeps telling me that you were in some train accident? That you were bedridden? But as soon as this viejita's husband dies, rest his soul, you are conveniently back to good health. Now you're gonna rip her off too? ¡Cuervo!"

Attorney Ruiz walks a few more feet and stops. He is now in front of the bushes where la sombra is hiding and far enough away from the tiny dwellings. Leaning in to the Chicana, he whispers loudly. "Look, I hate to tell you this, but I lost your money in a bet." The Chicana's mouth drops open.

"If I'd've won, you'd've of won." He shrugs matter-of-factly. "We took a chance and lost. Let's try to be good sports." He chuckles.

The Chicana raises her voice in anger. "Why don't you have the guts to say it out loud, so that everybody can hear what a professional liar you are?" She rolls her eyes. "You gambled our money away? You worm!" She looks at his wristwatch, gleaming with gold. It matches his diamond-studded cufflinks. "You don't look like you lost out on anything to me!"

He turns away and starts walking quickly. Then he stops and turns to her, his face red with anger. Whispering loudly, he shakes his finger. "There's nothing you can do about it! You have no proof, no knowledge of the law! So, if you defame my name, which is my business, I will gladly drag you into court for defamation of character and bury you for good!" He walks away, then turns with authority. "Oh, and it's a felony to threaten an attorney of the law!" With his head held high, he strolls off.

"You gutless bastard!" The Chicana resigns herself to her defeat. "I trusted you because you are Raza. Pero, I've seen tecatos que eran más hombre que tú!" *But I've seen drug addicts who were more of a man than you!*

The mother walks back, crying softly to herself, heartbroken.

As the cold wind gusts up into the trees, making the Christmas lights sway in the eaves of the tiny homes, the little girl looks back over her mother's shoulder at el abogado as he briskly walks away. A dark figure creeps up behind him and follows the attorney around the corner.

Attorney Ruiz arrives at a sleek silver Mercedes parked on the curb. Fumbling for his keys in his pocket, he finds them and beeps the car alarm off. As he gets ready to walk to the driver's side, he feels the barrel of a gun press up against his back. Someone whispers loudly in his ear. "Let's get in on the front passenger side, marrano." *Pig.*

The attorney freezes with fear, tries to look behind him. From the darkness the voice whispers coldly, "O si quieres, te destripo aquí mismo." *Or, if you want, I can gut you right here.*

Attorney Ruiz is shitting in his pants. He starts mumbling hysterically. "Please! I'm a Hispanic. I'm-I'm doing some charity work in the varrio! Tengo gente que me necesita," *I have people here who need me,* he mutters with a Hispanic twang.

"¿Si? Pos, on this bet, you're gonna lose it *all.* Súbete, Mr. Attorney of the Law." La sombra whispers death in his ear.

The attorney is startled by his words, which cut a crevice through his being and sharpen into focus the crushing cost of evil. With nervous hands he opens the front passenger door.

As he slides into the driver's seat, he tries again to see who his judge is. La sombra leans in to his ear. "Si me miras la cara, te voy a tener que matar! Me la rayo…Vamos a dar un vueltón." *If you see my face, I'm gonna have to kill you. I swear it…Let's go for a cruise.*

Attorney Ruiz, shining with sweat, makes sure he doesn't look at his accuser's face as he fumbles with his keys. Finding the ignition, he fires her up, driving off slowly and looking away.

Nearby, the evening train yelps its warning, chilling the nerves and stirring in the attorney a premonition of his approaching doom.

La sombra leans in to the attorney's ear. "Tienes un appointment con un train accident. Te acuerdas?" *You have an appointment with a train accident. Do you recall?* He directs the trembling attorney towards el tren approaching the railroad yard under the Guadalupe Bridge.

"Please! I'll give you money, or my jewelry! I've never hurt anybody in my life! You can have my car. Pleeassse!"

La sombra leans in to him again. "Si me canso de tu pinche chillería, va a ser tu última!" *If I get tired of your damn whining, it's gonna be your last!*

Abruptly the attorney loses his tongue.

They arrive under the bridge.

It's pitch black where they come to a stop. Railroad tracks intersect and run parallel to each other in front of the Mercedes. The warehouses are all shut down for the night. Not even a wino or drug addict around to hear screams for help. With a slight breeze to chill the bones, the place looks as deserted as a graveyard.

"Quítate el saco." *Take off your coat.*

The attorney jiggles like jelly with fear as he complies.

La sombra tears off the attorney's neatly pressed white shirt. He blindfolds him and ties his hands behind his back with the shirt rags.

"Please, don't do something you're gonna regret. Let me go. Por fa—"

"Cállate el hocico!" *Shut up!* Opening the driver door, la sombra pushes him out face-first into the gravel.

The train siren yelps out. The attorney's heart does a flip inside his chest. The chopping of the engines can now be heard. "What are you going to do?" He pouts for mercy as he blindly looks around.

He gets dragged between the two rails of a railroad track and dropped on his exposed belly. Ten feet away, on a curve in the rails, a stationary row of boxcars hides him from view of the approaching train. "Wwwhhhooooa!!!" The incessant chopping of the engines sounds like a wild mechanical beast bearing down on its prey.

As Attorney Ruiz starts to whimper, la sombra leans down to his level. "Mi vida, ahorita, no vale madre. Si este tren te hace cagada, tal vez me sienta mejor. Marranos como tú, con tus pinches *leyes,* no deben de andar sueltos entre gente decente." *My life, right now, ain't worth a damn. If this train makes shit out of you, perhaps I'll feel better. Pigs like you, with your damn* laws, *shouldn't be running loose among decent people.*

While la sombra talks, the attorney feels with his feet for the rails. Fear grips him like a vise and he gasps for breath. "Please, I help our gente." He squirms into a kneeling position.

"Like you helped that poor mother?"

Attorney Ruiz abruptly shuts up, nodding his head for mercy.

"Antes que te lleve la chingada, vas a conocer la ley de la Raza. Lo que le hiciste a esa pobre madre te va a costar más que tu pinche nombre, desgraciado." *Before you fucking check out, you're gonna know the law of la Raza. What you did to that poor mother is going to cost you more than your fucking name, asshole.*

"Wwwwaaaauuo!!!" The growling monster assaults the senses, just seconds away. Unable to control his calzón-gripping fear, Ruiz shakes his head uncontrollably and yelps out.

"Pleeeasssse!!!"

Placing the end of the pipe barrel to his head, la sombra yells above the train's engines. "Si te mueves de ahí, te volo la pinche cabeza!" *If you move from there, I'll blow your fucking head off!* With his foot he pushes Attorney Ruiz face-first into the gravel.

The ground now trembles from the thundering giant. He shakes his head feverishly. "Nooo!!!"

A few feet away, la sombra yells at him amid the monster's thunder. "Mr. Attorney of the Law! Apostaste con la Raza y perdiste! *You gambled with our race and lost!* Be a good sport!"

The train's deafening blast drowns out the attorney's widemouthed shrieks and screams. The attorney convulses and writhes around, trying to squirm away on his bare belly as the monster is now on top of him.

The train goes rumbling past on the track parallel to his, six feet away.

He is a pitiful mass of defeat as he lies there whimpering for a few minutes, the boxcars creaking and squealing past.

La sombra calls out, "Al rato pasa el tuyo." *Yours comes by in a few minutes.*

Attorney Ruiz surprisingly struggles to his knees, unable to bear his situation another second. He weeps and shakes his head. He finally cries with abandon, "Pleeeeeassssee!!! Take everything I have! Don't kill meee!!!"

The train passes through, leaving him in uncontrollable spasms of shock, on the verge of a heart attack.

La sombra approaches him. He leans down to the attorney's level and pulls out his wallet. "Esa señora que arruinaste es amiga mía. Si algo le pasa, entonces si te va a llevar el tren. Yo sé donde vives, pinche marrano!" *That lady you ruined is a friend of mine. If something happens to her, then the train will take you away. I know where you live, damn pig!*

Feverishly, the attorney nods his head yes and no, anything to please.

"Dame todo de valor que traes." *Give me everything of value that you have.*

He gives up his gold rings, gold-studded bracelets, and a Lucien Picard watch worth about twelve thousand dollars. La sombra opens his wallet and finds over three thousand dollars in cash.

"¡Esto no es suficiente! Mañana quiero que vayas y vendas ese pinche carro de culeros racistas. No quiero volver a verte en él. Y mándale todo ese dinero a mi amiga. Por correo. ¡No te le vuelvas a acercar!" *This is not enough! Tomorrow I want you to go and sell that damn car of racist chickenshits. I never want to see you in it again! And send all that money to my friend. By mail. Never go near her again!*

The attorney wouldn't think of disagreeing.

"Me voy a quedar con tu billetera. No hay ningún pozo donde te puedes esconder. ¡No *vuelvas* a chingar con la Raza!" *I'm keeping your wallet. There isn't a hole you can crawl into. Don't ever fuck with la Raza again!*

He leans in to the attorney's ear. "Y en la noche, cuando estés en tu cama rascándote el culo, acuérdate...del tren." *And in the night, when you are scratching your ass in bed, remember...the train.*

La sombra leaves. Another train starts moaning from the other direction. Ruiz starts squealing and rolls off the tracks, only to land on another pair of rails. He squirms away, trying desperately to free his hands with pathetic whimpers.

La sombra fades into the night.

mundo oscuro

Fourteen

El otro ojo
The other eye

In the darkening varrio the black '59 Impala rolls up to Ortega's Grocery and Market in the heart of la Tripa. The windows and doors are covered with iron bars. Brujo, in the back seat, leans in to Diablo riding shotgun. "Jefe, este pinche viejillo se va a tener que mocharse con un dies y ocho." *Boss, this damn old man is gonna have to chop himself off for an eighteen-pack.* Brujo and Sapo climb out from the back seat and stroll, bién chingónes in their Pendletons, towards the entrance. Sapo is also sporting a grey-green juvie jacket.

Sapo walks in first. Brujo gets stuck at the doorway with an old, jittery, frail viejita on her way out. She does a little dance with him as she tries to figure out if he's going left or right. Brujo quickly tires of her indecision and yells in her face. "¡Házte a la verga!" *Get the fuck out of the way!* The viejita winces and trembles from his verbal assault. With a whimper she scurries away.

Inside, Sapo is picking out the bironga. "Chinga, Brujo, ¿Pa' qué le gritates así a la pobre viejita? Te sales." *Damn, Brujo, why did you yell at that old lady? You're outta line.*

"Pos sí, hombre. Pinche viejilla, si no sabe andar que se quede en la pinche casa, la babosa." *Well yeah, man. Damn old lady, if she doesn't know how to fucking walk, she should stay at home, the idiot.* Brujo pulls out a frosty eighteen-pack of Budweiser from the store's cooler.

They both walk to the front of the store and start out the door. The old señor behind the cash register sees them walking out without paying and lifts a trembling finger to them.

Brujo stops cold and stares at him. "¿Qué chingaus? ¿Me quieres dar toda la feria también? No empieces conmigo, culero." *What the fuck? You wanna give me all your money too? Don't start with me, chickenshit.*

The viejito drops his head and they head out the door.

Meanwhiles, a couple of Stop-N-Gos away: "¡Hola! ¡Esperen!" It's Luna stepping off a bus. She sees Chuy and Plutarco locking up Prieto's and walks quickly to them.

"Hola m'ija." Chuy looks away.

"Por favor, ¿No tienen razón de Nazul?" *Please, do you have any word about Nazul?* She seems breathless with anxiety as she whispers loudly. "Tengo que saber. Por mejor o por pior." *I have to know. For better or for worse.*

Plutarco tries to act as if they don't know what she's talking about. "M'ijita, es mejor que te olvides de Nazul." *My daughter, it's better to forget about Nazul.* He nods his head.

The words tear at her heart. Chuy and Plutarco try not to look at her. She searches their faces. "¿Por qué no me dicen la verdad? ¿Está muerto?" *Why won't you tell me the truth? Is he dead?*

"Luna—" Before Chuy can continue, Luna darts off across the street to the sound of honking horns and braking tires. "Luna! M'ijita!" Chuy drops his head, then glances at Plutarco as she fades out of sight. "Chinga, ¿Qué vamos a hacer con ella?" *Fuck, what are we going to do with her?*

Plutarco nods his head. "¿Qué sirve que le demos esperanza? Don Pablito dijo que antes de que sepulten a Elías y su familia, algo grave va a pasar." *Why give her any hope? Don Pablito said that before Elias and his family's funeral, something tragic is going to happen.*

Chuy stares into the darkness where Luna went. He turns seriously to Plutarco. "Ahora me voy a tener que poner una parranda bien dada." *Now I'm gonna have to go on a drunken binge.* Trying to lighten him up, Chuy bulges his eyes out, contorting his face into a butt-ugly frown. "Una parranda que te deja como zorrillo ciego." *A binge that leaves you like a blind skunk.*

Plutarco gives him a cool varrio glance back. "Te aguitas." *I dare you.*

A teenage Chicano stares at the news on the glowing screen of a cheap TV. The newsman addresses the camera. "In today's news, one of the richest couples in the world has announced the donation of close to a billion dollars to philanthropic causes. Their highest priority, they stated, is to give to organizations that take care of animals. Annnd, the release of another film about vampires is set to hit the big screen this weekend."

The teenager turns to check out the sound of paper tearing at the other end of the small room. His dad sits in a wheelchair wrapping a tiny toy soldier in Christmas paper. The chavalo glances at the cheap-looking Christmas tree made out of tin foil and the meager array of lights. Underneath, a few presents lay scattered. It looks like Santa is going to be poor again this year.

The one-bedroom unit in the Alazán-Apache Courts is small and decorated with cheap furniture. A small portrait of the boy's dad in a Marines uniform sits on the TV.

Just then the mother walks into the room from a back bedroom. "Guys, did you see where Matilde left her teddy bear?" She digs under the cushion of the torn couch where her son is sitting and finds it. As she walks off again, she glances at her son. "M'ijo, that cable is gonna be cut off any day. I'm sorry, but you don't need to be watching those spoiled brats on TV anyway."

There's a knock at the front door. "It's probably another bill collector, chinga." She reaches the door and puts her ear to it. "Who is it?" No answer. She looks out the front window to her tiny porch lit by the pale lightbulb, but doesn't see anyone. She opens the door and looks around. In the dim glow of her porch light, she notices something on her steps. It looks like a piece of a white shirt in a bundle with a few red rose petals on top. She leans down and sees a fancy gold cufflink attached to the torn sleeve. It looks like the ones Attorney

Ruiz was wearing. Carefully, she unwraps the bundle. A neat stack of hundred dollar bills, a watch, and some jewelry. Her mouth open, she stands on the porch for a moment, looking around at the windy, dark varrio street.

"Honey! ¡Mira!" She runs inside screaming, startling her husband so much that he falls back off his wheelchair. She and her son help him back up.

"Honey! La Virgencita heard my prayers! Look!" The rose petals and bills roll off her hands and drift down to the patched floor. All three investigate the loot with trembling hands as the little sister and two-year-old brother come running in from the bedroom to see about the commotion.

The mother rolls the Lucien Picard watch and cufflinks in her hands. "These belonged to that culero, Attorney Ruiz." She walks out the front door and looks around at the cold darkness.

"Thank you! Whoever you are! ¡Muchísimas gracias! ¡Qué Dios lo bendiga! ¡Y feliz navidad!"

Osito and Payaso, two students from Los Vryosos Community Center, are getting off a city bus in the heart of la Tripa, at Trinity and El Paso. All is quiet as they walk down the dimly lit calle in the icy night.

Osito is chubby, with a street-smart attitude. He's wearing dark work pants and a grey Azteca Tire Shop work shirt smudged with grease. He trudges along at a confident pace.

Payaso looks younger and thinner. He's more cautious. He's sporting a dark blue gas station uniform smudged with mud and grease. "Chinga, I hate walking around here this late at night. We shoulda left the tire shop earlier."

"Yeah, but like I said, my jefita needs the feria to pay the light bill. I had to put in as many hours as I could." Osito walks quickly.

They hear the screaming tires of a car tearing ass a few blocks away. The noise gets closer and their stride quickens.

Just as Payaso feared, a dark '67 Nova rounds the corner with the pounding bass of a rap hit pulsating through the night. They look for a place to run and hide, but before they can react, the headlights hit their backs.

The Nova peels up to them.

Payaso and Osito keep walking.

The punk in the front passenger hangs his tattooed arm out the window to them. "Ey! Ese, what rola do you click to?" The punk senses fear. His snarl is full of confident evil.

Osito and Payaso keep their stride.

The punk in the back seat leans out to them. "¡Ey! ¡Jotos! He axed you a question. Why do you act like a couple of ugly rucas, like you're too good to talk to us?"

Osito takes a deep breath. He stops and turns to face them. "Do I owe you something, verga-face?"

Payaso freezes with fear, holds his breath.

The punks look at each other.

"Do you think I wanna be culeros like you? Throwing my shit around and shooting little kids in their sleep? Any pendejo can be an asshole! My Raza is the rola I click to." He stares them down.

The front passenger yells in his face. "Chinga tu madre!" *Fuck your mother!*

"Pos, chinga la tuya." Osito returns the most suicidal phrase you can say to a Chicano.

Flashing and cocking, the punks stick their plomeros out the window. Osito and Payaso take off running. The Nova tears away after them with the gangsters shooting recklessly.

Half a block down, the vatos reach Guadalupe Street with the Nova a few feet away. Except for El Gallo Giro Lounge pouring out a dreamy polka, the area is dead.

As Osito and Payaso sprint around the corner of a building, the windshield of the Nova suddenly explodes. Unable to see, the driver crashes into a pickup truck parked outside the lounge.

The two punks who were in the back seat now lie in a heap on top of the two in the front. All sit silently inside the smoking car trying to remember where they are. Slowly the two punks on top stagger off amid grunting and wincing.

"What the hell happened?" The driver is bloody-mouthed and dazed.

The front passenger has a bleeding gash on his forehead and a busted mouth. "Did somebody shoot at us?"

Just then the front passenger window shatters into a thousand pieces, startling the driver, who takes a dive down to the console.

The passenger next to him looks down to a weight that has fallen on his lap. "A rock?"

Down Guadalupe Street, Osito and Payaso have heard the crash and stop momentarily to catch their breath, the freezing air like acid in their lungs. Sneaking back around the corner, they hide between two buildings in the dark and wait to see what happens.

Payaso is ready to split. "Let's make a run for it, Osito. Now's our chance!" His hot breath turns to steam in the cold night.

Osito is more curious. "Wait. Something weird happened." He peers around the old, graffitti-covered wall, breathing heavily.

"*You're* weird." Payaso rolls his eyes.

Down the block, in front of Gallo Giro's, the punks get slowly out of the wrecked Nova. A few señores from the lounge cautiously step out to view the damage. When they see the punks holding the plomeros, they quickly scramble back in.

"It was those two jotos! Where are they?" The punk with the gash on his forehead looks around.

As they start to walk towards them, Osito and Payaso panic and make a run for it again.

"I told you, stupid." Payaso takes off like a shot.

"You're dead! Jotos!" The punks boldly shoot at them.

As fate would have it, Luna is cruising by with her sister and mother in Consuelo's four-door, '87 white Chrysler. Consuelo is in the front passenger seat while Estrella sits in the back seat, munching on some tortilla chips from an open grocery bag beside her. They hear the shots and cautiously look around through the few parked cars that frame the street.

Suddenly Payaso and Osito are in Luna's headlights as they dash across the street. Luna slams on the brakes. More shots ring out. Luna and her family see the four gang members chasing them and firing automatics. Consuelo and Estrella duck down to the floorboards.

"Osito? No!" Luna swerves away. The .25s ricochet, ping off of the Chrysler's wide chrome bumper, and puncture her right rear tire.

"Osito! Payaso! Get IN!" With a flat tire she takes off in their direction down the dark varrio street.

She catches up to Osito and drives alongside him. Payaso runs ahead like a track star. Consuelo opens the back door to him as Estrella scoots over to make room. Luna slows down and Osito climbs in. Pieces of black rubber fly off the Chrysler's tire as it rumbles after Payaso.

Payaso jumps into Osito's lap with a grunt.

As the Chrysler tears away, Osito looks back. "Luna, wait!"

"What?" Puzzled, Luna turns to him and cautiously slows down. A dark figure has intercepted the gangsters' enraged pursuit. Two vatos are already sprawled on the pavement. The dark figure is definitely a vato, a shadow that seems to melt into the darkness only to appear again by surprise.

He's caught the punks off guard.

One of the two remaining punks points his gun at him only to have it shoved down. It fires into his homie's foot! As the punk tries to run away in his baggy, low-hanging pants, the shadow steps on his pant cuff. The punk's pants fall to his ankles and he crashes to the pavement.

Osito jumps out of the Chrysler. "Did you see that? Who the hell?" He takes off running.

"Osito! Damn!" Payaso drops his head for a minute and rolls his eyes. "This vato is gonna give me a short lifespan. ¡Cómo le gusta el pedo!" *How he loves to look for shit!*

Down the street, the dark figure notices Osito approaching cautiously and dissolves into the darkness between two buildings.

Osito jumps over the four vatos who lie on the sidewalk moaning, too preoccupied with their wounds to care about their plomeros. He cuts in between an abandoned barbacoa shop and an empty lot.

A neon light glows blue-green and reads 'POOL' in front of El Bottoms Up Lounge. Osito catches a glimpse of the figure. He's dressed in a black topcoat with a matching chuco hat. "Ey! Carnal! Wait!"

The red flasher blades of two silent speeding squad cars slice through the night. The shadow ducks into the blackness beside the old flaking building. The cops rush to the scene of the Nova wreck around the corner.

Just as la sombra appears again, Osito gets close enough to call out to him. "Ey! Pachuco!" He runs after him.

La sombra slows down as he reaches a blanket of darkness in an empty lot littered with trash. He doesn't acknowledge Osito, keeping his back to him as he flows away.

Osito is out of breath. "Ca-carnal, I just wanted to say gracias for your esquina."

Thirty feet away, la sombra's silhouette turns to face Osito.

"Who are you? Are you el Gato Negro?" Osito has to bend over and rest his arms above his knees to catch his breath. He peers up to him.

The vato is motionless, his face hidden in obscurity. Dark mad-dog sunglasses glint, reflecting a blade of bluish light. His deep voice breaks the silence. "Todos somos del mismo rancho."

Osito looks to the ground for a split second, contemplating his words. When he looks up, la sombra has disappeared. He scans the area carefully. A chill travels up his arm and spreads throughout his body.

The headlights of Luna's Chrysler turn the corner, shining directly on Osito's face. Osito trudges off to her. He gets in and the Chrysler takes off.

Inside, Payaso checks Osito, who is unusually quiet, still out of breath and contemplating his encounter. "Well? What happened?" The car thumps down the street with its flat tire.

The girls silently wait for an answer.

Osito looks out the window. "I don't know…He didn't want me to know who he was. It was strange. I mean, he just *disappeared*. I-I looked up and—I think…he's hiding from…something." Osito is half talking and half mumbling to himself.

"Man, you don't make any sense." Payaso just wants the facts. "Did you *talk* to him, vato?"

"When I asked who he was he just said, 'Todos somos del mismo rancho.' That's it. Then a split second later I look up and he…like the ground swallowed him."

Luna comes to a halt. She looks at her mom, her heart in her throat…then to Osito.

"Luna, what's wrong?" Consuelo.

She takes a deep breath, barely able to hide her emotion.

She turns around to face him. "Osito, did you get a look at his face?" Hope starts to build inside her.

"No, he didn't want me to see who he was." He's puzzled by her inquiry.

"That's *all* he said?" Luna drives slowly.

"Luna, do you think you *know* this vato?" Payaso leans in.

"I don't know."

The gang exchanges puzzled looks about Luna.

"Man, Luna, you're making this even weirder." Osito is perplexed. "I asked him, 'Are you a pachuco?' and that's all he said."

As the Chrysler cruises along, Luna glances out her window at the darkness that swallowed him up.

Blocks away, Pato's Lounge pours out a sad rola about a long lost friend into the cold night.

In an inky void outside the lounge, a dark figure hides, reminiscing.

"¡Oyes, Blue-Boy, m'estás matando! ¡M'estás matando!" *Ey, Blue-Boy, you're killing me! You're killing me!* Elias would smile his impeccable smile, except for the gold front tooth. "Tú no puedes arrear este pinche '57. El méndigo cloche te avienta la pata p'arriba como resorte." *You can't drive this '57. The damn clutch kicks your foot back up like a spring.* He laughs. "Es que ese cloche está bién apreta'o. Te vas a dar un rodillaso en la garganta." *It's that the clutch is too tight. You're gonna slam your knee on your throat.* Laughter.

Elias had an artful way of taking the most frustrating problems and turning them into a chiste, custom-made for the varrio. He hardly ever laughed. When he did it was because Nazul or Chuy was rolling on the ground. He would laugh at them. He didn't like small talk, except with his wife and kids. With vatos he would not answer a petty question or add to a chiste. "Y tú ¿Qué chingaus sabes de eso? Te debes de fijar en el espejo," *And you, what the hell do you know about that? You should have a look in the mirror,* he would blurt out as he walked away from the wagging tongues. If you had low opinions about others in their absence, Elias had a low opinion of you.

In the dead of night, in the heart of la Tripa, a burly and unshaven señor in his fifties walks out of a convenience store toward an old, beat-up '58 Buick. He wears a maintenance-man uniform and carries a bag of goodies. Cautiously he looks around as he quickly climbs onto the torn upholstery of his carrucha and starts her up, throwing the bag into the seat beside him. Fizzle-sticks and toy action figures mixed in with a couple of little girl's dolls in their packages spill out onto the seat. Hanging from the rearview mirror beside a couple of black fuzzy dice, a portrait of his young family swings as he backs away.

A cloud of white smoke billows out of his muffler like a flour mill. The car radio sports pieces of wire hanger for nobs. A polka gurgles out.

The clanking pile of junk looks like it was put together at home, one piece at a time. It defies the laws of motion just by rolling down the street. He reaches into the bag. Amid all the kiddie goodies he finds a frosty quart of beer. As he's about to open it, he is blinded by the headlights of an oncoming car that swerves to cut him off.

Three gangsters jump out of a dark '78 Cutlass and head right for him. El señor shifts into reverse, but the grinding gears won't engage. The gangsters reach his door, open it, roughly drag him out by his collar, and throw him to the street.

"Did we get paid today, papi?" asks a vato wearing a black paño and baggy dark pants and shirt. "Orale, no te hagas culo. *Come on, don't act like an ass.* Show us your feria!"

El señor huddles in a ball, enduring the beating from the pack of varrio mafiosos. He tries to fight back. "¡Pinches bueyes! I have five kids. ¡Denme quebrada!" *Gimme a break!* He sits firmly on his wallet.

Another gangster climbs out of the dark Cutlass with a pair of jumper cables. He wraps them around the man's thick neck and tries to choke him. "You're gonna give it up, daddy! ¡En la Tripa, todos se mochan con los Muertos!" *In the Intestine, everybody chops something off for los Muertos.*

Kicks, punches to the head, and choking don't convince el señor to give up his wallet. He sits there and takes it. One gangster pulls out his cohete and fires three rounds inches from his feet.

The front passenger door of the black Cutlass is kicked open from the inside. A tattoo-covered hand pops a push-button fila. The face is hidden from view. "¡Chinga! No despares, baboso. Van a venir los juras." *Don't shoot, you idiot. The cops are gonna come.* He trots to them. "¿No pueden con este viejito? ¡Háganse a la verga! Yo voy a abrir este bote de frijoles." *You can't handle this old man? Get the fuck away! I'll open this can of beans.*

Shaking, el señor looks up a tattoo-covered arm to the inhuman, scarred face of Diablo. Dark maddogs devoid of life.

Before he can act, a loud Mexican grito cuts through the night, making the hairs on the Muertos' necks stand at attention. "AAAYYYY-HA-HAAA!!!" It resonates through the night, bouncing off buildings, coming from nowhere and trailing off to nothing but silence again.

They look around to some abandoned buildings where tall trees sway in a sudden blast of wind that sweeps down on the area. The gust blows through their clothes and makes them shiver with superstitious fear.

Suddenly a fist-sized rock comes hurtling down. It strikes the vato who is choking el señor with the jumper cables on the side of his head. The rock knocks him off his feet and onto the street with a grunt.

Los Muertos look at each other. Two more rocks come flying out of the darkness. Both of them hit their targets, one on the head and the other on the shoulder. One falls back. "¡Desgraciado!" *Bastard!*

"Brujo! Huevo! Find that culo!" Diablo orders with a scowl.

Brujo, the overweight, vulture-looking vato, pulls out a Glock and cocks it.

They approach the inky blackness. Two smaller rocks come flying out to meet them.

Brujo catches one with his right eye. "AHHHH!!" He clutches his face as he falls to his knees from the pain. "¡Chingadamadre!"

Huevo grabs his Glock and shoots aimlessly at the buildings just as the sounds of police sirens close in a few blocks away.

"Vámonos a la chingada. No valen verga." *Let's get the fuck outta here. You ain't worth a fuck.* Diablo struts back to the Cutlass, pissed.

Loading up their wounded, the vatos climb in. The Cutlass pulls back, burning rubber as it tears away.

El señor gets up, rubs his throat with his hand, and walks over to his Buick. Leaning in, he pulls out his cold quart of beer and brings it up to his anxious lips. Before he can taste the brew, two squad cars come squealing around the corner and stop in a cloud of exhaust and burnt rubber, inches from his knees.

All four rookies jump out with their Glocks ready and point them at el señor. "GET 'EM IN THE AIR!"

El señor tries to sneak a sip, but the cops won't have it. "NOWWW!!!"

Regretfully, el señor drops his quart to the ground. Sighing and raising his hands in defeat, he rolls his eyes heavenward.

Later that night, drunk as skunks, two older señores make their way home in an old, flaking-aqua, '69 Chevy pickup. Their slurred singing can be heard through the wet December night in the heart of el Weso as they weave through the dead varrio streets. Sparse Christmas lights on the tiny shacks hint at the coming holidays.

One of them sees a dog by the curb. The dog looks back. He waves at it. He looks down for a minute, then sideways to his partner. "Oiga, compadre…le saludé a un pinche perro…" *Hey, compadre…I just said hello to a dog…*

His compadre looks back at him after slowly digesting the information. "No, ¿qué tiene que ver? Pero si te saluda p'atrás…no le hagas caso." *It don't matter. But if he waves back…ignore him.*

"Aaah, chinga su madre. Vamos a cantar." *Aaah, fuck it. Let's sing.*

"Dos vatos sin jale querían pistiar,
Pero ni uno ni otro podía pagar.
Declara un vato, '¿Por qué es así?
¿Qué gente decente tiene que sufrir?
Pa'qué voy a trabajar, para soportar a los pinches rico-o-os,
Mejor me voy a pistiar.'"

Two vatos without jobs wanted to get drunk,
But neither one could pay.
Declares one vato, 'Why is it like this?
That decent people have to suffer this way?
Why should I work to support the damn rich?
I'd rather go get drunk.'

Los señores are lost in their magical moment, swaying to their crooning.

"Declara un vato, 'Yo fui a trabajar,
Por la pinche K-Mart cinco años o más.
Pero me enbotaron no pude pagar
Mi pinche car insooranse, mejor me fui a pistiar.'

Declara el otro, 'Yo quise estudiar
Pa'que me respeten y no trabajar.
Pero un Mexicano no puede hallar
Jale de gabacho-o-o, mejor me voy a pistiar.'"

Declares one vato, 'I went to work,
For the damn K-Mart five years or more.
But they threw me in the can 'cause I couldn't pay
My damn car insurance, I'd rather go and get drunk.'

Declares the other, 'I wanted to study
So they would respect me and I wouldn't have to work.
But a Mexican can't find
A gabacho's job, I'd rather go and get drunk.'

The red flashers of a squad car in their rearview mirror sober them a bit.

"A la chingada." The driver slowly pulls to a stop in the deserted varrio street. He looks around. They are in the abandoned warehouse district of Frio City Road and Commerce Street. Not a living soul around.

Concerned at his predicament, the driver glances over to his swaying partner. "Ben, tú hablas por mí. No sé mucho inglés." *Ben, you talk for me. I don't know much English.*

Two white cops step out of the squad car with weapons drawn. Flashlights light their way as they flank the truck.

Ben looks at his partner, his eyes half-lit. "Nooo, Juan, ahorita yo no me acuerdo nada de ese pinche idioma." *No, Juan, right now I can't remember nothing of that damn language.* He hides his quart of beer under the seat just as the cop taps on the window. The other officer hangs back with his Glock aimed at their fogged-up back window.

"THIS IS A POLICE OFFICER ORDERING YOU TO ROLL DOWN YOUR WINDOW, NOW!!" The six-foot-five cop, in his late twenties, is pumped up. His huge arms bulge out of his short-sleeve shirt in the freezing night.

El señor slowly complies. "Jes?"

The cop looks in. "Are both of you U.S. citizens?" He shines the tube of blinding light in their faces. Los señores just look at each other, waiting for the other to interpret.

Juan, slurring to his crony: "What deed he said?"

Ben just shrugs his shoulders ignorantly.

"Step out of the car, both of you." Both cops open the pickup's doors and pull los señores out by their collars.

"¡MANOS ARRIBA!" *HANDS UP!*

Los señores stick their hands in the air simultaneously. Benjamin steals a line to his partner as the thin cop walks over to investigate the front seat with his flashlight. "Eso sí saben decir, los méndigos." *They know how to say that, the jerks.*

The big cop clubs Ben on the head with the flashlight. "SPEAK ENGLISH OR SHUT UP!"

Ben is stunned by his anger. He rubs his head, confused. "Eyyy, boyyy."

"I'M NOT A BOY, WETBACK!" the cop yells in his face.

Ben looks him up and down. "Well, you no man."

"Ohh, shit!" The wimpy cop hears Ben's remark and shakes his head with a grin as he strides to the musclebound cop, who is turning red with rage.

"Goddamn it! That's it!" The cops handcuff both of them. "You wanna piss me off, beaner? You just did!" After frisking them for their wallets, they stand the two men facing the tailgate of the truck with their backs to them. The big cop fingers through the wallets and finds their licenses.

Leaning in to the skinny cop's ear, the big one whispers, "Let's show these wetbacks what happens when they piss off a cop." He struts to the squad car and jumps in the front seat behind the steering wheel. Cutting off the flashers, he grabs the mic.

The skinny one stands guard with his Glock ready.

Ben looks at his compadre and whispers, "¿Qué chingaus tienen estos pendejos?" *What's wrong with these idiots?*

"Anybody out there wanna join us in a little workout?" The cop on the mic looks down at their licenses.

Juan is now half-sober and concerned. "Estos cabrones nos pueden matar." *These bastards could kill us.*

"Speak English!" The skinny cop whops Juan on the back of the head with his Glock.

"Ay, chingau!" He rubs his head with anger. "Ey, pendejo, I fights in World War II. Why you treat me bad?"

The big cop deletes some entry in his computer with a smile. "We got the burro by the tail. We are under the Commerce Street Bridge. Y'all come now, you hear?" When he looks up, his partner is gone. "What the hell?" He jumps out with his Glock ready.

He cautiously looks around the darkness. Not a sign of his partner. Just los señores standing there with their backs to him in the glare of the headlights. He struts up to them. "Where's my partner?"

Los señores look around, puzzled. They shrug innocently.

The cop pulls out his billy club and strikes the two men hard on the backs of their legs. He sticks a gun barrel to Benjamin's ear. "Tell me or I'll pull this trigger."

Another cold gun barrel comes to rest behind the cop's ear. "Go ahead, '*officer.*'" The deep voice is dead serious. "Just don't *shit* on my calcos."

The cop starts to shake. "Now don't do anything you're gonna regret."

"Hand it over and I won't." The barrel presses harder.

Cautiously, the cop hands over the gun. "You don't know what you've gotten yourself into—"

"Speak Spanish or shut up." A fist comes smashing into his face. Groggily, he looks up at una sombra standing over him as he lies on the ground.

"Just tell 'em a burro made an *ass* out of you."

With that message, the cop passes out.

The shadow pulls the cuff keys from the cop and sets los señores free. They are shook up by his boldness, but relieved to be free.

"Es mejor que se pierdan por un buen rato." *It would be better if you got lost for a while.* La sombra hands them their wallets and licenses.

"No, sí, somos de Alis. Andamos visitando a gente aquí." *No, sí, we're from Alice. We're visiting people here.* Juan looks for a face on the shadow in the darkness. "Esta misma noche nos arrendamos pa' trás." *This very night we'll head back.* He looks down at the passed-out cop. "Deedn't we beat dese Nazis in pinche WWII? Para que murieron tantos hombres?" *What did so many men die for?* He turns to la sombra.

"Váyanse pronto." *Leave quickly.* The shadow ushers them into their truck.

Minutes later two silent squad cars, their headlights and flashers off, round the corner.

In the back seat of the parked squad car they find two unconscious cops with their pants pulled down around their ankles, piled on top of each other doggystyle.

"Mercy! Mercy me." In the front passenger of the arriving squad car a cop shakes his head at the pitiful sight. "They'll never live it down. Where's the camera?"

Ben and Juan pull out two fresh cans of beer from a secret compartment under the passenger seat as they cruise away.

"Mira, tú, Juan, yo no manejo mal cuando ando pedo. Pero yo tengo mucho cuidado, y casi nunca tomo. Nomás en Chreesmas." *Look, Juan, I don't drive bad when I'm drunk. But I'm very careful and hardly ever drink. Only on Christmas.* He burps loudly and hiccups, his eyes landing softly on Juan's pensive face. "¿Qué no?" Hiccup.

"No, Ben. Ese vato que nos salvó el culo, se me hace que es de los Kuculkánes...de Robe. No te acuerdas de esa leyenda en los cuarentas?" *That vato who saved our asses, I think he is one of the Kuculkánes…of Robstown. Do you remember that legend from the '40s?* He gives his partner a Pedro Infante gaze.

"El Gato Negro?"

"Si. Pero yo pensaba que el Gato fue un vato que salió de pedo con unos policias porque se llevaban a su esposa que era del otro lado. ¿Te acuerdas que lo pararon a él cuando andaba con ella? Y después de esposarlo por nada, empezaron a violar a su esposa en frente de él." *Yeah, but I thought that el Gato was a vato who got into a hassle with the police when they were taking his wife away because she was from the 'other side?' And after handcuffing him for nothing, they started violating his wife in front of him.*

He eyes Ben.

"Pos ¿no era el cuento," he lowers his chin to his chest for a burp, "que ella estaba esperando cama?" *Well, wasn't the story that she was expecting a child?* Ben takes a big swig.

"Yo nomás me acuerdo que cuando la estaban violando a su esposa, él los atacó y los mató a puras patadas." *I just remember that when they were raping her, he attacked them and kicked them to death.* Juan takes a swig of his. A bluish blade of lightning in the clouds lights their weather-worn faces for a split second. The pickup glides down the highway.

From his back pocket, Ben takes out a bent frajo from a squashed pack of Camels. "Sí, algo así. Andaban como cien Texas Rangers y cherifes y yo creo que toda la pinche Ku Klux Klan también detrás de él. Cuando un Mejicano se defiende, todo el tiempo sale todo el racismo en fuerza. Y todos somos culpables. Y mataron a varios Mejicanos, pero cuando atacaron a una familia en un ranchito y estaban listos para asesinar a las mujeres y los ninos, entonces apareció el Gato. Y cuando pegó el grito, se asustaron tanto que se fueron corriendo a pata por todos rumbos como gallinas traumadas." *Yeah, something like that. There were like one hundred Texas Rangers and sheriffs and I think the whole damn Ku Klux Klan after him. Whenever a Mexican defends himself, you always see all the racism come out in force. And we are all guilty. And they killed several Mexicans, but when they attacked a family in a small ranch and they were getting ready to assassinate the women and children, that's when el Gato appeared. And when he let out el grito, it terrorized them so much that they fled on foot in all directions like traumatized chickens.* He has trouble lighting his Camel.

Juan pulls it away from his mouth and attempts to light it.

"Y ¿Por qué se traumaron las gallinas?" *And why did the chickens get traumatized?* Swaying, Juan strikes a damp match to no avail. Ben grabs it back. He pulls out a Bic lighter from his worn-out jacket and flicks it. Nothing. Just then Juan gets one of the matches to light with a damp, dim flame. Before Ben can react with the frajo, it goes out.

Juan looks at Ben. "Es mejor no fumar, compadre." *It's better not to smoke, compadre.*

Ben throws the Camel out his rolled-down window. The old pick-up enters the 281 South expressway to Robe and Alice as the thunder barrels and the lightning flickers in some far-off county, the dark clouds slowly swallowing the horizon to the west.

Juan remembers. "Oiga compadre, y ¿Qué les pasó que se escamaron tanto?" *Listen, compadre, and what happened that scared them so much?*

Ben makes a confused gesto. "Ya te dije." *I told you.*

"No, no, compadre. Nomás me dijiste que se escamaron y se fueron corriendo a pata como pendejos y traumaron a unas gallinas, o comieron gallina, o algo." *No, no, compadre. All you told me was that they all got scared and went running on foot like idiots, and they traumatized some chickens, or ate chicken, or something.*

Ben rolls his eyes. "Comieron gallina." *They ate chicken.* He shakes his head. "Que se escamaron y se fueron corriendo como gallinas. *Como* gallinas. No que *comieron* gallinas." *It's that they got scared and took off running like chickens.* Like *chickens. Not that they* ate *chickens.*

"Bueno, como una chingada! ¿Qué pasó? Porqué se escamaron?" *Well, then, like a fuck. What happened? What scared them?*

"Bueno." Ben squints his eyes, trying to remember. "Se escamaron…Se escamaron." *They got scared…They got scared.* He turns to Juan.

Juan rolls his eyes. "No me digas que no te acuerdas." *Don't tell me you don't remember.*

"Oh, sí! Ahora sí se me está viniendo a la mente." *Oh yeah, now it's coming to me.* He clears his throat. "Bueno, dijeron que el Gato, no se movía como humano. Era como un fantasma…y no se le miraba cara. O que no tenía cara. Dicen los cherifes de aquí que parecía que algo oscuro lo cubría como una ilusión y que dió un grito muy feo, algo así. Yo no sé. Que los perros persiguieron el olor del Gato. Y sabían que era el hombre que mató a los dos chotas. Pero cuando apareció lejos de ellos y de repente bien cerca, los perros perdieron la razón y se fueron corriendo por todos rumbos llorando de susto. Pero, oí también, que los caballos se asustaron tanto, como que se volvieron locos, que aventaron a los Rangers y cherifes y se fueron corriendo por el bosque." *Well, they said that el Gato did not move like a human. He was like a phantom...and you couldn't see his face. Or he didn't have a face. The sheriffs from here said that it seemed like something dark covered him like an illusion, and he let out a very scary scream. Something like that. I don't know for sure. The dogs tracked the odor of el Gato. And they knew it was the same man who killed the two cops. But when he appeared far from them, then suddenly very close, the dogs went berserk and fled in all directions, crying of fright too. But I also heard that the horses got so scared, they went crazy and bucked off the rangers and sheriffs and fled through the woods.* Ben takes a swig of his beer in the silence of the humming truck. "Dicen que los caballos andaban con tanto miedo que se topaban contra árboles en su desesperación para huirse de ahí." *They said the horses were so scared that they were running into trees in their desperation to get away from there.* Ben turns to Juan, who is openmouthed with drool hanging from his lower lip. He closes it, and wiping his mouth with the sleeve of his jacket, takes a huge drink.

"Cabrón." *Damn.* Juan stares straight ahead. "Y ¿Qué chingaus es eso, compadre?" *And what the hell is that, compadre?*

"Pues yo he oído que hay cierta gente que todavía sabe los secretos de nuestros antepasados." *Well, I've heard that there are still some of our people that know the sacred arts of our past.* He takes a swig. "Y ese poder que conocen es nomás para gente de hembra fina. Nomás ellos pueden aprender esos secretos antiguos." *And that power that they know is only for people of fine lineage. Only they can learn those ancient secrets.* He nods his head. "Pues, sí. Yo he visto cosas en mi vida que nunca he podido explicar. Y esas leyendas, siempre han estado al centro de eso." *Well, yes. I've seen some things in my life that I've never been able to explain. And those legends have always been at the center of it.*

casa de luto

Fifteen

Casa de luto
House in mourning

A dark figure floats across the lawn of Don Pablito's house and comes to hide behind some bushes outside his window in the windy night.

It's late and all the lights are out except for an eerie glow emanating from the curandero's altar room.

A phantom consciousness investigates the dark, quiet interior of the tiny home.

Slowly, like an ant crawling across the wall, the intelligence inspects the grateful, smiling faces of the photos and memorabilia on the living room wall. Bullet holes have pierced some photos like a brutal force.

In the altar room the eerie glow blends with the warm radiance of a few lit candles. The candlelight flickers on the powerful presence of the santos studded on the walls. They seem to look down with unconditional love on a soundly sleeping Don Pablito curled up on his couch.

Outside, Elias' house is a cold dark shell…The wind whips through the trees above it.

In the darkness Luna stares at her ceiling, lying motionless in her bed at the mercy of the noisy bar down the street. A ranchera pours out its grief into the night.

Flasher blades slicing through the varrio, squad cars and ambulances zoom by on the street below, creating dancing patterns of red, blue, and yellow on Luna's ceiling.

Luna lies in a soft trance.

In the other bedroom across the hallway, Consuelo tosses and turns. She stares at the framed photo of her late husband on the dresser and worries. 'Ay. Algo está pasando. ¿Qué carga esta muchacha? Es algo serio.' *Ay. Something is happening. What is this girl carrying? It's something serious.* She remembers that Estrella also spoke to her yesterday…Luna is worrying about someone. Does she love him? If so, he must be the only man she has ever shown any deep emotion about. A la mejor he is a vato associated with the recent gang violence. Like so many others, he must have disappeared like a plume of smoke. If only her father was here. Especially right now. She glances once again at Jesus' photo. She sighs and her mind wanders.

They often argued at the beginning of their relationship.

He wanted to be a cop and she didn't want to live with that threat to her family. She had vivid nightmares of him dying in the line of duty. The soul knows. He had filled out the application without consulting with her.

Driving down the highway they argued viciously, their arms so animated they attracted the attention of a cop. He pulled them over. He approached their vehicle and Jesus rolled down his window.

"Is everything all right?" he asked the pair.

"Yes, officer, it's just that this woman drives me up the wall with her nagging." Jesus gives Consuelo a hateful look.

"I see. Can I see your driver's license?"

Jesus reaches into his back pocket and comes up empty. 'Good day for it.' He sighs defeat. "Officer, you're not gonna believe this, but I left it in my other pants because I was arguing with this woman!"

Consuelo leans forward to the cop. "No, it's because he doesn't have one."

"What?" Jesus rolls his eyes, hanging on to reason by a thread.

"Officer, don't listen to her."

"Well then, can I see your auto registration?"

Jesus thinks for a second and nods. "It's also in my other pants. They're both in my wallet."

"He's lying, officer. He doesn't have that either." Consuelo bats her eyelashes.

"I told you to keep your big...be quiet!" Jesus squirms with anger.

The cop puts his hands on the window frame and leans in past Jesus to Consuelo. "Ma'am, does he always talk to you like this?"

Consuelo stares straight ahead. "No, only when he's drunk."

Pulling the sheet up to her chin, she grins in the dark. It was a dreamy marriage. She could never have imagined love like this existed, for her kids and him. Then came the affair. That's a hurt she can never get over. He was a good man and a perfect father. But in his line of work, reality becomes distorted and even perverse. You are bombarded with the ugly side of life every day.

Seven years and he had refused to stop seeing her. He had loved somebody else. The only way for her to forgive was to become the unforgiven. So she looked for someone else too. Foolish revenge.

One night Jesus woke up sobbing uncontrollably. Consuelo and even the girls were startled from their sleep. He later told Consuelo he had a nightmare that he was...drowning the girls. "How can my mind be so cruel?" he had asked. After that night Consuelo knew death was coming. There was something out there in those streets that scared her. She felt that a premonition was soon to be fulfilled.

The morning of the day that he died, they both had decided once and for all that splitting up was the best thing for the family's sanity. She wonders what his last thoughts were when he needed the strength of his familia. According to Fischer, as he lay there bleeding to death, Jesus had tried to talk. Only blood came out of his mouth.

Years later, when Luna was old enough to date, Consuelo noticed that her daughter found herself unable to get close to anybody. Even today. The trauma to her innocent heart had been deep. She would build a concrete wall around her where the delicate love of a mate could never take root.

Except for someone who came out of nowhere. A love born on the edge of hell.

The light night drizzle sprays several cars waiting at a light at Brazos

los muertos cruise the varrio streets

and Laredo in the heart of the west side. The screeching tires of a black '59 Chevy Impala round the corner and zoom right through the red light, nearly causing an approaching vehicle to crash into the corner of La Gloria, a classic '30s-style hacienda-like ballroom steeped thick in Weso history.

Mosco, Brujo, and Tripa are crammed in the back seat. Two are sporting their black paños low on their brows. Brujo wears a dark wool cap pulled down around his ears and eyes. Bad-Boy is driving. A dreamy west side rola, "Vestida de Blanco" by Los Fabulosos Cuatro, pours out of the stereo and soothes the moment as they pass around a fat joint butt on its way out.

In the front passenger, Diablo, with his maddogs and flipped black cap, glances out the open window impatiently. "We ain't copped any lana tonight. We need some grasa para las guías!" *Grease for the gears.*

Tripa is still wearing the same jacket with the bullet hole and blood caked around it from the Guadalupe Bridge shooting. "Chinga, Mero, todos los chavalos se han agüitado gacho. No han hecho nada de desmadre." *Fuck, Main Man, all the chavalos have lost their nerve. They haven't pulled any fuckups.*

Crammed in the middle, Mosco lights up with an idea. "Ey, I know what. Let's cruise by my ex-old-lady's house. My suegros have a brand new stereo in the back bedroom. Nobody sleeps there." He shrugs. "She said she wanted me back."

The vatos exchange hopeful glances. "Simón, pero don't make it so easy." One of the vatos.

Looking stupid with his battered, swollen eye, Brujo is cautious. "I don't know, ése, your suegra is dangerous. I'd rather get caught and killed by Diablo than her any night!"

Roaring laughter.

They drive a few blocks and snake down a dark alley. About the middle of the callejón they stop. Bad-Boy turns the radio down.

Peering past Tripa and a five-foot chainlink fence, Mosco checks the dark, modest, but well-kept three-bedroom home. Only a bright light glowing at the top corner of the roof lights the area. His eyes half-lit and puffing on the joint butt, Mosco is feeling goofy. "They always leave a window open. They think they're in Alamo Heights. Tee-hee."

Brujo whispers loudly to Mosco, "Cállate el hocico!" He is more nervous than ever. "You'll wake up the pinche varrio dogs!"

They cut the engine off. Bad-Boy opens the door and leans forward, pulling on the back of his seat to let Mosco out. Mosco clumsily crawls over Brujo, jabbing his tender, swollen eye with an elbow.

Brujo throws his head back and winces with unbearable pain. "Baboso! Ahhh!!" He struggles to keep it to a whisper as he squirms with agony, shoving Mosco past him with a boot.

Mosco lands outside the driver's side door. He gets up with muddy khakis and works his way behind and around the Impala by Diablo. He does a comical chuco-surfer stance. "I'll be cruising back with the rack, Jefe," he blurts out.

"Cállate el hocico!" Loud whispers.

He slithers over the chainlink fence and tiptoes across the nice lawn like Sylvester sneaking up to Tweety's cage.

Arriving at a back room, he picks a window. He glances back at his homies and grins Chinese-style, bringing his index finger to his lips. "Shhh."

He unhinges the screen carefully.

In the other yards around him, a dozen dogs suddenly start barking. With his open mouth, Mosco looks around for a second.

Suddenly a pail of hot, steaming water comes splashing out of the open window, drenching his upper body. For a stunned moment Mosco freezes, his eyes wide open in excruciating pain. He wants to yell, but nothing comes out.

The vatos are openmouthed, watching the wispy trails of hot steam rise up from his upper torso like exorcised souls leaving the body.

"Ahhh, aaahhh!" He starts to shift back into gear. Looking around, he tears back to the Impala with his arms up in the air like a renegade lobster who just cheated a boiling death.

From the Impala his homies yell, "¡Aguila!" *Watch out!*

As he clears the house, Mosco glances back and catches a glimpse of his suegra slapping open the back screen door with a shiny butcher knife in her hand. She glares at him half-crazed.

Fear grips him and he leaps over the fence, only to get his exposed boxers hooked on it.

"Aguila!" the vatos yell.

Dangling, Mosco pushes against the fence while his suegra starts walking quickly down the steps. Wildeyed and whimpering, he yanks and tears his chones right off, leaving them blowing in the breeze on the fencepost. He lands in the mud. As Diablo opens the door to him he jumps up, only to bump his head against the door and fall back again on his ass.

Yelping with subdued cackles, his homies yell again. "Allí viene!" *She's coming!*

Wild with terror and not wanting to waste a millisecond to look behind him, Mosco leaps in through the open window. Tripa and Brujo struggle weakly to pull him in. The Impala tears ass down the alley filled with the pack of demented hyenas limp with hysterical laughter.

Nazul ponders the rain falling on the tall magnolia trees on the riverwalk below his window. Hundreds of Christmas lights flicker and reflect on the river.

'Joey, Oralia, all your dreams are on their way.' He struggles with their memory.

Nazul exists in a dark void as he stares at the Christmas revelers down on the riverwalk. He takes a deep breath. 'Luna…' Casting his gaze downwards, he shakes his head. 'Yo creo que no se va a hacer.' *I don't think it's going to happen.*

Restless sleep. Lying on the floor on the Indian blanket, Nazul tosses and turns. He sweats, engulfed in a pesadilla. *Waking dream.*

In his dream, movement and sound are distorted. Time creeps at a strained pace as he climbs through a huge glass window into a long, hazy, '40s-style room that eludes his focus. As he settles into the surroundings, he finds that the wind is blowing. Pieces of paper are flying through the room, which is lit up by a smashed lamp on the hardwood floor. A huge oval Aztec rug covers the center of the floor. He catches glimpses of rooftops outside between the spaces of curtains blowing around hypnotically. Is he high up? He looks down behind him and sees a pair of beams from a car's headlights cruising by in a slow, lethargic motion about seven stories below. He's in the casino building.

A woman's moan makes him turn his attention back to the endless interior, to the red, heavy curtains twirling in the wind and casting eerie shadows across the walls and ceiling.

He tries to focus on a female figure lying on a black leather couch across the room. Her face is obscured by her dark hair blowing around her face. His heart aches for her…But why?…With a fleeting attention span he struggles to concentrate on her features.

'Luna?'

la bomba

Nazul tries to walk over to her, his steps feeling forced and cumbersome. As he crosses the long, barren room, he walks in front of an oval mirror, the only décor on the wall, and sees his reflection.

Dark maddogs, chuco brim, and dark topcoat flowing in the constant stream of air. He's el Pachuco.

Luna's moan distracts him again and he approaches her, concerned.

Leaning down to her, he comes to rest on one knee. "¿Luna? ¿Qué te pasó?" As if spoken by another entity, his voice seems far away and deep in a well. Close by, an open door slaps open and shut from the force of the wind.

"Luna!" Getting more worried now, he holds her cold hand. "¿Qué te pasó? Who was here?"

Breathless, she can barely mouth the words, "La—la—boomm—mm—baaa…"

As suddenly as the message sinks in, a white flash followed by a thunderous force blows them both out a huge window. A shard of flying glass pierces his right hand, and the deafening power stuns his senses, leaving him with a sharp ringing in his head.

Nazul is startled from his sleep. Breathless, sweating, he sits up. '¿Qué chingaus?' *What the hell?*

He holds his head in his hands, troubled. He slowly lies back down. He can still feel her presence.

Don Pablito crosses his mind.

"Sueño mensajero…" He covers his face with his hands in resignation. "Otra ves." *Not again.*

"These problems are a little harder. So if you aren't sure of the answer, research it, don't guess. Guessing is the cheap way out." Luna strolls down the narrow aisles of her class. "Today is Saturday, so you get extra points for coming in and showing initiative. These are keys that unlock the doors of success. Are you willing to really work for what you want? This is the challenge."

Toward the back of the class, Silent opens his folder. A piece of paper folded into a triangle falls out. He looks around. Everybody's busy working, and Luna has strolled back to her desk.

He unfolds it. Inside is a written message along with a small ink drawing of a black cat's eye. 'El Gato Negro has targeted you for termination. ¡Wáchate!'

Silent looks around again. Everybody's still engrossed in their work.

Osito glances at him and motions with his eyes to his jacket pocket. Silent nods. He understands.

Luna stands up. "All right, class. Time's up. Bring all your work up to my desk and you can take a break. No sugar with your food."

As the class breaks up, Osito and Silent cross paths. Osito sneaks something to Silent which he quickly hides in his jacket.

The class pours out into the eating area. They start helping themselves to guacamole tacos and fruit in takeout bags and boxes on the long tables. Señoras in the varrio constantly prepare food for them and bring it to the center. They sit down to eat and talk.

Silent is sitting next to Osito and Payaso. Suddenly, across the table from him, Azteca-Boy stands up dramatically and pulls out a red plastic water gun, aiming it at Silent.

Silent is trucha and quickly ducks down as squirts of water shoot over his head. He pulls out a lime green plastic water gun from his jacket and shoots back at Azteca-Boy under the table, wetting his crotch good.

The whole class bursts out with excitement at the attempted hit, yelling, "El Gato Negro strikes again!"

Sitting at her desk, on the phone, Luna is startled, but then smiles when she sees what the excitement is about. She tolerates this game. Teenagers need to show off, to test their skills at being independent and always alert—a good reaction mode in their volatile surroundings. They need to have dramatic fun without hurting anyone. Luna laughs with them.

Except for a dreamy polka in the background, the dimly lit art studio is quiet. A lone silhouhette works feverishly in front of a huge canvas.

The five-by-five-foot face of Pachuco overwhelms Chico. Snaking around his tapita and maddogs, the jumper cables seem to have a life of their own. The flashes from the sparks light up the image, imprinting negative Xs or crosses across his face. Chico applies brushstrokes loaded with wet cobalt-violet oil paint.

Blocks away, Diablo stands in front of a smoky mirror in the dim bedroom of the ganghouse. Shirtless, his muscular, wiry body is a visual record of his vida loca. Puckered, healed bullet holes pepper his torso, punctuated by the numerous cicatrices up and down his back and front. Outside, night is falling. Deep in thought, Diablo is studying something, or someone, in himself. All is quiet except for a strange sound. The mirror reflects a ruca squirming behind him, passed out on the bed, snoring, her bare ass sticking out of the thick blanket. Diablo lowers his head with a weight in his heart.

"Si no cuida a la Chata, me la voy a llevar!" *If you don't take care of Chata, I'm gonna take her away!* Diablo seethes with anger at his tecata mom.

"Pos ¡llévatela! ¡Cómo una chingada! Así no tengo que darle de tragar. ¡Así puedo comprar más chiva!" *Well take her! Like a fuck! That way I don't have to feed her. That way I can buy more scag!* A rail-thin hag of a woman curses back with hatred.

"Ahora que 'Apá está en la pinta usted nomás anda de puta. Ni sabe de ella. ¡Vieja descarada!" *Now that Dad is in prison, you're just whoring around. You don't even know she exists. Shameless hag!* Diablo had just gotten out of el rancho. He went home to see if he still had a few things to collect. Pulling a flaking one-by-six off the wall of the tattered shack, he grabs his hidden .44 and sticks it in the belt of his worn-out navy blue work pants. He lifts up an old, soiled mattress and grabs two rounds and sticks them in his pocket. "¿Pa' qué nos dió vida? Nomás para hacernos sufrir. Yo me voy a llevar a Chata a la verga de aquí. Nunca nos va a volver a ver. ¿Me oyes? ¡Nunca!" *Why did you bring us into this world? Just to make us suffer. I'm taking Chata the fuck away from here. You're never gonna see us again. Do you hear me? Never!*

"Qué bueno. ¡Váyanse mucho a la chingada!" *Good. Go to fucking hell!* The hag draws a huge gulp from a cuarto de bironga. She digs through a butt-infested ashtray and finds one with a hit left. She lights it up with a kitchen match and starts coughing with hacks.

With a sickly, groggy, malnourished eight-year-old girl in dirty Nike workout pants and black sweatshirt on his arm, Diablo slams the door on her face.

"Me importa verga si es de María. Yo tengo que hacer esta feria." *I don't give a fuck if it's María's. I have to take this money.* Diablo grabs an ounce of coke and and stuffs it in a paper bag. "El ni sabía que ese buey que mojé tenía esta carga. El nomás me dijo que lo enterrara." *He didn't even know that idiot I wet had this on him. He just told me to bury him.* Cracking open his sawed-off, he slides two cartridges into the chambers. Through deep, dark maddogs he glances at his homie. "Si fuera él, hiciera lo mismo." *If it was him, he'd do the same.* "Diablo, María se da cuenta de todo. Tú sabes eso. Carnal, cuando estabas en la pinta, los jales cambiaron." *Diablo, María finds out about everything. You know that. Carnal, when you were in the can, things changed.* His homie puffs on a joint and sips on an Old Milwaukee, trying to keep warm. He rubs his hands. "Y ya no se emparejan nomás con los vatos como antes. Estos pistoleros hoy, les importa verga de la familia." *They don't square off only with vatos like they used to. These gunhands today don't give a fuck about family.*

Diablo stops his hurried slapping of cartridges into his sawed-off and stares at him. "María controla estos babosos. El nunca se ha hecho culo!" *María controls these idiots. He has never turned ass!*

"Carnal, ¿Cómo te puedo hacer entender? María anda bién entrado con la chiva. El vato ya ni sabe de esos puñatas." *How can I make you understand? María is in deep with the scag. He doesn't know shit about those assholes anymore.* He tries to warm his frigid hands on a single lit vela sitting on a crate turned into a coffee table. He searches his jacket pocket, pulls out three rounds, and hands them to Diablo.

"Yo siempre lo he respaldado, y todas las mojadas que hice por él lo hice porque los culeros lo merecieron. No por la coca. Pero por andar matando a pinches chavalitos en sus camas con sus culero drivebys. Me pagan o no, ellos saben que yo vengo a colectar. El sabe de que chingaus soy yo. Y yo nunca le he pidido madre. Dile tú que controle a esos pinches huerquillos culeros hasta que me empareje con él!" *I've always backed him up. And all the hits I did for him I did because the punks deserved it. Not for the coke. But for killing damn kids in their beds with their chickenshit drive-bys. Whether they pay me or not, they know I'm coming to collect. He knows what the fuck I'm about. And I've never asked him for shit. Tell him to control those punks 'til I square off with him!* Diablo stuffs the ounce into the inside of his jacket, grabs his sawed-off, and heads for the door. He turns to his homie, then glances at his little sister lying motionless on the old mattress in the corner of the small room. Bullet holes riddle the walls and broken furniture litters the dark interior. A pale blue string of Christmas lights sways in front of the cracked window, providing the only light aside from the vela. The cold wind is whipping through, chilling the bones.

"Chucho, si algo me pasa a mí, te encargo a mi carnalita. Tiene algo grave y tengo que llevarla a este curandero en Puebla. No dejes que nada le pase a ella. ¿Trucha?" *Chucho, if something happens to me, I entrust my little sister to you. She's got something serious and I have to take her to this curandero in Puebla. Don't let anything happen to her. Cool?*

Chucho nods back. He wraps himself tightly in his Salvation Army jacket, shivering. "Nomás no te dilates tanto. Bust the deal y ponle en chinga pa'trás. ¿De aquella?" *Just don't take too long. Bust the deal and head back. All right?* Diablo nods yes, chingón, then disappears out the beat-to-shit door, slamming it behind him.

"Okay tough guy, bend over. Let's see if you're still a virgin… Mmmm-hmm. Captain! This one's clean. Send in the next one. Okay, bad hombre, into the cell." A naked Diablo steps in and the cell door is slammed shut.

"Officer, my sister is dying on the west side. I need to get her to a doctor. She's only eight years old," Diablo pleads through the bars, trying hard not to lose his cool. Diablo knows these cops are just waiting for him to give them a hard time so they'll have a better excuse to take turns giving him a death beating. Or hang him in his cell, then say he committed suicide. What poor Chicano family is going to prove them wrong? He seethes inside, feeling totally useless. Any hint of a way out and he would take it. Most of these culeros are soulless parodies of human beings anyway. A choice between them and his sister, he wouldn't think twice.

The cop doesn't even look up as he fills out the paperwork. "Yeah, yeah. My mother's dying on the north side. She's already seen a doctor…and it's killing her."

"Chinga, ruco. This is no bullshit. I'm begging you!" He can't remember ever begging or saying please to anyone. He feels like tearing apart everything in this concrete box.

"Sorry, killer. You're gonna be in here for a while."

A vato in his twenties, covered with viaje tats, is escorted by two jail guards into a twenty-by-thirty-foot cell packed with restless vatos. He steps in and has no room to do anything but lean his small, rolled-up mattress against the corner where he came in and sit on it.

As soon as the jail guards slam the iron door, Diablo rushes over to him. "Chino! ¿Mi carnalita? ¿Cómo está?" *Chino! My little sister?*

How is she? When he hangs his head to him, Diablo grabs him by the hair. "¡Dime!" *Tell me!*

Tears start to well up in Chino's eyes. Grief or fear for his life. He swallows hard and closes his eyes with agony. He nods his head with the dire news. "Carnal…se murió." *Carnal…she died.*

"¡Esa no es la verdad! ¡Vale más que no sea!" *That's not the truth! It better not be!* Diablo grabs him by his jail-issue shirt and pulls him up to eye level against the bars. He breathes murderously. "Quiero saber todo. ¿Cómo chingaus murio?" *I wanna know everything. How did she die?* Chino can't bear his fierce stare. He could easily be next. He hangs his head and nods.

"¡¡Dime!!"

The cage is crammed with mostly Raza and a few blacks. Not one white face can be seen in the smelly cell. Two filthy toilets sit against the graffiti-covered cement wall in plain view. Flanking every available space, vatos lie around them, clocking the intense conversation.

"Y Chucho?" Diablo demands.

"Diablo, mira, yo no tuve nada que ver con eso. Me tienes que creer." *Diablo, look, I didn't have anything to do with that. You have to believe me.* Diablo's scowl is like death about to snatch your last breath. Chino swallows hard again, praying for mercy under his breath. "A Chucho…también." *Chucho…too.* He can't endure Diablo's glare. He covers his eyes with his trembling hands. "Lo mataron esa misma noche." *They killed him that same night.*

"¿Quién?"

"Los pinches pistoleros de María. Andan como pendejos matando a cualquier pinche jale que se les atraviesa." *María's gunhands. They're going around like idiots killing everything that crosses their path.* He nods his head.

"¡María me la va a pagar!" *María is gonna pay!* Diablo grabs a black dude sitting by his feet and throws him across the cell on top of the vato-covered floor.

Chino puts his hands up in defense. He looks away. "A María… también…lo mataron." *María…also…they killed him.*

"Lo mataron, lo mataron! ¿Quién chingaus?" *They killed him, they killed him! Who the fuck?*

"Chucho." He rubs his hands over his head nervously, trying to make sure he doesn't leave out any detail important to Diablo. "Dos pinches pistoleros de María llegaron ahí donde estaba tu carnalita y

Chucho y nomás empezaron a tirotear todo! A tu carnalita la mataron, los babosos." *Two of María's damn gunhands went there where your little sister and Chucho were and just shot up the whole place. They killed your little sister, the idiots.* He wrings his hands. "Y luego Chucho, bién herido, los mató a los dos y fue por María." *And then Chucho, badly injured, killed them both and went for María.* "Chingadamadre!" Diablo's rage makes those close to him coil away with fear, climbing on top of each other or stumbling away. "¿Y Lalo? ¿Por qué chingaus no hace nada?" *And Lalo? Why the fuck doesn't he do anything?*

"A Lalo lo asesinaron bién gacho por la General McMullen." *Lalo got assassinated really bad on General McMullen.* He drops his head in grief. "He got ambushed by cinco huerquillos culeros and they had a pinche shootout en la four-lane. Se los metió a todos." *He fucked 'em all.* He looks Diablo in the face. "Carnal, nomás te tengo puras noticias de muerte. Como estás torcido, no hay miedo en las calles. Solo que hacen loquelesdalachingadagana!" *Carnal, all I have is news of death. Since you're slammed, there's no fear in the streets. So they do whatever the fuck they want.*

"¿Y tú? ¿Cómo salistes de esto tan enterito?" *And you? How did you come out of this so nicely intact?* Diablo's eyes are like microscopic radar, scanning ruthlessly for any hairline cracks in the smooth surface. Most vatos, it's not what they say, but what they leave out that means anything.

"¿Entero? Me plomearon todo el cantón de mi jefita. Ayer la enterré. Ya iba a esquitarme con esos culeros cuando me paró la pinche ley. Y hallaron todas las armas en mi carrucha. Pero aquí estoy, Jefe, a sus ordenes." *Intact? They shot up my mom's house. I buried her yesterday. I was gonna square the deal with those chickenshits when I got stopped by the cops. And they found the weapons in my car. But here I am, Chief, at your service.*

"'¿A mis ordenes?' …Mataron a mi carnalita!" *'At my service?' … They killed my little sister!* Diablo yells in his face.

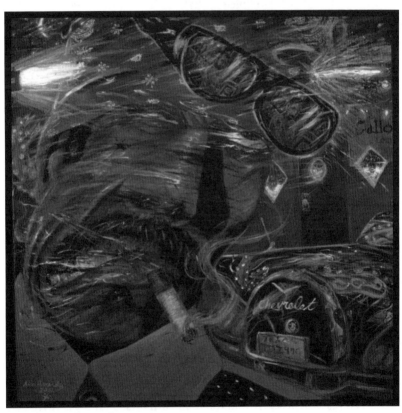

un balazo en la noche

Sixteen

Diablo viene a cobrar
Diablo comes to collect

"Dicen que ya salió Diablo y que viene a cobrar." *They say Diablo is out and he's coming to collect.* From the night a breathless seventeen-year-old vato rushes into a fortress-like rock house that is being re-modeled in the deep west side. He folds up his slick silver cell phone. Eight younger punks decked out in gang regalia lie around on a thick black leather couch. They are watching *Blood In...Blood Out,* a varrio cult film. They spring from their comfortable positions and grab their armas. Red paños and sporty jackets and caps with workout pants are the fashion. AKs, Uzis, .44s, and boxes of ammunition are scattered throughout the gaudily decorated room.

They cut the lights and nervously look out into the deep, dark cold through the curtains and iron-barred windows.

"¡Qué venga el culero!" *Let the chickenshit come!* One vato tries out his newfound huevos to hide his fear.

"¡Aquí estamos y no los vamos!" *Here we are and here we'll stay!* Another slaps a clip into his AK and takes a huge gulp from his tallboy. "I've been waiting for this culero. They say he's all chingón. Let's see if he can dance with my prieta." He slaps a sloppy kiss on his weapon. All are coked up and a little drunk.

The cold sweat trickles down the backs of the vatos' necks as they silently cover their positions in the dark room.

They wait. And wait.

Silence. Nerve-wracking silence. Time seems to have almost stopped its march.

"No va a venir," someone whispers. *He ain't coming.* "Sabe bién que hemos hecho desmadre y medio." *He knows we've done fuckups and a half.* He chuckles. "He knows we go all the way." With a cigarette dangling from his mouth, the chavalo clinks open his lighter and rolls out the flame. The blast of a .44 Magnum and the bloodcurdling slap of lead against bone make him disappear from view in a streaking liquid flash of crimson.

For a long minute, nothing but heartbeats in a vacuum. Then the oldest vato crawls across the wet floor to the window where the red curtains have started to twirl with the chilly, wet night breeze from the bullet hole.

As he looks up at the moonlight slicing through the gaps in the curtains, he sees the barrel of an AK coming through. Blinding, deafening, red hot lead sprays the room with flesh-ripping muerte.

Cinco vatos are mowed down like weeds. The cushy leather couch turns into a cloud of snowy plumes, slapping hard against a counter and continuing a sickening trajectory as it is ripped to shreds up the bullet-riddled wall.

The oldest vato by the window sticks his .44 out the opening and unloads seventeen blasts. The AK falls, a few rounds tearing chunks of rock and shattering the eaves on the outside of the house.

Silence once again. The smell of gunpowder, blood, guts, piss, and shit invades the senses inside the room.

The vato sneaks a lightning peek out the window. Again. He doesn't see shit. That doesn't mean a thing. He can sense him out there. A soulless force. Your last breath its relentless purpose.

In the other rooms he hears crying and blasts from a sawed-off.

His heart starts to choke his throat. The flashes of light from an Uzi around the corner slice the darkness for split seconds...as the stillness...once again returns.

Moments later, the slapping of the screen door leading to the backyard. Then yells and blasts. Someone begging...for something. Begging.

The blast of a .44 brings the deafening quiet back.

'What's it like, dying? I'm not ready! It can't be. How did it get this far? Diosito mío, por favor, perdóname, perdóname por mis pecados. Virgencita, Virgen—'

There's a light knock on his door.

Diablo takes his time answering. "¿Qué chingaus quieres?" *What the fuck do you want?*

"Mero, soy yo, Sapo. We're ready to go hit those two little punks."

Diablo doesn't budge from the mirror. With a pair of tweezers he plucks some hairs from his moustache. "¿Quién?" he answers, annoyed.

"Osito and Payaso. Their esquina kicked our homies' asses ayer."

"Y ¿quién chingaus era esa esquina?" *And who was their backup?*

Sapo: "Some pachuco."

"¿Y el señor del 7-Eleven? ¿Esas piedras eran cometas? ¿Necesitan una calculadora? Tapados." *And the señor from the 7-Eleven? Were those rocks comets? Do you need a calculator? Dumbasses.*

"Pos ¿Entonces? ¿Qué vamos a hacer? Es Saturday night." *Well, then. What are we gonna do? It's Saturday night.* Sapo sighs at flaking paint and graffiti on the beat-to-shit door, waiting for an answer.

"Andamos de malas..." *We're on a bad roll...* Diablo turns away from the mirror. "Esta noche, tengo ganas de chanclear, no balacear. Vamos al Andaluz a pisotear el cucaracho. ¡Alístense!" *Tonight, I feel like dancing, not shooting. Let's go to el Andaluz to smash the roach. Get ready!*

Sapo turns to leave, then remembers something. "Pero, Mero, no hay lana." *But, Main Man, there's no coin.*

"¿Qué?"

"Our clicka hasn't been able to score. They're fucking afraid of the dark," Sapo answers cautiously.

Diablo opens the door and sticks his head out. "¿Por qué chingaus?" *Why the fuck?*

"El—el Pachuco no—" Before Sapo can finish, Diablo slams the door in his face.

"¡Chingadamadre!"

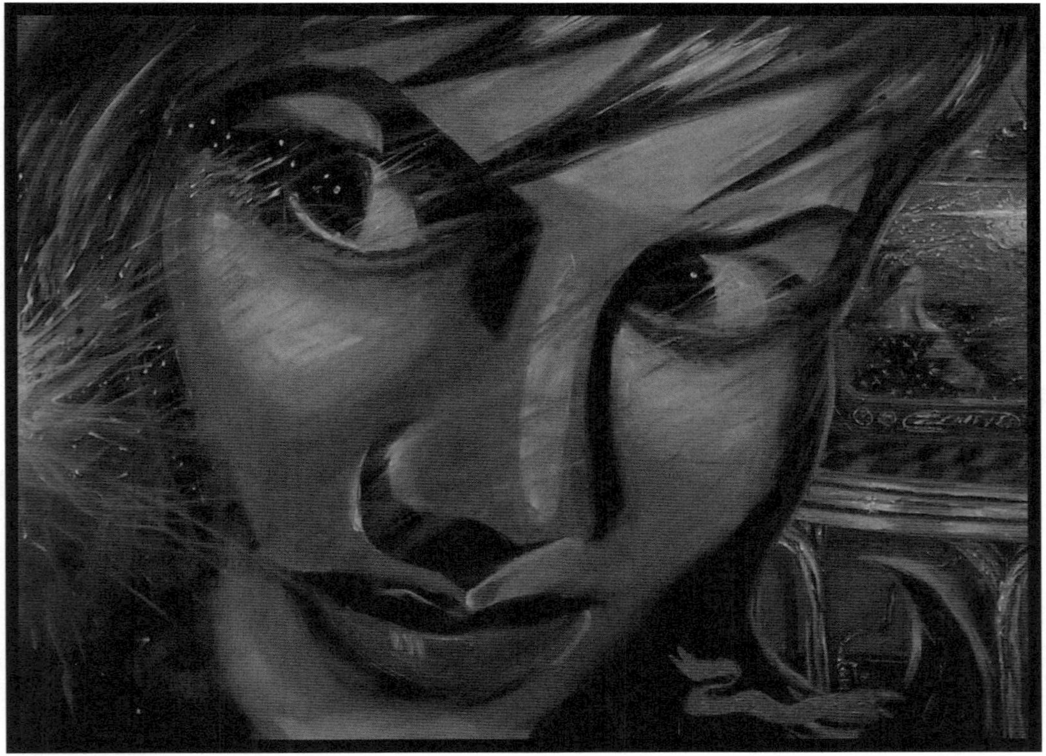

los invisibles

Seventeen

La noche tiene ojos
The night has eyes

The old, fluorescent, flaking sign of Ray's Drive-In glows pink and aqua in the misty night, twenty feet high. Down below, the place is booming. A classic malt shop, hamburger joint, and Mexican food drive-in, Ray's is as much a part of the west side as Raza. The parked cars getting curbside service, a few classic lowriders with their rearview mirrors decorated with rosaries and fuzzy dice, are a tradition at Ray's.

This is the night out for entire families. Kids chomp on burgers and sip on shakes while teenagers, doodied-up, check out the place for love. A young boy, accompanied by his little sister and his beat-up guitar, works the cars; they play polkas and rancheras like professionals for a dollar.

Ray's is also a classic hielería where older señores love to hang out and talk about old times.

Snatches of conversation here and there give rise to the notion that Pachuco is the man of the hour.

A group of older señores sits at a picnic table sipping on beers. A stocky señor who looks like Pancho Villa has the floor. "Pues, ya era tiempo. Cada en cuando, aparece de nuevo el Gato y repone la fe en lo bueno. Yo oí que esa leyenda del Gato Negro originó en la costa. Es un castigo que manda el Señor. Decía la gente que puede matar con el puro susto." *Well, it's about time. Now and then he reappears and restores our faith in good things. I heard that the legend of el Gato originated on the coast. It's a punishment sent by the Man. They say he can kill you with terror.* All are listening attentively.

"Yo oí que ni las balas lo detenían." *I heard that not even the bullets can stop him.* Another varrio-distinguished señor adds his two cents.

A third, wearing a cool burnt sienna tapita, looks at the families enjoying themselves. "Pues yo te digo un jale. Era tiempo que la Raza saliera de sus casas con la familia después del oscurecer en Saturday night sin tener cuidado de las gangas, que casí no se han visto, ¿no?" *Well, I'll tell you one thing, it's about time that la Raza came out of their homes after dark on a Saturday night without fearing the gangs, which really haven't been seen lately, right?*

"Verdad que no, compadre." *Isn't that true, compadre?* Another señor checks out the patrons.

Inside a nearby car, two teenage girls sit in the back seat, their parents up front, and trade secrets. "Chango said that the reason he can't be killed is because he's already dead."

"No way, wow, that's creepy. Well, I heard that a girl in the varrio is *in love* with him."

"Who?"

"That's what *I* said, but I couldn't get anybody to tell me. Pero, qué romántico, ¿no?"

"Wow, can you imagine what a varrio novela that would make?"

"But is he really dead? Must be alive if she's in love with him. If that's true."

Inside an old Buick, a ten-year-old chavalo leans in from the back seat as he talks to his parents in the front. "Daddy, when can I get a black chuco hat?"

His dad is turning up the news on the radio. "Wait, m'ijo, listen. They're talking about him right now."

"Sources tell us that a gang attacked the officers while they were trying to arrest two drunken drivers. The heroic efforts of the officers, who defended themselves without even resorting to using their weapons, is what really saved their lives. Police are on the lookout for these hoodlums, and now more officers have been assigned to the west side."

"Is that true, Daddy?"

"Not even, m'ijo. Gangs never attack the police for trying to arrest some drunk drivers. And when it comes to Raza, cops *always* resort to using their weapons."

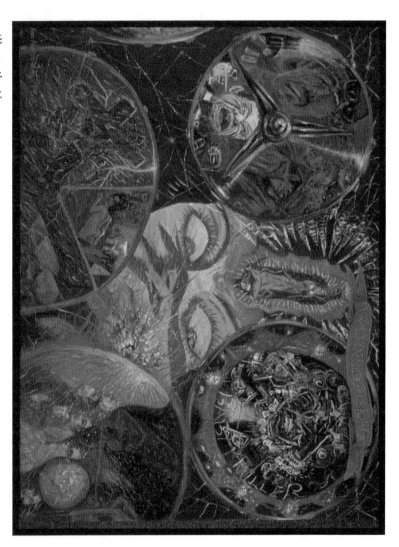

Eighteen

Vrillante ilusión
Brilliant illusion

Headlights approach dreamily and glide past. Slick streets. Raindrops streak red past the back lights and fall through the smoke trails of the muffler, mixing with the soot and oil on the rain-drenched, crater-covered calle. Nightfall brings out the varrio dogs that run wild in packs. Their numbers, hunger, and boldness seem to increase as they desperately search for food in the storm. Gangas de perros gnashing their teeth for any scraps. With growls and fierce yelps they leap at each other in murderous fury, a fleeting blur of iridescent silhouettes. As the '59 Impala rolls near, they scatter into the streams of rainwater flowing over the street. Estas calles where reputations for vatos are viajes for survival.

Los Muertos cruise. A constant breeze adds mystery to the inky night. A cunning pack of predators, they look for a weakness in the varrio's armor.

Bad-Boy is driving. Diablo rides shotgun, thoughtful, silent. In the back seat, Brujo, Huevo, and Killer are discussing how they're going to hijack a tourist. "Un pinche turista es chichón." *A damn tourist is like sucking titty.* "Simón, pero los pinches juras méndigos te ponen una putiza bien dada!" *Yeah, but the fucking cops give you a damn death beating!*

Bad-Boy is flipping through the radio stations. He comes across some hyper white dude yelling his ass off into the mic: "Bring a friend! Bring the family! Bring the whole neighborhood!"

Bad-Boy's face quickly sours. "Cállatelhocico." With a roll of his thumb he shuts him up. He comes across a white chick advertising a restaurant.

"Here at Billy Bob's teneemoos una comeedo muy bueeno para tú. Y see ablauw esp—"

"Ya, babosa." Sourly, Bad-Boy glances at Diablo. "Y se burlan 'cause we can't speak English." He flips through the channels.

Huevo smirks. "No que no querían que habláramos en español. Estos culeros ahora hasta se muerden la lengua para vendernos su pinche mugrero." *And they didn't want us to speak Spanish. These chickenshits now even bite their tongues to sell you their damn junk.* He glances at Brujo coldly.

Brujo nods chingón, his eyes half-lit from the toque. "Por la feria, hasta te acarician los huevos, los putos." *For the skins, they'll even caress your balls, the whores.*

Cruising down Brazos they glide by the cleaners and see something. The owner, a viejito, is trying to start his stalled '95 Lincoln Continental. Leaning into the open mouth of the slick carro, he fiddles with the terminals of the battery. In the driver's seat his viejita is on the ignition.

Bad-Boy: "Eyyy, maybe they need a jump."

As soon as the viejitos see the vatos, they quickly retreat into the safety of the cleaners, which is like a jailhouse, with wrought iron bars guarding every opening.

"¡Chingau! Are we that ugly?" Huevo pulls out his .44 and rifles through his dark, torn jacket for another clip. Nodding malías, he sideswipes a glance at Killer. "That's okay. I've been hurt before."

Brujo glances at the lanky vato next to him with a scar across his tacuache face. "Those viejitos are loaded. Last time me and Killer hit 'em, we took their payroll."

Killer looks behind him through the back window as the Impala rolls around the desolate corner. "No es nada. Like picking a chato off my culo." They come to a stop in the darkness between two abandoned buildings. Lights cut off.

Bad-Boy checks the clip to his automatic. In the back seat, Huevo does the same with his TEC-9.

Oblivious to the slick pace of experienced but edgy nerves around him, Diablo stares out the windshield with his darkness.

Both vatos step out and make their way back to the cleaners for an ambush. The Impala, still purring calentado, waits in the dark around the corner.

Killer: "To get some lana chingona, you need a vato frío like Bad-Boy. He'll cut off their lenguas if they don't say thank you."

Carcajadas. Diablo, still silent except for a clink from his heavy metal lighter, fires a Lucky in the dreamy stillness. He blows his cool indifference out the window.

A Weso rola by the Royal Jesters streams out of the car stereo. Diablo cleans his fingernails with his fila while the frajo sends plumes of blue grey curving around his black maddogs. With his cold-blooded menace he turns his gaze sideways to the vatos behind him. "Ya estoy hasta la riata con estos pinches huerquillos que todavía ni les salen pelos en el culo, y ya andan que quieren rolar con los Muertos." *I'm up to my prick with these little punks that haven't even grown hairs on their asses, and they're already nagging that they want to roll with los Muertos.* He heaves deep down and spits out the crack in the window.

Killer: "Simón, aquel Jetas tiene un pinche daycare center de pistoleros." *Yeah, Jetas has a damn daycare center full of gunfighters.* He grins. "Pinches huerquillos están todos puñatas. Usan los trama'os acá entre las pinches rodillas y cuando cargan los cohetes," he runs two fingers beside his thighs on each side, "andan los pinches cañones arrastrando por el zoquete." *Damn punks are all dumbasses. They wear their pants hanging around their knees, and when they carry their hammers, the damn barrels drag through the mud.* They laugh, but Diablo, his frajo glowing red, just pulls a tirada.

Brujo is leery, looking behind him at the darkness, the pain of the rock still fresh in his mind and swollen eye. "Oyes, Mero, you don't think we'll get hit by rocks again, do you?"

Diablo ignores his pathetic whining and just keeps cleaning under his nails. He's wondering why esta gente take so much shit from vatos like him. Where does that patience come from? ¿De dónde chingaus? *From where the fuck?* They sweat and even bleed, most of them, just to endure another day of suffering. Diablo never knew this grace growing up. Grace…to do what is right first, before any personal gain. ¿Qué chingaus es eso? And all their pláticas concerning the pursuit of their ambitions are always laced with: "Pero, no lo hice por el *dinero, compadre*…No fue por el dinero…" *But I didn't do it for the* money, *compadre…It wasn't for the money.* Hmph. They know that ill-gotten gain is evil and blackens the soul, preparándola for its doom.

He glances up at a lightning bolt that cracks the void of Prussian blue. The thunder explodes, goes rumbling with roaring convulsions across the deep slumber of the night. Diablo nods his head slightly, grooving also to la rola. He thinks, 'Y no les *ganas.* En toda la pinche vida, no les ganas. *And you can't beat them. In your whole fucking life, you can't beat them.* Where do you get the huevos to be like them? Any baboso can lose his razón in a second and be cagándose all over himself the next. Yo estoy wachando que así es. *I'm realizing that that's the way it is.* It takes a real human being to stay silent to pendejadas and continue su compromiso at hand. That's what that means. Simón.' He nods to the night. 'Simón.'

Diablo's parents and grandparents were all ganga. The drugs ripped their souls of any grace. All that is good and gracious was never seen here. Nothing but backstabbing and deceit.

Except for Chata.

His preciosa eight-year-old sister would look up at him as he was getting ready for a mojada.

"José Angel, ¿te van a matar?" *José Angel, are they going to kill you?* Her dark, penetrating eyes were the only holy thing in his world.

She was his reina. He would kill or die for her in the deafening flash of a hair trigger. Torn with guilt he has never gotten used to, he exhales hard. "No, 'jita. No pienses así." *No, baby. Don't think like that.* The cops wouldn't even investigate the killings between gang members. To them it was all good riddance. Let them kill each other off all they want. Nobody gave a damn about their lives.

Her dark hair always seemed to be unkempt. Like the unmade bed her jefita never even changed the sheets on, until he would trash them and steal some new ones.

"Pero a tío Gerardo lo mataron con una pistola como ésa." *But Uncle Gerardo got killed by a gun like that one.*

"Sí, porque el no se llevó su backup. Cuando no." *Yeah, 'cause he didn't take his backup. Of course.* He sits on the bed beside her and tickles her tummy 'til she giggles. He varrio-frowns a glance to her chest. "¿Qué es esto?" *What's this?* As she looks down, following Diablo's questioning finger, he flips his curled digit up at her nose, playfully. "Ahh! Te triquié otra vez!" *I tricked you again!* He grabs her by the ribs and scoots his hands up under her little armpits for more giggles. Taking a huge breath to swallow his concern for her, he leans in. "Chata, when I get back, ¡te voy a traer un surprise bien chignon!" *I'm bringing you a badass surprise!* She brushes her hair away from her chubby cheeks with her hands. Her big brown eyes light up when he talks about a surprise. Not a day would go by that he didn't plot some way to get her out of this drug-infested world and get her a decent home. Every day.

'That day is coming soon, Chata. Ya verás.' *You'll see.*

"José Angel, tú sabes como agacharte pa'que no te peguen las balas?" *José Angel, do you know how to duck down so the bullets won't hit you?* Her frayed innocence should turn any vato loco around to a decent life. To live like a real human being. A vida of honor and grace, como la gente de este varrio. *Like the people of this varrio.*

But it didn't. And he lost her to las calles. Las pinches calles. Now, no le importaba verga. *Now, he didn't give a fuck.*

'Que se mueran todos con ella. La vida no vale nada.' *Let them all die with her. Life is worth nothing.*

Maybe that's why he had survived such hopeless odds. He wasn't gonna make it easy for any baboso with only pendejadas on his chompa. In a morbid way it was amusing to him to make vatos del mero atole tread the edge of no return. To make some huerquillo hocicón crumble at his feet from the paralyzing fear of el Diablo.

Diablo had been shot at so many times that he could gauge a pistolero's nerves and know what he was capable of doing with his cohete. Uno que otro were Apaches machin. Simón. He knew damn well the deep, paralyzing assault of lead slapping into flesh. His flesh. Diablo was a battle-hardened soldado de las calles. *Soldier of the streets.* Now the most notorious of the streets considered him 'el Rey de las siete muertes.' *The King of the seven deaths.* A living legend who was already rotting in the grave. That's how many times he had survived the certainty of getting torn to shreds. After siete you had to be protected by la Virgen. Either that, or you must be el Diablo. And to someone like him, la Virgen ya se le había desaparecido. *The Virgin had already disappeared.* So he must be el Diablo. Either way, they would never mess with one or the other. All he wanted was to go out a balaceadas, to mow down anyone he suspected could be responsible for Chata's death.

He was also willing to check out frío for the next vato chingón of the varrio. Alguién con huevos de Villa or Emiliano. *Someone with balls like Villa or Emiliano.* So far nobody had filled those tramados. *Pants.* Porque buscaban nomás la feria or a cheap thrill and didn't give a shit how they got it. Or they were envious of his name, and then it was about their pinche egos. Diablo didn't give a shit about his starmatón status. A él le importaba verga. *It didn't mean shit to him.* He did what he wanted and mowed down whoever got in his way. Las calles sensed that, adding glory and mystique to his corrido.

Solo que la muerte was never merciful in catching up to José Angel. El Diablo. Porque este corrido, tan castigado…parece que no tiene fin. *Because this ballad, so tortured…seems to have no end.*

Brujo breaks his moment. "Oyes, Mero. ¿Quién chingaus será ese vato? Tiene buena puntería, ¿no?" *Hey, Mero. Who the fuck could that vato be? He's got good aim, right?*

Killer: "Man, I've heard some shit about that Azteca."

"But who the fuck is he? None of our clicka have been able to find out. All they know is he had stars around him." Brujo acts semiconscious, rolling his good eye back in his head.

Diablo holds up his nine-incher. "Yo te digo un jale. Nadie," he breathes in hard, "takes a shit en el Weso without chuco-dancing with my fila."

Brujo, looking stupid with his swollen right eye, grins with his two front teeth missing. "When you get through with that joto, va a parecer colador." *He's gonna look like a strainer.*

Killer and Brujo laugh and snort. Diablo ignores them as he slides to the driver's side.

Around the corner, outside the cleaners, Bad-Boy and Huevo hide in the shadows of a dumpster. They are tired of waiting in the freezing cold for the viejitos to come back out.

Bad-Boy steps out of the shadows. Peering through the window of the cleaners, he can make out the viejito on the phone, looking out with caution. Bad-Boy grits his teeth at Huevo. "That pinche viejillo is never coming out! He's prob'ly calling la jura. Let's drill 'em!" Without another thought they strut to the locked iron door and blast the latch off.

Before they can kick the door open, a roof air vent comes crashing down from above, causing a commotion as it bounces off Huevo's face and head. Huevo falls back with a grunt. Bad-Boy jumps away, looks up, and opens fire into the dark.

There's a tap on his shoulder. He turns with his automatic and comes face to face with a fist. He stumbles back. Swaying, he looks down at the pavement as it comes up and smashes into his face.

Suddenly the viejito comes blasting his way out of the cleaners with an AK-47 assualt rifle. His legs are shaking. His eyes wince, barely able to control the power. He peppers the immediate area, including his own car and the closed bakery across the street, with golf-ball-sized holes. For a few seconds the place is like the night Diablo was ambushed by seven vatos outside Pato's Lounge. Pieces of glass, stucco, and fiery metal fly off in all directions.

Shaking nervously, the viejito catches his breath and stands at the doorway, surveying the damage. Spraying radiator water and smoking, his glass-covered, shot-to-shit Lincoln looks like it just made a beer-run through la Tripa.

He scampers back inside.

Around the corner in the Impala, Killer and Brujo are staring at each other, openmouthed.

"¡Cabrón!" Brujo sucks up his drool and wipes his mouth with his sleeve. "Those viejitos musta forgot to say thank you, chinga!"

Diablo hits the gears. But before he can peel off, the back window explodes. A potato-sized rock hits Brujo on the back of the head, causing his face to go bouncing off the back of the front seat. His battered eye takes the full impact. The rock tumbles into his lap as he winces in unbearable agony, trying to see. "Ah-ah." He freaks. "A rock!" He brushes it off his lap like it's burning a hole through him.

Diablo jumps out of the Impala and empties his .44 at the darkness with flashes of thunderous claps.

After the smoke clears, the immediate area is suddenly and eerily quiet...The cold, wet wind gusts around the condemned buildings, swooping up leaves and pieces of paper and hurling them high into the night. Tattered aluminum roofs clank and creak restlessly nearby.

Inside, with Brujo whimpering and moaning, Killer peers out the window into the darkness like a scared ten-year-old. "El, el Pa-Pa-chu-co..."

Squad car sirens wail nearby.

Diablo jumps back in and the Impala tears ass around the corner. The headlights shine on Bad-Boy, crawling on his hands and knees in the middle of the street. Diablo rolls up and opens the front passenger door. "Where's Huevo?"

Bad-Boy glances behind him, trying to remember. He grabs his head. "Lo hicieron migas! *They made scrambled eggs out of him!* Let's get the fuck outta here!" Stumbling to his feet, he dives in.

The Impala's tires scream as it peels off and fishtails into the darkness.

Amid the groans of Brujo beside him, Killer leans in to Bad-Boy from the back seat. "Bad-Boy, what the fuck happened? Was it the Pachuco?"

Semiconscious, Bad-Boy holds his head in his hands. "Vato, all I saw was stars..."

Back at the cleaners, with flashers on and sirens blaring, two squad cars screech to a halt.

Shaking uncontrollably, the viejito manages to quickly hide his AK just as four white cops step out to the war-torn scene with their shotguns ready and question marks on their faces.

Timidly holding hands, the viejitos come out to meet them.

One cop scratches his head. "What the hell happened here?" He looks at the smoking Lincoln, whose car alarm is just now starting to sluggishly whoop and beep, then back at the viejitos.

They just shrug their shoulders innocently.

Nearby, another cop checks out the smoking AK shells on the pavement. "Damn! If Rambo gets his laundry done here, they musta pissed him off!"

"You don't know what happened?"

The timid viejitos just stare back blankly.

As they look around in the dark, they find Huevo moaning on the ground with a bloody face.

"What about him? Say something!"

Finally, the viejita speaks up. "We, we didn't *did* it."

The cops look at each other and burst out laughing to the scornful look from the viejita.

Outside the ganghouse, los Muertos are discussing the encounter. Sapo is working himself up into a lather. "I bet you mis nalgas that was the same vato who turned Demon into a drooling baby with that rock!" His breath and smoke turning to steam in the freezing air, he hands a fired-up joint to a paranoid, trembling Brujo, who has trouble holding his fingers still long enough to grab it.

Meco: "Simón. He's been kicking our asses all over el Weso! Our backup wants to sign up with him, or just spit-shine his calcos."

Sapo pulls his pants ridiculously low around his hips and thighs and tightens them with his belt. "It's gacho, but it's true. Ya andan juntando aluminum cans para comprarles toys a los chavalones del varrio pa' Chreesmas, chinga." *Fuck, they're already collecting aluminum cans to buy toys for the kids in the varrio for Christmas.*

Brujo nurses his sorry excuse of an eye. "Chinga, doesn't sound too puñata."

Diablo is pissed. He takes a deep, final drag and flicks the cigarette butt down hard into the street, causing sparks of ashes to fly off around the vatos' feet. "¡Cállenselhocico! Bola de viejas chismosas. Nomás andan con sus pinches cuentos. Vámonos a la verga al chancleo!" *Shut the fuck up! Bunch of gossiping hags. That's all you do is go around with your fucking gossip. Let's go smash the roach!*

El Patio Andaluz is a classic varrio nightclub dating back to the '60s. It is situated on the top floor of a two-story brick building on el varrio side of Commerce Street, a three-lane main artery which crosses the city east to west. On the top floor, an outdoor patio with picnic tables and wrought iron chairs overlooks the popular intersection below. The pounding bass from a live band pours out to the surrounding varrio.

The place is packed as los Muertos burst in like they pay rent. The beat sends shudders across the long room as Sunny and the Sunliners pour out one of their original hits.

Sunny's gruff voice awakens sweet memories from a world stashed dreamily away in a more magical antepasado. *Yesteryear.*

A mirrored disco ball rotates over the middle of the room, spraying little dots of light everywhere. Vatos and rucas, all dressed down in Weso fashion. Beehives, pink lip gloss, and loud eye makeup are everywhere. Most of the vatos are chucoed down. There are some white tourists who wandered in from downtown to catch what is really unique about San Anto. Not the Alamo. Raza.

Exchanging serious glances, a group of vatos malosos in khakis and white T-shirts, their arms covered with pinta viaje tats, take notice of los Muertos.

Diablo watches a sumptuous vixen walk by in tight, powder blue slacks that cling to her 'ooh-ooh, gacho-gacho,' Jennifer Lopez ass. As she makes her way to the dance floor with some Hispanic executive, all the vatos groan with lust, drooling over her luscious culo as it strolls by. She glances back and gives Diablo a caliente look, checking him up and down. The couple starts dancing as Sunny belts out the classic tune.

Diablo gulps down his beer like agua, and dropping the bottle to the floor, walks straight to the dance floor and grabs the masota away. He pulls her tight and starts to groove. Her partner grabs Diablo's shoulder. He almost stumbles back when he gets a full frame of Diablo's maddogs inches from his face. "Thanks," he mutters and dissolves into nothing. The vatos look around, puzzled.

Diablo grabs the Chicana and grinds into her pelvis as the vatos around him moan and groan. "Tú nomás andas castigando con esas nalgotas, masota." *You're just going around torturing vatos with those luscious cheeks, masota.* Diablo breathes into her ear through her thick black locks as she smiles and purrs.

Wanting to get his babe alone for some serious pichonazos, Diablo grabs her and heads out the side door to the patio.

The patio is dark and deserted, with rained-on wrought iron chairs and tables waiting for warmer weather. The thick, heavy, metal-covered door slams shut behind them, muffling the loud, driving rhythms as they step outside.

Now alone, Diablo plants a smoldering pichonazo on his babe as they lock in a hot embrace against the cold wet stucco wall. He runs his fingers down the crack of her ass, nestled tightly against the smooth material of her slacks.

The muffled bass thumps against the closed door. He hears the blast of music behind him as the heavy door opens and shuts. But with his masota grinding against his awakening monster, he doesn't bother to look.

Suddenly a beer bottle comes crashing down gacho on the back of Diablo's head. Pieces of flying glass and cold beer rain down on their passion. Startled, his ruca jumps away with a scream.

With a coronary-causing scowl on his face, Diablo slowly turns around. He clocks four vatos wearing matching white T-shirts and khakis with confused looks trained on his head.

The wet, swaying palm trees tower over them, and the cold wind gusts through, carrying the thumping rhythms into the night as they take their killer stance. The ruca wants to leave, but the vatos block her escape.

One tall, lean, rugged vato in the center pops his fila in Diablo's face and stares him down. "You killed my carnalito in front of Prieto's, Diablo. Eso no se queda así." *That's not the way it's gonna stay.* He breathes out the words with controlled rage.

The other three pop their filas.

Unmoved by the threat, Diablo pops his own out of nowhere in a split second, holding it up to eye level. His dark eyes seem to swallow all life around him as he trains them on the vato. His deep, gruff voice breathes out, "Tu carnalito tuvo huevos, Chacon." *Your little brother had balls, Chacon.* He nods his head chingón. "Fue una lástima." *It was a pity.* The dark surroundings shadow his fierce persona.

Just then another blast of music distracts them for a split second. Two white yuppie dudes in their twenties, wearing Gap sweaters and jeans with sensible loafers, peek out, sizing up the situation. Cautiously, they step outside, shutting the door behind them. More curious than scared, they keep their distance, eagerly hoping the vatos will let them play spectators.

Sighing with disgust, the khaki vatos roll their eyes. "Pinches tourists, they're everywhere, chinga."

Aztec warriors start their dance of death to the giddy witness of the yuppies and a nail-biting ruca.

Chacon is trained on Diablo. "Tu pinche lástima nunca se acaba. Me importa verga si rifas con huevos del Copetón. Nadie se chinga a mi familia y *sigue resollando.*" *You're fucking pity never ends. I don't give a prick if you throw down with balls of el Copeton. Nobody fucks my family and* keeps breathing. The vato macizo gets deathly close to Diablo's face, not showing a hint of caution for Diablo's explosive desmadre.

Known for his chuco cool, Diablo grants him a few more seconds of life.

"Me la rayo." *I swear it.* Fila swaying, Chacon backs away and looks for the opening.

Staring him down, Diablo cocks his head back like the vato chingón that he is, waiting for the inevitable moment. "Pos, ¿me vas a matar con el hocico?" *Well, are you gonna kill me with your fucking mouth?*

As if on cue, they all lunge at Diablo, stabbing and slicing. He jumps back, jabbing at their arms with his fila. He plunges the fila into a vato's neck. The vato runs to the door, slams into it, and squirms to the ground with wheezing sounds.

Now huddled together, the ruca screams and the tourists gasp in excitement.

Stepping around and kicking aside a couple of iron chairs, Diablo positions himself with the edge of the balcony behind him. He takes a quick glance down to the street below. A vato lunges at him and Diablo sidesteps, shoving him over the balcony.

A bone-cracking thud and the ruca's and tourists' screams echo in the back of Diablo's mind as he fights for his life with blades slicing him throughout his body.

He takes a gash on his chest. In return, Diablo plunges his fila into a vato's stomach for a split second. The target doubles over and collapses just as Chacon cuts Diablo's neck. Grabbing an iron chair, Diablo swats him, sending him stumbling back.

Diablo gets a handful of blood where he checks his neck. With rage he closes in on the dizzy vato and lunges in with his fila.

With perfect timing, Chacon jumps away and sends a roundhouse jab at Diablo's head.

The fila stabs his skull, breaking the blade.

As the confused vato checks his fila, Diablo grabs him by the hair and flings him over the side.

Chacon manages to grab on to the ten-foot-long neon sign. 'Patio Andaluz.' He hangs on as bulbs and wires burst under his weight. He short-circuits the lights, blacking out the whole place.

The ruca, in shock and gasping for breath, runs into the club. The two tourists are frozen in place as they clock Diablo wiping the blood off his fila on his pant leg and slipping it into his pocket in the windy night.

With his deadly maddogs he looks up at them and grins just enough to let his gold front tooth catch a glint of light.

The tourists suddenly get a dose of warmth running through their pampered bodies and smile back.

Diablo puts up his hand for a high five.

One tourist catches the groove and lumbers to Diablo, palm up and ready. Nervous and overreacting with enthusiasm, he slaps his palm forward with gusto. "Yeah! Duuuude!" At the last second Diablo puts his hand down, and the tourist goes stumbling past him and over the balcony with a yelp as his friend watches in horror. "Stanley!"

As Diablo reaches the door, a chile-relleno-shaped security guard, trying to figure out what killed the lights, peers out. He sees the stabbed vato lying on the ground. Before he can react, Diablo grabs him by the shirt and thrusts him past, shutting the door behind him. As Diablo enters, shots ring out as two more vatos in khakis aim, but they hit the metal door and blast the disco ball into pieces as Diablo zigzags through the club.

Screams, darkness, flashes of sparks. Los Muertos head for the door as the crowd, lighters lit, kisses the floor around them. Their silhouettes streak like giant spiders across the walls and ceiling.

By the front door another security guard fumbles with his piece. Before he can use it, Meco and Bad-Boy tackle him to the ground. With painful grunts, farts, and snorts from the guard, all three go tumbling down the long staircase, crashing through the front door and out onto the sidewalk. Diablo, Killer, and Sapo follow right behind them as they run out into the night.

Crawling around on all fours, the security guard looks for his gun on the sidewalk under the dim glow of the street lamp. Diablo trots by and kicks him in the ass, shoving him face-first into the concrete.

As they reach the corner, los Muertos almost trip on a vato lying on the sidewalk. Exposed wires crackle with electricity inches above him.

Sapo sniffs the air as they dash by. "Oyes, huele a barbacoa." *Hey, it smells like barbecue.* He chuckles. Above them, looking over the balcony and out the now-open windows of the club, the patrons have ringside seats to the action below. By now the two security guards have regrouped and fire at los Muertos as they jiggle and waddle around the corner.

In their breathless, wheezing zeal the guards trip over the smoking body of the khaki vato, barely visible in the dark, and stumble like idiots onto the sidewalk.

Los Muertos reach the Impala just as the security guards find their guns. They watch the vatos fire up the Impala and give chase again, only to trip once more on the body of the tourist. A gun goes off as they tumble to the sidewalk like bowling pins.

In the dark they crawl around again looking for their guns. The crowd above, limp with laughter, roars at their predicament.

Just then the Impala goes cruising by. Sapo hangs out the window and yells at the guards. "Par de marranos! We click to la rola, los Muertos, por 'onde pasamos, se tropiezan con los cuerpos. AAAYYYY-HA-HAAA!!" *You pair of pigs! We click to la rola, los Muertos, wherever we pass through, they trip over corpses.*

The crowd cheers them on and someone yells out: "¡QUÉ VIVAN LOS MUERTOS!" *LONG LIVE THE DEAD!*

los muertos burst out of el patio andaluz

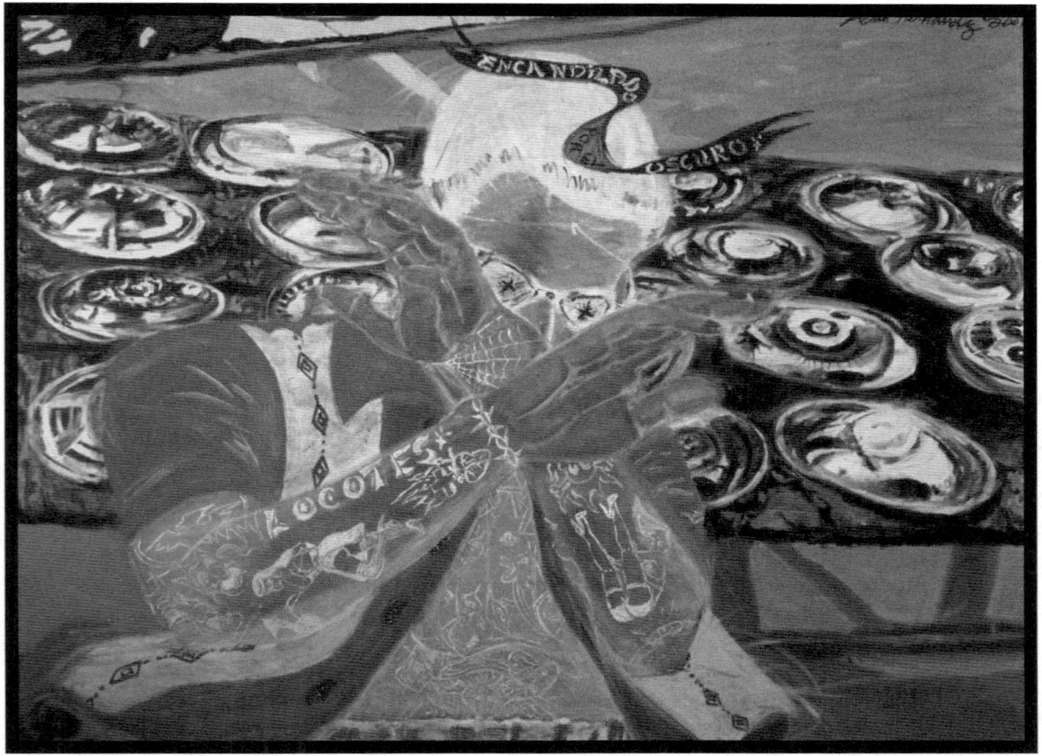

encandilado por el oscuro

Nineteen

Encandilado por el oscuro
Blinded by the darkness

It's Sunday morning. The sun streaks through the clouds in a vain effort to bring warmth to this cold and muggy day.

Mini flags flap in the wind on the hood of a sleek white limo escorted by two motorcycle cops as it races down Highway 281. It glides uninterrupted toward downtown San Anto.

Inside the Hilton Paseo del Rio Hotel, a group of news reporters has gathered around a podium with microphones and a small, select crowd.

The crowd applauds enthusiastically as a suit steps up to the mic.

"Today we have in our city a very distinguished guest, a giant in the communications and broadcasting field, and CEO of our national

news network, TNN. I'm honored to present to you Mr. Ed Turnip!"
More applause and cheers.

"Before he addresses you, Mr. Turnip has graciously given me the privilege to announce that he is here to personally donate fifteen million dollars to his alma mater, the prestigious Texas university, YU. I'm sure some of you heard the news. This is all going to happen… *tomorrow!*" Applause and cheers pour from the crowd.

Ed Turnip beams with pride at the Hispanic suit as he steps to the mic. "Thank you, Mayor."

One of the reporters is notably unenthused. Maria Rosales stands with dignity, confidence, and grace. The mayor eyes her nervously. Maria is the head newscaster for an independent TV station which doesn't dance from any political strings.

Mr. Turnip, with polished flair: "Thank you again, Mr. Mayor! Thank you San Antonio! Well, the mayor said it all! We will hold a ceremony tomorrow morning on the campus. Meanwhile, I'd like to enjoy your beautiful city, the riverwalk, and the Alamo."

Applause.

Roberta Roberts, a young, blond news reporter with heavy make-up, speaks up with her Texas drawl. "Mr. Turnip, what an amazing and generous individual you are! I also graduated from YU, and to show my appreciation, I will be more than happy to be your personal guide."

Laughter and applause.

An older, seasoned, male reporter: "Mr. Turnip, we know you came from a very enterprising and distinguished family. What advice do you have for students from, say, the upper middle class, who make up the majority at YU, but don't have the clout or connections for the really lucrative business deals?"

"Take my money and run!" Applause and laughter. "That is why I am here, to offer greater opportunities for less fortunate students who have what it takes, but need that extra lift from a friendly, helping hand. These are obstacles that are very real. And these are students I can really identify with."

Cheers and applause again.

Maria has stopped applauding altogether and speaks up, her voice cutting through the niceties. "What about students who can't even hope to go to college because of the pathetic education in our poor school districts?" Silence. "What about the student who, although he or she has had to grow up in a war zone plagued by the nation's worst poverty, still manages to get straight A's? Where is the friendly helping hand for them? I think these are the real obstacles at hand, don't you?"

The mayor cuts her off. "Ms. Rosales, is this the appropriate time for this? For your personal war on poverty?" He eyes the whirring cameras.

Mr. Turnip is speechless.

"Right now this city's poorest school districts, where Mexican Americans make up the majority, are run by colonized Hispanics. Their relentless agenda is to teach the gory glory of westward movement. Teachers who question the curriculum are silenced. The truth about our history, the children's history, is suppressed. The last thing on their minds is the well-being and competent education of those kids. It appears they have nobody to answer to. The state lets them police themselves. Now even the implementation of bilingual education is left up to each district. Where are our opinionated leaders?" The crowd is openmouthed and in a trance. "Nobody does anything. Our elected politicians waste no time in selling out poor people for a fast buck. One after the other. If a concerned parent requests a meeting with a principal, she is told to leave. If she protests, she is arrested by the police. Parents have also been threatened with the INS. All in perfect view, of course, of their kids. Can any of you here identify with this? I doubt it. These kids don't even feel safe in their learning environment. Why are you all patting each other on the back?"

Mayor Gus Garsa does a 180, deciding on a gentler approach. "Ahh, ah, Ms. Rosales, we will meet with you later and discuss this."

Maria ignores the mayor. "Let's focus on real obstacles and adversity in education. The majority of the population in this town is Mexican American. Most have had to live in economic and educational squalor. Would that qualify as adversity? But I guess you can't identify with someone like that either. Your friendly helping hand is for the slick white entrepreneur who can come here from anywhere and in no time have access to the best real estate and tax abatements this wonderful town has to offer."

"Ms. Rosales!" The mayor throws his hands up.

Mr. Turnip takes a deep sigh, urgently eyeing the mayor to do something. The crowd mumbles 'How dare she?' and 'The nerve of her.'

Maria ignores them. "What a pity that such celebrated men of vision can only see the petty whining of privileged America."

"Ms. Rosales, nobody is more committed to solving these problems than I am. My colleagues work tirelessly on these very real issues." The mayor is sweating.

"*Really.*" With a raised eyebrow she looks around the huge lobby at the frozen mannequins. "Sounds to me like you're polishing up for another election."

"That's it! This news conference is over!" The mayor is furious as he tries to escort his esteemed colleague away.

Mr. Turnip refuses to leave.

"Ms. Rosales, you have insulted a very distinguished man!"

Maria ignores his fury and stares down Mr. Turnip, who is glaring at her with anger. She looks at him as if he stepped in dog poo and the smell has reached her. Turning her back she walks off, defiantly twiddling her fingers adios.

As the mayor whispers apologies in Mr. Turnip's ear, Mr. Turnip ignores him, eyeing Maria as she and her cameraman walk away to the exit.

Mr. Turnip looks at the mayor as he sits down to console him. "I came here to give away millions and I feel like a total idiot!"

The crowd of reporters starts to disperse with its equipment.

"I'm really sorry." The mayor eyes Turnip nervously, unfolds his compact cellular, and starts punching numbers. "I'm gonna call her boss right now. She's gonna regret this, believe me." He pulls out his handkerchief and pats the sweat from his forehead. "Uh, hello, Ms. Payne? This is the mayor, Gus Garsa. Do you know what your reporter, Maria Rosales, just did?" Mr. Turnip stares straight ahead, thinking. "She publicly humiliated not just me, but Mr. Turnip. The communications giant, Mr. Turnip. I want her fired immediately!"

On the other end of the line, a worldly, attractive white woman in her early fifties, tall and lean with a light brown bob, leans back on her plush leather chair with her shoeless feet resting comfortably on her massive oak desk. Her brass nameplate reads 'Lila Payne.' Behind her, a panoramic view of the city skyline. "Mr. Mayor, Ms. Rosales is my best reporter. She speaks her mind. She is not my robot. And as you well know, this TV station is here to give a voice to the people. *Real* people, Mr. Garsa. I, I, Mayor," she winces from his verbal assault. "All right, I'll talk to her. But she has never apologized yet for anything she's said. Have a nice day," she sings as she hangs up. She leans back in her chair, her fingertips touching, and snickers mischievously.

la muerte de chuy

Twenty

Azteca Tire Shop

Osito and Payaso, dressed in their grungy, grey, grease-stained work uniforms, are busily dunking a huge, two-ton truck tire into a three-by-five-foot pan of dirty water, looking for the leak. Their asses point to the varrio street. Inside the walls of the tiny, grease-stained building of Azteca Tire Shop, a polka gurgles out of a cheap radio that sports a coat hanger for an antenna. Of course.

Out of nowhere the vatos hear a noisy engine. Before they can look, a wrecked bumper that looks like it rammed into a telephone pole rolls up to kiss their asses. They jump away.

With varrio frowns they look up at a clanking pile of junk that was once a car. Behind a cloud of muffler smoke, they see Pete in the driver's seat with his toothless, shit-eating grin.

"Aguila chavalones! That's how Santa Ana lost the war to Davy Crooket." He slaps the car door on the outside to them. "Wacha, ando castigando gacho with dis slut!"

Osito and Payaso are trying to adjust their vision to absorb the belching, smoking, '64 Nova in front of them. With mouths open they walk around it as Pete, unable to open his door because it is tied to the car with coat hangers, crawls out his window. Bullet holes riddle the once-classic body.

Osito shakes his head with disgust. The beat-to-shit Nova has, without a doubt, seen its share of killer parrandas, gangster shootouts, crippling car chases, and cracked windows and ripped seats from a pissed-off ruca. Duct tape seems to be the only adhesive holding the park lamps and headlights in place. With burning, watery eyes, their sour faces turn to Pete.

Pete challenges their perception. "¿Qué?" He brushes them off with a flick of his wrist. "Vat-vatos envidiosos!" *You're just envious.*

Shaking their heads, Osito and Payaso believe it, but yet can't believe it. Both doors seem to have been amputated and sewn back with coat hangers à la Frankenstein. As Pete follows them around, he trips on a pair of vise-grips sticking out of the rim, which hold one of only three lug nuts in place. He almost falls in the pan of dirty, cold water, but Osito catches him just in time.

Like a proud papá Pete surveys his carrucha, which is convulsing to stay lit. "Orale, you know you're jealous of my trucha-mobile."

Osito winces his watery eyes in the smoke as he gives Pete a disgusted frown. "Trucha es el vato que te lo vendió." *The slick one is the vato who sold it to you.*

Payaso is taking a disturbing liking to the taped-together, smoking bomb. "Is it fast?"

Pete looks down his nose at him. "Sheet, the payments are already tree monts behind."

Osito is having a hard time finding fresh air. "So you got a flat tire, or what?"

Pete grabs his huevos. "Chale, I gotta use the crepa."

Osito rolls his eyes. "Me lleva el tren." *I can't believe this shit.*

Pete runs inside the tiny building and opens the door to the three-by-four-foot restroom. Pete lets out an 'ahhhhh' as he tries not to pee on his shoes. On the walls, calenders of Aztecs with their passed-out rucas decorate the tire-smudged enclosure.

Outside, Payaso and Osito are dealing with Pete's latest consentida. *Favored one.*

Osito yells at Pete, twenty feet away, "Chinga, vato! Turn off this pinche factory!"

"Chale. It won't start again. The battery ain't wort a fuck."

"Me lleva el pinche tren." Osito rolls his eyes.

Like a byproduct of the killer smoke, a dirty, haggard-looking tecato and tecata emerge from the cloud. The ruca, her hair matted with what looks like dried-up puke on one side of it, is a skeleton. Tattoos on her frail arms fail to hide the track marks of a veteran junkie. The tecato, a dead-man-with-tattoos-walking, carries a football-size bundle wrapped in a dirty white cloth under his arm. Paranoid of even the tires lying around, they slither up to the vatos.

Osito sighs in defeat. "Me lleva —"

"Eyy, carnales." He rubs his dripping nose. "You vatos wanna buy a ham?" With filthy hands he holds out the bundle.

The vatos are perplexed.

Osito: "A, ¿Qué chingaus?"

Trembling, he holds it out to them and delicately unwraps it. "A honey-baked ham." The tecato rolls out the syllables with a dragged-out professional advertising voice as he peels off the moist layers.

He unwraps the prize and presents them with the Christmas ham. A ham some other tecato must've lost in a Tripa craps game. The out-of-place, homely looking delicacy seems like it's been through a parranda or two with them already. It looks like it's been sat on, wrestled over, and even a few sneaky bites have been taken out of it. The ruca looks around suspiciously like they're selling nuclear secrets to the Russians.

The tecato is eager to close the deal. "Gimme five bucks y es tuyo." *And it's yours.* He thrusts it into Osito's stomach.

Frowning, the vatos stand back, away from the smell of all three.

Just then Pete returns, fiddling with his verga and adjusting it back into place as he waddles back. He sees the offering. "¿Qué chingaus es eso?" He grimaces with a puzzled frown as he wipes his fingers on his pant legs.

The tecato sees his ticket. "A honey-baked ham. Orale, tres bolas."

"A pinche ham?" He digs in his pockets. "My jefita would like a pinche ham." He comes up with three wadded-up dollar bills. He pulls out one. "How about two? I need a bola for gas."

Sharply, the tecato grabs the feria and stuffs the ham into his stomach so quick that Pete fumbles it and the ham ends up tumbling to the dirty, oily gravel. The haggard pair disappears back into the toxic smoke.

Without a thought Pete picks it up and smells it. "Huele a verijas." *It smells like crotch.* He makes that sour puss face of his.

Osito: "Shit, it's probably got AIDS."

Haphazardly Pete wraps it up and throws it in his front seat. "Ah, I'll take it to my jefita anyway."

Their eyes watering, Osito and Payaso can't take the smoke any longer.

"Cabrón!" Payaso rubs his eyes on his shoulder, his hands covered with guck from the tires. "Apago ese pinche volcano!"

The Nova, shaking like a washing machine in the spin cycle, now starts making a clanking noise in the engine. Pete turns to the vatos with his varrio frown. "A la verga." *I'll be fucked.*

Osito rolls his eyes. "I bet the only thing that doesn't make a noise is the pinche horn."

The Nova finally belches its last gasp and dies.

"¡Chingadamadre!" Pete sighs and turns to Osito as the smoke clears. "You got cables?"

As the smoke blows away, Osito takes a deep, grateful breath. He nods. "Chale."

Pete: "Ey, you oughtta be glad I'm here. The Chit Maggots are out to wet you."

Payaso: "The Chit Maggots?"

"Simón. They're a punk clicka that do hits for los Muertos." Pete nods his head varrio-style. "Right now you vatos are hot!" He breathes in their faces, making them stand back with disgust.

Payaso: "Yeah, like we got a fucking choice."

Pete looks around suspiciously. "Right now they're trying to find out who your esquina is."

Osito: "Simón, so are *we*. We heard he's been kicking culos-culeros all over the varrio."

"Pos, wáchense." Pete leans in with this one. "I heard they're gonna do a drive-by on Los Vryosos Center."

Payaso: "¡Chinga! What's wrong with those babosos?"

Now that they can see farther than a foot, they clock three vatos walking by across the street. Two are wearing sensible lana for el Weso, with their Stacies, pleated khakis, three-quarter-sleeve lisas, and dark gafas. But one of them makes them do a double take. He's wearing gafas, but he's also wearing a ridiculous pair of bright, flow-ered Bermuda shorts that flap in the chilly breeze.

Bien-chingón, all three ignore the vatos as they strut by.

Osito grins as he yells out, "¡Ey! ¡Menso! ¿A quién le jambates esas cortinas?" *Ey! Idiot! Who did you steal those curtains from?*

The three vatos stop dead.

Payaso can't believe Osito. "What the hell are you doing?"

Osito just grins like he can handle himself.

Across the street the two chucos stare straight ahead, looking kill-er, while the vato in shorts turns with a deadly stare to Osito.

Payaso and Pete swallow a lump.

Dead serious, with his head cocked back, the vato stares Osito down through his gafas. "¿Qué pasó, culo?"

Osito hasn't lost his grin. "Que no estás en Hawaii, menso." *That you're not in Hawaii, dumbass.*

Payaso wants to slap Osito's face. "Shut up, man!"

The vato's homies now turn to Osito with death looks. The Bermuda takes off his gafas to Osito.

His knees shaking, Pete tries to talk sense to Osito. "Cálmala…"

It's too late. The three strut towards them with deadly purpose, ignoring the screeching brakes and honking horns of the traffic as they cross the two busy lanes of Zarzamora Street.

The Bermuda walks right up to Osito's nose. Osito doesn't budge.

The air is taut with tension.

Bermuda: "Who you calling a Hawaiian, culo?" He breathes heav-ily with murderous rage.

Osito is trying to keep from laughing at the confusion of Payaso and Pete.

"Anda fíjate en un charco." *Go look in a puddle.* Osito points with his chin to a puddle nearby without taking his stare off of him.

Payaso feels he has to stop this. "Man, Osito, shut up!" Nervously, he looks at the vatos. "He didn't mean it, está retardado." *He's re-tarded.*

Bermuda slowly turns to Payaso with a look that could cripple. "Tú cállate el hocico y súmete el mamón!" *Shut your trap and stuff your pacifier!*

Payaso freezes with fear. With wracked nerves, Pete is thinking about taking the ham to his jefita.

The Bermuda's homies now try to hold him back. One vato rubs his heart to try to soothe him. "Cálmate, Tres Muertes, it ain't worth it, ese."

But Tres is now shaking with rage. He reaches in his pocket and flips out a lock-blade knife. Payaso and Pete stand back.

Osito stands his ground. Grinning, he glances at the blade, then turns bien serious and shakes his head like it's already too late. "Yyyy, vato. Ya cruzates la última vida. Te la voy a sumir toda en el culo." *You've just crossed the last life. I'm gonna stick it all up your ass.*

Before Payaso and Pete can react, the vato grabs Osito by the front of his shirt and plunges the fila into his stomach.

Payaso gasps and Pete's eyes bulge out.

With spit rolling out of his mouth, Osito makes a death face. Clutching the blade, he falls to the gravel and rolls on his side. He gasps for air and starts to tremble violently. Payaso is frozen in disbelief.

"AAHHH!! Osito!" Pete throws himself down to Osito's side, fearing the worst. "Osito! No!" He slowly turns Osito over.

Suddenly Osito lunges at him with the blade, stabbing at him wildly, like *Psycho.*

Pete lets out a terrified shriek as he stumbles back, skipping like an idiot to avoid plunging butt-first into the pan of water. He falls, then crawls backwards on his ass.

To Payaso's amazement, the vatos and Osito burst out laughing at Pete's near-fatal experience.

It's only a rubber knife.

Payaso's heart is still trying to jump out of his chest. "Babosos."

The vatos laugh until they cry.

Pete gets up, feeling his ass for shit. Embarrased, he looks at the convulsing hyenas. "Pinches vatos, no tienen corazón." *Damn vatos, you have no heart.*

Out of nowhere a primer-grey '73 Monte Carlo rolls up to them with rap music blaring. Inside, three punk gangsters aim assorted fire-power out the windows at them. The vatos dive away for their lives.

Pete, already spooked, recklessly leaps away and lands in the pan of cold, dirty water. He comes up gasping from the miserable, grimy, wet cold.

The vatos in the Monte Carlo laugh at him. They were just bluffing.

Riding shotgun, one vato leans out to Osito. "Sleep good tonight, teddy bear."

They back up and peel away with their obnoxious music thumping.

Pete climbs out shivering. "Pi-pinches vat-tos."

campesino

Twenty-One

Mil años sin ti
A thousand years without you

The late Sunday morning misa lets out a crowd of mostly Raza from the San Fernando Cathedral in downtown San Anto.

In the middle of the crowd, holding their coats on their arms, Luna, Consuelo, y Estrella pull their veils off and fold them with care. Wincing in the light drizzle, they help each other put their coats back on.

Luna looks around at the gente as she helps Estrella. She does a double take and locks her gaze with a vato in the crowd for a split second before the people block her view. Her blood turns cold.

Her eyes search the crowd nervously. He's nowhere to be found. She swallows hard. She can't feel her face. Her heart starts beating faster, making it hard for her to catch her breath. She takes off aimlessly, leaving Consuelo and Estrella with confused looks. They try to follow her through the crowd but lose her.

Around the side of the church, they find Luna standing on the sidewalk of the narrow side street with her back to them.

"M'ija. ¿Qué pasó?"

Luna turns her watery gaze to her. "'Amá." She swallows hard. "I saw him."

"Who?" Her mother checks the immediate area for a clue. "Not... *him?* Is he the one you've been worried about?"

"Sí." Luna drops her head and cradles her stomach.

"Really?" Estrella looks around with awe.

It hurts Consuelo to see Luna in this state. She ponders the cracks in the pavement..."M'ija, sometimes we want to see someone *so bad* that we think we see them in a crowd. That happened to me with your father. For a moment I even thought it had all been a bad dream." She seeks out Luna's eyes, which are still cast downward.

Luna brings one hand to her face and rubs a tear away. "Ni lo conozco. ¿Por qué me siento así? Parece que he pasado mil años sin él." *I barely know him. Why do I feel this way? I feel like I've lived a thousand years without him.* The concrete monuments behind her loom, indifferent. Consuelo just stares at her with mouth open.

Luna's rare desperation is starting to make Estrella get teary-eyed. "Luny, I prayed that you would, that you could one day...see him again." She hugs her over her thick black coat and presses up against her neck. Consuelo joins their embrace.

"Ay m'ijita, que Dios te proteje el corazón." *Ay my daughter, may God protect your heart.* Consuelo's tears flow down her smooth olive cheeks.

A flock of noisy hurracas squawk and squeal as they fly overhead and float down to the naked pecan trees in the park across the street from the church. Luna's cloudy gaze follows their trajectory with little hope.

Back at the front steps of the church, holding her veil up to shield her face from the light drizzle, Maria Rosales slips on her smart black leather coat. She is accompanied by a Chicano couple, fiftiyish and well-dressed. The woman opens an umbrella.

Maria is looking around for someone. "Oyes. ¿Pa' dónde se fue Luna y su familia? Aquí andaban." *Where did Luna and her family go? They were just here.*

Her friends just shrug.

Maria checks her pager, then looks at the pair. "I'll have to skip the huevos rancheros at Dora's, guys. My boss is paging. Plus, I still have to edit my six o'clock. Tell Luna I'll catch up with her later, all right? Nos vemos." All three hug goodbye and part ways.

Sipping on a latte, Lila Payne is intently watching a news piece authored by Maria Rosales in the screen-filled communications room of AZTC, Azteca TV. On the screen, Maria Rosales is in the heart of the projects close to downtown on a chilly, damp afternoon.

"I'm Maria Rosales, coming to you from the San Juan Homes, where gang violence is increasingly threatening the lives of families and innocent children." As the camera follows her view, she looks beside her to a disheveled Chicana mother in her early thirties. "We have here a resident. Now, Ms. Rodriguez, you say that gang shoot-outs have occurred here in broad daylight, even by the playground where your own children play? That break-ins occur weekly?" She levels the mic to Ms. Rodriguez.

Ms. Rodriguez is a little embarrassed to be on TV, but she knows that it's something she has to do. She takes a deep breath and speaks up. "Si. A few days ago a teenager was shot ahí." She points to an area not even ten feet from the playground. She folds her arms in front of her chest to hide the moth-holes in her sweater. "Last week there were three shootings around here. Two other teenagers and a twelve-year-old girl were shot and stabbed. I've lived here for five years and it seems not a week goes by that we don't have to grab our kids and run."

"What about the police? Don't they patrol this area?"

Ms. Rodriguez gives her a puzzled look. "Police?" She looks around. "I never see *any* police around here. They only come *after* someone's been shot, and then they usually end up beating and arresting some hardworking parent who's fed up with the violence."

The camera pans a group of kids looking on a few feet away. "We are going to try to find the officers who are assigned to patrol this area. I'm sure there are police, somewhere, who are supposed to protect these citizens."

Picking their teeth with toothpicks, a couple of police officers, one white and one Hispanic, exit Los Reyes Mexican Restaurant on Laredo Street, near downtown, and stroll contentedly to their squad car. Close by, four other patrol cars are parked in a group.

With camera rolling and mic ready, Maria and her camerawoman approach the pair.

"Excuse me, officers, I'm Maria Rosales from Azteca TV. Are you two supposed to patrol the San Juan Homes?"

The pair looks at each other with guilty frowns. They know they're on.

The Hispanic cop's nametag reads 'Muñoz.' He speaks up. "Yes. Why?"

"Are you aware of all the violence that threatens the lives of the innocent children there? This year alone we have gotten reports of gang violence and drug dealer shootouts yards away from those poor families. There have been excessive robberies reported in the last month alone."

Milam, the white cop, throws his hands up. "Hey, we're supposed to be where we are. We can't be everywhere at once!"

Maria sees two more cops emerge from the restaurant. When they notice what's going on, they quickly make their way to their squad car. She turns her stern face on Milam and Muñoz. "Officers, how much time in the last six months, say, would you estimate you have spent inside Los Reyes? Just a ballpark figure, officer. I'm curious because I drive by here often and see up to six squad cars in the lot. It makes me wonder."

At this, officer Milam throws his hands up and leaves for the squad car. "Hey, I don't have to deal with this shit!"

Muñoz tries nervously to defend their actions. "Look, there is violence here. But we often have a hard time getting witnesses to come forward and give descriptions of the suspects."

"Well, that's why you were hired. To patrol those streets and get your own descriptions. Would you talk to the police if you knew there'd be retaliation on your kids' lives? Are you going to stand guard at these witnesses' houses if they do testify? When a concerned parent calls you for help, can you say that you respond with the same thorough investigation you would perform in, say, Alamo Heights?"

"Well, yes, I'd hope…" he fumbles with his words. "Look, what do you want us to do?"

"To do your job. The job you are paid to do. Protect the taxpayers. The children! We've heard of instances where you peace officers beat and kicked concerned fathers in the street, in front of their kids. These witnesses are supposed to look to you for protection. Do you think their children are going to grow up respecting authority?"

The camera rolls.

Muñoz is redfaced, pissed. "Lady, I don't know who—"

Maria puts her hand up to his face. "Maria Rosales, para servirle. *At your service.* Next time you do your job, the cameras might be rolling." She turns to her camerawoman. "Let's get our culos outta here."

Lila nods her head in disgust just as Maria walks in. "Those culeros."

In an adjoining office the phone rings, and Lila walks off to answer it. "Hello? This is Lila. Who? Oh, Mayor. Uh-huh. All right Mayor, please don't yell. What? Listen carefully. I," she points a finger to her chest, "I do the firing around here. This is my business. Yes, I did talk to her. What did she say? That no matter how much you and Mr. Turnupnose beg her, she won't give you her autograph." She winks at Maria, who is listening with a snicker. She pulls the phone away from her ear at the mayor's response and grimaces. "Don't yell at me, please. I'm not your cleaning lady, Mr. Gerrssa." She slams the phone down and squeals with laughter. "I love to piss him off. I sleep better." She starts to sashay away.

The phone rings again and Lila checks the caller ID. She grins and rolls her eyes upward. "Maria, it's your loverboy."

"Oh no. Don't answer it."

Lila tilts her head at Maria with sympathy. "Maria, why don't you like that Attorney Benavides? He's always showering you with gifts."

Taking a deep breath, Maria looks down and makes a four-inch measurement with her index finger and thumb. "Tú sabes. *You know.* He just doesn't hit the *spot.*" She grins at her audacity.

"Ay Maria, you're incorrigible." Lila slaps her hand on her thigh, laughing.

Again the phone rings. Lila sprints back and checks the caller ID, then rolls her eyes to Maria. "It's you-know-who again. Mr. No Hablo Spañol."

"Let me answer." Maria lets it ring as she takes her time walking over to answer it. "Hello? Ohhh, it's Mr. Turnupnose."

Mr. Turnip is on the other end of the line. "Look, Ms. Rosales, I know we got off to a bad start. I don't want an apology. What I'd like to know is if you'd join me for dinner?"

Close by, sipping on a martini, the mayor rolls his eyes.

Mr. Turnip continues. "Yes, dinner. No, I know you're not Roberta Roberts. Please. Will you join me? What I have in mind is I'd like to discuss further this problem you say we have with our children in the barrios. Our Mexican American children. Yes, I care. All right? Let me make some preparations and I'll call you right back. Ciao." He hangs up.

Lila is openmouthed. "Dinner?"

Maria smirks. "No, hey," she puts her hands up defensively, "if there's even a slight chance of getting some feria for the varrio, I ain't gonna pass it up. I just want to feel good about myself for a change. I have selfish reasons."

Smiling, Lila starts twiddling her fingers lightly on her lips. "Do you think this might lead to something? He *is* between wives." She studies Maria's reaction with high school curiosity.

Maria rolls her eyes. "Do I look like a two-by-four? This talking marshmallow isn't interested in me. He'll probably stand me up, chinga."

A sleek black limo pulls up to the front entrance of the Hilton Palacio del Rio. The bellman quickly rushes over to open the back passenger door. Before he can grab the handle, it swings open, almost knocking him on the knees as he jumps away.

Maria Rosales exits, looking gorgeous. She smiles at the bellman. "That's okay, I'm not crippled."

As she strolls into the lobby, a maître d' ushers her to a cozy table by the wall of long windows overlooking the riverwalk, which glitters with thousands of Christmas lights. Mr. Turnip sits waiting in a smart black suit.

A streak of classy excitement lights his face and he stands. "Maria, you look stunning."

Maria gazes into his eyes. Electricity. "I bet you're just saying that because it's *true*." She smiles and bats her eyelashes playfully.

Turnip laughs out loud. "Oh, my. You're wonderful!" Settling down, he gazes into her eyes sincerely. He takes a deep sigh. "Thank you for coming."

"My pleasure. But let's not forget why you invited me. The second highest poverty rate in the nation?"

"Oh, no. Of course not." For a moment he takes in her presence.

Then he gets serious. "Maria, it's not very often that I've been ashamed of myself. Today I was." His green eyes study the marble floor.

Maria holds his chin up to her eyes, giving him a warm smile. "I don't know what to say. This is the last thing I expected." She's kinda, sorta starting to like this guy.

Unexpectedly, Turnip snaps back to his usual self. "But Maria, I'm really out of tune with these problems. How can you help those who don't care?"

It's short-lived. She interrupts sharply. "Mr. Turnip, you have a very short attention span. I really can't stomach this."

"Maria, I—may I call you Maria?" He's afraid he's losing her.

"Right now I prefer Ms. Rosales."

"I'm sorry. Please inform me. What do these kids want?" He shrugs at his lack of understanding. He tries to find common ground.

She sips on her wine. "You know, Ed, last year the mayor asked Chicano teenagers from the nearby Victoria Courts that very same question. But it wasn't because he gave a damn. It was 'cause a few days earlier there had been a gang-related shooting at our swanky downtown mall. Of course, the well-being of the wealthy and the tourists is his number-one priority."

Ed is listening intently.

"Can you imagine a highly educated man asking dirt-poor kids a question like that?" She gauges his interest.

"What do they want? I'm ignorant too."

"What *you* want! What most privileged people take for granted in America. A real chance to make it in this country. For the affluent to also recognize and reward our talents. We don't want charity. Charity is given so people like you can sleep at night." She leans in. "It must be nice to live in a country where, if you work hard and use your ingenuity, you can *succeed*."

"But they were breaking the law."

"You know, Ed, this law which you so righteously defend is quick to protect the rights of a privileged citizen or a filthy-rich corporation. But it has no problem with a poor child living in perpetual misery and mortal danger. Now *that* should be against the law, *first*." She's not through. "And, Mr. Easy Money, this law has a murderous history of ruining Chicano families. Don't defend your law to me!"

"So what are we gonna do, disregard the law?"

"Ed, the law lets every fast-buck artist and shyster take full advantage of poor, working-class Mexican Americans. They are conned out of their meager earnings and often ruined financially by electric companies, insurance companies, and let's not forget legal drug companies who enrich themselves with their suffering and death. What law protects them? These are taxpaying citizens, Ed. Yet for them the law is a farce."

"I asked." He sips his wine. "But I come here and see a lot of Hispanic-owned businesses flourishing, raking in millions. What's holding them back from rushing to the aid of such a terrible existence?"

"Good question. Most rich Hispanics are quick to forget where they come from. White American culture is very seductive for a weak personality. These idiots are quick to jet off to Spain to 'find themselves.' And the Spanish-language TV stations are owned by rich families in Mexico and Miami. They could care less about our poverty. We're up against the prejudices of race and class."

Ed sits back and sips his wine, contemplating her comments. His respect for her is growing even further. He admires her solid sensitivity. She's not petty. Definitely a high-caliber mind. "Maria, after dinner, how about joining me for a stroll on the river to see the Christmas lights?"

"Sure. But I don't want to miss the ten o'clock."

"No problem. We can watch it in my suite. If that's okay."

"That would be convenient, wouldn't it? We'll see." They lock into an intriguing gaze as they sip their wine.

tormenta nocturna

Twenty-Two

Tormenta nocturna
Nocturnal tempest

A bluish electric cross glows in the rain above a hacienda-style building on the corner of Frio and Guadalupe Streets, close to the overpass of the I-35 expressway, bordering the west edge of downtown San Anto. The cross is radiant, with raindrops traveling down to the main entrance of Rodriguez Funeral Home.

Elias and his familia are lying in state on this drizzly Sunday evening. The morning will bring their trip to the San Fernando Cemetery, where they will be laid to rest.

El rosario has just ended, and out of the front doors of the '40s-style building a couple of dozen people in black slowly drift outside. Muffled, weary weeping fills the night as gente of all ages trudge out with swollen eyes that haven't seen rest. What's supposed to be a joyous time of year is instead a nightmare of cruel, unreasonable sorrow.

Don Pablito and Chuy are among the mourners. Don Pablito wears his thick grey wool coat with richly colored Aztec designs. Chuy is in varrio attire: dark blue work pants with a navy blue work shirt under a thick Salvation Army jacket and a dark sienna chuco hat of felt. Trying to stay dry, they are sitting by themselves on a bench off to the side under an overhang. They seem frozen in pensive solitude.

"Este es un domingo muy triste." *This is a very sad Sunday.* El curandero squints up at the heavy clouds. '¿Qué castigos tan negros son estos?' *What dark omens are these?* he thinks to himself. 'Que falta de luz.' *What lack of light.* Suddenly he blinks uncontrollably. He struggles to maintain coherence in the midst of this intrusion into his life. A sharp ringing in his ear distorts the present. Chuy says something, but his voice falls away into a deep well. Don Pablito's soul feels like it's leaving his earthly body. His vision gets cloudy and a brilliant light blinds his mind's eye. The rush of winds whips through his being, invading all his senses. Cold, hot, wet, and musky, like the furious climates of centuries. Or are they whispering voices…talking in urgency?

"Don Pablito, oiga!" Chuy is shaking him frantically, trying to bring him back.

As he slowly comes to, el curandero reassures a puzzled and frayed Chuy. "Estoy bien, m'ijo." *I'm okay, my son.* He holds his hand to his heart, taking a deep breath. "Es que fui en un viaje a mi palacio…a tocarle el corazón a mi Creador." *It's that I went on a voyage to my palace…to touch the heart of my Creator.* He nods his head, his eyes moist. "Cómo me hacía falta eso." *How I needed that.*

A few concerned gente are relieved everything is okay and amble off.

El curandero had these visions rarely, usually when a grave crisis would darken his optimism and he needed help. Like now. His extensive life seemed to require this tune-up. It was common knowledge in parts of Mexico and Peru that there existed shamans who were hundreds of years old. Our bodies are built to last forever. Don Pablito was only three hundred and fifty. These episodes left him emotionally exhausted, but with his will strengthened. He knew that he was being prepared for impending challenges.

"¡Hijo! Yo pensaba que se me estaba acabando." *I thought you were leaving me.* Chuy pulls out his pack of Luckies, shaking. Taking a relieved drag, he turns his gaze to the sound of car doors shutting and sits up at attention when he sees Luna, Consuelo, and Estrella getting out of their car. They slowly make their way to the entrance. Chuy leans in to el curandero. "Mire, Don Pablito, esa es la muchacha que buscaba razón de Nazul." *Look, Don Pablito, that's the girl that was asking about Nazul.* He starts to sink his face down into his cocked collar.

El curandero squints to see her. "Sí...pobrecita...¿Qué esperanzas cargará?" *Yes...poor girl...What hope she must carry?* He looks down at his hands as he rubs them together, feeling the tingling sensation as his blood rushes back through his veins. "Amor sagrado siempre sufre en este mundo." *Sacred love always suffers in this world.*

The three make their way to the front doors of the parlor.

Luna pans the faces of the gente. She's looking for someone. She gazes toward Chuy, but he is hidden in the darkness. Chuy lowers his head, further hiding his face under his chuco hat.

Don Pablito gauges their pace. "Busca a alguien en particular. Ella siente que él anduvo aquí." *She seeks someone in particular. She senses that he was here.* He squints upwards at the drips from the awning. "Pero ya no importa." *But it doesn't matter anymore.*

Scratching the side of his ass, Chuy looks around.

Ten blocks away, in the heart of la Tripa, a dark figure descends on two Muerto lookouts passed out in the front seat of the Cutlass, parked out front on the curb. Dark maddog sunglasses train on a faint light glowing from the front of the ganghouse. The window is cracked and barred.

La sombra approaches. He chooses a broken window on the side of the ganghouse and peers in.

Inside, a group of vatos and a few rucas pass around a joint as they sip on beers and try to stay warm. La sombra melts into the darkness of rosales and bushes.

Diablo sits on a La-Z-Boy with two rucas on his lap. Sporting his dark maddogs and flipped black cap, he is deep in thought as one ruca lights a frajo for him.

On the TV a snowy, staticky image of a soap opera gurgles with yuppie drama. A spoiled rich white dude whines to his fiancée, "Oh Brooke, why is this always happening to me? I can't believe they kidnapped my mother! How will I live through this?"

From outside the cracked window, la Sombra pans the disgusted, ridiculing faces of the vatos.

Mosco: "Ay, flor, no se te vaya rosar el culo." *Oh, flowerbud, I hope you don't get a rash in your ass.* He fits a fat joint between his lips, already holding a frajo, and takes a deep drag.

Sapo sips on a quart of bironga. "¿Pa' qué quiere a esa pinche vieja, wina? *What does he want that wino bitch for?* This is the only channel? Chinga! We need cable."

Bad-Boy: "Shit, if we had five hundred channels it would just be more shit like this! Pinches wimps. We always have to suck on their joto whining!"

Brooke comforts the young man. "Everything will turn out okay. You have your medical practice to think about. Pull yourself together."

"These culeritos are always doctors. The last time I saw one, he killed my 'buelita." Brujo scratches his balls with aggravation. "Mawfuckers."

The young man collapses to the Persian rug on the marble floor. "Oh Brooke, why has my life always been so wrought with strife? I can't bear it anymore."

Sapo can't stand the whining. "Compared to who? The queen of England? Pinche culito."

"'Rot with,' ¿Qué chingaus?" Killer, with his pinche varrio scowl.

Bad-Boy: "Chinga, the queen of England probably has more pelos en el fundillo than him. Lo que quiere es una buena cojida en el culo, el joto." *What he wants is to get buttfucked good, the wimp.*

Diablo couldn't give a shit about the pathetic drama. Instead está entrado in the nice backdrop for his thoughts of something else. "Cállenselhocico!" Dead silence. He takes a huge gulp of his bironga. A ruca holds the fat joint butt to his scarred lips. He takes in a thoughtful drag.

The drama continues. "Oh, Travis, you still have me."

"Simón, culito, get that pussy while it's hot!" Half whispering, Mosco's careful not to raise his voice.

The rucas giggle.

Outside, Pachuco winces at the cold wet ground. His feet feel numb. Dramatically, Travis lays his arm over his forehead. "Oh Brooke, I feel faint. Everything's going dark. Call the doctor!"

The music takes over the scene. "Will Travis truimph over yet another crisis? Tune in tomorrow for *Hollywood Drive.*"

Bad-Boy: "Who gives a fuck. Bola de maricones. Change it to that other culero channel."

Sapo grabs a pair of pliers and turns the channel. Another image barely manages to frizz into a coherent feed. A group of perfect lifeguards is meeting on a sandy beach for their daily instructions. Suddenly they hear some beachboy surfer yelling to them a hundred feet away about a crisis down the beach. The group of yuppie heroes springs into action. As they near an outcropping of rocks by the shore, they discover a screaming surfer babe in her twenties caught between some rocks that are getting beaten by the waves.

"Ah, la pinche ruca se le atoró el culo en las piedras." *Ah, the damn ruca got her ass stuck in the rocks.* Bad-Boy rolls his eyes. "Ya no hallan ni porque chillar estos puñatas." *They don't know what to find to whine about, these jackoffs.*

The vatos and rucas laugh out loud as the crack team quickly maps out the plan to save her.

"La deben de dejar que se ahogue a la verga, por pendeja." *They should let her fucking drown for being so stupid.* Brujo scratches his balls again.

Sapo goes for a sip of his beer. It's empty. Shaking ten beer cans lying around, he finds one with a few sips left and downs it. He gags and spits it out to the amusement of the vatos.

Bad-Boy: "I put out my frajo in that one."

Sapo picks the pieces of tobacco off of his tongue. "Eyy, we need to make a beer run." He heaves de asco. *In disgust.*

A thin, bare-chested vato stands up. He sports a tattoo on his chest that reads 'Gato' in a flowing ribbon. "Pos órale, mochense." *Well then, throw down.*

They all reach in their pockets for feria…Most come up empty.

Sadly, Gato looks at a few crumpled dollar bills and change on a coffee table. "Man, it looks like we gonna have to settle for Kool-Aid, chinga."

Sapo is disgusted. "That pinche Pachuco is cramping our onda gacho, homes!" He heaves back, then spits on the floor, making one of the rucas crinkle her nose in disgust. "He's even fucked up our homies on OJT." He scans the frowns. "Nosotros ni le hicimos nada." *We didn't even do anything to him.*

One of the rucas with beautiful, dark, flowing hair, grey Dickies pants, and a pink haltertop, speaks up. "It sounds like he's a soldado for la Raza to me." Mysteriously, she casts her fear out the beat-to-shit cracked window. "But everybody says que es un *fantasma.*" *That he's a* phantom.

Gato lights a frajo butt. "Ey, mi tía told me he kicked two juras' asses at Ray's Drive-In. She says que el varrio can't stop talking about it. And you wanna hear something else weird?" He puts the frajo out on his tongue. "Bueno," he winces at the smoke curling up into his eye from the last drag and blows it away. "For some reason that vato, el Blue-Boy, tengo un feeling, un pedo atorado, I dunno, pero tengo ese *jale,* que el Blue-Boy tiene somteeng do doos con el chuco." He scratches his armpit and smells his hand. "Que pinche cointidents que matamos al Blue-Boy y aparece el chuco." *What a damn coincidence that we kill el Blue-Boy and the chuco appears.* Eyes bulging out with intrigue, he nods his head. "It's a paraquat, ese. A *pa-ra-quat.*" He nods chingón.

"Cállatelhocico!" Bad-Boy rolls his eyes to the ceiling. "Paraquat," he nods. "*Paradox,* menso. Paraquat, chinga! Ya quiere hablar como los pinches Hispanics que nomás andan vendiendo el culo cuando votamos por ellos. *He wants to talk like those damn Hispanics that are always selling their asses when we vote for them.* Paraquat."

Gato throws up his arms. "¡Bueno, para mí es un paraquat, y qué!" *Well, for me it's a paraquat, and what!* He turns to the crew. "Pero, wacha, some rucas se *rayan* que lo han visto downtown. *But, check it, some rucas* swear *that they've seen him downtown.* And that curandero, Don Pablito, he ain't even in the hospita, homes. He just stopped his curadas 'cause of the cohetazos. La neta, dicen que el Blue-Boy es el Pachuco." *The net, they say that el Blue-Boy is el Pachuco.* He checks their solemn faces.

Now the vatos are eerily quiet.

"Naw, ese vato las dió. *Nobody* can survive that shit. He probably got ground into hamburger meat and the pinches varrio dogs ate him." Tripa checks his wounded shoulder and then pans the vatos' faces. "Pero, esa noche…cabrón! Nos pasó algo bien *espantoso…*Ese vato me *escamó.*" *But that night…damn! Something really* mysterious *happened…That vato* scared *me.* Tripa checks their inquiring minds. "He didn't even yell como aquel baboso on the way down." The vatos are now filled with superstitious fear. "Como que el susto de la muerte had no poder over him. *Like the fear of death had no power over him.* Is a *pa-ra-quat.*"

Abruptly Diablo stands up, knocking the two rucas off his lap and onto the floor littered with empty beer cans, vachas, and gargajos. "Ese fantasma es una ilusión. Si no, ya estuviera *enterra'o.*" *That phantom is an illusion. If not, he'd already be in the* ground. He walks to the side window where Pachuco is hiding in the bushes. "¡Ya estoy cansado de este pinche pedo!" *I'm tired of this fucking shit!* The TV features a syrupy preview of another yuppie drama: *Jake, Jenny, and Zoe!* Diablo turns around and puts a foot through the screen, smashing the tube and sending sparks flying. A cloud of blue smoke billows out of it. He trains his serious, dark eyes on the openmouthed vatos. "Esta noche…cierro todas mis cuentas." *Tonight…I'm closing all my accounts.*

Brujo, still looking stupid with his swollen eye, squints at him. "Mero, we're gonna have to make a list."

Mosco, half chuckling: "Cabrón, it's gonna look like a pinche grocery list."

Dwelling on more important things, Sapo: "Ey, y la bironga? Tenemos que pistiar." *Ey, and the brew? We have to drink.*

Mosco lights up. "Ey, I can go to the ATM and pull some feria out." The vatos glance with a glimmer of hope. "But I'm afraid they'll catch me."

"Baboso." Bad-Boy looks away, disgusted.

Diablo stares out the foggy, smoke-stained window, nodding his head. "Nomás andan con sus pendejadas." *All you do is go around with your stupid shit.*

"Ey, Diablo, I gotta go borrow my carnala's car so I can take my abuela to church for las Novenas. Tá de aquella?" *Is that cool?* Tripa groans as he pulls his still blood-soaked jacket on. "I gotta take a mierda first."

Diablo just flings his thumb and index finger at Killer. He glances back at him. "Ey, y quítale feria pa' un cuarto." *Ey, and get change from her to buy a quart.*

Shaking his head, Sapo watches Killer stagger to the head. "Chinga, what kinda clicka is dis eef our homies tienen que andar dándole rides a sus abuelas y la chingada." *Have to be giving rides to their grandmas and shit.*

Outside, Pachuco quietly stuffs a paño into the muffler of the Cutlass. He looks to the driveway and makes out the beat-to-shit Impala covered with a dark green tarp.

Lifting the tarp, he looks inside. In the back seat he finds some jumper cables lying rolled up on the floorboard. He crouches down as Tripa opens the front door and walks off into the night. Crawling under the Impala, Pachuco finds the starter and clamps the hot end of the cable to it. On the metal frame he clamps the ground. Running the other cable under the rear of the car and out the tire well, he unscrews the gas cap and sticks the red cable inside, closing the lid halfway. The ground is clamped to the leaf spring under the shock on the inside of the rear tire.

Chico's dark studio looks mysterious with only a strung lightbulb lighting the five-by-five-foot canvas that he stands back to study. The cocked collar of the pachuco gives him a ladrón look. Dark negative crosses play across the lit areas of his face and gafas, jiving with the positive of the blinding sparks.

Absorbing the work, Chico takes a deep breath and exhales. "'Pachuco con Jumper Cables.'"

Inside Rodriguez Funeral Home, Luna kneels down in front of Elias' casket. Beside her, Consuelo and Estrella pray silently for his beloved familia.

Luna is struck down by such utter tragedy, by the sight of Elias' face makeup poorly covering the assault of gunfire. She can't help but picture Nazul in this state. Clutching her rosary, Luna looks down and whispers to herself, "Nazul, como te he buscado." *Nazul, how I've searched for you.* Her emotion runs deep, makes her tremble.

She looks up again at Elias, her glassy gaze traveling down his torso, stiff in a black suit. She notices a piece of folded paper tucked neatly under his hands crossed on his chest. She looks around. Only a couple of people remain seated a few feet behind her.

Back at the ganghouse, Diablo comes bursting through the front door, followed by three Muertos. The rickety screen door rips from its hinges and comes crashing down on the gang. Cussing, Diablo grabs it and hurls it away. He sends it bouncing off the Cutlass. The two lookouts are startled from their sleep.

Los Muertos are all packing serious firepower.

Mosco leans in to the two in the Cutlass. "Go inside and warm up. We're gonna go wet la pinche calle." *The damn street.*

los muertos search for pachuco

Diablo, Mosco, Killer, Bad-Boy, and Brujo climb in. Bad-Boy revs her up. The Cutlass backfires a little, then takes off down the dark, deserted street.

A few blocks down, the parking lights glow red as it screeches to a halt. The vatos fall out, choking on the fumes.

Diablo: "Chíngadamadre!"

Through watery eyes, Mosco catches a glimpse of Pachuco as he steps out from the darkness. He freaks. "E-El Pachucooo!"

They squint. Their eyes burn. Looking around, they reach into the car for their firepower. But when Mosco turns around, he's gone.

Diablo fires a few rounds into the bushes and vacant lots. When he looks back to the vatos, he sees Pachuco appear behind Mosco. He fires. Mosco ducks as the round misses his head by a hair. Losing his Glock in the panic, he falls to the asphalt and crawls under the car.

A fleeting shadow crosses the headlights and the vatos open up. Pieces of branches fly away.

Bad-Boy levels his AK and sprays the immediate area.

Smoke, then silence.

"Cálmala." The vatos turn to Diablo, who has a Glock pressed tightly under his ear. Pachuco has grabbed him from behind and is using his body as a shield.

"Drop the cohetes y descuéntense!" *Drop the weapons and leave!* Pachuco orders them.

The vatos look at Diablo for answers. Pachuco presses the barrel harder into his jawline.

"¿Qué chingaus esperan? ¿Necesitan una calculadora? ¡Burros!" *What the fuck are you waiting for? You need a calculator?* Diablo tries to catch a glimpse of the face, but the barrel presses harder and won't let him.

As Mosco crawls out from beneath the car, looking back nervously, they slowly start heading back to the ganghouse down the dark street, leaving Diablo to his fate.

"¿Qué chingaus quieres conmigo?" *What the fuck do you want with me?* Diablo strains to look at his face. "Y ¿Quién chingaus eres?" *And who the fuck are you?*

Silence. Then, "Un fantasma. Una ilusión. ¿No es lo que dijiste?" *A phantom. An illusion. Isn't that what you said?* The hairs on the back of Diablo's neck stand at attention at the sound of those words. Pachuco lets him go so he can turn to face his judge, the darkness hiding his features under the chuco brim and gafas. But he can make out a teardrop tattoo under his right eye.

"¿Qué chingaus eres?" *What the fuck are you?* Diablo stares at the figure wrapped in mystery. Sirens wail in the background. The constant buzz of a chopper in the distance circles, then speeds away with its searchlight, adding urgency to the night.

"Tu muerte." *Your death.*

With that revelation, Diablo, todo marijuano, is suddenly stunned to see Pachuco's face radiate brightly. He steps back, tripping on his own heels, and falls to the ground.

Diablo hears the sound of a bullhorn and looks away to a silent squad car, no headlights, only the single searchlight, which was trained on Pachuco's face and is now trained on Diablo.

"Put your hands where we can see them!"

As the squad car squeals toward Diablo, Pachuco leaps away into the darkness. When Diablo looks back, he is gone.

Back at the ganghouse, the vatos arrive in a breathless strut. Mosco reaches the front door first and bursts through, startling Sapo, Gato, and the two vatos and rucas inside who are loading weapons to the loud blast of Latin-hop blaring from a boombox. "Eyy!! El-el Pa-Pachuco hit us! He-he's got Diablo!"

By then the rest of the vatos are inside breaking out the firepower. Bad-Boy opens the back door and sprints to an old, decaying shed behind the house. With a flashlight he pulls out the keys and opens the three locks. Inside, the flashlight beams on an amazing collection of weapons. A bazooka, Uzis, and grenades tumble down as he pulls out a few assault rifles.

Brujo trots out to help, followed by Sapo.

The vatos burst out into the darkness with vengeance. Bad-Boy hurries to the Impala and flings the tarp away. He climbs in as Brujo, Killer, Mosco, and Gato stumble out with the artillery and load up.

In the dark, Bad-Boy sticks the key in. But it won't turn. He pulls it out and looks at it. "Chingau! It's the wrong key!" He glances at Sapo standing outside. "Rana! Go find the pinche llave!"

Sapo drops AKs and a shotgun and trots inside. Desperately, he searches the littered living room, throwing cushions off the torn couch and Diablo's La-Z-Boy. Nothing but a vacha, a Lifesaver, two peanuts, a few pennies, and a crumbled Cheeto with hair strands. Nervously, Sapo picks up the frajo butt and lights it. The rucas and other vatos search in vain. They crawl on the floor in the dimly lit, sorry excuse for a living room.

Luna anxiously ponders the wrapped piece of paper under Elias' hand. She fidgets uncomfortably with an urge beyond her character and looks behind her. The last two people are leaving, along with Consuelo and Estrella.

She turns back to the folded paper. Nervously, Luna reaches under Elias' hand and slowly pulls out the note.

It's heavy. Something heavy inside.

Outside the ganghouse, Brujo, Killer, Gato, and Mosco decide to climb out of the Impala and look for the key in the front yard.

Sapo looks at Mosco as they crawl on their knees on the dark, cold, muddy ground, searching in vain for the key. "I think Diablo thinks we can't fucking think."

Mosco desperately looks under the stomped-on bushes by the front door. "I hate to fucking think what he's thinking, chinga."

Bad-Boy waits impatiently. "Fuck it!" He leans down to the floorboard and attempts to hotwire it.

'Rr-rr.' The battery's dead.

"Chíngadamadre!" He peers out. "Brujo! Get the pinche battery from the keetchen! Chíngadamadre!" He slams the door shut. With a pair of pliers in hand, he pops the hood and starts to loosen the screws on the terminals. Brujo trudges inside.

Trembling at her boldness, Luna's hand caresses the outline of the small, heavy object over the folded paper. It feels bulky, but the thickness of the letter-sized paper still shrouds its form. She looks behind her again. She's all alone.

Slowly, she starts to unwrap it.

Brujo waddles out with the battery as Mosco, Killer, and Sapo pick up the weapons and throw them in the back seat. They throw the battery into place. The terminals are tightened.

Bad-Boy jumps in the front seat and feels for the wires in the dark.

Luna carefully unfolds the paper. She unravels a metal crucifijo, the broken strand of a rosario with a few black beads still hanging from it. Her hands caress the familiar, sculpted body of Christ.

A nagging familiarity wells up inside her. "I know this." She sees some writing on the wrinkled paper, smooths it out. In pencil: "Adiós, querido amigo." *Goodby, beloved friend.* "Nazul." In a painful stir of dizzying emotion, she gazes up at the ceiling, holding the cross to her heart, hoping to feel him in it. "He was here? He *has* to be alive." She looks around as if expecting to find him in the shadows of the dimly lit room.

Bad-Boy finds the wires.

They connect.

A white flash blinds the night as the doors and hood of the Impala fly away in a violent explosion. Flaming bodies fly through the air.

The blast is close enough to the shed to rain fire on the grenades and ammo.

Another, more thunderous blast lights up the whole block.

The shockwave cuts across the varrio, rattling walls and blasting windows out of homes for blocks around.

Ten blocks away, tremors pound into the stucco walls of Rodriguez Funeral Home, causing the light to flicker.

Inside the parlor, within the trembling walls, Luna drops the crucifijo on the marble floor. It pings and bounces under Elias' casket. She looks up at the swaying lamps hanging from the ceiling and the dust floating down. The lights flicker out momentarily, then light up with a weaker glow.

Outside, the few gente left react with astonishment. Consuelo and Estrella can see the yellow glow and the reddish billowing smoke in the distance behind the parlor.

"Madre mía!" Consuelo clasps her hands to her mouth.

Chuy and Don Pablito stand up in amazement.

In awe, Luna leans down and picks up the crucifijo. She looks at it once again, bringing it gently to her mouth for a last, gentle kiss. Tears start to well up in her beautiful, dark eyes. "El Pachuco…"

She looks up in prayer. "Virgencita, por favor, si está vivo, no me lo quites." *Virgencita, please, if he's alive, don't take him away.*

"Hijo, ¿Qué sería eso?" *What could that have been?* Chuy looks at el curandero, puzzled.

Don Pablito crosses himself as they watch a cloud of reddish-brown smoke waft up into the thick sky.

Squad cars descend on the fiery scene from all directions. Pieces of light building material float down on a few scattered bodies lying sprawled in the street, close to the leveled ganghouse and crackling inferno.

The two rucas lie smoldering in the middle of the street, smoke billowing from their hair. Four cops jump out and drag them to safety as a police chopper buzzes down cautiously on the blackened area. It starts circling with its powerful searchlight.

In the dark brush of the vacant lot across the street from the ganghouse, Sapo grunts as he struggles to push Bad-Boy off of him. He staggers to his knees and looks at his homie. Smoking pieces of car metal are embedded in his face and head. No vital signs.

Shaking and cut up, his clothes burnt rags hanging from his torso, Sapo feels his head and body for wounds. He seems in one piece.

"Bad-Boy. Carnal." Sapo shakes him for a sign of life. Close by he makes out someone's smoldering leg. Trembling from the shock and cold, he weeps. "Chíngadamadre."

The light beam sweeps by, almost detecting him. He limps away into the surrounding empty buildings.

"Can you talk?" A white rookie cop checks out the ruca's war-torn face. "Can you tell us what happened?"

"Whe-rrr-mm-I?" Groggy and stunned, she tries to open her swollen red eyes to the hot yellow glow, her face covered with gashes.

Another cop arrives with a water bottle and squirts her face.

She comes around. "Uh, uhhha." She groans with pain, the deep ringing in her ears sending unbearable stabs of light deep into her brain. "AHHH! Ah."

"Now listen." He picks her chin up to his eye level. "We need *information*. What happened?"

"I-IIdoonnow." She opens her eyes and they roll back in her head. Her mouth drops open and a dark fluid drips out. "The stars fell down…They fell down. Da Pa-achu-uco-o—" She passes out again.

"Lieutenant!" Eager to impress, the rookie runs to his boss, who's on the horn with the mayor. "She said what you said. It's the Pashucoo."

"I knew it!" He turns to his sergeant, then back to his cellular. "Mayor, I'll call you back!" He walks past the burning, jagged shell of the Impala, dark smoke dancing in the breeze. "Put out another APB on him. Ultra-high priority. Seal off the area immediately. I want every car searched. Get the K-9 units out here. He's not gonna have a rat's chance in hell of getting away. This time we're gonna saturate this area with all the manpower we got."

"But sir, who is he? Nobody even knows what he looks like. If he never strikes again, we won't know who he is. We have no prints, sir. He might as well be a myth."

The lieutenant nods to the inferno. "We'll find him if we have to arrest every Mexican male eight to eighty, crippled or crazy." He scans the scattered piles of fire and smoke. "'Sides, somebody's gonna talk. Guarantee you that."

Five blocks away, at Guadalupe and Brazos, la sombra emerges from the alley as fire engines and ambulances noisily race by.

Black unmarked cars and mysterious station wagons with tinted windows cruise the area in a block-to-block search. Intermittent flashes of light illuminate their dashboards. Pachuco leaps away between some parked cars.

Everywhere gente filter out to see the commotion going down in their varrio and to assess the damage from the blast. Opportunity presents itself and Pachuco makes a run to Guadalupe Street, hoping to dissolve into the dozens of gente.

On a side street he stumbles upon a slick vato decked out to the nines in Armani threads. He's brazenly enticing a small group of teenage vatos and rucas with crack. When the teens see Pachuco they scatter, leaving the dealer puzzled. With a drugged scowl he looks around and notices the dark shadow approaching fast. "¿Ey, homes, you got *that* many kids, o qué chingaus?"

Pachuco answers with an uppercut to the chin, which propels the dealer against a chainlink fence. He falls cold.

Pachuco rifles through his pockets and finds vials full of crack, which he throws in a storm drain nearby. In another pocket, a wad of dollar bills. By then a group of gente have noticed him. They gather around. To them he is el Gato Negro. Señoras and señores shield him from view.

El Gato Negro hands the money to a señora who starts passing it around. The crowd of Raza civilly distribute the hundreds among themselves, careful not to attract too much notice.

A squad car rounds the corner and shines its searchlight dead on the group.

El Gato Negro looks down at his hand, which he just pulled out of the dealer's pocket, and sees a set of original car keys to a '57 Chevy. His eyes desperately search the area. Fifty feet down, across the street, he sees a customized, jet black Chevy Impala with red and purple flames.

"Run! ¡Descuéntate!" a vato in the crowd yells at el Gato Negro. The gente purposefully walk into the path of the oncoming cruiser. Pachuco now has a chance to run across the street.

In two more heartbeats he's inside the ride and tearing ass away. "Get the hell outta the way!" the bullhorn blasts. "You're obstructing justice!"

Forcefully weaving through the crowd, the squad car smokes away after the speeding Chevy, which makes a quick left on Frio Street close to the I-35 expressway.

They glide down a few narrow, two-lane varrio streets lined with parked cars. Pachuco is shifting gears with the gas pedal floored. He comes upon a van which makes a quick right, revealing three vatos pushing a stalled car in his lane dead ahead. In the opposite direction, a pair of headlights is closing in fast.

In a dizzying sequence the Chevy swerves to the left, then right, barely missing the vatos and clipping the outside rearview mirror of the oncoming car, blaring its horn as it jets by. He checks his rearview. The vatos leap over parked cars as the cruiser slams on its brakes and skids sideways, slamming into the stalled car. Pachuco glances back to see smoke, debris, flashes of light, and metal sparks.

At the intersection ahead, another squad car, its lights flashing and sirens blaring, tears after the Chevy as it zooms by. Quickly it catches up and speeds alongside. Rolling down the front passenger window, the cop sticks a Glock out at Pachuco as he shifts into second gear, slowing down enough to make a quick right at the next intersection.

Slamming on its brakes, the cruiser adjusts and peels back to the intersection to give chase. They catch a glimpse of the Chevy rolling up the one-lane freeway ramp to the I-35 expressway, which runs between el Weso and downtown.

Crackling lightning brings a downpour of rain. The Chevy has to slow to a crawl behind a '72 Buick.

Catching up from behind, the cop in the front passenger seat of the

pachuco glides down the varrio street with the squad car close behind

cruiser starts shooting recklessly at the Chevy.

Rounds ping off the chrome, and more hot lead punctures the trunk and slams into the back of his bucket seat. Pachuco bumps the Buick from behind, pushing it up the ramp until they merge into the two-lane expressway. Behind him the squad car catches up again and rams the Chevy's chrome bumper. Pachuco's knee hits the stereo knob and a loud melody pours out.

♫ "Estás sellado," Pachuco fishtails away, "por el destino…" The cruiser is kissing his bumper while the Buick scrapes the guardrail to get out of the way.

♫ "Que tú serás," a deep yearning in his soul toils with a revelation, "mi compañero…"

The cars race in the windy rain on the high, winding overpass as city lights strobe by.

♫ "Y qué iremos por un camino…"

Shooting wildly, the squad car zooms up next to the Chevy.

♫ "Hasta que alguno," another round cuts through the driver's window, inches from his head, and blasts the rearview mirror to pieces. "Se muera…"

Nazul remembers el sueño. Bracing himself, he grips the steering wheel tighter.

He has no choice but to swerve away to the right, crashing through the guardrail.

♫ "Se muera…"

A sense of falling grips his stomach. Time slows to an eerie crawl, and his actions seem like someone else's as he braces for the impact.

♫ "—muera…"

A giant wooden cross flows by. A violent jolt shatters the windshield. The sounds of grinding metal and cracking wood. Nazul is plunged into darkness.

There is a deep ringing in his ears. He shields his eyes, catching only a glimpse of his destination. Through the smoky dust and flying glass, illuminated by weak headlights, a faint image of la Virgen flows mysteriously upward in silence.

The Chevy lands with a bone-shattering crash. It juts at a ninety-degree angle, its tail resting on a partly crushed table.

The wrecked car sits smoking in the middle of a trashed altar, its headlights still faintly glowing in the dust. Above, rain falls from the gaping hole in the ceiling. A five-foot sculpture of la Virgen hangs

pachuco bumps the buick from behind

high on the wall, facing the opening above. Nazul is inside a church situated under the expressway at the edge of el Weso.

The santos glance down at the impossible guest. A small fire breaks out under the engine.

In the parking lot of Rodriguez Funeral Home, Don Pablito and Chuy are walking to the GTO, their heads covered with newspapers to shield against the rain. They hear the sirens wailing a few blocks away. Choppers race to the scene from different directions.

"¡Hijo! Qué noche tán guatosa." *What a noisy night.* Chuy unlocks the curandero's door and bounces over to his, pulling up on his baggy pants. He jumps in.

Behind them, Consuelo, Estrella, and Luna hurry to their car.

Chuy revs her up and shifts the souped up GTO into drive. A few blocks away a police chopper pans the scene below with its spotlight. Screaming cruisers and unmarked vehicles race past towards the church.

Don Pablito gestures his chin towards the commotion. "Vamos a ver que está pasando allá." *Let's go see what's happening over there.*

"¿Pa'ver que negocio es de nosotros?" *To see what business it is of ours?* Chuy gives him a sly grin as he pulls away.

The front doors of the church burst open and the SWAT team enters in combat-ready formation wearing gas masks. They clock the smoking Chevy with the small glow of fire underneath. Except for a group of five in the center aisle, the cops split up and make their way down the lanes in pairs, their flashlights searching for any sign of movement.

As they get halfway into the church, a bigger fire erupts under the car. The main team in the center aisle can now make out what they couldn't smell through their gas masks. A stream of gasoline has flowed down the main aisle, on which they are now standing.

"ABORT! FIRE!" the team leader yells as the flames now travel right for them.

"Holy SHIT!!" In the side aisles the members try to race the flames to the door. In the panic a round goes off, striking the highly flammable liquid.

The front doors of the church light up with a blinding blast that spits out a handful of bodies on fire. Screaming and yelling, they tumble out onto the sidewalk. Cops try frantically to douse the flames with fire extinguishers.

the chevy crashes into the church steeple

Around the corner, a block away, Chuy's GTO purrs to a stop on the curb. Both he and Don Pablito can make out the glow of fire through the row of huge, rectangular, stained glass windows of the church. Some windows are broken and black smoke is billowing out. "¡Madre mía! ¿Qué pasaría?" *What could've happened?* Chuy ambles out and over to help Don Pablito out of his seat and onto the slick pavement. Cautiously they start walking toward the scene.

The pouring rain has slowled into a nagging drizzle. Men in dark suits and SWAT teams in heavy armor run by, yelling back and forth, "Surround the church!" "Get that chopper on the horn!"

"Damn it, you idiot! Don't point that gun at my face!" A suit shoves the barrel of an AK aside.

"Goddamn it, get those K-9s over here NOW!" Another suit yells over their heads at a gang unit, "You people are supposed to be ready for war? Un-fuckin'-believable!"

At the corner of the church, a police and FBI dragnet directs some National Guard troops to start unloading roadblocks to seal off the area.

"Hey! Is that your car?" From the front of the church, a rookie cop walks quickly to them. Chuy nods. "Well, get it outta here NOW! Got fire trucks coming!"

Chuy and Don Pablito start walking back. Overhead, a police chopper shines its blinding spotlight on them and cuts away.

"Vale más irnos de aquí...antes que nos echen la culpa." *We'd better get away from here...before they blame this on us.* Chuy ambles faster to the car. Don Pablito walks with slow, relaxed steps.

As Chuy helps Don Pablito into his seat, he sees a dark, crumpled form behind his seat on the floorboard. The surprise causes him to reel up and bump the back of his head on the window frame. "¡Ay, chingau!" Behind him, barking German shepherds with their units race by.

"We got something! Yeah! It's him!" From the church, around a row of thick, twenty-foot pine trees that line the grass, flashlights slice frantically through the smoky garden. "Over there! He took off." The barking dogs, frantic yells, and stumbling bodies ramble aimlessly around the corner as shots go off. "You idiot! You almost shot me! Give me that thing!"

El curandero calmly looks up at Chuy. "No tengas miedo. Súbete." *Don't be afraid. Get in.*

Nervously looking around, Chuy walks over to the driver's seat and climbs in. Two blocks away, down a darkened street lined with vacant lots and condemned buildings, they come upon a cop setting up a roadblock. Chuy eyes Don Pablito nervously.

"No tengas miedo. Dale." *Don't be afraid. Go on.* Don Pablito nods.

With a flashlight trained on Chuy's face, the rookie walks up to them with one hand on his holstered Glock. "Get out! I gotta search the car." His nametag reads 'Kirby.'

Chuy opens his door to step out.

Suddenly, from the darkness, the cop hears a man's voice call out. "Kirby! I got him! Over HERE!" Silence. Then, "Hurry!"

Officer Kirby looks anxiously at the dark, brushy area. He shines his flashlight but can't make anybody out. "YEAH! Kyle! I'm coming!" He looks at Chuy, undecided. "Go on, get outta here." Chuy looks at him openmouthed, confused.

Pulling out his Glock, Kirby runs in the direction of the voice, but with caution. "Where the hell are you?"

No sound. Just the crackle of police radios, wailing sirens, and the buzzing chopper overhead. Thunder from the storm rolls eerily across the sky above him.

Suddenly a flashlight beams on the rookie's face. "What the hell are you doing over here?" An FBI agent appears out of the brush. "You're supposed to be manning that barricade!"

"Someone called me, sir. It sounded like my partner."

"I've been all over this area and ain't nobody over here!"

Officer Kirby isn't convinced. "But sir, I'm sure of it."

The agent points a finger at the barricade. "Now!"

Officer Kirby runs back, tripping over debris as he tries to reholster his Glock.

Inside the purring GTO, Chuy is perplexed by their narrow escape. He looks at Don Pablito. "Yo no oí nada. ¿Quién lo llamaria?" *I didn't hear anything. Who could have called him?*

El curandero looks away indifferently, shrugging his shoulders. He seems to glow slightly.

Chuy had noticed that when el curandero would pray, his body would radiate with a dim metallic light. When Nazul's grandfather, Julian, was dying, he knows that there was a period of about a month and a half in which Don Pablito hardly ever slept. Pero, he was functioning well, making decisions sensibly and even excellently. Don Pablito later told him that this was accomplished by praying without ceasing. He explained to Chuy how in this brainwave frequency a human being is able to request and receive messages, guidance, and the best solutions to the most debilitating problems from the ultimate power. And that is why an apparition like the Virgen de Guadalupe would request that a church be built in her name. Although most churches have always had their own monetary interests in mind and do little to ease the stark poverty around them, when a group of people would pray together with the same request in mind, they could build up powerful fields of consciousness. Chuy had come to understand that it was essential to be humble and trust in good, no matter how dismal things may seem. That the greatest truths to be learned are the ones which require that we lose our arrogance and open up our hearts like innocent, trusting children, within reason, of course. This attitude of humility is the secret to enlightenment, true wisdom, and power over adversity. There is an implicit order in the universe which governs mankind and all living things. We are all connected by a radiance. To most, its eternal purpose is a mystery, so it demands trust. To shamans, this purpose is revealed. We are eternal beings living many lifetimes at once. Every sacrificial experience is a stepping stone to a higher existence where we are capable of unimaginable power.

When Chuy met Don Pablito, el curandero was looking for Nazul. Somehow the curandero knew that Nazul's lineage, la de los Kuculkánes, was in grave danger of perishing from the earth. Don Pablito also knew that Nazul, Manco Capac, was soon going to face the worst peril of his life in his journey to become un 'soldado de la luz.' El curandero could help Nazul through this transition. The spiritual consciousness of the varrio, of society, had to change. Some souls, like Nazul's, are linked to this spiritual evolution. And Luna is vital to these horas luminosas.

After this varrio education, Chuy felt he was like Nazul. A pachuco, Ph.D.

To Chuy's amazement, he finds himself pulling up beside Don Pablito's house. How did they dodge the hundreds of cops? He thinks he even saw the National Guard out there. They were ten blocks away and arrived in some kind of time vacuum.

He's tired of scratching his ass.

———————

Back at the burning church, a Live-Eye news team arrives before the fire trucks and starts setting up to broadcast across the street. Roberta Roberts is there, fluffing her hair and getting ready to spring into action. She fusses with her makeup and yells at her help about every little quirk. "Goddamn it! Where's my eyeliner? Hurry!" Roberts struts around anxiously.

A mile away at the Hilton Palacio del Rio, Ed and Maria are looking out their seventh-floor balcony over the riverwalk, facing el Weso. They can see the glow from the fire of the ganghouse and the handful of choppers with their single sweeping eyes circling over the area like fireflies. The continuous sound of sirens wails close by the downtown hospitals, then faintly in the distance.

Ed is on his cellular with TNN National Broadcast News. "How long does it take to talk to somebody who knows what his job is? Damn! He's where? In the bathroom? Then get me the program director! Get me somebody, damn it! Now!" The balcony doors to their room are open and the TV inside is showing some tourists visiting a rose farm in some northern town.

"Yes. An explosion! Two explosions! Get one of our affiliates down there pronto! They are? Well pick up the signal! Run it through. Go international." He hangs up and walks Maria into the suite to see the broadcast just as a TNN newswoman interrupts the rose farm piece.

"We interrupt this program for this late-breaking news. We have just been informed that a series of explosions has rocked the west side of San Antonio, Texas. Our affiliate has a Live-Eye on the scene, so we are picking up the signal now."

TNN cuts to Roberta Roberts as she catches a last bit of information on her headset. "TNN? I'm on TNN?" She fluffs up her puffed, cotton-candy-like hair and glares at her entourage. "This is my ticket! Don't screw this up!"

The cameraman, a young Chicano, points a serious finger at her. "You're on!"

With a Texas twang, "This is Roberta Roberts coming to you live from a gang-infested varrio on the west side of San Antonio, Texas, where police say a cold-blooded hoodlum and his gang of murderers have been waging war on another gang here, as well as on law enforcement. Earlier this evening they boldly blew up a car full of rival gang members in the middle of this neighborhood. The police then chased the leader of the gang up an expressway ramp. When they caught up to him, he crashed his car through the guardrail," the camera pans the splintered opening in the guardrail of the expressway, which runs overhead, above the church and the thick smoke billowing out of the gaping hole in the roof, "and he crashed through the church steeple and into the altar! And just moments ago the gas tank in the car blew up. The church is now on fire. There is no official word yet on the exact number or extent of casualties, but it seems very doubtful that whoever was in that car survived."

The camera does a tracking shot of the Chevy engulfed in flames through the open doors of the church. Around them, firemen have trouble finding a fire hydrant that works. "Try the other one around the corner."

Roberts looks around for a police officer to interview. She sees a middle-aged cop nearby. "Officer Petty, have you located the body yet?"

The officer is in a hurry, but stops momentarily. "No, but I just want to say that we are doing everything we can to protect the good citizens of this city from these psycho killers. We'll be here all night if we have to." He takes off.

"Thank you, Officer Petty. Authorities have stated that this gang has been hard to catch because the residents of this area refuse to co-operate with police in providing information. We have one story of residents actually aiding the criminals' escape. I'm going to try and get some feedback from some of these *re-si-dents*."

Maria gives Ed a hard look.

"Excuse me!" From the crowd she picks what looks like a well-to-do Chicana teen.

The teen looks at Roberta doubtfully.

"Yes, you!" Roberts commands.

The teen marches to her and salutes.

Roberts glances uncomfortably at the camera, then back to her. "Are you from the area?"

"Sirol." Chewing on her gum, the teen looks Roberts up and down.

"Let me ask you, we have heard over and over again that the locals are hesitant to cooperate with law enforcement in these situations. Can you—"

The Chicana cuts her off. "'The locals?' As in wetbacks, gangbangers? What does that mean, 'the locals?'" She shakes her head with varrio charm.

Roberts is aghast. "Why do police have so much trouble getting descriptions from you, even though these murders occur in broad daylight?"

"Snapea. Re-ta-li-a-tion." She leans in to her face.

"Yes. We have heard that from others." Roberts cuts her off and turns away to the camera in resignation. She spots another Chicano teen who is dressed in trendy varrio threads. It is Silent from Los Vryosos Community Center. "What about you? Do you know the killer?"

A little embarrassed by the suddenness of the interview, Silent stammers a bit. "Uh-uh, no. But…I think he's the baddest vato in el Weso."

"Baddest what? In where?" Roberts nods her head to the camera in disbelief. "I wonder if the right hand knows what the left one is doing here."

As she turns her back to the teen to look for another interviewee, she absentmindedly reaches behind herself and scratches. The young vato, still within earshot and in the camera's background, speaks out. "Ey, pendeja, does your right hand know that your left one is scratching your ass on national TV?"

Roberts is oblivious. She tries to get someone with authority, but all are too busy. She sees Luna, Estrella, and Consuelo staring at her nearby. She focuses her attention on Consuelo and motions to her. "Excuse me, do you have anything to say about this cold-blooded killer?" She walks halfway to her, her mic reaching.

The camera trains on Consuelo, who doesn't budge from her spot. "No, because I don't know the *facts*…like *you*." The mic picks her up nice and clear.

Ed looks at Maria and shifts uncomfortably, but Maria is starting to smile.

"Well," Roberts shakes her head at the camera, "that's the local perspective for you."

She looks around at the crowd of Raza gathered close by to watch. She motions to her cameraman to get a shot of the gente. He looks away for a second, disgusted with her, but complies. "Once again, we are on the west side of San Antonio, Texas, a predominantly Mexican American community. It is clear that with tonight's explosion and ensuing chase ending in a violent wreck, the level of violence in the area is escalating rapidly. It appears the participants are sometimes very young teens. One has to wonder why these youngsters aren't in school, why their parents can't control them. The other important issue here, as the SAPD pointed out, is the general lack of cooperation on the part of the community in the identification and apprehension of these offenders. This is a phenomenon typical to communities of illegal aliens."

"Hey! I have something to say," a voice cuts her off.

Roberts looks at the crowd, puzzled. She sees Luna stepping forward.

Maria leans forward in anticipation.

"What?"

Luna walks right up to the mic. She stares right into Roberts' eyes, "That it is so tiresome to have someone like you come down here with your pompous attitude, and without so much as a sincere conversation with anyone, proceed to give the world your opinion about *our Raza*."

Roberts catches herself with her mouth open in front of the camera. She turns away.

"Wait. I'm not through." Luna follows her.

Roberts covers the mic. "Yes, you are."

As Roberts turns her back to her, Luna walks up from behind and yanks the mic away. Roberts is visibly struggling to sustain some semblance of professional composure.

Luna keeps Roberts at bay for a second and speaks into the mic. "The gente in this varrio," she fights Roberts off with her free hand, "are not necessarily the kind Miss Roberts does lunch with." Roberts loses her manners and becomes forceful. Luna puts her hand on her face, rearranging her makeup.

Roberts yelps and jumps away.

Ed and Maria are openmouthed in their riverwalk suite. Luna goes on. "I have lived here all my life. This is my community. A Chicano community. Mi varrio. I can tell you from firsthand experience that these people, and Raza *everywhere*," her eyes sparkle with heartfelt emotion, "¡son unas de las gentes más lindas en todo el mundo!" *Are some of the most solid people in the whole world!*

Tuning in across America, Chicano households and family-owned businesses are moved by a broadcast totally new to them. Prisons packed with Raza are glued to the live drama unfolding before them on TV.

Off-camera, Roberts orders her cameraman to pull the plug. "Goddamn it! Do it now!!"

The young Chicano shakes his head. "I can't! Ed Turnip wants this covered!"

Roberts then realizes that Luna is through with her message. She yanks a brush from her assistant's hand. "That bitch!" She brushes her hair viciously and struts back to Luna, who seems satisfied with her delivery.

She snatches the mic away from a docile Luna and turns to the camera, her false eyelashes askew. "Well," her breath is short and choppy with rage, "we don't have an *interpreter,* but maybe we shouldn't *need one* in America."

Now enraged, Luna walks back to Roberts and yanks on the microphone cord. As they struggle, Roberts yells to the cameraman, "Juan! Help!" When he just stands there, she calls for a cop. "Officer! This crazy woman is attacking me!"

Maria turns to Ed. "Let her speak. Believe me, she is *not* crazy. She's a teacher. You want competent information? She grew up there."

"But she has no authority to report the news."

"Ed, any authority your reporter Roberts had went up in smoke."

Ed takes a deep breath. As he exhales, he decides. He flips open his sleek cellular. "Get me the main man. Now!" He glances at Maria, who is starting to smile at him. "Yeah, Lou? Listen, I want Miss Roberts to let that girl give her opinion. But if she starts cussing, pull the plug."

"Cussing?" Maria's stare could melt butter.

"Lou, just let her talk. Do it."

"What??" Roberts, trying to regroup off-camera, gets the message through her headset. "You gotta be joking! Damn it! I can't believe this shit!! Why don't they let her do the news!?"

The cameraman looks away with a smile. "Looks like they are."

"Sonofabitch!" Roberts loses it. She stomps over to the receiver and pulls the plug herself.

The TV goes blank for a moment, then the TNN newswoman comes on holding a hand to her earpiece, listening. "We're having technical difficulties. It seems our reporter, ah…So let's go back to our rose farm and—wait, no, it seems we are going back to the live scene with Miss Roberts. Yes, we are."

Ed is yelling into his cell phone. "She is fired! Get her outta there!"

Maria throws in her two cents. "By force?"

"By force if necessary! Now let that teacher talk!"

Back in the varrio, Luna and her family are almost to their car half a block away when Silent breathlessly calls to her. "Luna! They want you to go back on the news!"

Luna looks back, puzzled. "What??"

"I'm not kidding! But hurry!"

Luna runs, then walks quickly back to Juan, the cameraman, who's waiting to hand her the mic. With a smile he says, "Remember, you're live on TNN, *nationwide!* Possibly *world*!"

Still surprised by the turn of events, Luna glances back to Consuelo and Estrella, who have caught up and are watching breathlessly. She turns to the viewer. "Well, I don't know what's going on, but I would like to respond to the *news* reporter's racist remarks about language. You know, these privileged Americans love to pride themselves with knowing another language. They know French, German, but even though they are surrounded by our culture, they can't speak *one* sentence in the language of this hemisphere. They act like they don't know where we came from, but we didn't come from *anywhere*. When they arrived, illegally, we were already here. Our parents and grandparents were belittled and scorned for not knowing how to speak English. Well, to me, people like Miss Roberts are the true illiterates!"

Across the nation, in their cramped homes, Luna's words bring grateful smiles from Mexican American parents and grandparents alike. In Paris, France, a crowd gathers outside a coffeeshop already packed. They strain to catch the live broadcast as it is translated. In Mexico and South America, gente from all walks of life tune in.

"Privileged America wants everybody to glorify white European history, language, you name it, but acts stupid when it's confronted by our culture. Why is that? We know everything about you. Why don't we count in our own home? Yes, we provided this land. A land built on the backs of *our* parents. Yet nobody gives a damn what we think! We have been here as a people since Spain colonized these lands in what is now known as the southwestern United States. Our elders suffered at the hands of U.S. law. Their lands were taken, and most were murdered or imprisoned. They went from being landowners to slave labor just because they couldn't understand this new language that was imposed on them by greedy land robbers. This is what this English language can still mean to those of us who respect their memory. To this day it is shoved down our throats. And when we do learn it, privileged America never includes us in anything worthwhile. Most of us are still slave labor. Mainstream America is like a wicked stepmother who shoved her way in, and when she couldn't get rid of us, ignored us and did everything possible to make our existence unbearable. She loves to exalt her own kind, but is maliciously wicked with her unwanted stepchildren. We have endured impossible odds and are the true heroes of adversity in this country, in this Cinderella story set in an epic scale. But we are not in your history books, films, TV shows, or art museums."

Ed's mouth has dropped open. Maria's eyes start to water.

"Some of us have seeped through the cracks and are now doctors, teachers, et cetera. But diplomas and Ph.D.s also rob us of our identity and devotion to our gente. We become mere puppets promoting the republican agenda in the varrios, which largely requires the suffering and extermination of Raza. We want education that benefits Chicanos too.

"This varrio is like countless others across America where crippling poverty—here, next to the highest in the nation—has been a constant companion to Mexican American families for longer than we can remember. Don't preach to us about hard work. We've reinvented it from the fields to the factories. But we refuse to break our backs at some dead-end job just to make some billionaire richer.

"Our prisons and cemeteries are full of dreams we've already lost. Hardworking parents who did everything possible to keep their modest homes, only to be beaten down by the system. Teenagers who saw no end to the hopelessness and lost their heads. Every day our kids are fed tales of lavish glory by mainstream America via the TV, about the privileged few who, with just some petty effort, can have it all. What awaits most of our gente, no matter how talented, is an indifferent and cold America who shuts doors in their faces at every turn. Privileged America, try telling your teenage sons and daughters they can't dream. I doubt if you can even imagine that. Believe me, you'll find that a child who can't dream can become a dangerous thing.

"Miss Roberts told the world about the violent kids who live here.

luna stands in front of the burning church and addresses the nation

It's true they lose all hope and reason. Wouldn't you? They live in a war zone wrapped in the self-destructive pitfalls of hopelessness." Juan directs Luna to stand with the front doors of the burning church behind her. He pans into the reddish inferno. "Roberts raised some important issues. Why is it that working parents can't make enough money to support their families and be there for their children? Even when both parents work? These kids have to raise themselves or they'll be homeless. Why is it that their schools don't acknowledge and embrace their history? Would your schoolchildren have self-esteem and stay in school if their existence and history was constantly ignored or belittled? I don't think so. These are issues that we need to address *now*.

"Our parents and grandparents worked themselves into the grave just to put food on the table. Yet most died feeling like failures because they couldn't afford us a better life." The camera pans the santos in the church as they are consumed by the flames, melting. "But we know it wasn't their fault. They were the most impeccable citizens this country could ever hope to have! This draconian system denied them their due. And now they are denying us."

Luna stands tall and grits her teeth. "Raza, we owe it to our gente to *unite*. Let's stop hurting each other, when each other is all we've got. If you've made it, we're happy for you. Pero don't forget that it was *your* gente who united in the '60s and made it possible for a few of us to dream. Without their heroic efforts your status here would have been below a dog's. They didn't just march for our rights, they risked and lost their lives, just so that we could be treated like human beings. Be thankful to your elders *first*.

"Right now our buying power is immense. Mainstream America loves to ignore us as much as they love our money. Let's boycott all products that shun our existence." Ed Turnip cringes. "From films, TV shows, trendy clothing, beer, et cetera. Let's show them how *invisible* we really are. We give them our money so they can use it against us. Buy goods made by our Raza first. Don't be a fool any longer!

"RAZA, UNITE. Let's finish what Emma Tenayuca, Cesar Chavez, and our abuelos started. We owe it to them and our children. And their rallying cry was," Luna raises a defiant fist, "¡ADELANTE! ¡ADELANTE CON LA CAUSA! ¡LA GENTE! ¡LA GENTE PRIMERO! ¡Y QUE VIVA LA RAZA!"

The gente in the crowd get chills down their spines. She jars a dormant resolve in them.

Goosebumps travel down Juan's back, and he can't help but let out a loud and long grito. "AAYYYYYY-HA-HAAAA!!!"

His grito stuns Raza across the nation into a wild frenzy of cheering and applause. All around the church, the gente burst out with wild yelling. "¡¡ADELANTE!! ¡¡ADELANTE CON LA CAUSA!! ¡¡¡LA GENTE PRIMERO, Y QUE VIVA LA RAZA!!!"

Maria Rosales sits in a trance with tears streaming down her face. She stands up, walks with purpose to the balcony, and yells out to el Weso, "MI RAZA, I LOVE YOU!! I LOVE YOU!!" Shaking her head, she chokes on her sentiment. "¡QUE VIVAMOS! ¡QUE VIVAMOS! ¡¡NUNCA NOS QUEBRARAN!!" *MAY WE LIVE!! THEY WILL NEVER BREAK US!!*

Stunned, Ed looks down at the floor for a moment. "*That* was the news?"

Outside on the riverwalk, Ed can hear hotel workers who have abandoned their slave work to pour out and cheer. He can't help but get caught up in the infectious enthusiasm spreading through San Anto. "I'M WITH YOU, BABY!! ¡¡QUE VIVA LA RAZA!!" Jumping up, he runs over and hugs Maria as they dance around like kids.

Across America, Raza are out in the streets in a wild and rare moment of unity.

At the burning church, gente are now cruising Guadalupe Street in a parade of honking horns, gritos, crazy cheering, and applause. Juan keeps the camera running. Pedestrians fill the sidewalks and streets with their revelry. Some Hispanic cops have to restrain themselves from getting washed away by the excitement of their Raza. Nearby, hardcore gangsters in front of their TVs jump up and throw down their weapons. They run outside to join the crowd invading the varrio streets.

The FBI and police are perplexed by this awakened giant.

Juan wipes his eyes with his sleeve. "Eso sí es...*news, man.* Tomorrow...the *whole world* is gonna know us." He nods his head. "Simón."

Ten blocks away, Chuy stares out the tiny window at the commotion on the streets. A moan nearby catches his attention. Down the narrow hallway a faint light glows from el curandero's altar room as he tends to Nazul's wounds. He applies a mud of hierbas to a four-inch gash on his forehead, close to the hairline. Dressing up the cut with a white cloth, Don Pablito then turns his attention to his bruised ribs. Nazul winces in pain as el curandero presses his hands against them.

Barking dogs outside cause Chuy to look out again. He sees the flashlights and K-9s down the street. Overhead, the chopper blades cut through the night as a searchlight scans the area. The FBI is now conducting a house-to-house search.

"Maestro, se está acercando la ley." *Master, the law is getting near.*

Don Pablito helps Nazul to his feet. He looks at the white patch on Nazul's forehead. Looking around, he grabs Nazul's pachuco hat and fits it on his head. "Son muchos. No hay tiempo para nada. Vete pronto." *There are too many of them. There's no time for anything. Leave quickly.*

Chuy rushes over to help Nazul, but Nazul waves him away, insisting that he can walk on his own. He turns to Don Pablito. "'Apá, su bendición." *Father, your blessing.*

El curandero gives the sign of the cross to them from the hallway. Both humbly cross themselves and head out the door to Chuy's mean-looking GTO.

Chuy revs her up, and with headlights off they cruise away from the invading dragnet.

Varrio dogs are going crazy in their backyards. The cops argue with the homeowners who don't want muddied dogs and cops trudging through their homes. In no time the cops start arresting the uncooperative gente.

Chuy and Nazul find the streets teeming with traffic and Raza. People are hanging out of car windows, yelling and cheering hysterically in the rain. Others spill out onto the sidewalks as the GTO arrives on Guadalupe Street. Chanting can be heard: "¡Adelante con la causa! ¡La gente! ¡La gente primero! ¡Qué viva la Raza!"

Chuy scratches his ass. "¿Qué chingaus está pasando? Esta es una noche, pero bien loca." *What the hell is going on? This is a really crazy night.*

The GTO rolls behind twenty cars to the traffic light as a steady stream of traffic rolls by on Guadalupe Street.

Back at Don Pablito's house, fists pound on his door. A team of cops demands entry. As el curandero opens his door, a flash of light from inside blinds them and they fall back on the mud, tripping on the K-9s, who start yelping with fear, trying to tear away.

Ten blocks away, a cracked street lamp glows down on a white '65 Malibu with a shattered back window as it rolls slowly to a stop in front of a row of abandoned warehouses on Frío City Road, by the railroad yards that border el Weso and downtown. The driver rests his hand on the steering wheel. The name 'Chino' is tattooed on his knuckles. Below, on his clenched fingers, the tattoo 'Weso.' He glances indifferently at the distant searchlights from the police choppers still circling the church area. Sirens wail and die out, only to start wailing again.

A moan behind him distracts his attention. In the back seat, Sapo nurses his countless burns and scrapes with a paño.

Chino grins. "Chinga, ese, parece que you had it out with a flaming gato from la Tripa."

"Simón. It's funny, ¿verdad? You weren't there to see our homies' body parts lying around." Sapo shivers from the pain and cold. He checks a chopper as it zooms noisily by overhead, on its way to the church. "Ey-ey, Chino, you think Diablo saw the news? That ruca?" He looks around uncomfortably.

The smoke from Chino's cigarette dances around his head before escaping out the cracked window and into the breezy night. "No sapo, Rana."

Just then, out of the fluid darkness, there's a tap on the front passenger window. Sapo leans in from the back seat and unlocks it.

Rubbing his hands to warm them, Diablo jumps in, cold and wet. "¡Jijo de su. Cabrón! Se me helaron los pinches huevos." *Damn! My balls froze.* He glances at Chino, who hands him a tallboy. "¿No traes frajos?"

Chino pulls a cigarette off his left ear and hands it to him. Diablo lights it and takes a deep, thoughtful drag. Popping the bironga, he takes a good swig. He glances back at Sapo. "¿Qué chingaus te pasó a tí?" *What the fuck happened to you?*

Sheepishly Sapo leans in. "Mero, hubo-hubo un *desmadre*. El Pachuco, nos acaba de mandar a la chingada. *Mero, there was a total fuckup. El Pachuco just got through sending us all to hell.* Yo y Brujo are the only ones left of our clicka."

Before he can absorb the news, a loud tap of metal on the window by Diablo's ear makes him turn. He stares into the twin barrels of a shotgun. Flashlights in the face from both sides of the Malibu blind

chino glances at a chopper zooming down to the burning church

him and Chino. A third flashlight beams in from the shattered back window.

Outside, four heavily armed cops surround the Malibu. "GET THE HELL OUT, GREASEBAGS! NOW!"

As Diablo and Chino open their doors, the cops simultaneously grab them by the collar, roughly pulling them out and throwing them down into the mud at the rear of the Malibu. Quickly they start frisking them. "You wetbacks need to all fucking die! Fucking leeches."

Just then Sapo sticks his singed face out the open driver door.

"Shit!" One cop sees him and jumps from the sight. He grabs him by his singed hair and throws him down too. "Damn! Anybody uglier than you in there?" He chuckles. "Well now…looks like you already been *interrogated*."

One cop has a knee on Chino's neck, pinning him down as another jura, next to him, stands and stomps on Diablo's head with all his rage. "Piece-a-shit cockaroaches!" His nametag reads 'Haley.' "Where the fuck do you come from? You know, we can kill you if we want and nobody would give a fuck!"

Suddenly Chino rolls over to the cop pinning him and bites him through his pants on the soft inner muscle of his leg.

The cop jumps away. "Shit! Motherfucker!"

Chino jumps to his feet and lunges at Haley, knocking him down and stomping on his head. "*You're* the fucking leeches! Pinches marranos!"

The other three cops rush Chino, attacking him with their flashlights and rifle butts. Chino keeps them off balance by kicking them in the shins as he gets pummeled to the wet asphalt. Getting up, Haley, wild with rage, kicks Chino hard in the nuts. Losing his balance, he trips back down. Chino manages to get to his feet and kick Haley's face. He is grabbed from behind. The other cops beat him senseless.

In the confusion Diablo unholsters a Glock from one of the cops. He pulls the trigger and a thunderous blast in the air rattles the officers to their bones.

All four lawmen snap to the new deal.

Diablo's gold tooth glints with controlled vengeance. His dark eyes, death. "Ey. You wanna be assholes? Todamadre," his voice is deep. "I can be an asshole too."

The cops freeze with fear.

One cop standing behind Chino is holding a pump-action shotgun, which is pointing to the ground. Though his face is bloody and he feels groggy, Chino is still coherent as his senses come fleeting back to him.

Groaning from the fuckup, Haley slowly stands up to Diablo. "There's four of us, wetback!" He struggles to catch his breath. "Nobody takes a gun from a cop and lives! Looks like you just bought yourself a deep dark hole."

In an instant the cop grabs Chino by the neck, using him as a shield, and levels the shotgun at Diablo. At the last second Chino deflects the shotgun down with his arm as it fires.

A puddle of water at Diablo's feet is blasted by the buckshot. Diablo stands unflinching, the water splashing up in front of his emotionless death mask.

Diablo answers with a stunning blast of lead that levels the cops as they thrash backwards from the force of the rounds striking their bulletproof vests.

The face of the cop with the shotgun streaks red as he flies backwards with a somersault. Chino's neck runs thick with his blood. His shotgun goes flying through the air and lands with a thud on Sapo's head.

"Ay! Abuela!" Sapo rubs his head in agony, cowering.

Diablo struts to the Malibu as if nothing, climbs in the front passenger, and slams the door. Chino follows, walking past Sapo, stopping only long enough to wipe the blood off his neck with one of the squirming cops' pant legs. He climbs in on the driver's side, revving up the Malibu.

Sapo looks up just as the back wheels start spinning, splashing his face with liquid mud. He jumps to his feet after the car. "Eyy! Cálmala!"

mi mano

Twenty-Three

En los hombros de mis padres
On the shoulders of my elders

The Malibu arrives on Guadalupe Street to thinning but rowdy crowds.

Diablo scans the noisy revelry with his disgusted frown. "¿Qué chingaus tiene esta pinche gente?" *What the fuck's wrong with these damn people?*

Cautiously, Sapo leans in from the back seat. "Mero, this ruca from el Weso got on TNN tonight, y, y le rayó todo el disco a los pinches racistas. *And she let all the racists have it.* And the varrio went crazy." Sapo leans out the window and yells with enthusiasm, "¡Qué viva la Raza!" He laughs. "¡Chinga! What a night."

Unmoved, Diablo stares ahead. He takes a swig of his tallboy.

Luna, Consuelo, and Estrella cruise in the slow, noisy traffic. Luna's at the wheel and Estrella in the back seat, all smiles.

"M'ijita, I think this time you really did change the world."
Consuelo glances at Luna with admiration. "For la reals."
Estrella leans in to stroke her big sister's dark hair. "Luny, tú eres maciza. *You are solid.* Like Dad used to say." Leaning in farther and giggling, she hugs Luna around the neck.

Luna squeezes her little sister's hands under her chin. "But I'm still wondering why they let me speak on TNN." She looks away at the news teams in their broadcast trucks. They still struggle to get to the scene of the burning church. She smiles. "Yo tengo una idea quién fue caprichoza." *I have an idea who was incorrigible.* Nodding, she checks Consuelo. "Mi carnala."

Luna glances at a team of law enforcement searching a señor's car with K-9s. The doors and trunk are open, and the handcuffed citizen is being harshly interrogated. "Estrella, find my cell inside my purse. I'm calling Maria about these Nazi cops harassing our gente." She holds her stomach. "Ay, 'Amá, I'm still worried about Nazul. My stomach is a knot. What if the cops find him? They'll kill him. I just hope he's somewhere far from here." Shutting her eyes tightly, she tries not to give her fear too much power.

Consuelo doesn't know what to say…"Dios mío, me too." She shakes her head. "But if he's not, I hate to say it, pero it looks very hopeless for that poor muchacho. Who could survive a crash like that? And when you hit a cop, ay, I don't want to think right now." Suddenly she sits up. "But I do know one thing, los rezos can change anything for the better. Let's pray for him."

Blocks away, Plutarco knocks on the rickety screen door of a tiny varrio house on a quiet street. A viejita peers out through the half-open wooden door. "Señora Martinez, Don Pablito les pide que todos se pongan a rezar por Nazul. Los chotas lo andan buscando para matarlo y necesito su ayuda. Y llámele a su gente, a todos. Gracias." *Señora Martinez, Don Pablito asks that everybody pray for Nazul. The cops are looking for him to kill him and he needs your help. And call your people, everybody. Thank you.* He takes off on his mission. The viejita humbly nods and shuts the door. As Plutarco steps back to the sidewalk, a dozen señores, chamacos, y señoras swarm around like ghostly sombras searching. They silently go house to house, knocking on doors. Teens run out from one of the homes up ahead and head for the other blocks in the misty darkness to spread the request.

The nagging drizzle bears down. Luna rolls up her window. Slowly, they drift past Chuy's GTO waiting at the light, first in line at the intersection.

Luna's lovely face glows bright in Chuy's headlights as they roll by, and she turns to them for a moment. The glare blinds her to Nazul's disbelieving eyes, staring right at her through the rain-streaked windshield.

He sits up. "Luna…" Her name escapes from his lips in a low and deep whisper.

Chuy checks him, then Luna, who is on her cell. Luna puts the cell phone down. "Ay, I can't get a signal."

Down the street, coming from the other direction, Sapo is sticking his ugly face out the window yelling, "Viva la Raza!" with the dispersing crowds, to Diablo's annoyance. He sees Luna roll by. "¡Wa-wacha! ¡Vatos! ¡Esa es la ruca que te'taba diciendo! ¡La que estaba en TNN! ¡Simón!" *Check it out! That's the ruca I was talking about! The one that was on TNN!*

For a few seconds Diablo couldn't give a damn. Then he glances back to catch a glimpse of her face. With all the coolness of a vato chingón, he stares straight ahead to Chino. "Trucha, él que no se pone trucha." *Watch out, whoever doesn't watch out.* His mouth forms into his trademark scowl.

Chuy and Nazul have ringside seats as Chino brakes and steers the Malibu into the oncoming traffic right in front of them. Chino worms his way in to the sounds of screeching brakes and angry, honking horns as he follows Luna, a couple of cars behind.

Nazul: "¡Chuy! ¡Pinche Diablo! ¡Persíguelos!"

The GTO obnoxiously cuts into the stream of traffic behind a pickup. Moving slowly, it ends up two cars and a van behind the Malibu.

Up ahead, Luna comes to a red light behind a wrecker truck at Brazos, across the street from the Guadalupe Theater. "Mom, let's talk to Dad's friend Arnold Fischer about Nazul. Maybe he can help us." A flash of lightning reflects on her windshield.

"Ay, m'ijita, I really think this is way over his head. Besides, how are we going to get ahold of him now?"

"I know. That's too bad because Fischer es un soldado por el varrio." *Is a soldier for the varrio.* She checks her rearview in time to make out two dark figures approaching on each side. "Mom, Estrella, lock your doors!"

All three quickly lock all four doors.

"What is it, m'ija?" Consuelo strains her neck to see.

"It's Diablo." Her heart thumping in her throat, Luna braces herself as he arrives at her window.

Gunmetal taps on the glass. "¿Te acuerdas de mí, masota?" *You remember me?* Through her window, Diablo cocks his head maloso and peers into Luna's face, fogging up her vision. "Wacha."

She looks around through the rain-streaked window and sees Diablo's .44 pointing not at her, but at Estrella in the back seat.

"No, please. I'll get out!" Luna looks at her terrified mom, who's holding on to her, not knowing what else to do.

"Luna, no!"

Outside on the sidewalk, across the Chrysler from Diablo, Chino points his plomero at the driver in an Econoline van behind Luna, a middle-aged Chicano who shakes his head to shame at Chino. Inside his van he feels for a tire iron under his seat. He finds it. Gripping the tool, he waits for just one pendejo move.

With all the noisy activity of confused police teams running like mensos back and forth, the wrecker driver is oblivious to the hijacking behind him. He leaves slowly as the light turns green. Behind the van and Malibu, the cars start to honk their horns even louder.

On the sidewalk behind Consuelo's car, Sapo pleads with Diablo for Luna. "Por favor, jefe. She's Raza! She's my hero."

Diablo ignores Sapo with a grin. "Cállatelhocico."

Sapo shakes his head with guilt. "Chingadamadre…Tuve que mover el hocico." *Motherfucker…I had to open my trap.*

Nazul is distracted by a squad of police across the street that starts stopping and searching the cars going by the other way. He ducks down, wondering if he's going to have to take off running for his life any second.

Across the varrio in their tiny homes, gente of all ages, even children, pray to their sacred altars. A divine humming seems to rise up above the homes to brave the murderous rage of this fateful night.

"Ya sabes, I got chit for patience." Diablo smashes the back passenger window with his .44. Estrella screams and jumps back, curling herself in the far corner of the seat.

Despite Consuelo's protests, Luna opens her door.

Diablo grabs her and pulls her out, shoving her around by her hair as Estrella and Consuelo scream and plead for her. From across the three street corners, señores stepping out of their carruchas are already clickiando, picking up rocks as they approach Diablo and Chino cautiously.

Grinning at the señores, Diablo tosses the plomero to Chino and pulls out his nine-inch fila. "Vamos a tirar un welton, chingóna." *Let's go for a cruise, badass.* He holds the fila up to her neck.

"No! Don't hurt her!" Consuelo and Estrella scream and plead.

From the GTO, Nazul hears the screams up ahead and sits up. He grabs Chuy hard by the collar, startling him. "Chuy. Tú no te metas en esto. ¡Descuéntate!" *Chuy. Don't get involved in this. Take off!*

Trembling and bugging his round eyes at him, Chuy slowly regains his nerves. "¡ 'Ta'bueno, 'ta'bueno!" *All right, all right!* He pulls his face away from Nazul with his varrio frown. "¡Si no me matas de susto primero! Chinga." *If you don't kill me of fright first!* Straightening his crumpled collar, "¡Pero, son tres vatos, homes!" *But they're three vatos, homes!*

"Hazme este favor." *Do me this favor.* His stare is dead serious from under the brim of the beat-to-shit chuco hat as he nods to Chuy. "I need for you to take care of my jefito." Nazul slides out of the red and black checkered bucket seat of the humming '68.

Before he can close the door, Chuy calls out, "¿Que lo cuide? ¡Chit, él mejor me cuida a mí!" *To take care of him? Shit, he takes care of me instead!*

As the señores cautiously approach, Chino points both plomeros at them. Behind him, the vato in the van steps out with the tire iron in hand.

Consuelo yells to Estrella, "M'ija, run and hide!" Estrella takes off as a señor directs her to his car across the lane. Consuelo opens her door and approaches Diablo, begging for Luna. "Por favor, don't hurt her!" She tries to block his getaway as she pleads with him. "Noo... take me!"

"'Amá! Get away! He's crazy!" Luna yells.

Diablo struggles to pull Luna away as she grabs on to the open window frame. He quickly tires of Consuelo in his face and coldly shoves her aside, knocking her down to the pavement.

Consuelo isn't about to give up. Lying on the wet street, she grabs Diablo's legs and won't let go.

He tries to kick her away, cussing, "¡Házte a la verga!" *Get the fuck away!* He can't get his balance with Luna also struggling to hold her grip.

Sapo is the first to catch sight of el Pachuco, his topcoat catching the brisk wind a few feet away. He freezes.

Pachuco struts by and closes in on Chino, who has his back to him. Without missing a step, Pachuco sends a vicious uppercut into the back of Chino's head, causing it to slap hard against the telephone pole next to him. He crashes to the sidewalk, losing the cohetes as Pachuco kicks them away.

Diablo shifts his focus from the angrily approaching señores when he hears the slap of bone on the telephone pole and slowly turns his maddogs in that direction. Screeching tires bring his attention back to the street, and he tracks a cherry red GTO barreling towards him, barely squeezing between the rows of cars in the traffic.

He loosens his grip on Luna, bracing himself for the impact. Luna jumps away and grabs Consuelo, making a clean getaway.

Chuy honks his horn loud as the GTO zooms past, inches from Diablo's ass. Diablo tries to make out Chuy's face as he races by. When he turns around he gets an ant's-eye view of the soles of a pair of calcos as Pachuco leaps off the trunk of Consuelo's Chrysler and comes crashing down on his leather face.

Diablo is still holding his fila as he picks himself up off the street, his shattered maddogs in several pieces around him. His fierce eyes still spark stars as he focuses on Pachuco. The faraway moaning of an approaching train stirs in Diablo an uneasy dread.

It seems for a moment as if the entire area is suddenly silent. Out of nowhere a thick fog descends, cutting visibility to twenty feet. Luna looks around.

Consuelo ushers her a safe distance away, near the señores and Estrella. They all start to scatter a bit, trying not to attract too much attention to Pachuco.

Luna won't go very far. "'Amá...that's Nazul," she whispers breathlessly. Consuelo tries to make out his face, but it's in shadow under the low brim of his chuco hat as he trains on Diablo.

"C'mon m'ijita, the cops are driving by," Consuelo whispers to Luna, trying to get her behind a station wagon with Estrella.

A mournful groan again from the train seems to spark a blinding flash of lightning that makes everyone around Luna cringe. Roaring thunder goes rolling across the sky over the tense vatos as they stare each other down.

Diablo holds his fila up.

Pachuco slowly slips off his belt and holds it hanging by his side, ready.

"Aquí se acaba tu pinche corrido." *Your damn ballad ends here.* Diablo's stare es el último desmadre. *Is the last fuckup.*

"¿Pos, pa qué me la cantas? Aquí estoy." *Well, why sing me a tune? I'm right here.*

Diablo can't readily remember where he's heard that reply as he grunts with rage and lunges at him with his fila, slicing the air with death.

Pachuco whips his belt in front of him.

Diablo lunges at Pachuco, but he uses his topcoat to deflect mortal injury. The belt whips around Diablo's head and ends with the belt buckle snapping under his right eye.

Diablo winces, jumps back, and sends a death kick to Pachuco's nuts. Pachuco doubles over with a grunt as Diablo tries for another. Pachuco jumps away and catches the heel of Diablo's calco underneath, shoving it high and causing him to fall back on the street, breaking the fall with the back of his head.

In a split second Diablo executes a Rayo-de-Jalisco flip, his legs coming back up like a rewind of the fall. Pachuco is waiting with a punch to the side of his head. Diablo's rage numbs him as he tackles Pachuco against the van with punches and stabs at his upper body. Desperately, Pachuco shields himself with his elbows and forearms under the thick topcoat, catching painful slices but diverting jabs.

Consuelo and Luna try to muffle their screams for Nazul twenty feet away. Around them, though, the area is now strangely devoid of the law.

Brutally, Pachuco thrusts his knee into Diablo's nuts twice to get some breathing room. Diablo staggers back, out of breath. Pachuco leaps forward and lets loose all his vengeance, his fists pummeling. Diablo endures knee-crashes to his head, kicks to the groin and stomach, and bone-crushing punches to his face. He spits blood, splattering Luna's Chrysler and the van's windshield behind it. He grunts and staggers to stay up, refusing to fall.

Blocks away, squad cars battle with uncooperative drivers, their walkie-talkies garbling conflicting intelligence about a Pachuco sighting.

Both vatos are sopping wet from the persistent downpour. Diablo staggers back and flings off his Bexar County jail-issued rayon jacket. His torn, dirty undershirt reveals an array of tattoos covering his arms and upper body. Wiry, powerful muscles glisten in the rain. Peeking out of the undershirt on his chest is a face of Jesucristo holding two .44s across his chest, tears dripping from his eyes. As Pachuco checks the tats, Diablo lunges at him, zigzagging at the face, slicing him on his chin and neck as Pachuco jumps back, barely avoiding lethal injury.

Pachuco sends his belt whipping, but Diablo grabs it with his free hand and pulls him in. Pachuco's hand blocks a death stab to his heart. The fila goes through his left hand.

Diablo pulls it out and away, ready for another try.

Without a sound, Pachuco grabs Diablo's hand holding his belt, turns away, and bringing it over his shoulder, crashes Diablo's elbow down. A loud, bloodcurdling snap makes everybody in the street wince. Diablo's arm is broken.

His strength sapped, Diablo doesn't react. Pachuco grabs his knife hand, forces it behind him, and buries it deep into the back of his ribcage, holding it there. Blood red runs down Diablo's pants.

Luna and Consuelo look away.

The vatos both stumble back onto the sidewalk, tripping over Chino and crumbling against the tall, wooden double doors of the '40s-style corner botica, its entrance right at the corner of the block at Guadalupe and Brazos.

Pachuco falls forward on top of Diablo. Diablo lands with his hand still holding the fila in his ribs under him, too drained to even lift his arm. Breathing heavy clouds of steam, they are face to face. Across the street, the Guadalupe Theater's neon tubes glow pale violet in the mist.

Sapo watches in awe down the Guadalupe Street side of the sidewalk. The honking horns grow quiet. Corre la palabra. *The word spreads.* A trucha witness of the varrio, he feels like history is going down in front of his eyes. He nervously looks around, wondering why Pachuco isn't detected by the army of cops now running around just across the street.

Several blocks away, SWAT teams with heavy firepower and K-9s join forces, ready for war.

"Who the hell said he was here? What the fuck's going on?" An

FBI agent throws his hands up in disgust.

A sergeant: "Sir, I think our talkies are wet or something. They either don't work at all, or we get garbled info and conflicting sightings, sir. We thought we heard he was cornered here at Brazos and Chihuahua streets."

"Wet? These talkies are waterproof, you idiot. Shit! It's like a carnival out here!" The agent puts his hands on his hips and looks around impatiently. "This is embarrassing!" He throws his hands out. "Spread out again! Find that motherless sonofabitch or I'll have your ass!" As he watches everybody scramble, he mumbles to himself, "All that damn training, for what?"

Three small children pray quietly, warmed in the glow of velas adorning an altar in a quaint home. Behind them, viejitos y viejitas with their black veils seem transfixed on the santos as they kneel in prayer, reciting a rosario.

Pachuco wraps his belt tightly around the neck of Diablo, who lies almost helpless. He squeezes tight. Morbidly, Diablo's tongue starts to stick out, gasping for air. Pachuco twists the belt even tighter, whispering into his face. "En la vida," he nods his head, "*todo* se paga." *In life, we pay for it* all.

Amid the wailing sirens, train yelps, and police choppers zooming past low overhead, Pachuco hears a familiar voice.

"No! No more killing!"

His mouth bleeding and bruised, eyes swollen half-shut, he turns to Luna through the rain dripping over his chuco brim, trying to focus. Consuelo has her arms tightly around her across the street.

"Please…No more killing." Mouthing the words, Luna pleads to him, shaking her head. She stares into his eyes with a look that unsettles his vengeance.

Pachuco turns back to Diablo just as a lightning bolt cracks the darkness and illuminates his face for a split second.

Diablo makes out his features. He blinks in disbelief. "Blue-Boy." Breathless. His voice deep and guttural, he's barely able to speak. "¿Qué chingaus? Tú estás…*muerto.*" *What the fuck? You're…*dead. Diablo struggles with the revelation, a superstitious, yet deep-seated dread of the impeccable law of the land, a law by which our grandparents lived and died. He stares blankly at Blue-Boy. For once in his

Rey-de-las-siete-muertes life he looks defeated. "Estás…muerto…" He can barely utter the words as they are drowned out by the train's wail. His soul, bruised and bloodied, arrives at comprehension. It's too late; his blood and life are draining away into the cracks in the pavement, mixing with the rain, running over the edge of the sidewalk and into the stream of dirty water along the curb, pouring into the swollen drains.

"Sí, me mataste. Y peor." *Yes, you killed me. And worse.* Pachuco whispers loudly into his face. "Así lo quisiste, ¿Qué no? Pero no tuviste los huevos de matarme como un hombre." *Isn't that what you wanted? But you didn't have the balls to kill me like a man.* Breathless, he nods his head chingón. "Chale."

"Pos…ya hice lo que hice. ¿Qué chingaus quieres…que haga?" *Well, I did…what I did. What the fuck…do you want me to do about it now?* Diablo struggles to stay conscious. He stares at el Blue-Boy.

Blue-Boy tightens the belt again, but just enough to get his full attention. He leans in to Diablo and whispers chingón, "Elías y su familia, eran amigos míos. ¡Ellos eran gente vryosa, de hembra ligera! Hombre como él, tú nunca vas a conocer. En estas calles nadie le tiraba parada…Su esposa se llamaba Elsa. Y sus niños, ¡por ellos nunca podrás pagar con tu pinche vida culera! ¡El y su familia no merecieron morir a manos de cagada como tú! Yo estoy aquí de parte de él…para cumplir con tu desmadre." *Elias and his family were friends of mine. They were radiant people, of fine lineage. The man that he was, you're never gonna know. In these streets, nobody stood up to him…His wife's name was Elsa. And his children, for them you will never be able to pay with your chickenshit life! He and his family didn't deserve to die at the hands of shit like you! I am here on his part…to seal your doom.* He glances at a tearful Luna, their future together evaporating helplessly into the mist of the dark night…

The train lets out a painful yelp as it crosses under the Guadalupe Bridge three blocks away. Diablo coughs blood, uttering, "Yo…nunca comprendí, homes." *I…never understood, homes.*

Nazul gives Diablo a cold stare. "Pero ya…" nodding, he glances at Luna, "ya estamos *cansados* de ver la sangre de Raza en las pinche calles." *But now…we're* sick *of looking at the blood of Raza in the streets.* He slaps the belt off his hand, pissed, and starts to get up, then leans back in to Diablo's ear again, whispering, "Te rayates, culo." *You lucked out, asshole.* He grins. "No que te creías tán chingón." *Didn't you think you were all badass?* Nazul's stare reduces Diablo to a culero tecato's worthless level. "Wáchate ahora." *Look at you now.* He nods disgust. "Chale, tú ya no *paras pilón* aquí. No *vales verga!" Naw, you don't stake any claims here anymore. You ain't worth a* fuck! Pachuco hears urgent screams from Luna as Sapo flees. He blinks at blinding police flashers just yards away as he slowly looks around, exhausted from the battle, the walls around him now flashing washes of red tint. Before he can react, a calentado squad car comes screeching to a halt inches from his shoulder, its bumper almost over Diablo where he lies mortally wounded on the sidewalk.

As Pachuco sorely gets up, three cops jump out and rush him, knocking him hard against the tall doors of the building. Enraged, one cop throws a paralyzing kick but misses in his fury. His foot goes zooming up into the air and he crashes to the street on his ass. They handcuff Pachuco roughly. Pachuco winces from the cut on his hand but doesn't resist.

Luna and Consuelo scream, "NO! You cowards!"

Time seems surreal as Diablo's head echoes with the wailing train tearing through his soul. He squints up at the warm headlights, which shine like heavenly beacons over him, streaks of rain falling and melting into his face as his existence ebbs out, then fades back to the unbearable present.

It's like the cops are unable to control their rage long enough to get him alone. Two grab Pachuco's arms from behind as a third pulls out his billy club and strikes his head hard. Again. He kicks him mercilessly in the nuts and stomach.

"EYYY! Pinches cowards, you call yourself police officers?" Los señores once again take up rocks and sticks and approach the cops with loud protests.

The headlights from the cruiser cast enormous shadows of Prussian blue that contrast against the weathered burnt lavender of the botica's stucco walls. A small crowd gathers to watch the beating of Pachuco in horror as it is projected in giant proportions. They join Luna and her family y los señores in yelling at the cops. "You cowards! You're gonna kill him!"

Luna pulls out her cell phone and starts punching numbers.

One of the cops holding Pachuco pulls his Glock out and points it at the angry señores. "Just give me a reason!" He's out of control with rage. "I'm ordering you to disperse! That's an ORDER!" His hand is shaking, "I'm warning you!"

"Hello, Maria?" Luna strains to listen to her cell.

Weakly, Diablo comes to and focuses up on the cop with the billy club, his back to him a few feet away. The cop bends his legs and sends a powerful blow to Pachuco's head. Luna screams at the top of her lungs, "MURDERERS!"

The cop is seething. "You like to hit cops? Huh? This is what it feels like!" He leans back and delivers a blow that could crack a skull. The blow splits Pachuco's hat, the force thrashing him from the cops' grip. He falls to his knees facing Diablo, blood trickling down the side of his face from under his crushed and torn chuco brim.

Luna's screams bounce off into deep canyons in his mind and drift away. Darkness dragging him down to a depth that has no dimension or form. He feels like he's vanishing into an abstract space. A deafening whirring sound builds up inside his head, glimpses of his childhood echo in his brain. They melt, form, and dissolve again. Running through the house wearing his six-shooters and banging at everything in sight…His 'buelita urging him to eat his lunch. "Nazul, ya siéntate. Ven a comer. Ven acá. No te voy a llevar a la labor mañana, mañana. Nazuul—" *Come sit down. Come eat. Come here. I'm not gonna take you to the field tomorrow.* The hazy presence of Elias and his family coming to greet him from some journey comes into focus…He gasps as he observes them, then himself. He is a radiant presence? His soul filled with relief, Nazul hears familiar giggles and looks around him to Joey and Oralia as they run and hug his legs like they used to…He almost bursts into tears, but is comforted somehow.

It's Elias now. Nazul is speechless for a moment, then blurts out, "Carnal." He doesn't seem to be breathing. He feels like it's someone else forming what he thinks are his words. "Pero…¿están todos bien?" *But…is everyone all right?* He hears himself say in a flow of energy… "Están todos—"

He gazes at Elsa, who comes in and out of view with an almost fluid, embracing light right behind her face. She never looked more beautiful. "Nazul, como te han hecho menos los niños." *Nazul, how the kids have missed you.* Her smile is life itself. Around him, the sweet breeze is like a caressing veil on his skin.

Elias now stares back at him. "Simón, carnal." He smiles wide. "Estamos bien felices. No tengas cuidado, ¿eh? Ya verás. *Tú vas a ser feliz* también…" *We are very happy. Don't worry, huh? You'll see.* You're going to be happy *too.* He seems to affirm that belief.

"Ya verás, ese Blue-Boy," *You'll see, ese Blue-Boy,* he chuckles. "Ya verás." Nazul feels all alone again, not wanting to accept his fate. He knows deep inside and without question that he's got to go back. "No te aguites, carnal. Aquí estamos todos a tu lado." *Don't give up hope, carnal. Here, we are all on your side.* Elias reassures him the way only he could. "No…" he utters as they fade eerily away, "no." Darkness. The glowing face of Don Pablito now illuminates the deep. He stares at Nazul with the candle flame dancing in his eyes. Behind him the santos emerge on his wall and converse in strange languages.

Demons now gnash with growls from the shadows as fierce winds and a desolate landscape threaten to intrude into his space. As he struggles with this abstract world, the vivid image of his beloved Don Pablito overwhelms everything else. His tender stare sends the shroud of fear skipping, tripping, and sliding through the murk in its terrified escape. "M'ijo, la ley de la tierra está a tu lado, esstaa…a-a tu-tu la-la-lado-oo…" *Son, the law of the land is on your side, isss…on-on-on you-r-your side.* His words seem to stretch out forever, then emerge as a fleeting event, zipping by at an inconceivable speed. Don Pablito gazes up at a statue of the Virgen, who comes alive and smiles at Nazul. Her motherly love is overwhelming. "Nazul…acuérdate del dicho en la tumba—la tumba…de Cuauhtémoc…Solamente…solamente las horas…las horas…luminosas cuentan en la vida…" *Nazul…remember the epitaph on the tomb—the tomb…of Cuauhtémoc…Only…only… the illuminating hours…count in life.* Echoes. Then the words fade to nothing but a sharp, urgent beep. The painful whirring in his head starts again, and voices come in and out…possibly from that place. That godforsaken place…

The Outside.

Someone is waiting for him there in that hell that now seems to hold a thread of hope. Luna's screams, yells from los señores, pull him back to his destiny.

"Look at you now! Piece of shit wetback! Where's all your shit now? Crawl on the ground, motherfucker!" The cop's ass is three feet from Diablo as he plants his feet firm and raises his club high for another murderous blow to Pachuco, who is still helpless on his hands and knees. Silently wincing in pain, Diablo pulls his hand out from under himself. He still holds his fila. Leaning up with the last ounce of his strength, he shoves the bloody nine-inch blade into the cop's ass, all the way to the handle.

The cop freezes for an instant, then yelps horribly. He stumbles off and knocks the other two cops down as he does a semicircle and crashes onto the hood of the cruiser. He shakes his ass around, desperate to find relief.

One of the cops gets up and blasts three shots from his Glock into Diablo's chest.

The .44s slap Diablo back down to the pavement. His body slides slightly on rainwater mixed with his blood.

The shots jolt Nazul back to the present as his senses collide again in the painful realization of his hopeless situation. Still on his knees, he focuses on the world around him. With a whirring sound in his head, he trains on Diablo's eyes. They stare back at him, a grin on his bloody mouth.

Blood and rain running down his face, Pachuco squints to see the alarming red blood on Diablo's chest and ripped undershirt. The events fall into place in his mind, and he starts to realize what just happened as his hearing returns. He holds his gaze on Diablo for an eternal moment. The faint moaning of the distant train seems to hush all the ruckus as it wails its departure. The sound waves are momentarily muffled by the passing buildings and homes on its lonely, never-ending journey.

Diablo's eyes glaze over. His grin still defies all the odds.

A persistent whimpering catches Nazul's attention, and he turns to his left and focuses. On the hood of the cruiser he sees the cop with a blade stuck in his ass laid over as the other two cops try to pull it out. "Shit! Stand still! Don't move! It's gonna hurt worse!"

"NO! Just leave it there! Call the medics! Call for backup!"

"We don't need no fucking backup. This cocksucker's mine!"

Walking back to the sidewalk and standing over a handcuffed Nazul, the cop who shot Diablo holsters his Glock and pulls out his billy club. "Playtime's over, you sumbitch!" Just as he grunts with rage, ready to deliver, something snaps inside Nazul. He lunges at the cop's midsection, picking him up and throwing him on top of the other two on the hood. The blade gets shoved deeper into the cop's ass and he cries with abandon.

The one on top gets up and tries to attack Nazul with the club. Nazul sends a death kick to his nuts that doubles him over with a grunt. Nervously unsnapping his Glock, the other cop pulls out his weapon but clumsily drops it in the puddle of water. He turns around, pulls the knife out of his buddy's ass, and lunges at Nazul. He's off-balance with rage and goes stumbling by as Nazul sidesteps him and kicks him in the throat. He gasps for air and falls to the sidewalk.

A bleeding, handcuffed Nazul runs past Luna, Estrella, and Consuelo to escape. The crowd cheers him on. "¡Dales en la madre, Gato Negro!" *Give 'em hell, Gato Negro!*

Luna calls out to him through her tears. "¡Vente conmigo!" *Come with me!* She gulps with grief. "¡No te vayas! ¡No!" *Don't leave!* As he disappears into the darkness down the street, the crowd disperses in different directions.

More cops arrive on foot and try to make sense of the situation. Their colleagues writhe in pain, crawling around gasping for air and whimpering uncontrollably.

One seasoned cop checks the threesome and mutters to his two partners, "Anybody bother to check his wallet? Figures. We don't even know what the hell he looks like. Just that he was a Mexican. Well there's a shitload of Mexicans here. And they all look alike. Fuck."

Two rookie cops on the street see Luna and her family getting in their car. They run to them and grab Consuelo and Luna roughly by their arms. "Where is Pashuco? We know you know!" Luna and Consuelo stand silent as one of the cops pulls out handcuffs. "Tell us! We know you ain't blind. We're placing both of you under arrest!"

"Get your damn hands off of 'em!" A deep voice with authority booms behind them.

The two cops turn to see a six-foot-three silhouette wearing a captain's cap approaching them with purpose. They lose their grip quickly.

Consuelo's face lights up. "Captain Fischer! ¡Ay, gracias a Dios!"

Fischer shoves the rookies aside. "These ladies are friends of mine! Now git yur ass out there and get the real criminal, you idiots!" The two rookies scamper off, mumbling yessirs.

"Arnold, listen to me. It's not the way it looks. Those cops were trying to beat him to death!" Luna pours out to Captain Fischer. "You gotta believe me."

Fischer stares at her, digesting the information.

The area is suddenly crawling with law enforcement.

"You three are sopping wet. Now come on." Fischer ushers them to their car. Consuelo hurries over to the driver's seat.

Fischer opens the back door to Luna. She pleads with him, "Please… don't let them kill him." Resting her head on his chest, she whispers, "Te lo pido…" *I beg you…* Her swollen eyes glance up, searching his. "Mujer, you are shaking." Fischer pulls off his black leather police jacket, wraps it around her, and sits her in the back seat. He shuts the door. Luna rolls down her window to him.

Fischer checks his surroundings, then turns to her, the rain pit-pattering on his cap brim, his shirt quickly turning darker blue and glistening wet. He reaches under her wet locks and moves her hair away from her eyes. "What's his name?"

Luna numbly glances at the weapons as the teams lock and load. "Nazul."

With his index finger he lifts her chin. He nods, "You couldn'ta picked…a quieter guy?" Fischer looks for a way to lighten her heart with his serious humor.

Luna smiles in spite of her fears…trying hard not to pout.

Fischer puts his hands on the window frame and glances again at the barking K-9s and rustle of police. "Damn! All these forces for just one vato? Unbelievable!" Taking a deep, long breath, he drops his gaze down. "Luny, me and your daddy…" He looks away, sighing deeply. "Fueron *muchos* años." *They were* many *years.* Looking down again, he shakes his head at the time that has passed. He looks deeply into her eyes and nods with resignation. "M'ijita, how can I promise you *anything?* I'm just a link in the chain. And these guys, ninety-nine percent of 'em, live by the saying, 'If you do the crime, your ass is mine.' And tonight you can multiply that a hundred times."

Never a quitter, her eyes study his handsome stare. Emotionally drained and shivering with cold, her trembling makes her stutter. "Nin-ninety-nine p-pe-percent. Tha-that leaves o-one." She nods her head to him. "Some-t-times *one*…is-is all it takes."

"Yeah," grinning, he looks around, "to start a damn revolución!" He looks at Luna deeply and nods his head.

"M'ija, ¿Cómo te puedo hacer entender? Es casi imposible. *How can I make you understand? It's almost impossible.* I mean, they could make up a dozen reasons why they had to shoot to kill. If by some miracle he is brought in alive," he looks away, "your boy is in a lotta trouble. Make no mistake, Luny." He is dead serious. He leans in to a tearful Estrella, and she comes for a hug goodbye as he glances to Consuelo. "You better get her outta here. Now." He looks back to Luna. "I'm sorry, m'ijita. Dispénsame." *Forgive me.* He turns and walks away.

Leaning out the window, she calls out to him. "Fish!" Slowly he turns around. His cap brim, shiny from the splatter of rain, casts a shadow across his eyes. "My father had a saying that *he* lived by: 'Cua-cuando las campanas de la justicia nunca suenan por el hombre pobre, pa-para ese hombre, no hay ley.'" *When the bells of justice never sound for the poor man, for that man, there is no law.*

Fischer stares for a long moment, then lowers his gaze to the street. Slowly he turns and walks away.

Back at the Hilton, Maria is on her cell with Lila. "Yes! They're arresting Chicano males and anybody that gets in their way."

Lila is in her pajamas in front of the TV, watching a live feed from el varrio. She grits her teeth. "Sorry bastards. I'm calling my attorney right now and telling him to send an army of civil rights lawyers to el Weso. Te wacho." She hangs up and starts punching numbers into her phone.

As Maria finishes talking to Lila, Ed Turnip is on the phone with Juan, the cameraman on the church story. "Put the word out about possible civil rights abuses and keep your camera ready." He hangs up and makes another call. "Hello, Lou? Put me through to the governor."

Maria is also on her cell. "Tell my news team to meet me in el Weso, now!"

A pack of wet varrio dogs growl and squeal as they fight over an old can of chili. Behind a dumpster they try to find shelter from the rain under a couple of twisted car hoods, which lean like a small roof across a chainlink fence, some decaying sheets of plywood, and a stucco building wall. The winner runs to the far end of the enclosure and growls viciously. He gnashes his teeth at the intruder on their turf, a crumpled, dark, and defeated form.

Down on his knees under the hood, Nazul is motionless. Overhead, chopper spotlights threaten to invade the area. Their blinding lights slice through the cracks. Barking K-9s seem to be everywhere. Nazul, still in handcuffs, awaits his doom.

Don Pablito's weathered eyes look ahead in a trance. He's lying on his side on the couch, facing the army of santos in his altar room. The candles, though now dim, burn for Nazul. A loud whisper escapes from his lips. "Nazul...no te muevas..." *Nazul...don't move...*

The wind whips up around Pachuco and whispers el curandero's words in his ear. As he reacts, he hears the dogs barking in alarm. A gun barrel comes to rest on the same ear from behind.

"No te muevas, Nazul."

Expecting it all to end in a fiery blast, Nazul is nevertheless comforted by the cop's familiarity.

"Levántate. Pero con mucho cuidado." *Get up. But very carefully.* He turns to face the voice.

The cop helps Nazul up to his feet, and walking close behind, leads him between the narrow walls of the two buildings he ran between earlier. Ahead, a maze of angry red flashers and sweeping beams of blinding light await him.

They reach the street, and the cop forces Nazul down on his knees between two parked cars just as a team behind him rushes past to another false sighting. "They found him! Over here!"

As Fischer ponders the fate of Nazul, he gets a call on his talkie: "Attention. Attention. This is the chief. We just got a call from the governor! If anybody violates any civil rights in this varrio, they will be prosecuted! Affirm now!"

With a smile, Fischer answers back. "This is Fish reading you loud and clear, Chief."

More voices come in on the talkies as a dozen more captains confirm the new orders.

The FBI agents get new orders from their superiors. "This is straight from the top! No human rights violations!"

Inside her car in the slow-moving traffic, Consuelo attempts to go around an old pickup truck that is jumpstarting an even older Ford Fairlane. "A ver...cálale!"—'RRR-rrrrr'—"¡Cálmala! ¡Ahora sí! ¡Dale!" "Nada." "Ta'bueno, cálmala..." As she maneuvers around the stalled vehicle, she sees a cop's silhouette step out in front of her from the row of parked cars. With a flashlight he waves her to a stop. Puzzled, she squints to get a look.

Consuelo studies the murky shadow through foggy windows as it walks to Luna's door on the sidewalk side and stands there for a minute. More police dash by on the street. Far away, yells can be heard amid the barking dogs and sirens.

The cop looks down on the crumpled black form at his feet. He reaches down and unlocks his cuffs.

Nazul looks up behind him, confused, as Fischer reaches over his shoulder. He follows the captain's hand as it presses the chrome handle teardrop button and slowly opens the car door. Luna is startled...She stares in disbelief at Nazul, just a few feet away.

The pain is still deep in Nazul's head. He stares at Luna in a trance, unable to comprehend. He blinks through the blood and the rain, frozen in time.

Captain Fischer helps Nazul into the back seat. Luna throws her arms around Fischer's neck, sobbing. "Yo te *conozco*. Te *conozco*. Te lo agradesco." *I* know you. *I* know you. *I am grateful.*

Fischer chuckles at her joy. "Me? Wish I could take credit for it, m'ija. It's either a strange twist of fate, or you got some powerful friends." He checks Nazul. "Better let me have that topcoat and hat. I'll try and get it back to ya soon. No promises." He pulls the battered, sopping topcoat off him and grabs the chuco hat, rolling the topcoat around it. "Now, you all need to get outta here and get home pronto."

Consuelo opens her window to him. "Fischer, I...You just don't know."

The captain leans down to her. "Well, I guess you owe me an enchilada dinner, ¿Qué no? And I'm coming to collect. Tomorrow. You can count on it. Now let's get moving. And don't panic. I'll getcha outta here."

They all hold their grateful faces on him as he pulls out his talkie and looks down to the roadblock five car lengths away. "This is Cap'n Fischer. Is Lieutenant Danny Ruggles still supervising this grid?"

"Yes sir, Captain. He's right here."

A crackle of voices, then, "Yeah. Fish. This is Ruggles."

"Danny, can you see me down here?" He waves. "All right. These folks in this white '87 Chrysler," he puts his hand on the roof, "are friends of mine. Some gung-ho cowboys roughed 'em up bad. Now I don't want 'em bothered anymore. Let 'em through. Pass the word."

"You're the captain. Will do. But you owe me a beer. Ten-four."

In the front seat of the Chrysler, Estrella looks behind her and giggles at the sight of Luna and Nazul holding each other in an embrace that seemed impossible just minutes ago, the rain dripping in from the cracked, foggy window. Consuelo glances into her rearview mirror, relieved, and smiles.

Luna holds on to Nazul as if he might fly away.

Our POV floats up behind their car and travels high to the electrical lines to reveal the massive dragnet. Christmas lights flicker from the windows and eaves of the tiny homes.

The Sunglows' "Fallaste Corazón" serenades their departure...

Y tú que te creías...el rey de todo el mundo...
Y tú que nunca fuiste, capas de perdonar...
El cruel y el despiedado, de todos te reías
Hoy imploras cariño, aunque sea por piedad
En donde está el orgullo
En donde está el coraje
Porque hoy que estás vencido
Bendigas caridad
Ya ves que no es lo mismo amar a ser amado
Ya que estás acabado...qué lástima me da

Maldito corazón...me alegro que ahora sufras
Que llores y te humillen ante de gran amor
La vida es la ruleta, en que apostamos todos
Y a ti te había tocado, nomás la de ganar
Pero hoy la buena suerte la espalda te ha volteado
Fallaste corazón...no vuelvas a apostar...

And you...who thought you were the king of the whole world...
And you who were never capable of forgiving anyone...
The cruel and uncaring, you laughed at everyone
Today you implore love, even if it's just for pity
Where is your laughter
Where is your hatred
Because today you are vanquished
You beg for love
Now you see that it's not the same to love and to be loved

Now that you are finished, what a pity I feel

Deadly heart…I revel in your suffering now
That you may weep and be humiliated, refused by great love
Life is the roulette wheel on which we all place our bets
And your chances have always been, only to win
But today your luck has turned its back on you
You lucked out, dear heart…don't ever gamble again…

fin

Glosario
Glossary

Though this is by no means a complete glossary of all the Spanish and Caló words and phrases that appear in this book, the author hopes it will be helpful nonetheless. A standard Spanish-English dictionary may also prove useful to the astute reader, and http://babelfish.altavista.net is a nice translation resource. Finally, Wikipedia at http://en.wiki.org has a good article on Caló.

abuela, abuelita—*n.* grandmother
abuelo, abuelito—*n.* grandfather
a la mejor—*adv.* maybe
andamos de malas—we were on a bad roll
ando castigando gacho wit dis slut—I'm punishing bad with
    this slut
'apá—*n.* father
aquí se acaba tu corrido—your ballad ends here
balaceadas—*adv.* in a hail of gunfire
bien chingones—*adj.* like hot shit
calentado—*adj.* warmed up, ready to go
calzón—*n.* underwear
chale—*adv.* no
chamaco—*n.* teenager
chato—*n.* crabs
chiva—*n.* literally "goat"; slang for heroin
como aquel baboso—like that other idiot
como un menso—like an idiot
con el chuco—with the pachuco
grito—*n.* a loud cry that signifies victory or machismo in
    Mexican culture
de buena onda—of good vibes
entrado—*v.* grooving
frajo—*n.* cigarette
frío—*adj.* cold
hazte a la verga—get the fuck outta the way
hielería—*n.* ice house
horas luminosas—*n.* illuminating hours

Glosario

huerquillo—*n.* little punk
huerqillo hocicón—*n.* loudmouth punk
huevos—*n.* literally "eggs"; slang for testicles
jalan—*v.* work
juras—*n.* police
labores—*n.* fields
los vryosos—*n. pl.* the radiant ones
machin—*adj.* badass
mal—*n.* curse
mascizo—*adj.* solid
meco—*n.* sperm
me lleva el tren—literally "the train takes me away"; idiom for "I can't believe this"
Mero—*n.* God, or the head man in charge
migra—*n.* Immigration and Naturalization Service
misa—*n.* Catholic mass
mojada—*v.* literally "dunked"; slang for a gang hit; "wet the street"
mojado—*adj.* literally "wet"; n. slang for recent Mexican immigrant; "wetback"
nalgas—*n.* butt
no sapo, rana—literally "I don't toad, frog"; idiom for "I don't know"
otro lado—literally "other side"; south of the Mexican-U.S. border
pa'fuera—*prep.* outside
parranda—*n.* drunken binge
pedo—*n.* fart
pedo atorado—a trapped fart
pelos en el fundillo—hairs on her ass
peor than a pinche cucaracho—worse than a damn roach
pero—*conj.* but
persígelos—*v.* follow them
pintar venado—literally "paint a deer"; idiom for "paint yourself gone"
pláticas—*n.* talks
plomazos—*n.* gunshots
porque buscaban nomás la feria—because it was only about the money
primito—*n.* little cousin
puñata—*n.* jackoff

que les dolía los culos—that their asses hurt

rancho—*n.* literally "farm"; "el rancho" is slang for prison

ropa indígena—indigenous clothes

se burlan—*v.* they make fun of us

se lo llevó el tren—literally "the train took him"; idiom for "swept
   away from the face of the earth"

señora—*n.* woman

señore—*n.* man

siete—*n.* seven

soldado de la luz—soldier of the light

sordo—*n.* deaf one

suegra—*n.* mother-in-law

suegros—*n.* in-laws

tecato/a—*n.* drug addict

tirada—*n.* hit

todo el pedo—all the shit

toque—*n.* marijuana cigarette

trucha—*adj.* hip to things, street-smart

vato—*n.* man, equivalent of "dude"

vatos del mero atole—guys with real balls

Acknowledgments

I would like to thank my gente for the resolve they instilled in me to make a difference. I was raised by a pueblo. Mi jefito, Juan, mis abuelos, and my beloved jefita, Olivia, te doy mis gracias. They all provided much of the material for this story. For most, the fields were the only thing they knew, yet their resilience, wisdom, and grace to this day keep my spirit solid.

I would like to thank my ruca, Andrea Greimel, who worked tirelessly on this story and helped me bring it back from the grave. To my homie, Mike Tapia, who was there at the beginning to teach me how to write. Also, my fiel carnal Felipe Vargas who made this book a reality. Eres chingón. My undying gratitude to Ruby Payne for believing in my vision when other Hispanic publishers wouldn't. Jesse Conrad, I thank you from mi corazón for your tireless support and ingenuity. And lastly, mil gracias a mi varrio for the incredible stories that have never been told but that I carry like a divine light en mi alma.

I dedicate this libro to my late wife, Debi Fischer-Hernandez. She believed in this story, though words can never reveal her radiance. This tale is about high drama, heroic courage in the dark face of doom. But then again, they are only words. She lived it.

Adan Hernandez 2006

Adan Hernandez grew up in Robstown, Texas, close to Corpus Christi.
When Adan was nine he and his family moved to San Antonio. Adan
has been a serious artist for thirty years. His work is included in the
permanent collection of the Metropolitan Museum of Art in New
York City and has been exhibited in museums throughout the U.S.
and Mexico. His collectors include many Hollywood insiders, and his
work is shown regularly in Los Angeles. Adan created all the original
artwork for the character Cruz in the varrio classic *Blood In...Blood
Out*. His work has also recently been included in Cheech Marin's
blockbuster traveling exhibition "Chicano Visions: American Painters
on the Verge," which has broken attendance records in museums
across the U.S. and will travel to Mexico, Europe, and Tokyo in the
next few years. This is his first novel.